The Eye of Heaven

JoAnne Soper-Cook

Dreamspinner Press

Published by
Dreamspinner Press
4760 Preston Road
Suite 244-149
Frisco, TX 75034
http://www.dreamspinnerpress.com/

The Eye of Heaven

Cover Art by Anne Cain   annecain.art@gmail.com
Cover Design by Mara McKennen

ISBN: 978-1-61581-733-7

Printed in the United States of America
First Edition
March 2011

eBook edition available
eBook ISBN: 978-1-61581-734-4

For Paul—again and always.

Author's Notes

Those readers most familiar with the history of the early Italian Renaissance will doubtless recognize the plethora of anachronisms that appear within these pages. Although the bulk of historical background is presented as it happened, there are some aspects of this novel that I have bent to my own purpose.

The bubonic plague first appeared in Florence, in the year 1348, and reports from that era (not the least of which is Boccaccio's *Decameron*) show that Italian trading ships returning from the East brought the disease with them. For the purposes of fiction, I have allied with this, but placed the character of Ysin-Hui (a Chinese trade emissary unknowingly infected with plague) in the opening pages of the novel. Thus, the unwitting Ysin-Hui (and not some anonymous trading vessel) becomes the plague's catalyst. I simply felt that this made for a more interesting story.

The character of Serenola is based on the fifteenth-century Italian religious reformer Girolamo Savonarola, the originator of the Bonfire of the Vanities. I found Savonarola's zeal compelling and rather frightening, and realized that although he would be the perfect foil for our heroes, he resided in the wrong century. So I moved Savonarola back into the fourteenth century, and changed his name. Throughout the fifteenth century, Savonarola was an ardent opponent of conspicuous wealth and excess—something he saw as a specifically Florentine vice! Although he recognized the doctrine of pestilence as punishment for sin, there is no record that he actually preached this— unlike his fictional counterpart, Savonarola appears to have been much more sympathetic to the suffering of his fellows, and even tended the sick monks during the plague. Like my character of Serenola, he was executed in the Piazza del Duomo by a Church grown tired of his preaching.

The personage of Geoffrey Chaucer is of course, historical. Those readers who love English literature will doubtless recognize him as the author of *The Canterbury Tales*. Various sources are unclear as to the exact date of his birth: some have it as late as 1340, while others as early as 1328. For the purpose of this narrative, I accepted 1328 as the appropriate date, simply because this would make him twenty years of age during the time that Dante and Rouen were in London, and of an age to be something of a contemporary. According to my sources, Chaucer served as a page to the Countess of Ulster, and doubtless would be in service to her during much of his youth. Again, for the purpose of this fiction, I moved him out of that household and placed him back in London.

The character of Fernando de Medici is a talented cross-dresser, employed in the flourishing medieval sex trade. The punishment for homosexuality during the Middle Ages was torture (usually the rack) and death—yet, there were inns like Lorenzo Tralini's all over Europe. The attitude toward homosexuality that is presented here (that intolerance which necessitated hiding one's true sexual orientation) is not intended as a reflection of my own feelings and beliefs. Rather, it is an accurate depiction of the intolerance that has unfortunately existed for much of human history.

That Fernando is a Medici is also significant; the Medici, originally skilled in banking and international commerce, rose to power slightly after the period indicated in this book, and in time became the ruling family of Florence, renowned for their patronage of the arts. In later years, artists such as Da Vinci and Michelangelo benefitted from their largesse, and for decades they were the predominant power on the Florentine landscape. Fernando de Medici would doubtless have been a young nobleman of great wealth and breeding.

During their brief time in Spain, Dante amasses a great collection of books. It is of interest to note that Dante owns a lot of books and is therefore a young man of means—a personal library such as Dante owns would have been impossible for the great bulk of medieval people, many of whom were also illiterate.

The depiction of the Spanish Inquisition and the destruction of the Juderia owes much to Bernard Hamilton's excellent book, *The Medieval Inquisition* as well as Jason Slade's *The Spanish Inquisition*, hypertext version. I am indebted to both these authors for their clear and concise reportage. Other sources of note include Barbara Tuchman's *A Distant Mirror*, Donald Weinstein's *Savonarola and*

Florence: Prophecy and Patriotism in the Renaissance, and Charles L. Mee Jr.'s book, *Daily Life in Renaissance Italy*, which, although dealing with a rather later era, nonetheless provided excellent detail about the social history of Renaissance and pre-Renaissance Florence.

And finally, there is Florence herself, and her resplendent architecture. The great Duomo (literally "cathedral") was the product of medieval architect Brunelleschi, but was not completed in his lifetime; much of the work had to be abandoned during the plague, when a declining European population decimated the available work force. The Campanile was also not completed during the time period in which this story is set; I have deliberately finished it myself so that Dante could tease Rouen about residing in its tower. All other features of Florence were intact at the time: the Ponte Vecchio (the great bridge over the river Arno), the Piazza del Duomo, and the markets, taverns and inns.

One important feature of 14th-century Florentine life that I have deliberately ignored is the curfew; in order for the story to progress, it was necessary for the people of Florence to be out and about in the evenings, rather than barricaded in their homes, as the curfew demanded. Otherwise, the details of life in Florence are as realistic as I could make them.

Wherever possible, I have used Italian words and phrases to enhance the authenticity of this narrative. I will allow, however, that my usage is overwhelmingly modern, and therefore devoid of the wonderful medieval slang that Dante and Rouen might have used.

I am forever indebted to Boccaccio's *Decameron*, from which I took my depiction of the plague; *The Cambridge Biographical Dictionary*, hypertext edition, (for the compelling portrait of Savonarola); and to artist Vittore Carpaccio, whose *Cycle of St. Ursula* provided me with a very real idea of what Dante looks like. Rouen, unfortunately, has not yet deigned to appear.

All mistakes, blunders, anachronisms, and oversights are absolutely mine.

JoAnne Soper-Cook, March 2011

Characters

In order of appearance

FLORENCE

Dante, servant of the house of Salvatore di Tuscano

Lilith, the ancient mother of all vampires, the first wife of Adam, and the consort of God

Ludmilla, Salvatore's cook and washerwoman

Salvatore di Tuscano, Dante's master and foster father, a powerful member of the Florentine ruling class

Ysin-Hui, a Chinese trader and friend to Salvatore

Rouen di Francisci, son of the noble house of Francisci of Prato, Dante's lover

Leonardo di Sforza, Rouen's friend, a patron of Tralini's inn

Valentin the Pardoner, former employee of Tralini, now a pardoner of the Church

Cardinal Gioletti, Valentin's benefactor, and a patron of Tralini's, friend to Ludovico Serenola

Captain John Anger, English sea captain who travels between Britain and the Italian coast, friend to Valentin

Fra Ludovico Serenola, priest of a mendicant (begging) order, Italian religious reformer and evangelical preacher

Fra Vittore, mendicant priest, novice and follower of Serenola

Niccolo, a novice, servant of Cardinal Gioletti

Paolo di Francisci, Rouen's brother, an idiot

Madonna di Francisci, Rouen's mother

Jacopo di Francisci, Rouen's father

Lorenzo Tralini, owner of an all-male brothel in Florence

Il Scorpino, the Summoner, emissary of the ecclesiastical courts

SPAIN

Pedro, owner of the wine shop, employer of Dante and Rouen

Isak, resident of the Juderia, Jewish scholar, neighbor of Dante and Rouen

ENGLAND

Geoffrey Chaucer, English poet and man of letters, friend to Dante and Rouen

Melina, friend of Fernando de Medici, Rouen's lover

FLORENCE

Cardinal Prosti, colleague of Cardinal Gioletti, protector of Fra Vittore

The Eye of Heaven

Prologue

Sometimes too hot the eye of heaven shines.

~William Shakespeare

DANTE

IN 1347, in the year of our Lord, there went out a proclamation from the Lord God, He who is called Jehovah, and it was noised abroad to all the corners of the earth. It was said that the angel Gabriel stood atop the Mount of Olives and blew his trumpet, and lo, the Earth melted like wax.

At long last, the promised end of the world. Our kind had proliferated, had now spread abroad so far and so fast that God must needs purge the land of our presence. Or so the prophets said. Our number had become too great, and we were infecting the mortal innocents, affecting them with our iniquity. It was time to change the course of our most necessary evil, and by so doing, eradicate all evil from the face of the earth. The means by which He chose to destroy us was a disease you now know as *plague*. The instrument of this destruction was a woman named merely, Lilith.

My name is Dante, of the house of Salvatore, and I am, at the time of this telling, in this, your modern age, some six hundred and fifty years old. I am immortal, one of a small and peerless number that nightly roam the world. When I was first brought over into darkness, I was but a stripling youth, and so I have remained. Our kind do not age;

despite the ravages of time, we remain the same as on the night that we first took that unholy cup.

I am forever twenty years of age. I still have a young man's smooth, square face, framed with dark chestnut hair that flutters around my shoulders and large dark eyes, heavy-lidded, flecked with gold. Arched brows that lend my face a permanently quizzical expression, as if I were questioning the gods. A mouth that hints at a hidden sensuality, the lower lip not quite pendulous but poutish, petulant. Tall for then—the Middle Ages—not so very tall for now, these modern times, this twentieth century.

In life I was the kind of face and figure that could meld into the masses. I exist now in death, and my immortal nature is well hidden. I am a template upon which my milieu inevitably sets its mark.

I have a story to tell you, one which I think you will very much want to hear. Because it concerns the nature of existence, the integrity of betrayal, and the astounding wrath of the vengeful God Jehovah. Pray, place your hand in mine and follow. You very much believe, even as you resist me, that nothing is as tender as the night.

Chapter 1

October 1347
Florence, Italy (Firenze)

DANTE

I HAVE heard the story told, in hushed whispers around the dining table, or in my master's chambers, that the holy God Jehovah made Lilith from the dust of the earth, created her as He created Adam. And Lilith, unwilling to subjugate herself to him, resisted, uttered the secret name of God, (that which is not given men to know) and flew high into the air. She traveled to the Red Sea and there, in a frenzy of evil, created demons, the diabolic children of her blood-lust. This was the seed of her rebellion against Him.

This was the beginning of our kind, this aberrant subspecies of blood-drinkers that nightly roams the earth. We are bound with chains as ancient as the universe.

When I met Lilith, she was already immensely old, and I have no reason not to believe the stories. I believe that she is the First Eve, the immortal wife of Adam. I believe she is as much evil as I have ever known.

"DANTE!" The tinkling crash of broken crockery; a shattered plate skittered into pieces across the hard tiles of Ludmilla's kitchen floor. "Clumsy oaf!"

Her hand cuffed me, briefly, a clever tap across the nape of my neck that nonetheless humiliated me. I bent to scrape up the broken fragments, brush them into a cloth to be taken away. I would never have dropped the tray except that I was in a frenzy of excitement, my whole body juddering with nervous anticipation.

"You've cut yourself! Ahhhh!" Ludmilla squatted in front of me, a huge shadow blocking out the morning light. "Little piece of it—" She brought my finger close to her face and picked the tiny shard away. Immediately the blood welled up and with it, the pain. "Here. Wrap it up." She passed me a strip of linen and bound it twice around my finger. "You should be more careful."

I had been careful, I had been *exquisitely* careful, but I was just so *excited*! The trader that my master entertained upstairs was not his normal sort of guest; this man was special, different. I sensed it. The entire household buzzed with unasked questions, humming like a beehive. We were each of us intensely curious about him.

"Now, need another tray for you to take." Ludmilla bustled about, a large shape at the dim edges of my vision. I wasn't listening to her. I was feeling the throb in my finger and wishing that she would hurry with the tray, so I could go in and see my master's strange visitor. "Take this—grip it, boy!" She curled my fingers around the handles, squeezed my hands until they hurt. "Don't drop it this time." She scrutinized me with her small, dark eyes, lips pursed. "So you've seen him, then."

"Who?"

"The *trader*!" She turned and pretended busyness with a basket of onions. "Cosimo says he has an extra eye, here." She pressed her thumb against the center of her smooth round forehead. "And an extra finger on each hand."

"Maestro Salvatore has an extra finger on each hand?" *Mio Dio*,

THE EYE OF HEAVEN

this was news to me. How was it I hadn't noticed?

"The *trader*!" Ludmilla glared at me with all the gravity of a disgruntled sow. "How is it you were raised at his side—" She jerked a thumb upward to indicate my master, in the rooms above us, "—and are so stupid?"

I pulled a face. "Cosimo talks nonsense." Cosimo was the master of horses. "He has no extra fingers, nor eyes either."

"Ahhhh!" She shoved me out the door. "Make haste with that, and don't drop it!"

I went up with my tray of wine and sweetmeats, careful on the stairs, my mind quivering with anticipation. I was now finally old enough to serve my master properly, as a man, to wait on him and bring him wine. I was no longer relegated to the kitchen with Ludmilla. I was a respected servant, very nearly a counselor, with the master's ear if I wanted it.

I pushed the door open furtively, peered around the corner. Salvatore was hunched over at his desk, gazing at a map.

"My Master." I waited in the doorway, as Ludmilla had taught me, and allowed only my gaze to rove around the room. It was indeed glorious, but then, my master was a man of wealth and position, and much humility. That he conducted his business in this gilded salon was nothing to him; its gorgeous frescoes and vaulted, coffered ceilings escaped his attention as surely as if they were mere phantoms of the imagination.

"Ah, Dante! Come in, come in." Salvatore looked up, smiling at me, and I was struck by how little he had changed since first he'd found me in the marketplace. And that was eons ago, ages since. I felt that I had come a great distance since then. "Dante, this is Ysin-Hui, the trade emissary from China. Ysin-Hui provides me with the spices and dyes I need, and in return, I supply him with oil from my groves. Here—" Salvatore uncorked one of several vials that stood in a row upon his desk, motioned me near, "—cinnamon, and cardamom." The heady smells rose and mingled, a delicious perfume.

"I have never seen such things…." I touched a hesitant finger to the side of the glass bottle; I expected it to be warm to the touch. There was anise seed, attar of roses, yellow turmeric, and saffron, impossibly expensive and much more precious than gold. There were innumerable rows of tiny vials, filled with things I had never seen before. There was the dried head of a monkey in a velvet bag.

"Young, Dante, I am pleasured by our meeting." He bowed to me, graciously, but I flushed hot and cold with embarrassment. My master's other friends, wealthy Florentines, knew not to bow to me, as I was but a servant. "Would you like something to take along with you?" He pushed the velvet bag a little closer to the table's edge. "Maestro Monkey, he smiles because he likes you."

I glanced at the animal's severed head with its thin dead lips, its fixed expression. The eyeballs had long since rotted and collapsed back into the hollow sockets, dried strips of crackling tissue that was plastered flat against the bone. My stomach lurched painfully, and I looked quickly away. "You are far too kind, Ser."

"Dante is my servant, but he is much more to me than that." Salvatore was speaking to the emissary, but I listened without seeming to. It was a trick I often employed, to apprise myself of the household business. "I found him in the market when he was but a child, and he has remained with me ever since. I expect that, because I am so very fond of him, I may need to purchase him a title." Salvatore often showed me off this way, proud that I belonged to him. "I have thought of petitioning the Medici. They are rising rapidly in prominence…." He trailed off, smiling, and Ysin-Hui smiled also, and nodded, a courteous mirroring. His keen, dark eyes watched me as I went to stand by Salvatore's side. "Ysin-Hui honors us, Dante."

I bowed from the waist and nodded to the emissary. "It is a pleasure to meet you, Ser." I employed the Tuscan honorific, since I had no idea how to greet him in his own tongue, but he seemed pleased with me, and smiled. In fact, he smiled more than anyone I had ever met. I looked carefully but could see no extra eye. His hands employed a mere five fingers each.

"Ysin-Hui will be staying with us for a few days, Dante, as he is a stranger in our city. Would you run and ask Ludmilla to make up his bedroom, please?"

I was being dismissed, but I didn't mind. I had performed my duty, and I had seen what was in the little bottles and indeed the monkey's head as well, and now, as was often the case, it was time to depart silently, as any worthy servant knows to do. "I will, Maestro."

The truth was, a prolonged stretch of time in Salvatore's presence made me uncomfortable. He often made much more of me than was appropriate, and his enthusiasm embarrassed me. His affection was an overwhelming thing, a nearly physical presence that enveloped me like a cloud, cloying, overpowering. I knew that his deep regard for me could smother me, without meaning to; he merely loved me far more than I could stand. I felt his hand descend upon my shoulder, and it burned me. I slid away from it, under the pretence of picking up my tray, and moved toward the door in guilty silence. I bobbed a bow and escaped, running down the back stairs until I reached the kitchen, out of breath.

When I was a child, he brought me sweetmeats from market every day, watched while I ate them, observed me with a frightening intensity that compelled me to swallow every one, until I made myself ill. He ordered clothing made for me, from the finest houses between here and Venice: cloaks and doublets, cut in the latest style, fashioned from the finest cloth, fine-woven hose of silken thread, leather boots dyed to match. When the other boys at my school made sport of me and beat me up, Salvatore hired tutors such as those employed by prominent *fiorentino*, so that I should be educated in his home, and not exposed to peril on my way to school. He boasted that I was tutored by such minds as those who created the erudition of the Medici, the Sforza.

He sat beside my bed at night until I fell asleep, even when I became so old that I no longer feared the darkness. Often I would be occupied in some task about the house, and I would look up to see him watching me, a curious expression on his face.

He supervised my activities himself, or if he was unable, sent a servant to go with me. I felt ridiculous, being followed about the town by Salvatore's hulking guards, as if I were his firstborn son, instead of merely his servant. If I went into a shop, a tavern, or a church, his emissaries followed me. If I sought sport with a fellow or a maiden, it was certain I was being watched, under the guise of his protection. Salvatore's presence followed me everywhere, he was with me every possible moment, as if he feared that I would vanish like a vision. When I knelt to say the *Pater Noster* at Mass on Sundays, Salvatore was there beside me, gazing into my face as if it held some kind of holy glow.

Salvatore loved me too much. It frightened me. There is love, and love again, and then the love becomes religion.

My EARLIEST memory is of being in the marketplace. I can't have been more than two. I don't remember how I got there, of course; I merely remember sitting in the dust behind an applecart and crying as if my heart were broken.

The market seemed so very huge a place, and I, so all alone. And I was hungry, I remember it now: that peculiar, gnawing hunger that feels as if it would eat right through you. This lent vigor to my screaming and I continued until I was fairly hoarse from it. Still, no one came.

I first remember Salvatore as an elegant shadow falling over me, a huge pair of hands reaching down. I was lifted up, into the sunlight of late afternoon, the ground falling away from me. He seemed so very tall, but then, I was a tiny child. To me, he would have seemed so. Even now, hundreds of years after his demise, he still seems huge, a tall, elegant shadow. Perhaps I will always remember him this way, as my savior in the marketplace, lifting me out of the darkness and into the light. He thought I would always exist in light, my wise master. But then, he could not have anticipated Lilith, her ancient blood that condemned me to this immortal hell. Perhaps it is best that he does not know what his servant, his sometimes-son, has come to.

Tuscany in summer is a glorious place; there is an ethereal quality about the light not seen elsewhere, I'm certain you yourself have seen it in the paintings of the Renaissance: Da Vinci, Botticelli, and Andrea del Sarto. There is a quality of stillness, also, of eternal waiting, as if the landscape held its breath. It is a place as perfectly the same as it has ever been, unchanged by Time, untempered by Fortune and by Fate. The green hills with their dappled olive groves roll into the horizon as ever they did; tranquil streams meander thoughtfully, unhurried; the sky in daylight is still a stretch of blue serenity. It is above all else, a place of peace, and a certain creature comfort. There are times when, in my self-imposed exile, I search for some solace, and it is then that Salvatore's villa establishes itself most strongly in my memory: a stately *palazzo* on the outskirts of Florence in which I was happy.

After he had found me, he installed me in his house under the care of a nurse—a washerwoman who had been with him as long as anyone could remember. She also cared for his only daughter, Sorcha, a plain and plump girl who cared little for anything besides prayers and holy books. It was whispered that she was bound for the convent. All I ever saw of her was her back, as it traveled hither and yon about the house. She was a fussy, petulant girl, much given to moods and rages; it was not unknown for her to scream the house down, when she was denied some trinket or bauble that her father might have brought from market. Her various attitudes changed as quickly as the wind. She spent most of her time closeted with her nurse and never went outside.

But I was as happy underneath his roof as I had been anywhere; indeed, I had no real recall of being either happy or otherwise, but then, I had been so very young when he found me. So perhaps my time under his roof is all the mortal memory I have, all the mortal memory I need. It is as if I was created the moment that he reached down to lift me into the light.

His house, with its myriad rooms and labyrinthine corridors, was a perfect place for a young boy, and I passed many a contented hour wandering there, devising imagined adventures in which I figured largely as the hero. In summer, there was the courtyard, lush with trees, cool and sheltered from the sunlight. If I climbed onto the topmost point of Salvatore's tower, I could gaze out over his olive groves and his vineyards, rich acres of green stretching as far as I could see: this was Salvatore's world, this was my world.

These olives had made him rich, and because of his wealth, I wanted for nothing. I was clothed in the same rich fabrics all in his household wore, I was fed and cared for as if I were his son, instead of the urchin that he had found at market. Like many a foundling who was forced to fall upon the kindness of strangers, I could never be sure of my place within the household, but with Salvatore di Tuscano, I was always sure of my place in his regard.

I was in service to him when Lilith came.

I had just passed my twentieth year, well into my majority, an adult now. You will remember that the span of time to make a life was much shorter then; at twenty I was as mature as ever I would be. I had reached the fullness of my height, my shoulders broad and strong, my muscles hardened from years of carrying and fetching, working with Salvatore's *cavaliere* in the courtyard. I had hair underneath my arms and elsewhere on my body, and I was compelled now to shave my face every morning with a blade.

There was a commotion in the house at that time: Sorcha was twenty-five and still had not married, and Salvatore seemed intent that she should go into contemplation. She had always been a quiet girl, immersed in reading, the study of Scripture, not overly inclined to gaiety, and certainly not interested in being courted. Salvatore had her introduced to several of his patrons, their sons, and their sons' cousins, but all for naught. Sorcha was not interested, she would not marry, and as the years passed, one upon the other, the time when she might wed dwindled down to nothing, and was gone. Salvatore considered sending her to the convent, but Sorcha wailed and wept, prevailed upon his mercies in the name of her dead mother, until Salvatore finally consented. Sorcha would remain here, would manage the affairs of the family after Salvatore had gone; since there was no son, I would assist her, as her chamberlain, and thus be assured of my livelihood for the remainder of my days.

Alas, it did not happen like that.

I WAS folding cloth for Ludmilla the night that I first saw her: a woman, tall and thin, with an unearthly countenance and eyes of blue that glittered. I shrank from her, my voice withered in my throat and died, and I knew nothing but this horrible, heart-pounding terror. Fear rose and filled my head, a wordless shriek, as she moved, one hand outstretched in front of her, the long nails gleaming in the dimness, eerily illuminated by my candle.

I knew she was something unholy. Yet I was powerless to flee; it was as if my feet had fallen off my legs.

"Dante...." Her lips moved to shape my name; she uttered it, a whisper like dried leaves, a murmur that died away like wind. She drifted, grew in height, hovered over me like some great, winged shadow. Her hair was long and tangled and reached nearly to the floor, a dark sheet, a shroud. Her mind pressed against me like a mouth, a great beckoning presence that insisted, that insinuated itself into my soul. And I sagged against the wall, drained of life, held pinioned by the terror I felt because of her. I was in a great, shrieking, mindless agony of fear, that horror that erupts when the mind can hold no other thought, no other impulse. As if from a distance, I heard the thudding cadence of my heart, the dark interior swishing of my blood as it slowed by degrees, like a timepiece running down.

I was suspended in death.

I felt her bend over me, felt the tendrils of her hair brush against my face, my neck. Fingers probed my face, my mouth, slipped into my nostrils, examined the insides of my ears. Fingers slipped into my opened shirt, sliced my nipple with a fingernail, a pain as keen as ecstasy. "You are mine. I have marked you for my own."

My mouth opened, my lips shaping themselves into an oval, a supplication. *Who are you?*

"I have come to bring about the end of the world." *Mystery, Babylon the Great, Mother of Harlots.*

Who are you?

"I am Lilith. The First Eve, the willful woman, the cast-off skin of evil. I am—" Leaning over me, her hair brushing my face, my blinded eyes, "—the very consort of God."

There was a fluttering rush, as if from the beating of a great many wings, and her nails slid into my neck. She wrenched my head around, bared my throat and sank her fangs into me.

My body rose in her embrace, floating. Her lips fastened onto my skin with a powerful suction that seemed to pull my soul to her. And I was filled with light: varicolored, beautiful, it streamed out of her and into me, a spiral thread. I existed in a perfect space, and I was safe, and every cold and lonely thing inside me was erased, replaced with love and heat. She was draining me, and it was the best thing, because what else was there except this love, this perfect peace? *Peace I give unto you, not as the world gives*....

"Dante, drink it, darling." A flood of liquid over me, against my face, my death-blinded eyes, dripping into my mouth. I was with my mother again, and I remembered what it was to be an infant, suckled at her breast and safe in her embrace, the milky smell of her. *Oh, my mother*.... Suckling at her breast and safe, and—

The slow thudding of my heart returned: gently at first, barely audible, a distant ticking like a watch. And then stronger, beating in my ears like the cadence of an enormous drum, pounding lustily and strong and *alive*!

The room resolved around me, and I saw that I was in her arms, my mouth at her breast, and I was pulling blood from her, as she had taken it from me.

"Enough, Dante." She disengaged her nipple from my mouth, pressed her fingers against the flow of blood, smeared them on my lips. "New-made revenant, I bless you."

I caught her fingers and sucked them, drew them deep inside my mouth and bucked against her, my whole being suddenly engorged with lust. I held her by her waist and rubbed myself against her hip, faster and faster, rubbing myself against the rough fabric of my hose, the silken fabric of her dress. Release hovered around the edges of my senses; I could feel it building underneath my skin, that telltale tickle in the brain, the soles of my feet: imminent now, building, building—

Bright stars danced behind my closed eyelids and I spent myself against her in long, tremulous bursts that left me weeping. She wrapped her hand around me and squeezed, and I shivered again, and ground myself against her.

The world was exquisitely painful, and jagged around the edges. If I opened my eyes, the candlelight would blind me.

"Dante."

THE Ancient Kiss manifests itself differently in us all, but for me, it was a horror from the start, an alternate reality that had stolen my own existence, replaced it with something that I did not recognize and could not navigate.

I awoke the morning after Lilith made me, lying on the floor of my chamber, half-blind from the beam of daylight that slid across the floor, my skin seared with the impending heat, the promise of the dawn. The sight of it nauseated me and seared my eyeballs; I feared to touch it because I knew it would burn the skin from my bones. I crawled into a cabinet and slid the door behind me, and there I stayed, unconscious, until the world had made its revolution into darkness.

When I awoke again, I crawled up from a nightmare. I was possessed of a hunger the likes of which I had never known: it throbbed along my very bones, it pulsed underneath my skin. Every fiber of my being screamed for nourishment, a hunger that was like the fever pitch of lust.

I crept down into the kitchen.

There was food here, I thought, yes, food. I would eat and then I would be appeased, the pain would stop. I was utterly demented, my need for nourishment possessed me: I was deaf and blind to all else and driven only by this. My gums ached furiously; the bones themselves seemed to change their shape.

I found a loaf of bread lying on a table, and I seized it greedily, tore into it with my teeth, stuffed it down my throat. This was food, it was good, it would help—my stomach recoiled around it, forced it back in a great, retching heave, a violent contraction, a revulsion that ripped its way up out of my chest. I vomited until I was empty, huddled on the floor and clutching my aching stomach, arms wrapped around my chest. "Oh God, it hurts…." My voice was loud, ringing in the stillness of the kitchen. I could hear rats running underneath the cupboards, the padding of their tiny feet upon the stones. Above me, I could hear Ludmilla, sewing: I could hear each tug and pull as she drew her thread, the hissing passage of the needle through the cloth. I could hear people sleeping, hearts beating in the distant rooms above the kitchen.

I was losing my mind! I clamped my hands to the sides of my head, squeezed my eyes shut. The room seemed to move; the whole house was breathing, I could hear them all, breathing like that. I could hear the shifting of the timbers as the house settled, the creaking of the stones. I could hear it, hear everything.

I found a pitcher and poured a little water, but I could not drink it—my stomach lurched as I passed the cup across my lips, and I knew that if I drank it, I would vomit as before. I was suddenly and violently afraid.

"I'm going to die," I said. I would starve to death. Despite the abundance of Salvatore's wealth around me, I would starve.

I wondered what I was supposed to eat, now that Lilith had

changed me, now that her blood had passed into me. I wasn't certain about what had happened, I only knew that I had changed. My body felt differently than it had the day before: lighter, but at the same time more inherently solid, as if it had been invested with some covert power. My blood hummed along my veins, throbbed underneath my skin; my skull felt full of light.

Ludmilla kept a glass against the door, just on the wall above the chopping table, and I went to it now, pulled it down and peered into it. I was curious to see how these myriad sensations had manifested themselves in me; I wondered if drinking Lilith's blood had altered my essential structure. I held the mirror in my arms and tilted it until my face came into view.

I was *changed*!

I recoiled from the glass, flattened myself against the wall, desperately afraid of the apparition in the mirror. That wasn't me, it couldn't be me, and if it was, then Lilith had worked dark magic on me. I didn't look like that, it wasn't me!

My eyes, though still brown, were flecked with rich gold; the irises were deep and velvet, the whites as clear as marble. Something moved in the depth of my gaze, something animate; my eyes themselves were warm, glowing, enticing.

These were not the only changes.

My skin was pale as bone, and my face was unusually mobile, less able now than ever to disguise its expression. My hair tumbled about my shoulders, as darkly glossy as the mane of one of Salvatore's finest mares. My lips, slightly parted, glistened with moisture; when I parted them to see my teeth, I noticed two tiny spikes emerging from my gums on either side. I was subtly altered, a metamorphosis so precise as to leave my features intact while perfecting every aspect of my being.

I was beautiful now. But still damnably hungry! And it was building by the second, this lust for nourishment, so that it had become quite exquisitely painful.

I thought about the woman Lilith, what she had done to me, how she had given me suck from her breast, how she had given me blood from her body, how she had taken mine in return.

My mind was working furiously. This thing I craved, could it be blood? Perhaps this was what I must now eat. Perhaps I could no longer tolerate Ludmilla's cakes or her good, doughy loaves. Perhaps I could not take fruit, or sweetmeats, or wine.

I could feed as Lilith fed on me. The thought grew, gained shape, solidified.

Lilith had taken my blood. And I had taken hers. Then it was blood I needed. I would have to eat blood, drink it, something....

"I can't do it." Whispering, my voice was as loud as a normal person's mumble: I heard a twitter in the hallway, in a moment I would be discovered. The hunger twanged my senses like an over-tightened lute string; in a moment I would snap—

"Well, Dante! What are you doing, hiding in Ludmilla's kitchen?"

I spun guiltily, upset the mirror, and it fell before I could catch it, shattered into a million, silvery pieces.

It was Luigi, the groom's son. "Mother of God!" He blessed himself hurriedly, hastened to ward off the bad luck that follows a broken mirror. He was thirteen, barely on the cusp of manhood, still superstitious and uncertain, still clinging to childhood ideas. I regarded him with a lofty contempt that was quite wonderful and new.

"Luigi... I don't feel very well." I pitched my voice low to beckon him closer, slid down the wall till I was sitting on the floor. The hunger pulsed in me like a living thing, and there was no whispering of conscience, not then. I was hungry, I would eat. It was as simple as all that. I had scarce thought outside of hunger; there was room for little else.

"Should I summon Ludmilla? Have her make a potion?" He came closer, he was kneeling in my vomit, and this amused me, somehow. I could smell him, and he smelled wonderful: his skin, his hair, his sweat, the dust of his day's labor. I could hear blood beating in him, swishing through the tiny tubes of veins and arteries. I wanted to devour him whole, and I thought how easy it would be to break his soft, thin skin, so very like the skin of a plum or a grape. It would be like biting through a crust of sugar to the pulsing sweet heart of him. I thought about this quite intently. And I noticed that he was moving closer to me.

Come closer, yes, that's it, like that.... I could draw him with just a thought, and now he was folding himself into my arms, and he was there in my embrace and oh! the sweetness of him, like a luscious candied thing, the rich blood-smell of him, rising into my nostrils. I held him delicately, afraid that if I squeezed him he would shatter.

My gums ached, the shape of them was changing, from either side the spike descending, sliding down out of the bone. But I was clumsy with them yet, and I couldn't pierce his skin, so I seized a shard of broken mirror and slashed his throat, groaned aloud as the blood streamed down into his hair. I sealed my lips over the wound, as the dark fountain of his life erupted into my throat. The hunger hissed a little less keenly, and a lambent desire rose to take its place, filled my belly with a heady languor like that left behind by wine, well-aged and red. I felt the way I did after I had pleasured myself, alone in my bedroom, after I had brought my own release: sated, warm, and safe.

I drank until I felt his essential being disengage, slip out of his body with a discrete click like the snapping of a bone. The death was a shock, a sudden, sucking pull that dragged at me with claws; I recoiled from him, cast his body from me. Perhaps I ought not to continue drinking until the death comes, I thought.

I crouched for a long time with my back against the wall and watched him, watched the slow process of mortal demise with some great interest. I could see things now that I had never seen before, and I could see more: all the varied shades of light and dark that move across the spectrum. I watched Luigi dying, saw the changing temperature of his skin as the life left him. I saw the varicolored, invisible gases rising from his flesh, the slow stiffening of the rigor mortis.

The body cools so quickly. Something I learned that Lilith never told me. I'm not sure why I'm telling you this now. But it does: cools, and stiffens, the limbs hardening, the face becoming waxen, like a doll. A thing. I leaned against the wall and regarded him this way, my arms clutched around my belly, the blood spreading its warmth through me. I pondered, idly, what to do with it, this empty shell. I supposed I ought to bury it, dispose of it somehow. There aren't any rules for such things, you know. I wondered if the dogs might take it, should I leave it outside the villa gates....

Murder is a mortal sin, I thought idly. *Murder. I have murdered him....* I rolled the word around in my mouth, sucked it back like blood. It had the shape of a small stone, rested easily on my tongue. It meant little to me, as did other supposed sins. Salvatore tried to civilize me, but I have never fully embraced the dogma of the Christ. I fear that my inherent sensuality precludes such a spiritual gesture, as I love pleasure far more than is proper.

I wondered if this was how Lilith felt after she had taken me. I wished that I could ask her, but she had long since left, and I was alone in my new state, with none to tell me otherwise. I tossed Luigi's body into a stream behind the house.

I MADE my way back into the villa and up the stairs, intending to sleep in my old room. I knew now that the light could harm me, so it was vital that I shutter all the windows and bar the door.

A sound startled me, and I turned to see Ysin-Hui, Salvatore's Chinese trader, coming up the stairs. He carried a pail and a linen towel, and looked as if he had been ill. His skin was as pale as wax, and in the dim light, I could see beads of sweat standing on his forehead.

"Are you unwell, Ser?" My voice boomed out in the stillness of the stairwell, rushing past my lips at unearthly volume. I clamped a hand over my mouth and smiled past my fingers. "May I aid you?" I whispered. I could smell his blood, it didn't smell right. He hovered, creaking in front of me, his dark, almond eyes hazy, his gaze indistinct.

"I wish only rest." He moved away and down into the hallway, walking with a certain hobbling gait, his arms held stiffly from his sides, as if his armpits hurt him.

I noticed that the linen towel was spattered with bright red blood.

Chapter 2

DANTE

THE night before he had arrived in Salvatore's house, Ysin-Hui, the Chinese trade emissary, departed from the port in Sicily to begin the journey that would take him to Florence, and to our household. He anticipated no catastrophe. Sometime in the early hours of the morning, while sleeping in the upstairs bedroom, he was finally bitten by the single flea that had ridden undetected in his clothing all the way from China.

I AWOKE the next evening, mad with blood-hunger, desperate to feed the screaming demons inside of me. I knew I would have to go out and hunt, and the thought repelled me. I had replayed Luigi's death in my mind, over and over, till I had nearly driven myself mad. His face had haunted my dreams all day.

I had since learned to shutter my windows tightly against the advancing light of day, and chink the cracks with spare blankets. I knew the light would kill me if I were exposed to it. I had tested this myself, that first morning after Lilith made me. So while the sun rode high in the sky, I must needs shield myself in some convenient crevice. With my room secured against any wayward beam of sunlight, I slept in my bed as I always had, and feigned the same security and peace of mind. But something in me realized that I would soon have to be gone from this place. I could no longer hide the truth of my affliction; I would be missed about the household, and there would be talk. I could no longer take my meals with the other servants in the kitchen, the sight and smell of mortal food now sickened me.

There were other things, as well, connected with the blood and with this new hunger given to me by Lilith. The blood I'd taken had been absorbed completely into my body, without waste. There was no usual urge such as I often had upon arising, to empty my bladder or bowels. This amused me; I wondered if I'd enjoy never having to shit. I liked the way I felt after I'd taken Luigi's blood, but I didn't like the way I felt upon awakening. The desperate blood-hunger clawed at the brain, eroded the soul. The skin of my face and fingers was shrunken, cleaving to my bones.

And I was hungry—God, the hunger! I could smell the blood and flesh of mortals as they moved about the house. Indeed, there seemed to be a great flutter and commotion on the stairs, and I let myself into the hallway, thinking to discern the cause of this sudden rush-and-stumble.

I flattened myself against the wall as three maids clattered past me, balancing a giant tub of water between them, its contents sloshing violently against the sides as they rushed it into an upstairs bedroom. Somewhere in a distant room, someone was shrieking, a great, keening wail, a wordless screech that bent the walls. The whole world had gone mad in my absence, it seemed, and I, but moments awake and hungry, could not discern the cause of this apparent distress.

There was something moving in the air, some miasma of disaster that would drive me from this house, as surely as if I were but some wayward demon. There were myriad flickerings and warnings around the edges of my mind. I sensed imminent catastrophe.

I hastened down the steep stone stairway to the kitchen, caught Ludmilla's sleeve between my fingers. "What's happening—what is it?" My blood was thrumming in my ears, disaster scampering along my skin. I needed someone to make sense of it for me.

"Where have you been all day?" Her fist shot out and slammed into my cheek, a vicious backhanded slap that drove me against the opposite wall. "A death in the house and you're hiding from it!" She turned aside from me, spat on the floor. *"Vigliacco!"* Coward.

The keening wail from upstairs filtered down through the ceiling, assaulted my ears with its constant murmur. My skull rang with the force of Ludmilla's slap. "What's happening?" I asked again. "What's wrong, Ludmilla?" It was vital that I know the name of this tribulation.

"Sandro!" She ignored me, turned to scream at the kitchen knave. "Blow the ashes into flame and boil more water." She muttered something, made the Sign of the Cross hurriedly, bent to heave the great iron kettle onto the hearth. Her small eyes were sunk back into her fat face, like raisins in a pudding, and her skin was pale with fear. I wondered for a moment if indeed the house had gone entirely mad.

I FOUND Salvatore in the upstairs bedroom, hovering over the supine—and very dead—body of Ysin-Hui. "My Master—" I rushed to his side, caught his hand between my fingers, eager for its warmth. "—what is it?" There was a peculiar odor in the air: musky, not unlike the reek of rotting meat. My hand moved instinctively to cover my nose, my mouth.

"Dante." He drew me close to his side, his hand brushing my hair absently. His body was trembling underneath his clothes, his calm composure a mere facade. I knew then that something was very wrong. "I've never seen this. I don't know what it is." I saw by his appearance that he had been summoned from his evening's leisure, that quiet time when he took a little wine and smoked a portion of the *hasheesh* that Ysin-Hui brought him. His doublet had been pulled on hastily over his shirt, his hose was wrinkled; his hair was rumpled and there was a favorite leather-bound quarto clutched between his fingers.

The body of Ysin-Hui was stripped naked and displayed on the sheets as if it were a cut of meat. I could see that no preparations for burial had been made; the body seemed to be in the same condition as when the emissary had died. The linen bedcovers had been pulled back, and what I initially thought was a decoration on the cloth, was in fact, great steaming streaks of dark blood and black bile, putrescent and filthy. Gouts of greenish pus clung to the blankets, exuding a foul odor that made me gag as I drew near. The bed underneath the emissary was black with filthy excrement and dark blood.

"Dante, don't!" Salvatore called me back to him, but I was oddly fascinated and pretended not to hear. The maids had laid the tub of water on the floor and fled, handkerchiefs clutched against their mouths to bar the stench. The air around the bed fairly hummed with it, the fetor of this new death.

"What is it?" I spoke mostly to myself as I leaned over him, drew each of his eyelids up in turn with my thumb. The eyeballs had rolled so far back into his head that only the whites showed, streaked with blood. His face was contorted in a rictus of agony, the characteristic death's-head grimace. I knew that he had suffered before he had finally succumbed, and it made me sad. I knew he had been a friend to Salvatore, a man of culture, a *literati*. I felt grief for him, regretting his death as I have often regretted the extinction of some pleasing, harmless thing. Yet in those days, I did not understand the death of mortals so entirely as I do now. Sometimes it is a blessing to go gentle, as the poet said, into that good night.

Instinctively, I blessed myself, a gesture of reflex rather than faith, a show of fealty to my master, those others of his household who remained to witness this. And then I again bent near the emissary's dead body, hardly able to believe what I was seeing.

A great black bulge of flesh protruded from under each arm, swelling out of his armpits like some enormous egg. The swelling on the left had broken and exuded a dark, sticky pus. The smell of it was overwhelming, and I was forced to turn away. I staggered to the corner of the room and retched dryly, my empty stomach heaving, as if I would turn myself inside out.

"All right, it's all right...." Salvatore's hands on my shoulders, guiding me to him, drawing me close to his body, protecting me as he had always done. His voice was a soothing timbre, just above my ear. The horrible stench pervaded the room, a mixture of blood, pus, and excrement, mingled with the stink of putrefaction. My gorge rose as I groveled against him, eyes blinded, my hunger suddenly, freakishly gnawing at me. In the midst of such sickening putrefaction, such overwhelming horror, I could still smell his rich, old mortal's blood, with a fragrance as heady as wine. I could feel his heart beating strongly underneath his skin, and I was *hungry*....

...mouth opening, fangs descending with a throbbing, delicious ache *oh the blood!* and leaning into him, my mouth opening over his neck and there, the other servants clustered around the bed, *they can't see me and I'm so very hungry and oh! the blood*....

"Prepare the body!" Salvatore lurched away from me as if on the spur of an abrupt decision, dislodged me from his embrace, strode toward the bed in which the remains of Ysin-Hui lay, dead and stinking. "I must send a missive at once to his household." His mouth twisted, and a great shudder ran through him. I gaped at him, the blood-thirst pounding through me, throbbing like a pulse-beat. *Hungry*....

And he was gone, striding out the door, calling for a scribe, the servants following after him, twittering in his wake like a flock of hungry birds.

I was left alone with the corpse of Ysin-Hui.

"Go and pour out the bowls of the wrath of God upon the earth."

Her voice, like a whisper of dry leaves, a barely audible presence. I turned, and there she was, materialized from the ethers. My body leapt in recognition, arched toward her, the core of me an unconsummated ache.

"My servant, Dante." Her fingernails dug into my face, one fingertip underneath my eye. I knew that if I moved, she would blind me. I felt her breath upon my cheek, heard the rustling swish of her dress as she moved. Spirit-sprite, demon succubus.

"Lilith."

"Yes...." Her hands tilted my face into the light. "I see the transformation is complete. Wonderful." The pink tip of her tongue slid out to wet her lips, and I watched it, mesmerized. I remembered suckling from her, drawing her blood into my mouth, and I burned with the memory, like a recollection of lust, a dream.

"Why is he dead?" I meant Ysin-Hui, the body in the bed.

"His wrath is poured out over all the earth." Her eyes, brilliantly blue, shone with some inner fervor to which I was not privy. Behind us, I could hear the bustle of the household: Salvatore yelling in the courtyard, the far-off clamor of hooves.

"What do you mean?" And I sensed in that instant, even as I asked the question, that the death of Ysin-Hui was merely the beginning of a plethora of horrors.

"I am come to bring the end of the world." Her eyes glittered strangely as she moved to release me; my legs quivered and I tumbled to the floor, my cheek coming to rest against the cold tiles.

When I looked up, she had vanished.

BY SUPPER the next night, Ludmilla was feverish, and had taken to her bed, the dark rash mottling the fleshy skin of her face, the deadly buboes already swelling underneath her arms. Salvatore summoned the best physician, one whose skill was much vaunted by the Medici, but to no avail. Sometime later that night, Ludmilla died.

The plague spread throughout the household, racing up stairs and along corridors like some demon assassin. After Ludmilla, it took the serving maids, the gardener, the groom. It took Cosimo and he died writhing in the stables with the animals. It took Sandro the kitchen knave, who tossed in his bed, screaming hysterically of the Devil every time I came near. After some hours of this, Salvatore came and ordered me to stay away from him. I was astonished.

"But, Master—"

"You stay *away* from the boy, Dante!" he roared, his hair and beard askew, his eyes wild. "For all I know you may be the cause of this...."

I stared at him, my heart throbbing in my throat. I felt an uncharacteristic anger pressing against the back of my eyeballs, as acrid as bile in my mouth. "I could not possibly—"

"Liar! I know you are in consort with the devil." He shuffled papers on his desk, ready to dismiss me. An opened pot of ink rested at his elbow, beside it a stained quill. He had written the missive himself, I was certain. One last act of gratitude to Ysin-Hui. My throat thickened at the thought of it, such loyalty.

"My Master, I could not possibly—"

"You lie to me, again you lie!" He rose, grabbed the lip of the great mahogany desk and flipped it against me, knocking me backward and scattering papers, spilling the ink so that it pooled like dark blood on the inlaid tile floor. The huge desk tottered for an instant on uncertain legs, then dropped back into its customary position with a resounding bang. The silence rang with awful possibilities. "You never are seen in the daylight, and the servants say you have left this house under the cover of darkness—"

"My Master—"

"And Ysin-Hui, my friend and companion, has died here, in this house! And you were *hiding* from it; Ludmilla told me that you have not been seen all day!" He stared at me, his eyes enormous in his old man's face, his mouth quivering as if he had taken with the palsy. "You ungrateful, little *bastard!*" He slammed his fist down upon the desk, a vicious blow.

"My Master." I was close to tears, my throat was thick and the back of my eyeballs burned. I felt his affection withdraw itself from me, slide back into his soul. His expression was hard, the cold bargaining glance of a stranger. I stared at him, wondering where I would go, now that he no longer loved me.

THRUST in your sharp sickle and gather the clusters of the vine of the earth, for the grapes are fully ripe....

She flew in through the opened window like an angel of wrath, caught Salvatore under the chin and held his head, her fingers digging into his flesh. "Shall I kill this one?" A great winged shadow, the archangel who shall announce the end of the world.... "I offer him to you."

I stood rooted to the spot, galvanized with fear. My throat had swelled so that I couldn't open my mouth, couldn't speak. Dread slithered over me, an insect swarm.

Please don't....

"Ah. You recant, then, on your faith?"

I had no idea what she was talking about. "Please, let him go." Salvatore stared straight ahead, eyes frozen in his face like inanimate glass balls, caught in the same strange thrall as I had been, that first time in Lilith's presence.

"He will soon enough be dead, Dante." She freed his forearm from the sleeve of his gown and with one sharp fingernail, traced a bright red circle in his flesh. *Ring around the rosy....*

Her mouth smiled, lips opening like a bloody slash, like a wound. "I am become Death, destroyer of worlds."

I WANDERED for a long time about the city, lost in the teeming streets. I was then, and still am, most at home in large crowds. I blend into the masses. I disappear. It was a useful talent to have, for one of my kind; I could literally hide in plain sight.

The autumn evening was warm, and so I could roam at will, seeking sustenance among the myriad faces that lined the streets, that supped at leisure in the inns and taverns. I was possessed for a moment of a mad desire, to catch one of them by the arm or by the shoulder, to fall in step with him, as comrades do, to turn his face to mine and smiling, say, "I'm going to kill you."

I shook myself, hastily disposing of the notion. The hunger must have made me a little mad.

I had not fed sufficiently since I'd drunk the blood of the groom's son, Luigi, still unable to use these new fangs of mine with any such utility. I'd gone out into the streets looking for more, and had badly mauled a peddler the night before, gnawing at him until finally, in frustration, I tore his throat with my hands, spilling most of the blood before I could get it. I'd cursed myself, my ineptitude; this was supposed to come naturally to me, this was the gift that Lilith gave me.

It was a difficult way to make a living, to say the least.

I WANDERED into a tavern, ordered a cup of ale, and sat beside the fire. There was a table of young Tuscans just across from me, all of them in the advanced stages of drunkenness, all of them—to my preternatural vision—strangely compelling, and really, rather beautiful.

THERE was a trio of minstrels playing near their table, one with a lute, the other with a mandolin, the third with some kind of timbrel. The music cut through the noisome din, high and sweet and intricate, and the fire was pleasant, entrancing. I watched it for a time, seeing colors and shapes in it that were not possible to mortal eyes. The tavern buzzed around me, a soothing racket.

Yet the hunger....

I turned my gaze toward the table full of Tuscans, their boisterous laughter commanding my attention, the scent of their heated flesh a perfume in my nostrils. They were loud and brazen, secure in their strength, their masculinity. They were the flower of Italy. Or so they thought.

There was one, at the head of the table, a dashing young bravo, expensively dressed in silk hose with but a strip of leather stitched to the bottom, a velvet doublet with deep, dagged sleeves. His black hair fell unconfined to his shoulders and was cut in the current fashion, feathering toward his face. His skin was as white as milk, and his eyes, dark green, like verdant, emerald forests. His expression was one of divine calm, the face of a sleepy Bacchus.

Come to me....

His head snapped up, his entire being suddenly infused with the idea of me, the silent summons that I'd sent him. It seemed that I now had only to think of something, and it would come to pass.

Come hither, love to me....

I WATCHED him rise, as if in a dream, push aside his chair with a certain deliberation, move across the room to where I sat, innocuous before the fire. The light contracted, pushing in on me; the music swirled dangerously as the blood lust crested to a roar. My fangs descended, slid throbbing out of my gums, and my desire rose to fill my head like smoke. *Come hither, love....*

His fingers splayed against my face, the soft pads sliding on my skin, flicking against my lashes. His leg pressed against mine, all hard bone and sinew; I could smell his delicious heated flesh through his clothes, and I arched against him eagerly.

I caught his face between my palms, turned his head to open the line of the throat, the sweet ivory column of it, the throbbing vein that pulsed like a tiny heartbeat. I kissed it, tenderly, smiled into his eyes....

Love me, yes you do....—leaned and drove my fangs deep into the artery, groaned against his neck as the dark fountain of his blood erupted down my throat—

Oh yes, so good, so good

—he was bucking against me, resisting me; his leg came across mine and pinned me to the bench, his hand pushed against my face, he was resisting me, even as I drained him, he resisted me!

"Stop it!" The heel of his palm slammed into my chin, "Stop!"

I pulled away from him, staring. His green eyes were bright with unshed tears. The wound I'd made was a violent red gash against the pale skin of his neck.

"Rouen…." Inexplicably, I knew his name.

"Leave me alone!"

There was a clatter at the door as he went out; the minstrels paused their music and every face turned to watch him leave, then turned to stare at me. The blood-hunger had left me, and in its place, I felt nothing but a curious emptiness, a spiritual sorrow.

The company were staring at me, at my bloody mouth.

I left, intent that I should find him.

I DID not return to Salvatore's house until the evening of the next day. I had spent the remainder of the previous night searching for Rouen all throughout the streets of Florence, but he had vanished as surely as Lilith vanished into mist. Yet, my thoughts returned to him again and again. I could not fathom how he had the strength to resist me, to pull away while I drained his life's blood. Perhaps there were mortals that were stronger than our kind. Perhaps this Rouen was one of them.

The first thing I noticed as I approached the villa was the bright red cross painted on the door, hastily daubed and still fresh. It was curious, I had never seen anything like it before, and I didn't know what to make of it. I wondered if the doctor had come, and if he had quarantined the house.

Perhaps there had been other deaths, then, in my absence.

I wandered into the kitchen, which was empty save for Ludmilla's boy Lorenzo, a lumbering behemoth of fifteen years who cracked nuts between his teeth and coupled with the kitchen maids behind the granary, as was his custom.

He was slumped at the table, half a loaf of bread before him, and a flagon of wine. His great moon face was wet, and his protruding eyes red about the rims. I despised him. He was nothing but a great useless lump of animal matter.

"Where is everyone?" I asked him sharply. The house was unnaturally quiet. The sight of him irritated me beyond comprehension, but then, I noticed that my emotions had taken on a new quality these days. I felt things far more intently than I had when I was mortal: love and pleasure were an overwhelming madness, lust and anger, a dangerous obsession. So the blood changes us, whether subtly or overt.

"This new death has taken them," he answered, his gaze averted. He raised the sleeve of his jerkin and scraped it across his nose, leaving behind a long trail of mucus, viscous and green.

I wanted to kill him right then. "How many?"

"Seven today." He would not meet my eyes.

"Is my master well?" I strode over to him and yanked on his forelock. "Look at me!" I forced his head up to meet my gaze, but he cringed away from me, shut his lids. I felt my fingers ball into a fist, my arm draw back reflexively. One blow would kill him. I would probably be doing him a great mercy.

"Lorenzo, where is the master?"

But he would not answer me, and so I broke his neck out of sheer anger, disposed of him with the rest of the dead. I threw the bodies behind the house, covering each with a layer of dirt. There was no fear that they would be disinterred by happenstance, as nobody had come near the villa now for days.

After I had done this, I went looking for Salvatore, found him in his chamber, alone. The room was filled with the stench of mortal decay, senescent flesh, and I knew in an instant that he had not long for this earth. He had the look of death about him; already the creeping pallor had drained his face of color.

"My son Dante." He raised one bone-thin hand and beckoned me to his side, drew me down against the bedclothes. His long fingers were cold in my grasp, and curiously fragile, like the dried bones of animals. "You have served me well." His voice was weak, a thready whisper in his throat.

"My Master." I could not speak for the tears that clogged my throat, and blinded me. I must needs turn away from him. Sorrow is a thing we feel most intently....

"Ah, my faithful servant, Dante." His old eyes peered at me in the semidarkness. "Where have they gone, my family, my servants? The house is quiet, too quiet now."

I thought about Lorenzo, whom I had just murdered in the kitchen. "I do not know, my Master." Lies, of course, but lies were kindest now. How could I tell him that some preternatural monster had come into their midst, sowing death?

"My body pains me, Dante. And I cannot catch my breath."

I had heard him coughing, seen the crimson spatters on his handkerchiefs, the bedclothes. His skin was mottled with the same dark rash as that which killed Ludmilla. I knew it was this sickness that devoured with a terrifying swiftness. I knew also that he would die a painful death. I wondered if the mortal part of me that still existed could allow it. "Can I aid you, my Master?" I thought there was some kindness I might give him, a tincture of darkness that would ease him into death.

He stared at me for a long moment in the gathering darkness, his old eyes quizzical. "I wish only mercy," he said, with deadening finality.

He did not struggle when I took him, and I was careful to take him as gently as I could. I drained him swiftly, drawing his wise old mortal's blood deep into my throat until his feeble heart was silent.

I had given my last service to my master.

The villa was dark behind me as I slipped out into the night, determined to vanish into the city, if such a thing was at all possible for me. There was nothing here for me anymore; what connection to this mortal world I'd had, now lay dead in an upstairs bedroom, his decaying flesh exuding a deadly plague. My idyll here was over. I was no longer Salvatore's servant, or his son. I was merely Dante.

I had no real thought as to where I might go; I only knew what I was looking for, that it was all bound up with a word that repeated itself like a chorus in my brain.

Rouen.

Chapter 3

December 1347
Florence

ROUEN

My name is Rouen di Francisci, and I am six hundred years old.

My God… written down like that it looks rather shocking, I must admit, and yet, it is a truth from which I cannot run. It is the central fact of my existence; I am immeasurably old because of him, and without him I would not have become the thing I am now.

Nosferatu, vampyr, the undead… the names are all the same, no matter where you roam, no matter where it is you find these legends. There are even modern fables, penned by lovely Southern ladies, who think they know these things, who postulate that we are very numerous and powerful, and that we can fly. I have read these tales.

I can fly, and yet I choose to only when I must, for it pains me, reminds me of how far I have fallen from my mortal nature. But Dante flies as often as there is opportunity. Dante has no such moral difficulties. Clearly, he is the stronger of us. But he is also beautiful, at least to me.

Often, when I lie awake at sunrise and gaze at him, his immortal beauty nearly stops my heart. I know scarcely more of him now than I knew then, and when is then? Eons ago, forever. Are we powerful? I think that Dante must be, simply because I am so bound to him by this eternal love... that is his sole power over me. As for our numbers, there are to my knowledge, no others, or at least, no others that remain. There is only Dante, and I. Yet Dante speaks often of before, when Lilith came, brought with her the terrible curse that very nearly wiped us off the face of the earth. Perhaps this is why Dante and I are so very insular and cold; perhaps this is why we cling to each other in the hope that, if Lilith lives still, she will not find us. Or at least, I cling. Dante does not cling to anyone. He does not need to.

You want to know of us; yes, I can see you there, leaning close to this page. What does he look like? Your mind is asking, does he do the same things he did when he was mortal? I will answer all of this: I will tell you that yes, I once was mortal, but it was so very long ago that I can scarce remember. My powerful family, my father and his olive trees, his grapes, his ancient name, and the hidden sin of which he was so proud, are long dead and gone to dust. Such is the way of things, and the sleepy Tuscan village from whence my little mortal soul was born is also gone, dissolved like all things in the strong broth of Time and whispered away on the wind. What is it the poet said? "At my back I always hear, Time's winged chariot, hurrying near". Andrew Marvell, whose only temporal worry concerned the affections of his coy mistress! But such are the concerns of mortals. When last I opened mortal eyes to the sunrise, men walked behind oxen carts, pulled hand barrows full of fruit, lived and died by the sun and by the seasons. Life was short, brutish, and unequivocally nasty. I do not long for it.

But I want to tell you about Dante. He has no name, at least none given in baptism. He calls himself Dante because his master long ago chose it for him. He has no family, no kin of which he speaks. If ever he had a mother—and I think he must have—he has never mentioned her. His earliest mortal memory, he told me, is of lying in the dust of the marketplace and crying. "Everything seemed so very large," he said, his dark eyes recalling it as we sat and talked around the fire. "Everything."

I also found him in the market. I remember that it was the dead of winter, the advent of the Christmas feast, a chilly evening, just at twilight. I had gone out, reluctantly, and at my father's bidding, to buy a bird for the holy meal, a task I hated, but one which fell to me anyway. The servants claimed they were frightened of the markets, they feared plague. I suggested to my father that he might wish to dismiss them all, instead. My suggestion was ignored. He treated all my words this way, as if they were weightless feathers, fluttering about him, meaningless. I merely watched him warily and waited, as I always had, for any chance to expose him.

I had walked for hours today among the crowded, muddy stalls; I had traveled, footsore, up and down the intricate side streets and the convoluted alleys of Florence, and I had finally gained nothing for my troubles. I did not want to linger long in public; there was always danger of the plague, and I had no way of knowing which of the filthy commoners that passed me might be infected.

I passed the alehouse, doubled back to view a stall of jewelry; there might be something there that Mother would like. I had purchased small tokens for both her and Father, but I knew she would enjoy the bright silver brooches, so I bought one. Mother enjoyed shiny trinkets, and was happiest when decked out in her finery, glistening like the sun. This was most ironic, for my mother was blind from birth. Yet she contemplated little else, but how she might best adorn herself to please my father, to somehow sanctify their unholy union. His greatest pleasure was to lavish her with gifts of gold and jewels, to keep her simple and submissive, and most important of all, silent. So far, his ruse had worked. Their apostasy remained hidden from the incisive gaze of the Church.

I paid for my purchase and waited while the vendor wrapped it in a piece of cloth for me. My gaze wandered as I waited, eventually lighting on a ragtag group of people standing nearest the arcade. They intrigued me, these remnants of the market rabble. "Who are those people?"

"Which people, Ser?" His gaze followed mine, picked them out easily. "Oh, those people." He turned aside, spat on the ground. "Merchandise they are, as well as this." He swept his arm wide, to indicate his wares. "Selling themselves. They know it's busy here, despite the plague." He handed me the package, securely wrapped in burlap. "A blessed holiday to you, Ser."

I murmured something, I'm not sure what, and drew away, my attention elsewhere. I was suddenly fascinated with the whores, and I wasn't sure why. It wasn't like I'd never seen any before.

That young man leaning against the arch... who was he? I knew that I'd seen him somewhere before, his face was as familiar to me as my own... his large, dark eyes, pale skin, arched eyebrows. Yes, I knew him.

I wondered if he were one of the patrons of the inn I frequented, but I couldn't be sure. That he was selling his favors meant nothing in this case, and surely gave no indication that he was a gentleman of my particular persuasion. Some of the inn's gentleman whores sold themselves purely out of economic necessity, and I supposed it could be so with him.

But where had I seen him? It was positively eerie, I knew this man as surely as I knew myself.

I drew closer, hid myself behind a wall, and peered at him. He was poorly dressed, but not in the usual way. By that, I don't mean that his clothes were simply cheap, or badly made—that lack of workmanship that so characterizes the clothing of the lower classes— no, he wore garments that had at one time been luxurious, but were now threadbare. He looked like the servant of some good household, who had fallen on bad times.

I watched as he called out to passersby, leaning against the archway. He was shivering, drawing the remnants of a tattered cloak around him, crouching against the wintry blast. His fingers and the tips of his ears were white with cold. I wondered if he would survive the night, or if he were as doomed as all the other hapless unfortunates without homes or kin to take them in.

A vicious pang of pity lanced through me. I felt sorry for him, probably because he held some unknown familiarity for me, or because he was close to my own age. Something about him reminded me of myself, somehow. His face was beautiful, but innocent. I wasn't used to that. The faces of Tralini's painted boy whores with their multitude of knowing glances were nothing more than a pretty procession of used-up jades. I had seen them too often. The trouble with Tralini's inn was that the buggers never changed: always the same faces, the same fetishes, the same noises and smells. It bored me, an endless parade of pointless fucking.

"Rouen!"

I turned at the sound of my name, jolted out of my reverie by a familiar voice, a smiling pair of hazel eyes that I knew as well as my own. "Leonardo!" I caught him and embraced him, leaned back to smile. "You have no fear of plague, then?" Like me, Leonardo was of a noble household. I couldn't think why he was in the marketplace today.

He grinned. "Nor do you, it seems." He nodded toward the arcade. "Browsing, or are you thinking to buy?"

I laughed. "Lower your voice, buffoon." I cuffed him playfully on the back of the head, dislodging his velvet cap. "As if I would consort with filth like that!" I pointed toward the shivering boy, the dark-eyed one, the one whose eerie familiarity I couldn't place.

He was watching me.

"He likes you, Rouen." Leonardo nudged me, playfully from behind. "Go on, buy him. A little sport would be fun." He fumbled at his waist for his purse. "Or better yet, let's purchase him together...."

And before I could stop him, he was striding toward the boy, a handful of florins in his fist.

"Leonardo, no!" I dashed after him, but it was too late; he was negotiating a price. Before I knew what was happening, we were all three of us in the upstairs bedroom at an inn: Leonardo, the nameless boy, and me.

"This is nonsense!" I hissed at Leonardo, pulled him over to the side. The whore was warming himself by the fire, stretching chapped and chilblained hands toward the flames. "He could be riddled with plague for all we know!" I was suddenly and inexplicably furious. I normally enjoyed such sport, it was the popular thing with those of my circle. But I preferred to sport with Tralini's painted boys; at least I knew that they were clean. This kind of consort was beneath me.

"Well, fuss if you must." Leonardo was busily unfastening his hose. "I paid for him, and I intend to have fun with him. Come here, boy!"

I watched him cower close against the fire, still shivering underneath his tattered cloak, and pity rose in me, a great roaring wave. "Leonardo, stop...."

Leonardo turned, stared at me. "What did you say, Rouen?" He cocked a hand behind his ear, adopted a comical expression. I was sickened, suddenly, and wished I had never come here. I should have gone straight home; my mother's brooch in its burlap wrapping pressed against the inside of my pocket, reminding me of duty.

"Please, Leonardo. Let him go." The boy's dark eyes gazed at me, no expression in their depths; his mouth was set, a thin colorless line. I could neither tell if he hated me or desired me.

"No, Rouen." Leonardo peered at the boy, speculatively. "I think I might like to see him dance."

Something cringed, deep inside me.

"Dance, boy!" Leonardo leapt at him, poked him in the shoulder with a fingertip. "Dance for us, go on! I'll sing and you can dance." He started humming, some tavern ditty that we knew.

"Leonardo, stop this now!"

He spun around, seized me viciously. "Why, Rouen? Are you no longer interested in this kind of sport?"

"It's cruel, you're humiliating him—" I felt sweat gather in my armpits, the small of my back. "—stop this!"

His face hardened, his intelligent, dark eyes becoming cold and empty, the eyes of a marble statue. "I don't care. I'm enjoying myself."

I watched as Leonardo grabbed the shoulder of the boy's shirt and ripped it viciously, exposing the pale skin beneath, the naked landscape of his shivering torso. He preened before the boy, adopted an imperious manner and a mincing tone of voice. "Dance, minion! I, Leonardo di Sforza, command you!"

The boy ignored him, cowered further into his tattered rags, and Leonardo slapped him, a savage backhanded smack across the mouth, a blow violent enough to shatter his teeth. I watched, cringing, waiting for the inevitable retaliation, but the boy merely stood his ground, tears slowly filling up the rims of his eyes... tears that were tinged with blood.

"Plague!" I roared, pointing to him with a quivering arm. "He's riddled with plague, Leonardo... his eyes, his *eyes!*" I backed away until I felt the wall between my shoulders. I was shaking, terrified. This was the judgment of God upon us, punishment for our unnatural ways. "Don't touch him!" I warned, "He'll kill you."

As if in slow motion, I saw Leonardo turn and grin at me, unfastening his hose, slipping out of the codpiece, baring his erect member. He laughed as he tore away the boy's tattered hose, laughed as he bent him double, laughed as he rammed himself hilt-deep into the boy's unresisting body. The boy jerked, gasping, pain and disbelief etched on his features. He had not expected this.

"Oh, Rouen, you should try him!" Leonardo swiveled his hips, driving himself deeper. I watched in horror, unable to turn away from it: Leonardo's grinning face, the boy's helpless body, jerking with the violence of the thrusts, his averted face contorted in agony. "He's really quite superior to Tralini's boys...." His eyes flickered closed, his face working, a grimace lingering about his features. His mouth twitched, pulling at the corners as he neared climax; I had seen this often enough when he fucked the whores at Tralini's.

"Stop—" The boy gasped, reached clawing for Leonardo. His spine stiffened, and something in his posture chimed warning in my brain.

"Leonardo, he's—"

Leonardo slammed into him again, arched his back, and crowed as the climax took him, and ground himself against the boy's naked buttocks. "Oh, Rouen, truly—" He wiped his face in his sleeve, "—are you certain you won't try him?"

I turned away, sickened beyond measure, unable to speak for the words that stuck in my throat. I heard Leonardo fastening his garments, adjusting his hose, tying the laces to his doublet.

"Really quite a wonderful fuck, Rouen. Thank you for finding him." A burst of laughter, the clatter of retreating footsteps, down the narrow staircase, out into the street. A wave of sickness gripped me, and I retched, emptied the contents of my stomach onto the floor beside me. I felt cold all over; I felt evil. Surely God would judge us for this, just as he would judge us for our unnatural lusts....

Someone was sobbing.

I pulled myself up and went to him, hovered near, uncertain as to how I might assist him. I couldn't meet his gaze. "Did he hurt you?" I asked. It was a stupid question; the answer was patently obvious.

He turned his head, his face wet with his strange bloody tears, and hissed at me, "Get out!"

And in that moment, galvanized with horror, I knew him. He was the young man who had assaulted me in the tavern, who had somehow called me to him and then...drunk my blood. His lips against my neck, his mouth pulling at me, like a baby at the breast.

I drew back as if burned, recoiled from him. "I know you!"

"Get out!" He buried his face in his arms and sobbed, his naked shoulders shaking. I saw that his thighs and buttocks were streaked with bright red blood, the white skin of his back dappled with finger-marks.

"Who are you?" I whispered, but I knew even as I asked it that he wouldn't answer me. I stepped close to where he lay and removed my cloak, draped it over him. "I'm sorry," I said. It seemed woefully inadequate in the face of our brutal treatment of him, but I didn't know what else to say. "Please, take it, it's Christmas." I dropped a handful of florins on the floor beside him and retreated, hastening into the darkness.

His sobbing echoed behind me, chased me out into the night.

SEVERAL weeks later, I was working late in my father's study, adding the week's profits in the ledger, when he was suddenly there. It was the beginning of the New Year, mid-January, and as cold as it ever became.

"Rouen."

I turned slowly and beheld him, as if in a dream, standing near the shuttered window, his cloak—my cloak—wrapped about him. He wore a long winter doublet over heavy woolen hose, new leather boots, and a velvet cap upon his head. His hair was clean and pressed at the ends, and waved about his face in feathery wisps. He stood as still as a statue, and as silent.

I rose slowly from the chair, moved toward him. "I am Rouen di Francisci." I waited for his introduction, was annoyed when none came. "You must have a name!" My nobleman's patience was ill-suited for this. I watched as the smile spread slowly, a little wistfully, and he turned those incredible eyes to mine. "My name is only Dante. You may call me as you wish." The words hung in air, naked. His expression was bemused. "I am quite adaptable, you see: I can be either peasant or nobleman, king or churl, depending on your wish." He bowed, mockingly, slipped out of the cloak and handed it to me. "Your cloak, Ser."

I remembered how he had been selling himself to survive, there in the market. "You are afflicted with the plague." I reached into the drawer for my handkerchief, pressed its scent against my nostrils. "Go away!"

"Ah." He nodded. "You wish me to keep your cloak, then? A small gift in exchange for my trouble?" He began to slowly walk toward me, his feet silent on the tiled floor. "You do remember my trouble, Ser?"

I felt cold fear like a lump of ice in my guts, cast about wildly for an escape.

But he was on me, his hands like bands of iron around my arms, holding me where I was. "Plague," I whispered.

"No. Not plague, Rouen." He moved me to the couch, and sat us both down. His expression was curiously gentle. "You must listen to me."

"I remember you," I whispered. "The tavern. You tried to drink my blood."

"I did drink your blood...." He raised his hand, and I cringed, afraid that he would strike me, but he merely smoothed my hair away from my forehead, his touch very gentle. There was a curious grace about his movements, something not entirely human, and his skin was heated as if with fever. Myriad wondrous colors swirled inside his eyes.

"What are you?" I wondered if he were some kind of demon.

"You need me."

He sounded mightily certain, I thought. I turned and stared at him, his alabaster face, his fathomless, brown eyes, his sensual mouth, the spray of pale-gold freckles across his nose. But God! The luminescent beauty of his face, that ancient angel's face. The great artists of antiquity, infused with holy fire, could not have painted more perfect a Lucifer than he. He was indeed more beautiful than Tralini's painted boys. I could no more turn and go than I could summon the winds to do my bidding; I sat rooted to the spot, staring at him.

You must understand: as Rouen di Francisci, I was the eldest son of a noble family, one of the wealthiest in the country; my father, with his vast stands of olive trees, his gilded palace, was rich beyond belief, a wealth accrued through his incestuous—and illegal—marriage to his own sister, my mother. I had been educated by the very best tutors that his money could buy, in the hope that a thin veneer of civility might gloss over the fact of my bastardy. He brought me scholarly books from foreign lands so that I would be enlightened, and thus compound his duplicity further. Every effort was expended to the end that I might prove a credit to his name—his name, which, if the truth were noised abroad, would become the name of the filthiest of liars, a pagan who coupled with his own sister and produced cretins. How fitting that I had sullied myself by associating with this urchin. The thought pleased me.

Thus was the curse of my own perverse nature, the desire that favored my own sex, and shunned women. I had been this way as long as I could remember; I preferred the pleasures of a hearty young bravo to the delights of a maiden. It had taken its toll on me. I was often melancholy, a melancholy that gave way to cruelty and vice; I suffered through fits of ennui and did damage to myself. I got drunk and broke things. I made my mother cry.

"You need me."

I gazed at him for a long moment, remembering him as I had last seen him, lying bruised and bloody on the floor of some anonymous inn. "I should have stopped him. I'm sorry." I spoke, of course of Leonardo, the rape.

"Rouen, you need me."

I took him to my lodgings in the city, smuggled him past the landlord, one of my father's patrons. Only when he was safely inside the room did I dare to breathe a sigh of relief. If I had been seen with him, I would have been utterly undone; my father, for certain, would have been publicly shamed if word ever got around that I was fraternizing with the underclasses. Yet it would go still worse for me if my father ever discovered the truth of my perverse nature.

He hovered near me, his breath warm against my cheek. I immediately thought of the tavern again, his mouth against my neck. *Come hither love to me....*

"I would like to bathe." He pressed his fingers against my lips, pushed the unspoken question back into my mouth. "I promise I'll tell you everything soon enough, but I've traveled a long way. I would like to bathe."

I hid him in the garderobe while I summoned the chambermaid with bucket after bucket of hot water to fill the bath. I pressed a couple of florins into her hand and told her to bring up the best soap and some thick towels.

I busied myself at the desk while he stripped, not trusting him enough to leave him alone, but wanting to give him some small measure of privacy while he bathed. I sensed that luxuries such as privacy had been notably absent from his brutish existence; I wanted to remedy that. My curiosity, however, was aroused, and thus I was careful to position myself in front of the mirror, the better to see him clearly behind me.

He shed his clothing like a skin, left it lying in a pile on the floor. He slipped out of his boots, laid them side-by-side against the wall, folded everything neatly and placed it on a chair, even his drawers. This was probably the only suit of clothing that he owned.

I forced myself not to stare at him, but his body was exquisite, the form of an Adonis. He was potentiality, a template of perfection, standing naked over the washtub, gazing down at his own reflection. Narcissus at the pool.

"Please, get in. The water, it cools so quickly." I spoke to him over my shoulder, glancing up into the mirror. He hovered naked at the edge of the tin bathtub, waving one hand back and forth along the surface of the water, drawing ripples through his own reflection. I thought I saw him smile.

"Are you watching me?" He stepped into the tub, stood for a moment, and then folded his body down into the water gracefully. "I ought to make you pay for the privilege of looking, I suppose." His expression was suddenly coy, and I was struck with the memory of him, leaning against the archway in the arcade.

I snorted in disgust. "I assure you, I am not interested in you." I turned, pointed to the soap with my pen. "Wash yourself."

I found I couldn't turn away from him; he seemed to have bewitched me somehow, so that I must watch him in the mirror, follow the clean lines of his muscled shoulders, the shifting landscape of his chest and his flat belly. His hair spilled around his shoulders, a chestnut mane. God! but he was glorious!

I watched him in silence for a moment, let him have the luxury of hot water, soap, these little comforts. Apart from the unfortunate incident with Leonardo, I knew nothing about him, and wondered if he were not some kind of madman, bent on having sport at my expense. "You said I needed you." I bent over my ledger, printed out a neat line of figures, the totals of last week's profits. As always, Father was doing well. "What did you mean?"

He laughed shortly, a surprisingly pleasant sound. "Of course you need me." He ducked his head underneath the water, rubbed his soapy palms into his hair.

"Do you know something about me? Is that what this is about?" I was terrified that he was some sort of blackmailer, sent to spy on me and extort money. I knew that if my father ever found out about my unnatural desires, he would kill me himself.

"I know everything about you. Your past, your future." He ducked his head, rinsed the lather from his dark hair. "I was once like you. Somewhat." There was a trace of bitterness in his voice.

"Nonsense." I felt the tiny hairs nearest my scalp prickle.

"Truly." He lathered his body, began scrubbing vigorously, and sluiced himself with water. "Which is precisely why I chose you. We are all chosen, you see, each one forced into the steps of the dance." He smiled, faintly. "Someone wise once told me that."

I noticed that the nipple of his left breast had been slit neatly in two; it was healed now, the wound covered with a thin layer of tissue, a curious scar, like a small sealed mouth. It was an odd wound to have, and I wondered how he came by it.

"Rouen."

I had not blinked, and yet there he was behind me. "You need me." His voice was a velvet caress, utterly sensual.

I cringed away from him, leapt out of the chair. "Enough of this!" I roared. "Who are you?" My heart was pounding in my throat, blood singing in my ears.

He did the strangest thing, then. He took my hand and pressed my palm against his naked chest, laid my fingers on his damaged nipple. "I am become Death, destroyer of worlds." His whisper barely stirred the hair at the sides of my face. I was suddenly cold with a profound and death-deep chill. Why had he said that? Had this urchin even access to literature? The phrase, my mind recalled, was from some Hindu thing, the *Bhagavad Gita.*

There was no heartbeat. At least, no heartbeat that was mortal. The cadence was altogether wrong, there was no warmth, no essential pulsing throb; there was nothing human in it.

I could not even speak, my voice was stopped in my throat, words clotted together like so much dried blood—

Blood.

"You need me." His fingers stroked the side of my face. I was powerless to stop him. "You have always needed me."

Heat flooded me, rising up from deep within my belly, and I dimly heard myself groaning as I reached for him, clasped the muscular perfection of him to me. I keened aloud when I felt his teeth go into my flesh, a discrete hiss that slid along my skin, flowed off my fingertips like water. I bucked and strained against him as his lips pulled hard, sucking. Lust stiffened me, my whole person was engorged with blood. He took one last pull and I arched toward him, exploded in an eager burst, my spent desire seeping wetly into my drawers, my hose. He turned his mouth to mine, still wet with blood, his tongue wrestling bluntly with my own. "You must take the blood." His hands slid down, and with a thumbnail, he slit the damaged nipple so that it bled freely. "Take it."

"I don't understand...." My head swam dizzily, there was no projection of normalcy for me to grasp.

"Your friend Leonardo is infected with the plague. When you kissed him, he infected you. If you do not take the blood, you will die." His gaze was steady, unwavering. I knew somehow that what he said was true. Poor Leonardo....

I stared at him. "You want me to drink your blood?"

"Rouen, already it works its dark will upon you!" he said, impatiently. "Now take it, please, I beg you!" His dark eyes drew me into his embrace. *Come hither love to me....*

I was falling, drowning in him; I felt him lower me to the floor, and I was kneeling before him, a supplicant at the feet of Christ. "Dante...." He was beautiful, he was everything I wanted.

I fastened on to him, caught his nipple between my eager lips and sucked, felt the essence of him slide into my mouth and trickle down my throat. I wrapped my arms around him, clutched his body tightly as his hips began to grind against me, our flesh locked together. So good this, so warm, like light.

I did not know then that I would never see the light of day again. Even as I held him, kneeling on the floor, even as my mouth drew his vampire life, even as he made me what I am, I still knew nothing. Dante himself knew nothing. I was brought over in a state of purest ignorance, under the most dire necessity.

"WHAT do you mean, the end of the world?" I turned to stare at him, lying beside me in the bed. His eyes were hazy with sleep, half-closed. It was nearing the dawn; he'd told me how he could not stand the sunlight, how the advent of the day brought a death-like sleep.

"This new disease, this plague, Rouen." He shifted in the bed, rolled up on one elbow so that he was facing me. "It is but the beginning of a surfeit of horrors."

"I don't understand," I told him, but I was suddenly more afraid than I have ever been, with a terrible premonition of disaster. "How is this woman—"

"Lilith."

"How is this Lilith going to bring about the end of the world?" I felt vaguely sick. Whether it was his unnatural blood, working in me, or my own precognition, I couldn't tell. I just knew, somehow, that what he told me was the truth. And it frightened me terribly.

He shook his head, his eyes filling with tears. "I don't know, Rouen. But she will."

I lay back among the pillows and watched him fall into his death-sleep, knowing that as the sun crawled higher into the sky, this earth turned another measure into eternal darkness.

For the first time in many years, I prayed to God to save me. I felt dark unconsciousness tugging at me like a summons, and I resisted it, terrified that if I closed my eyes to it I might never open them again. I lay as if at the center of a dark, sucking crater, paralyzed by fear like I have never felt. My father's brutality to me, my mother's blindness, their awesome and terrible sin, all of it paled in the face of this.

Mystery, Babylon the Great, Mother of Harlots....

I turned, and with the last of my strength, I raised myself in time to see the great winged shadow of a woman, hovering over the bed, eyes glittering in the darkness, fangs poised to strike.

"She—"

Darkness claimed me, but not before I heard the telltale flutter of wings.

Chapter 4

February 1348

London

VALENTIN

I HAVE seen the face of holy vengeance, and she is the sickle in the hand of God. Blessed be His name!

I am Valentin, and I am a pardoner. Some years ago, I was a paid whore in the house of Lorenzo Tralini, but now I serve Jesus Christ our Lord. I consider myself among the blessed.

Some years ago before even that, I was the favorite of the nobleman Rouen di Francisci, the bastard who was the son of his uncle. Rouen would visit often, and he found me beautiful. He preferred my awkward foot to the slender ankles of the others, and he didn't mind when I fell down on the floor and thrashed about. He knew I couldn't help the swoon, when it chose to take me. And he liked to fondle my twisted foot, lightly stroking it with his fingertips. He would do this until I felt light, and then I would do the thing that he liked best, which was to caress him with my mouth. I did it because Tralini paid me well, and was honest. There were some houses where the masters were not honest, I regret to say. But Messer Lorenzo was most kind to me, and did not insist that I wear paint, as the others did. Messer Lorenzo cropped my silver hair close against my skull, for I had lice, and when he discovered how much the patrons liked my short-cropped hair, he demanded that I maintain it. I was fifteen when he found me. I stayed with Messer Lorenzo for nearly four more years, and then I left.

I left Messer Lorenzo because a cardinal told him that he thought me pretty. I wondered if he would purchase me, to use me for himself, as happened with some of the other boys. There would be a certain commotion, and then a trunk upon the stairs, a clatter in the night. Those who were taken away were bought by gentlemen of culture, for a very great price. I do not know what was done to them after they left Messer Lorenzo. I do not like to think of it, because it frightens me.

Messer Lorenzo's house was set far back at the end of a narrow street, so that it could not be seen. Messer Lorenzo joked that the Devil could not find his way to the doorstep. I hoped that it was true, because I knew that what I did for Messer Lorenzo and his patrons was a sin. If the Devil came, I knew that I might go to Hell, and then I would be lost. I realized that I was already lost, of course. But this is another matter.

The cardinal who came to see us was a young man, strong through the chest and very stout. His breath was scented with cloves. Messer Lorenzo said this was because his teeth were bad, and I was not to mention it. Messer Lorenzo said his name was Cardinal Gioletti.

Cardinal Gioletti entertained me in a private room, where he first requested that I strip for him, so that he might inspect me. I stood naked for a long time, while he walked about me, the scent of cloves a wreath about my head. I dared not breathe the odor of his bad teeth. I prayed to the Virgin that the swoon would not take me then, and I was spared. Blessed be the Lady.

"How old are you?"

"Eighteen, Ser." I was ignorant, and knew not what to call him.

"Are you a strong boy?" He peered at me, slid a finger into my mouth and felt my teeth. His finger tasted of sweetmeats.

"Yes, Ser, I am."

"Would you like to leave here, Valentin? Would you like to come with me?"

My heart throbbed in my breast. I was afraid; what would happen to me if I went with him? "I don't know, Ser." I felt the dizziness, the clammy hands that gripped my skull, the prelude to my swoon. I took a breath, prayed, and clenched my teeth.

"Would you like to serve our Lord Jesus Christ, Valentin?"

I stared at him, dumbfounded. What was he asking me? "Oh, yes, Ser! Of course, I would."

His eyes flickered over me, lighting on my torso, my secret parts, my naked shivering legs. "Get dressed."

He turned and left me alone there, and I felt blessed indeed. For he had left a shiny florin on the table, and I had done no service for it! I hastened into my robe and followed him, running down the stairs to freedom.

GIOLETTI made me a pardoner of the Church, an emissary of the grand ecclesiastical courts. It was my task to go about and furnish indulgence to those who, pious, purchased pardon, and I traveled the road between London and Canterbury, selling indulgences to those who were on pilgrimage. I was suited for this, because I liked to talk to people, and Cardinal Gioletti liked my voice. I liked to sing, I sang often when I was traveling by myself, to pass the hours. I traveled alone, and most of the time at night, that I might reach each parish by the daylight. But I preferred to travel in the night, with the great vast expanse of sky above me. I was happiest under the cover of darkness, when I could see the stars, and the moon with his smiling face. In the darkness, I was nothing more than another person, no different from the others. I was not Tralini's whore or my family's shame. I was simply Valentin. And I took my new task seriously, for now I was in England, where the parishioners were especially pious.

She found me in a tavern. Blessed be her name! It was the depth of bitter winter, the New Year's second month, and I was nodding at my meat, nearest to the fire. I had my jar of relics and a wallet full of pardons, and I was hungry, having traveled all the day from Canterbury. I was closer now to London than I had been, but still I had a ways to go.

I had asked the landlord for some bread and cheese, and a little jug of wine to warm my stomach. I thought I might have taken with a weakness, because I felt ill. And I was dizzy, but it might have been the hunger. Cardinal Gioletti had instructed me to skim the excess from the price of pardons that I sold, but not to take it for myself. He said I was to bring the extra to him always, and not to touch the coins because they were destined for God's holy work. So I lived from what I garnered doing other tasks besides my sacred duty: I might chop some wood or draw some water, drive the oxen to a farmer's pasture. Sometimes I worked very hard, but I fed myself in this manner for some time. Cardinal Gioletti had warned me not to speak of our arrangement, because he feared for me, that my reputation as one of Tralini's boys might jeopardize my position as a pardoner. He said he wanted only to protect me, and I was grateful.

"You are far too good to me, Ser. I do not deserve it." I had knelt in front of him, to ask his blessing before departing on my journey. I felt his hand stray to my head, his fingers sink into my hair, caress my skull.

"Pretty Valentin…." He tilted my face up and gazed at me for a long time, chewing thoughtfully on a clove. For a moment, something flickered in his eyes, an expression that I recognized—I had seen it in the patrons that came to visit at Tralini's—but then he was himself again, smiling and benevolent, and I was glad.

I HAD eaten but a little of the bread and cheese the landlord gave me, and now a great heaviness had come over me. I turned myself sideways to the fire, gazed into the flickering heart of it. And then the swoon came down.

It felt the same as always, as if two great hands had seized me underneath my chin and dashed me savagely against the wall, and then I felt my eyes go up, slide back into the darker regions of my skull. I heard the clatter as my jaw snapped shut, and then my spine crackled like a whip, and I rolled away and out of it, and up....

Mystery, Babylon the Great, Mother of Harlots....

From my vantage point above the city, I could see the fires of destruction. People screamed and ran, already burning. I turned, and I was in the midst of it, standing on a slimy cobbled street while buildings burned about me. Bodies toppled out of windows as wooden houses crumpled; I saw a woman toss a baby from an upstairs bedroom, watched it fall slowly, tumbling end-over-end, its swaddling loose and streaming in the wind. Its cries sliced my soul with horror; it hurtled toward me, and I stepped aside to catch it, watched it slam headfirst into the stones, its head bashed in and leaking brains.

I stumbled backward, gibbering with fright and speechless, and somewhere in the insanity I heard my own voice... *a dream, Valentin, this is the swoon, remember how it takes you....* My shoulder crashed into the wooden slats of a high-sided cart, and I stumbled, hands grappling for purchase. My fingers sank into something soft that gave way under my grip: the rotten carcass of a dead man, his eyes wide open, empty, and staring.

A chant started, somewhere in the distance, the sound of children's voices singing, high and pure: *A ring around the rosy, pocket full of posies, ashes! ashes! we all fall down!*

There was a bong of a bell, and the cart started moving; I jerked away, but I was on it, I was pinioned under bodies, and I couldn't move. The wooden wheels jerked and slithered on the slippery cobbles, slimed with blood and filth and excrement, and I opened my mouth to scream but chanted it instead: *A ring around the rosy, pocket full of posies....*

The cart, I can't get off the cart, oh God, help me, they're taking me, and I'm not dead, I'm not dead....

I filled my lungs and screamed with all my might. Slowly the light resolved around me. The cart was gone, and so was the awful bonging bell. There were no fires, no stench, no dead babies. I lay shivering for a long time, terrified to move lest the vision return and swallow me whole.

When the world was sane about me once again, I found that I was on a little bed, and I was frightened, because I had no money to pay for such a room. But I was very sleepy, and sore, as I am always when the swoon comes. There was a fire, and I was warm, and I felt safe.

"Valentin." A woman's voice.

I turned my head upon the pillow and gazed as she lowered herself to sit beside me. She was an uncommon woman: tall and thin, with long, unbound hair that brushed the ground, her breasts unkirtled underneath her gown, her feet as bare as any summer maiden. "My lady?" I tasted blood upon my lips, it is usually so when I fall and thrash about. I pressed a finger to my mouth. "I'm bleeding...."

Her hair brushed against my cheek as she moved over me, the sweet perfume of her rising into my nostrils. I felt desire, and I moved toward her, wondering if it were sin to couple with her, here in this bed that she had bought for me.

Her lips pressed against my own, her tongue a flickering shape that lapped away the blood, took it into her own mouth. And as she drew away, I saw twin flames behind her eyes, the unnatural pallor of her, smelled the scent entangled in her long, dark hair—

"I am the abomination of desolation...." *Mystery, Babylon the Great, Mother of Harlots.*

I bolted from the bed, the remnants of a scream echoing in my throat, threw open the door and ran as far as I could.

The acrid taste of her was still in my mouth, lingering like the scent of smoke, burning things. I could still taste it by the time I reached the church in town.

I KNEW this church, it was a safe haven for me—just days ago I had offered pardon here, and sung the offertory for the congregation. I like to sing. I would often sing when I was with Messer Lorenzo, but those were bawdy songs. I liked the way the hymns sounded, and I knew them all by heart. This church on Sunday past was full of people, and all of them had heard me sing. I confess to a little vanity in this; Cardinal Gioletti once told me that I sang like an angel. I was glad, because I only wanted him to look on me with pride. I only wanted to make him happy, and never to betray his trust in me. But I confess, there are times when I have sung for him that his eyes filled up with that look that I have told you about, the one I'd seen at Messer Tralini's, and I wondered, secretly in my mind, if indeed he lusted for me. Perhaps he would not want me if he knew of my strange swoon, the way I fell and thrashed about and bit my tongue.

I remembered now. The swoon had taken me here, in this church, last Sunday. After I had sung the Offertory, after I had offered pardon....

I wept quietly, ashamed. I realized that where once my swoons had occurred only seldom, now they occurred more often. I wondered why this was happening to me, and I decided that I must have sinned.... God must have seen fit to punish me by bringing the swoons more often, I was being punished for the things I'd done at Messer Tralini's house, the sins I'd committed.

Sodomite....

That ugly word! But truly, it described me fully. And it made me angry, that life had led me to debase myself in myriad ways, abase myself in service to a succession of wealthy patrons, who only wanted me because of my large pale eyes, my short-cropped silver hair, my clubbed and useless foot. My twisted foot, that made me useless to my family of peasant farmers, that led my brothers to sell me to the landlord for a florin, that he might use me until I was broken, and then turn me out to starve.

I wept, kneeling near the altar, near the statue of the Blessed Virgin. I wept, appealing to the Holy Infant to absolve me of my sins, to save me if such a thing were possible.

A breath upon the back of my neck, the scent of flowers, a stream of light....

Te absolvo, Valentin....

I looked, and she was there, the Holy Madonna, tall and pale and utterly magnificent, her long, dark hair streaming past her, vanishing into the light.

Her eyes, bright blue and glittering, slowly filled with tears, even as I watched....

...bloody tears that welled up and streamed down her face....

...and the Holy Infant cradled in her arms, his throat torn and gaping, a bloody hole...

...Her lips, wet with blood, her mouth a glistening crimson

wound....

Te absolvo, Valentin.

I opened my mouth and screamed, and I screamed until I felt the great hooked claws come down and grip me underneath the chin, dash me against the wall. I screamed until I felt the glassy chitter as my jaw snapped shut, the whiplash crack as my spine rippled under it, and then my eyes rolled all the way back, and I was gone.

"DEMON! He's taken with a demon!"

The cold stone floor of the church underneath my back, chilly through my clothes. I was lying on the flagstones, reeling from another spasm in the brain. I rolled over onto my side, tried to get up. My mouth was wet with bloody froth. There were several people from the church, and the priest, all standing there watching me. It made me frightened, like a stone in my belly.

"I saw the Blessed Virgin," I told them. "In a vision." I pointed at the altar, the great marble statue of Our Lady. I felt that I was speaking from outside myself, as if I were watching myself say these words. "With the Holy Infant in her arms." I cradled my arms to show how she had held Him... His throat a gaping, bloody hole from which she drank his blood. *Te absolvo, Valentin.*

My heart throbbed painfully in my throat.

The priest gazed calmly at me, wordless. I looked about at all the people, turned my gaze upon them, one by one. And I was suddenly afraid, I knew that something bad would happen.

The priest nodded. "Take him."

Two of the men moved toward me, their hands outstretched, and memory flashed across the surface of my brain, *Te absolvo, Valentin.*

I scrambled to my feet and burst through them, head down and running. I caught my satchel as I raced past, clutched my sack of pardons to my chest and ran as I have never run before. I can run fast, even though my foot is crippled.

By morning, I had booked passage on a ship bound for Sicily. Rouen di Francisci had once promised me protection if I ever needed it, and I intended to collect on that promise.

BY FIRST light the next day, I realized that I was on a plague ship. I tell you this now, in retrospect, although I had no such word as *plague* for it, not then. I had so few words in those days, I was practically illiterate. The offertory I could sing because I had memorized it. I could barely read.

But it was a plague ship, crammed with passengers from China, the Far East, even those traveling from England, as I was. People coughed and spat up blood, people became seasick from the incessant rocking motion of the rough, midwinter crossing. People vomited great gouts of black bile into buckets, which rotted and stank and gave off deadly fumes.

I spent much of my time up on the deck, braving the icy blast and the freezing rain to get a breath of air. I could not stand the stink belowdecks, the constant noise, the groans of the dying. Little children screamed and cried and ran about, sometimes ankle-deep in vomit, filthy water. There was no privy, and so people relieved themselves wherever they happened to be sitting, squatting or lying. Men coupled with women on the narrow bunks at all hours of the day or night; men coupled with other men wherever there was space belowdecks. The searing cold and icy winds that buffeted me topside were preferable to the stinking hell I faced below.

I took my meals alone, sitting with my back against the wheelhouse, my feet braced against the side. I drank only water and chewed the same hard tack the sailors ate. I passed the daylight hours staring at the horizon, until I fell into a stupor, dreaming while I was still awake.

Sometimes in these dreams I saw her: tall and poised and deadly. She appeared above the masthead, floating in the air, her long hair streaming out behind Her, trampling a serpent underneath her heel. Blessed be her name, I thought, too weary to escape her. If such was my destiny, then it must be God's intended will for me. To fight it would be heresy and sin.

My swoons increased after we had put to sea, and I was afraid for my own safety. I thought that I might fall overboard and drown, because I was not able to help myself when the swoon chose to take me. I had been taken with it twice since we departed England, once privately, when I was on the deck alone (Thanks and praise to our Lord that I was spared from harm!) but the second time, I swooned in the presence of the captain and the bosun. I was standing at the railing when I felt the claws come down, slice into my skull behind my eyes. My spine arched, my limbs rigid, and I felt my eyes roll up—

But someone caught me, lowered me gently to the decking, and placed a clean handkerchief between my teeth. "Leave him, stay back." A man's voice, kindly. My spine whiplashed, and I was gone.

I SAW her in my swoon, riding toward me on air, her eyes flaming as they had been when I'd seen her in the church. She clutched a sickle in her right hand, and held a star suspended between the fleshy cage of her fingers. *Mystery, Babylon the Great, Mother of Harlots...* I saw her open the palm that held the star, releasing it, so that it flew high over land and burst into a flame of fire above a great domed cathedral. A flock of doves took flight, pure, white birds with bleeding breasts, wheeled high above a parade of mourners led by a screaming priest with fiery eyes and a long, red beard...

Te absolvo, Valentin.

I snapped awake, suddenly alert. My heartbeat was throbbing in my throat. "Where am I?" I didn't know this place; the smells were different.

"It's all right. You're safe. Just rest." It was the same man's voice, the one whose hand had slipped the handkerchief between my teeth. I felt my lips; I was not bleeding. "You should carry a handkerchief with you, and slip it between your teeth when you feel it coming on. That will save you from biting your tongue all the time." He spoke Italian, but with an accent like the English. I wondered where he came from.

I sat up on my elbow, saw that I was in the captain's cabin, lying covered on his bed. I felt ashamed. He had seen my swoon, had seen me fall and thrash around. He might even put me off the ship!

"Please, do not bestir yourself. It's all right. You're safe." He moved into the light: a tall, thin man with white hair and a neat, white beard. His face looked like pictures of ascetics I had seen. His eyes burned like Cardinal Gioletti's, but in a kindly way. He seemed very sad.

I relaxed a little bit, allowed my coursing glands to still themselves. "You saw my swoon, Ser." I spoke to him in English, to show him that I had facility in both tongues, and could speak to him in his own as well as mine. I wondered why he was not afraid of it, like others were. My family claimed that the swoon caused me to exude bad humors, and therefore kept me confined when the spasms came. They feared I would contaminate the air with choler.

"My younger brother—" He paused to pour me a cup of hot, spiced wine. "Is subject to swoons very like your own."

I took the cup, sipped it gratefully. I was very hungry, as I often was after the swoon had passed. The wine was thick like milk, and sweet. I drank it all. "You aren't afraid of me?" I asked him. "Most people think I have a demon."

He laughed gently. "I don't think so." He filled my cup again. "What is your name?" he asked me. He gave me a thick piece of bread, a handful of figs.

"Valentin of—" Of where? I was rootless; I had no kin who would be proud to claim me. "Merely Valentin." It was difficult to talk around the mouthful.

"Merely Valentin, I am the captain of this vessel. John Anger is my name." He smiled, rose to go. "Rest awhile and come out onto the deck when you feel fit. I'll show you how to handle the wheel, if you like."

I brightened, felt myself quicken. "Thank you, Ser. I'd like that."

He nodded, was gone. I finished eating, lay back on the pillows, and fell immediately asleep, exhausted.

I BEGAN spending a great deal of time in the company of the captain, learning how to handle the wheel, how to guide the ship into the teeth of the wind so that the great sails filled. I was given a hot meal with the sailors for my efforts, and a warm blanket to cover myself on the deck. I was as reasonably happy as I could remember.

But by the time we first sighted land, fully a third of the passengers had died. At first, when the deaths came singly, the captain insisted on a Christian burial: the body would be shrouded in linen sheets, wrapped carefully as if it were precious and handled with all reverence. The captain would recite a service, and the body was tipped overboard while the bosun played a dirge upon his flute.

But the deaths increased, and instead of dying one by one, people dropped like flies. Children played happily at noontime and were dead by evening. Women and men rolled senseless out of bunks and died in the filthy water that swirled about belowdecks. And in time, there were no careful Christian burials, with Bible verses and music on the flute. Bodies were dumped where they had lain in piles near the railings. There was no service. There was no music. There was merely death. I wondered if any of us would make it to Sicily alive.

At night, she began to appear to us, just above the starboard bow, a flaming apparition with a sword in each hand, bared fangs poised to strike. The deaths increased, taking victims from among the crew: hardened old sailors who had faced down deaths of many kinds fell ill and died within a day; the bosun, eating breakfast with the captain, suddenly doubled at the waist and vomited black bile; the ship's navigator abandoned his sextant and went below to die.

It was surely the end of the world.

I AWOKE to a clear, calm Sunday when there was scarcely wind enough to fill the sails. Far out, close to the horizon, the water was as flat and as featureless as oil. It was a very bad sign. We were within sight-distance of Sicily. I prayed to the Lord Jesus that we might make it safely, but with a hollow place inside me. I realized that I did not believe as I once had, and it shocked and frightened me.

I folded my blanket, shivering with a sudden chill, and went to wash myself. Standing at the basin, I noticed the rash: a bright red ring upon my forearm. *Ring around the rosy....*

So now it had me. Panic rose in me, an evil serpent that uncoiled in my belly, hissing. I felt hot color mount upon my cheeks.

"Valentin." It was the captain, calling me. I rolled my sleeves down carefully, washed my face and dried it, and went into his cabin.

He was lying curled upon his bed, his cheeks hollow, his eyes bright with fever. He looked very ill, and I was afraid: I knew the fate that awaited him, and now me as well. "What can I get you, Ser?" I covered him with the blankets, touched his forehead with my hand. His skin was burning.

"I am dying, Valentin."

"No, Ser. It's just a fever. Let me make you an infusion." I had some small knowledge of potions that I'd gleaned at Messer Tralini's— mostly remedies for ailments of the private parts—but I thought I might ease his pain somehow.

"Valentin." He grabbed my wrist and squeezed it, pulled me closer. "I want you to hear my confession. I cannot die unshriven." His expression was frantic, as if he had seen into Hell itself...

I stared at him, fumbled behind me for my wallet. I had forgotten that I was a pardoner. I didn't know what he wanted me to do. "Ser, I can't—"

"You are a pardoner!" His voice was hoarse, strained. The skin of his face was mottled with black patches, the rash that this death brought with it. A horrendous swelling distorted the skin of his neck, bulging over the collar of his doublet, black and scabrous. "I pray you, grant me pardon."

"All right." I nodded furiously, pulled out my sheaf of pardons, stuffed it back into my wallet again. What was I thinking? Was I going to sell him an indulgence? I retrieved my rosary, passed it to him. "I will hear your confession." The beads trembled in my fingers, clicking.

I stayed with him until the last breath left him, my rosary clutched in his fist. I left it there. I closed his eyelids and then I covered him, made the Sign of the Cross over him. *Te absolvo.* I pulled the blanket over him and closed the door. And then I fastened it with a lock and chain I took from the quartermaster's storage. It was not fitting that any should disturb him in his rest. I wrote an epitaph upon his door, a cross. I could not write his name because I did not know the letters.

I went out onto the deck. The storm was coming; I could feel the rising wind upon my face. I leaned over the railing and cried, very frightened and all alone. I didn't know what to do. There was none to whom I could tell it; there was no one to listen. I had been infected with the plague. Either way, I would die before the morrow.

Chapter 5

Late February 1348
Florence

LUDOVICO SERENOLA

I MAKE this testament with my own hand, so that it will stand as proof of my existence when I am gone. If there be men upon the Earth after the Great Destruction has been wrought, then let them read my words and tremble! Such is the devastation of the Lord God, He who is called Jehovah. I doubt there will be men to read my words, because I know within my soul that this plague which ravages the Earth is the will of God made manifest, the wisdom of Jesus Christ our Lord. His is the necessary judgment, to rid the Earth of the evil that has encumbered us in latter days.

I ought to have known at the right beginning that this increase of evil was but the manifestation of Satan upon the people of the Earth. The ways of men are wicked, and they love the darkness because their deeds are evil! But I was immersed in worldly things, an altogether improper contemplation of the secular, and so the revelation of our Lord passed unbeknownst to me. Until the messenger brought word of it, like the angel to the prophet Jeremiah.

"Fra Ludovico!" I was contemplating during matins when Pietro burst into the nave, stumbled on the flagstones and genuflected clumsily. He was fumbling, overly tall, surely a monster. I wondered what sin lay upon the soul of his mother, that he should be thus. The tiny chapel was too small to hold him. "The news, the news!"

I started up, blinked the sleep away. I could hear the far-off tolling of the Duomo's bells, the end of matins. I had been immersed in considering the frescoes opposite the altar; surely we might spend a little coin to refurbish them, the colors were quite faded. "Pietro, what is it?" I brushed the dust from my cassock, kissed my beads and placed them safely about my neck. "Surely you might have wiped your feet." The mud on his boots was crusted thick; he must have dallied near the Arno's slushy banks.

"The wrath of God, Fra Ludovico!" He prostrated himself before me, arms spread, his great, fleshy body sprawled upon the flagstones as if felled by force. "Disease, a plague—"

I hauled him to his feet with an effort, grimaced. He was filthy and stinking, an unlettered serf with the intelligence of a barnyard animal. I thanked our Lord that He had chosen to gift me with His grace, that I was not thus. "What plague?" I snapped. I genuflected, backed away from the altar, my contemplation of the frescoes. My skull had begun to ache most abominably, and it was but early in the day. Perhaps I might retire to my cell and rest before my necessary labors. "Have you come to pester me with nonsense?" I moved briskly through the nave, stepped out into the bright sunshine of the winter morning. A chill wind blasted me, shivered through my clothes, and I hastened to my quarters. Pietro of course followed, not having the sense to recognize when he was being dismissed.

"Fra, there is a dispatch...." He fumbled inside his cloak, extracted a slip of parchment, folded once and sealed with fine red wax. I found my spectacles (I resist them even though my sight is failing; it is my one small vanity, I admit) and slipped them on. The world slid into focus.

The wax had been imprinted with his seal, the Holy Pontiff Clement VI, and had traveled over land from Avignon. I sat down at my desk and pulled it open hurriedly, nearly tearing the parchment in my haste.

It was indeed from the Holy See. A mere handful of words, scant justice to its lengthy journey. I read it, and as I did, the confirmation of my suspicions settled in my belly like a lump of lead.

"What is it, Fra?"

I had completely forgotten Pietro. "You may go," I told him, my level gaze daring him to ask coin of me. He assented, bowed himself out.

I pulled my spectacles off and laid them on the desk. Immediately my vision blurred, softened round the edges. Truthfully, I preferred the world this way, devoid of essential detail. The parchment quivered in my hand.

I took my volume of St. Thomas Aquinas, laid it open. Its illuminated borders swirled into gorgeous chaos, blurred before my failing sight. I traced the gilt edges, rubbed the fine page between my fingers. St. Thomas knew, as did our Lord, the necessary penitence for apostasy and sin. It was but fitting, I knew, that our Lord Christ should choose to dispense His holy judgment now, when mankind had reached the peak of degradation. I knew that He could no longer tolerate such carnal disobedience as that which I myself encountered in the taverns and the inns of Florence—some of which were transgressions of the most unnatural sort.

But still, I was frightened. I wandered to the window, sat upon the bench, and gazed out at the morning, the parade of busy Florentines in the *piazza*.

It was surely the end of the world.

"Ludovico...."

I started up, jolted from my grim imaginings. "Vittore, what is it?" He was but a novice, a yet unbearded boy, one of the many who came from noble houses to take instruction from our order. I hoped he would be spared the destruction of the Judgment. I hoped he would be among the saved. At once, my heart was squeezed with a great agony of tenderness and I went to him, enfolded him within my arms, and gave him the holy kiss of peace.

"Fra Ludovico...," Confused, he backed away from me. "Is there something wrong?" He caught my hand. "You have been weeping."

So I had. I touched my face, felt the moisture there. "Vittore, it is the Judgment of our Lord." I handed him the letter, watched his face as he read it. A great fear leapt into his gaze.

"This cannot be." He crumpled the letter against his chest. "Ludovico, this is an error, some aberration...."

"No, my brother." My body was suffused with a great weariness, a profound sadness. I thought of those that He would be compelled to toss screaming into Hell. I thought of those unnamed millions in undiscovered lands who did not know His gospel, or His truth. I thought of those who frequented the inns and taverns, whose dearest pleasure lay only in these dens of iniquity. And I wept again, as our Savior wept when He gazed upon Jerusalem. "Now leave me," I told Vittore. "I wish to spend the day in prayer and contemplation."

I accepted his embrace and waited till he had gone out. Then I donned my cloak and set off into the throbbing center of the city.

CARDINAL GIOLETTI had just risen when I arrived, and was bathing in his great, copper bathtub as I was shown into his quarters. The novice who ushered me in was slight and silent, another of the pale boys that Gioletti favors.

"Ludovico! Pray come and give me a holy kiss." Gioletti rose upon his knees, his considerable belly rising from the murky waters like an island. I pecked his cheek delicately, stepped back. "You are risen early this morning. What brings you?" He soaped his armpits and his chest noisily, splashed water over the sides. The tub was carved with scenes of the Fall of Man, beautifully hand-tooled by some bastard relative of Brunelleschi. Gioletti had paid handsomely for it. The room was tastefully—if a little abundantly—decorated. The walls hung with fine tapestries depicting worthy religious scenes. This morning, a fire burned briskly in the grate. I went to it and warmed myself.

"I received a letter from His Holiness the Pontiff." I moved to the table, upon which had been set a selection of bread and cheese. "May I?"

"By all means. And wine as well, if you wish it—in the flagon, there." Gioletti stepped out of the tub, descended a small flight of steps to the carpet. "Niccolo!" he barked at the door, which swung open to admit the pale slim boy, this time bearing a thick towel. I seated myself and ate sparingly, poured a little wine.

"Doubtless you have heard of the sickness from the East," I said. I fished in my purse for my spectacles, slid them up on my nose. "The letter concerned this; His Holiness postulates that this might well be an early sign of impending Judgment."

"Judgment!" Gioletti snorted. He lifted his arms as Niccolo moved around him with the towel, vigorously rubbing water from his chest, his belly. "I hardly think so."

"My lord, I would insist that you take this seriously." I poured a little more of the wine, cut a piece of cheese. Gioletti always kept the best of meat and drink. "My servant Pietro this morning brought me word of this new illness. It spreads in Florence, even as we speak."

"Are you certain it isn't some new sort of sexual disease?" Gioletti laughed uproariously. Niccolo knelt before him and dried his private parts, slipped the towel between his thighs. Gioletti rested a hand on the boy's pale hair, his fingers curling familiarly around his neck. "Ah, Ludovico. Too much time you spend in Tralini's whorehouse inn." He tapped Niccolo on the forehead. "Enough now. Stop playing with my cock."

The boy gathered his towel, stood to go. "It begins with a rash, bleeding in the nose. Some say it kills in hours, others say days." It was vital that he understand the seriousness of this. "I think we should prepare the faithful for the apocalypse, my lord. Doubtless this is the judgment of God upon us all."

"Ludovico! Far too serious for so early in the day." Gioletti fondled Niccolo's bottom, sent him from the room. The cardinal's member was partially erect, dark purple between his thighs.

I looked away hurriedly, busied myself with the food. "Still, my lord, it is possible. And I find that my thoughts turn ever to those beloved of the Lord who will need succor in these dark days."

"Fra Serenola, you need release from your oppressive dogma." He seated himself on the bench opposite me, thankfully clothed in his dressing gown. "Or perhaps...," He glanced over his shoulder, toward the door. "...You might like to sample Nicco's charms?"

"No, my lord." I swallowed what was in my mouth, wished nothing more than to be gone from here. "I find I have not the stamina to pleasure sharp young boys."

I RETURNED to my cell to find Vittore waiting for me, and with him several others of the novices. I had been gone most of the morning; I hadn't realized how long it would take me to return from Gioletti's house. "What is it, what's the matter?" I hung my cloak upon a hook, stoked the fire till it burned vigorously. "Vittore, come and sit, and you—" I gestured to them, a huddle of serious young men, "—crouch about the fire and be warmed."

"Fra, we have something to show you." Vittore's eyes were red-rimmed, damp with unshed tears. "This morning, Italo awoke to find this." He pushed back the sleeve of his companion's dark cassock, revealed the red rash, the characteristic ring. "He is cursed by God." Vittore's dark eyes appealed to me, as did the eyes of all of them, looking to me for the answer that I could not possibly give them.

I glanced about the circle, gazing into each pair of eyes in turn. I realized that there were twelve of them in all, the same number as those of His disciples. I knew that He was trying to send me reassurance, and suddenly, I knew what to do.

"Don't worry," I told them, and drew them all into my embrace. Something kindled in my belly, and I knew that, far from being an anonymous servant of His Church, I had been chosen for a special task. It would begin with these twelve young men. "There is indeed evidence of judgment, but we are the blessed of God." I took the hands of the two closest to me—Vittore and his young companion—and bowed my head. "Let us pray that God will lead us to His purpose."

We prayed the *Pater Noster*. Outside, the bells tolled, announcing the strike of noon.

Chapter 6

Late February 1348
Florence

DANTE

"Rouen, it's getting worse." I deliberately pitched my voice low so that those around us wouldn't hear me and think me insane. Hysteria was running high these last dark days. "Did you see that red-haired folly in the streets?"

"Dante." Rouen was annoyed with me; his brows were knit in a manner that I had come to realize was characteristic of him. He had the true nobleman's instinct for subtlety, and was never as overt in his emotions as I was in mine. The blood has not changed him so much, after all. "It is the carts going by, again. And Serenola."

Serenola. There was a name that I was uneasy to hear, I confess— the red-haired priest's evangelical fervor reminded me far too much of Lilith's own dark zeal. He was popular with the masses, but I wanted nothing to do with him, and besides, I had given up my faith long ago. "Yes, Serenola. Another sacrificial lamb for the supplicants to pin their hopes upon. As if anything could save them from this." Serenola was well-versed in demonology, they said, and professed that the entire cause of plague was the existence of "unnaturals" among the *fiorentini*. He had promised to rid the city of Jews, homosexuals, and those heretics he called "the devourers of the living". I could guess what he meant by that—clearly, he intended harm to our kind—but I wondered if he knew that beings such as us did exist. Perhaps Rouen and I might pay him a covert visit....

"I think not." Rouen glared at me across the table; he was becoming most adept at divining my thoughts. "I intend to stay away from him, and so should you."

"But, Rouen, a careful visit might impress upon good Fra Serenola that he should turn his thoughts to matters holy." I pretended to sip my ale; it was vital that we keep up the appearance of normalcy in the face of such hysteria. "Think of how instrumental we might be in turning his thoughts back to God!"

Midwinter now, the plague had abated somewhat—some said it was because the cold killed all the fleas. If that were true, I reasoned, then, the plague would come again when the cold subsided in the spring. And what then? Another holocaust, more deaths, more crowded plague ships arriving at our ports bearing thousands of dead and dying that, turned away by the authorities, sat festering until every soul that lined the decks was dead. And always the carts, the terrible clangor of the bell, when Rouen and I retired in the mornings, *Bring out your dead, bring out your dead....* The fleshy slap of bodies landing on the cart, the oily squeak of wheels greased by the stinking fluids leaking from the corpses. It was enough to make the skin crawl.

As if that were not bad enough, now there was this priest, Serenola, who with his fiery-red beard and his maniacal expression, resembled the Devil more closely than anything else. An evangelical reformer, he had made it his business to follow the carts through the musty morning streets of Florence, crying aloud and beating his breast over "the evil, the evil". He was attended, as far as I could tell, by a coterie of young novices, all stripped to the waist and flailing themselves with whips, in some bizarre attempt to make recompense. They made me severely uncomfortable.

"Oh yes, Serenola," I replied, pushing my tankard toward Rouen. "Crying always of apostasy and sin." I felt the corners of my mouth pull down, the way they always did when some emotion took hold of me like this fear did now. "Have they been to question your father yet? Lying in that fusty bed and fucking his own sister...." I opened my mouth to yawn, was suddenly seized about the throat.

Rouen was as angry as I have ever seen him, but he had been uneasy lately, as we all of us were. "Pewling bugger—"

"Let go!" I hissed at him, my fangs descending, slapped his hand away. "So superior, Rouen, with your noble title and your name, your pretensions to Medici connections... does Serenola or his disciples know that you are a bastard, with no real father but your uncle? Hmmm?"

He sat back, and as I watched, the rims of his eyes filled up with bloody tears. He fumbled in his pocket for a handkerchief, dabbed his face quickly. "Damn your eyes," he whispered, his mouth pulling down into a sob. "I know you have no real love for me anymore."

Something stabbed me quickly, in the heart, and in one shameful moment I saw myself as Rouen saw me, and I knew that I had become a spiteful bastard. "Rouen...." Truly, he deserved better; he had taken me in and given me a home; it was his money that kept me warm and housed. He had found good lodgings for us over a tavern in the heart of Florence. There was always wood for the fire, and sumptuous coverings on the bed, clean white sheets. I ought not to be so cold-blooded.

"You still blame me for what Leonardo did to you." He buried his face in his tankard, pretended to take a great swill of ale. He was getting rather good at maintaining the illusion; he could no longer ingest mortal sustenance and had replaced his once prodigious appetite with an exemplary lust for blood.

"Leonardo raped me." I thrust the knife in..."And you stood by and watched, you let him do it!"

He gazed at me in silence, his hazel eyes enormous in his bone-pale face. The blood had drawn all human color from him; now he resembled nothing so much as a gorgeously perfected fresco, an image from the life of some obscure Tuscan saint.

I turned as the tavern door opened to admit a fleet of workmen, idle and garrulous at this late hour of the day, just moments after sunset. There was little for them to do now; stonemasons and construction laborers, they were at loose ends, awaiting the completion of the half-finished Duomo while the plague had its way with Florence. Mostly, they roamed about the streets these days, hammering on the doors of shops and workhouses, demanding to be given employ. Many of the guilds had disintegrated into rabble collectives, much given to civil disruption and disorder.

They shuffled in and ranged themselves around a table, shouted and pounded until the landlord came to quiet them. He joked and smiled as he laid foaming tankards of ale in front of them, summoned a wench with a loaf of bread, some cheese.

I noticed Rouen watching them intently, eyes narrowed, his tankard clenched in his fist. Something in his posture alarmed me; I leaned forward to touch my hand to his. "Rouen? What is it, *mi cuore*?"

"You see that mason over there." He pointed. "No, the one with the curly, red hair."

"Yes." I glanced at them, dismissed them and their noise. "Rouen, don't point. You'll draw their attention."

"That red-haired one, he used to work at my father's villa."

I didn't see the problem.

"He stole from us and disappeared. I always wondered what became of him."

"Well, now you know: he procured gainful employment and has probably become infected with the plague." I sounded rather more sarcastic than I'd initially intended.

"I wish you would be serious," Rouen hissed, "just for one moment, I wish you could—"

"What are you staring at, my pretty?" The red-haired mason had seen Rouen's narrowed gaze and took exception to it. "Perhaps you'd like to come and sit on my lap, eh?"

The masons laughed uproariously, shouted abuse and filth at us.

"Rouen!" I cursed softly. "Just turn away and pretend you were looking for someone—" I glanced up as the landlord appeared at the table. "Yes?"

"Bread and cheese, Ser?"

I glanced at Rouen, quickly. It might be necessary if we had planned to stay, but right now I had no other thought but getting Rouen out of here as soon as possible. "No, thank you." I wished him away with the strongest mental gestures, and he went.

"Stop staring at that mason, Rouen, or we will be forced to leave." I lifted my tankard to my lips, sucked in a great mouthful, then turned to the side and quickly spat the foul stuff upon the floor.

There was a commotion at the door, the clamor of running feet. I lifted myself to the window and peered out; I could make out nothing in the darkness but a great stampeding mob.

Rouen was at my side. "What is it?"

I squinted, cocked my ear and listened, caught the essence of it, Plague ship put in at Sicily, port side stove in, everybody dead on board....

They were running away, even though the ship was miles from here, with nothing alive aboard her. She had probably been in port for days. Such was the quality of the new hysteria.

I dropped down from the window, slipped into my chair.

"Lord God!" I recoiled from him, fangs descending, at the ready. "What are you?"

A ghost.

He was standing at our table: tall, gaunt, with huge blue eyes so pale that they were colorless, and eerie, silver hair chopped so short that it stood out in spikes about his head.

I turned to Rouen, a question in my eyes, and siphoned the answer easily from the surface of his mind….

Valentin.

Clearly, he was dying of the plague, his skin badly mottled, his eyes glazed with fever. "Rouen." He toppled forward, caught himself with a palm against the table. "Help me. Please."

As I watched, his body was seized in a fit of violent shaking, as his eyes rolled back in his head and his spine arched like a whip. I grabbed and held him down, thinking I would help him, but Rouen pulled me away. He reached into his pocket and slipped a cloth between the young man's teeth. "He swoons," he explained, "but you cannot touch him, lest he harm himself and you."

"My God, what is it?"

"Brain spasm. Don't touch him—it will be over in a moment."

The noise went on around us unabated, as Rouen and I crouched around the young man and shielded him from the gazes of the curious. I watched him shaking in his peculiar swoon, his teeth clenched, body arched as tight as any bowstring. "Rouen, he's going to hurt himself!"

It was a brief seizure that left him trembling on the dirty floor, a filthy bag of bones. "Who is he?" I seized Rouen's arm, I was determined not to let him go until he answered me.

"His name is Valentin," Rouen replied. He pulled the shaking youth into his arms and held him tightly, with affection. "He and I were lovers." His hazel eyes caught and held my gaze, begging me to understand, and not to chastise him.

The youth rolled his huge pale eyes to look at us, smiled at Rouen faintly. "Once," he whispered. His voice was a shade above a whisper, a crackling like dead leaves. "We were lovers once."

I wrapped my cloak around him, bent and caught him into my arms, a fevered bundle of bones and flesh. Rouen and I bore him away into the night. I knew he would not live till morning.

Chapter 7

ROUEN

VALENTIN had returned to me, but I did not know how long he would remain. Already his pale skin—the skin I so loved in years gone by—was black and mottled. Already the fever was mounting, and when he coughed he spat blood.

And the fits, always Valentin's scourge, were coming now with greater frequency. He had been in and out of consciousness since Dante and I first brought him here.

"Be careful." I reached toward the bed. "Don't tip the basin, Dante." The overfull pan of water teetered dangerously on the bedside table. Dante was washing Valentin with the reverence normally reserved for corpses. It irritated me.

The candlelight glowed eerily along the walls, increasing our shadows so that we were reflected enormously. This was a bare and chilly room, but a good place to stay because it was inconspicuous. We could not afford, in the midst of the swelling religious hysteria, to be discovered. An encounter with Serenola—such as we had had mere days before—could never again be risked. While I knew that Dante and I were possibly immortal, I did not think that we were indestructible.

"Rouen, look." He lifted Valentin's arm, held it flexed away from the body to show me the dark bubo swelling from my darling's flesh. "I'm astonished he survived this long."

"Does it cause him pain, I wonder?" I pressed my palm against

Valentin's pale cheek, remembering how I had seen him at Tralini's, so very long ago.

I turned at the sound of footfalls on the stairs, and saw Emilia, the serving maid that we had hired to attend us. She carried a jug of hot water, which she poured into the basin, and a set of clean clothes for Valentin. Her rooms were down a flight and adjacent to our entrance. She knew whenever Dante or I was coming in, and that she was to appear immediately to attend us. She also knew not to come into our apartments during daylight, and indeed, we had ensured that the door might be barred and bolted from the inside, before we ever leased this place.

"Your friend is ill." She spoke quickly through a handkerchief soaked in cologne.

"He is dying." Dante's voice was flat, angry. He disliked Emilia, thought she was a stupid woman. "If you were at all clever, you would leave now."

"Dante!" I hissed at him. Our gazes met and clashed before his eyes slid away from mine. Emilia stood in silence, her handkerchief pressed against her mouth, her eyes enormous above it. She had never questioned our strange habits, but she knew that Dante and I were different, somehow. She simply dared not ask in what manner, and for that, I was grateful. I knew about Serenola's campaign against "unnaturals" and how vulnerable Dante and I were now. I also knew that the careless talk of a household servant would be sufficient to betray us.

"Messer Rouen, if there is nothing else…?"

I nodded, pressed a coin into her palm. "Thank you, that will be all." I watched her disappearing down the stairs before I spoke again. "You are sometimes an ignorant cretin."

"She should not be here. He is infected and dying with the plague." Dante slapped the washrag into the basin, splashing water at me. He did not look at me nor speak for several long moments. His square face could not conceal his expression of distress.

I was compelled to ask, "What is it?"

He lifted Valentin as if he were a doll, slipped the soiled shirt off, rolled the pardoner's filthy hose and discarded them. He was being infinitely gentle, lifting and moving Valentin with care. "You never said anything about *him*." He nodded toward Valentin, lolling insensible in his arms. "You never said anything about Tralini's whorehouse." His wide mouth, normally so sensuous, was compressed into a hard white line. His fangs had descended, and the tips were pressed into his lower lip, sharp white points. He hadn't fed yet. I knew he would have to hunt soon, I could see his hunger, pressing against the underside of his skin like pain.

"Dante...." I leaned closer, peered into his bent face. "Are you *jealous*?" I was incredulous; I hadn't thought him possessed of sufficient feeling....

"Never!" he snapped, fangs flashing. He circled Valentin's waist with one arm and pulled the pardoner toward him, so that Valentin was facing him, his chin on Dante's shoulder. He rubbed a quantity of soap into his palm and applied it to Valentin's scalp, his spiky, silver hair. "Why would I be jealous of some dithering boy whore that you buggered at Tralini's for a florin, now and then?"

"You *are* jealous." I caught his chin between my fingers, lifted his face. "Dante!"

"I am busy. Rouen, if you don't mind...." He jerked away from me, busied himself with washing Valentin's hair. I watched them in silence: my immortal darling with my dying mortal lover cradled in his arms, gently washing that filthy, corrupted flesh with unearthly patience.

"Why do you care like this for him?" I rested my hand on Valentin's naked shoulder. "He is nothing to you, Dante, but a tragic dying mortal."

"He is something to *you*." He slanted a gaze at me as he slipped the clean nightshirt over Valentin's head. "And you were so infected when I found you. This 'tragic dying mortal' might be you, Rouen, were it not for my unholy intervention." He smiled bitterly. "Don't you think this is the fate that eventually awaits us all?"

Panic leapt and fluttered in my throat. "You said we were immortal! You said we couldn't get this—"

"Yes." He laid Valentin back upon the sheets, drew the heavy blankets up around his chin. His fingers lingered on the pardoner's pale forehead, briefly. "Maybe this is what Lilith meant when she spoke of her abomination." He rose from the little bedside stool, opened the casement to pour the dirty water out. I listened to it hit the cobbles. "Perhaps this plague…," his hands fluttered in front of his face, gesticulating, "is the punishment of God upon us all." He laid the basin on the table, folded the washcloth. His face was a mask carved out of stone.

"Listen to the words you say!" I stared at him, aghast. Surely he had gone insane—this plague had nothing to do with us, it—

"Rouen." Dante knelt in front of me, caught me by the shoulders. "That night that Lilith made me, do you know what she said? 'I am come to bring the end of the world'."

"Rhetoric!" I scoffed. "Mere sophistry from the Queen of Lies!" My bluster belied the belly grinding fear I felt.

"Do you believe in God, Rouen?" He knelt beside me, his hand upon my thigh. His fingers were warm with that immortal heat. "Did you know that we burn, forever and ever?"

"I don't know."

"Don't you think that if He so desired, he could effect judgment?"

"Why?" I couldn't fathom it; this was insanity, surely.

"Because He can. Because He wants to. Because He has been invoked so many times and in so many differing ways since the world began. Jehovah has finally gone mad with power!" Dante laughed: a short, bitter sound. "And Lilith is His instrument."

"You've been listening too much to Serenola." I rose from my chair and stalked across the room, laid my arms upon the casement.

"Listening to him talk about 'unnaturals', Jews poisoning the wells."

Florence was silent; even now that it was midwinter, people feared to leave their homes. The inns and taverns closed their doors at sunset; it was becoming more and more difficult to hunt.

"I have to hunt...," I stared into the deepening twilight. "I haven't fed yet." I turned to see Dante crouched over Valentin. "You should hunt, Dante."

He nodded wearily. "Yes." He adjusted the blankets over Valentin, slid a warming pan underneath the covers, at his feet. "Stoke up the fire so he won't be cold while we leave him."

"He is a pardoner," I told Dante. "Blessed of the Church, an emissary of the Lord. Do you think, if this were judgment, that God would see fit to visit it on him?"

He didn't answer. Perhaps he had no answer to give.

WE WAITED outside an inn for what seemed like hours. It was freezing, and it had begun to snow: great wet flakes that stuck fast and melted in our hair. Dante was shivering and so was I; despite our winter cloaks, the chill struck straight to the bone.

"Let's go home," I pleaded. "I'm not so hungry that I must needs feed tonight."

"Rouen." Dante's eyes glowed at me across the darkness. "Remember what I told you: every night you go without the blood weakens you. I cannot protect you from the plague if you continue to defy me!" He broke off as the inn's door opened to admit the last of the evening's stragglers: two bull-necked masons and a scrawny boy. Dante and I fell in step behind them.

I caught the boy and bashed his head against a wall, tossed him senseless into the street, and then grabbed one of the masons by the throat, my fingers sinking deep into his fleshy neck.

It was the red-haired mason, the one who'd stolen from my

family. I grinned at him in the dim light as my fangs descended, sliding down out of my gums. "Justice," I whispered, "I do believe you owe me, Ser." I wrenched his chin back and slammed my teeth into the artery at his neck. The blood spurted, rich and hot, erupted down my throat. I gorged myself on him, drank until I felt the discrete snapping click as death engaged him. I dropped his body in the gutter, looked about me to see if there were any more.

The boy was struggling to consciousness, crawling away, hands and knees against the cobbles. I lunged and caught him, broke his back across my knee and delved into his chest with my fingers. *I want the heart, where is it—*

"Rouen!" A hiss in the darkness, Dante materialized above me, disheveled. His fangs gleamed from the crimson crevice of his mouth.

I smiled at him. "Magnificent monster...." He appeared beautiful to me, more so then than at any other time. Everything about me was more fluid, I was moving ever so slowly. I could hear each minuscule noisome flicker with devastating clarity.

"Stop *that*!" He grabbed my wrist, pulled my hand out of the boy's chest. "Digging around in him like that—" He yanked me savagely to my feet. "—get rid of the body!"

He kicked the dead boy into the gutter himself, pulled me by the wrist. I could hear the rolling clatter of the carts upon the cobbles, just behind it, the sonorous bellow of Serenola, preaching the judgment.

The convoy came around the corner and caught us unawares: Dante dragging me by my wrist, our bloodstained faces showing darkly crimson in the dimness. The front of my cloak was spattered with great gouts of the dead boy's blood, my fingers flecked with bits of flesh and sinew from where I'd dug into his chest. Even to myself I appeared fearsome, demonic. *Jesu Maria, what a time to be caught like this!*

"*Heresy*!" A roar from the crowd that followed; the cart rumbled closer, enclosing us against the crouching facades of nearby houses. "Bloody monsters, demons!"

I glimpsed the enigmatic priest, his red beard waving as he ranted, arms high above his head. The crowd of flagellants pressed in on us, wailing and beating themselves, and I clutched Dante's arm. "They're going to destroy us!" It was a spectacle altogether horrible, young men stripped naked to the waist and streaming blood while they struck themselves with iron-baited leather whips. It was like some bizarre panorama, the Passion of Christ reenacted for Holy Week....

"Shush, Rouen." He wrapped an arm around my waist. "Whatever happens, promise me you will not be afraid." His body trembled like a reed. "We have no quarrel with you, Fra Serenola!" His voice rose above the crowd, clear and pure. "I pray you, take your followers and leave us."

"The demon speaks!" Someone near the back of the crowd roared. "Listen to the unholy canting of the unnaturals!"

I stared at Dante. "What are you going to do?" Surely, he ought to do something soon, or we would be in a most unpleasant situation....

The crowd surged. Somewhere behind me, a light was struck; a pitch-coated torch ignited with a hiss, I could feel the heat upon my skin. "Dante..." Serenola unwrapped the wooden rosary from about his waist, held the crucifix toward us.

"Hold tight!" His fingers tightened on my waist.

We rose into the air.

It was making me sick, floating and whirling above it all; Dante hadn't yet learned, it seemed, to control his flight. We caught an updraft and floated uncontrollably upward; we slid into a cold wind and dropped like a stone.

I could see lights in the windows of houses below us, the slow crawling progress of wagons and carts. We floated low above a church and heard the women wailing. We drifted past a bawdy house and listened to the sound of mortals dying. Florence crouched underneath us, terrified.

"Dante." I buried my face in his neck. The cold wind and rapid flight had cleaned the blood from him; his preternatural flesh was as hard and white as it ever was. "Let's go down."

We descended rapidly, plunging out of the sky like some freakish, double-headed monster. My feet touched cobbles gently. I opened my eyes. We were standing in front of our house.

"I think you ought to practice a little more," I told him. "But otherwise, it was exhilarating." I was shaking uncontrollably.

He was smiling, proud of himself, and preening a little. "Thank you, Ser. It was my pleasure."

We hastened up the stairs. Dante lit a candle and led us into the bedroom where Valentin lay. I could hear his raspy breathing, easily discerned the smell of dying flesh.

His color was very bad: his eyes had sunk back into their sockets, his lips were as white as paper.

Dante lay for a moment with his head against Valentin's chest, listening. "Rouen." He beckoned me, bade me lay my head next to his. "His heart is giving out."

I sat back on my heels. "What are we going to do?" I whispered.

Dante made an irritated noise.

"So we just allow him to die."

"What other choice do you see, Rouen?" He gazed at me for a long moment, his expression beautifully delicate, his large, intelligent eyes thoughtful and sad. "There is no cure for this, and, Rouen, there are no doctors that will come here." He clasped his knees, looking very like a small boy. I wondered what sort of mortal he had been. "He has probably an hour left to him."

I laid my palm against Valentin's pale cheek. It was already cooling, the life draining out of him. I remembered the years when I was seeing him at Tralini's, when, for a florin, I could treat him as I pleased, and how, for a florin, I never treated him with anything but kindness, because I loved him. There was something gorgeous about him; his large, pale eyes held innumerable possibilities in their depths. When I talked of anything at all he listened to me, as if eternal truth spilled wanton from my lips. His regard was unconditional.

I turned at a sudden, rapid motion in the darkness, and Dante was on him. Fangs extended fully, he struck at the carotid artery, fastened onto Valentin and drained him. It was over in an instant, before I could protest or agree.

"And now he throbs between two lives...." He gazed at some point beyond me, his lips darkly wet. "What choice will you make for him, Rouen? This mortal, your late-lamented lover." He grabbed my shoulder, "Quickly! Make your choice."

I think I nodded, but I can't be certain. I watched as Dante tore open his shirtfront, sliced his corrupted nipple with his fingernail. His movements were quick, painful to look at.

Time slowed to an inky crawl, the planet hesitating while we enacted our dark rituals.

Do this in remembrance of me....

Valentin, *Te absolvo*.

They melted into one another like faded images, like ghosts: Valentin's pale head against Dante's paler torso; they embraced with the chilly joy of statues. Valentin's waxen lips closed around Dante's nipple as he pulled the blood into himself, as his body moved to clasp his savior closer. I watched it flow back into him, the blood that stained his cheeks with delicate color that gave his eyes the same eerie animation as Dante's.

"This is my body, this is my blood." Dante gazed at me, Valentin nestled in his arms. His eyes were half-lidded, weighted with the delicious languor of it. This giving of ourselves to mortals is a precious thing, and it pleasures us. We delight to make new revenants, again and again.

He laid Valentin back upon the sheets, pulled the nightshirt over Valentin's head, and lay down upon the pardoner. "Take the heat from me, you're dying."

Valentin wrapped his limbs around Dante, his clubbed foot stumbling for purchase against the white expanse of Dante's back. He clung to Dante desperately, the tips of his fingers digging into Dante's skin and leaving marks. "Cold, I'm cold."

I drew the blankets over them both, went to stoke the fire. When I returned, Valentin had fallen asleep, clutched in Dante's arms. Both were lying side-by-side.

"Rouen." Dante beckoned me. "The blood has taken hold, and he is sleeping now. But I must needs stay to warm him." His fingers pressed against my lips as his eyes filled up with bloody tears. "Rouen, why did you not tell me of him?" He sobbed quietly, his fingers still against my mouth.

"Dante, you're weak. Rest, now." I found I could not answer him, because the answer was painful for me to contemplate, and I knew he was exhausted.

"He took everything I had, Rouen." His eyelids fluttered closed, hiding his luminous brown eyes from me. His fingers loosened their hold upon my face, fell lifeless against the blanket. His breathing became deep and even.

I laid another blanket over them and left to walk the streets of Florence until daybreak.

Chapter 8

February 1348

Florence

LUDOVICO SERENOLA

VITTORE came to me at nightfall, when I sat musing at my meat. I knew it was Vittore because of the way his footfalls lie upon the flagstones; he walks limping ever since we first initiated our cycle of holy flagellations.

"Fra Serenola." He waited on the threshold, a young man veiled in darkness. I thought about St. John the Baptist, the messenger of the Lord.

"Come in, Vittore." I sliced a piece of bread for him and cheese, poured a cup of wine. "Have you eaten yet?"

"I am fasting this eve, my lord." He seated himself with difficulty, bracing himself against the table's edge. His face was pale with strain. "And I will spend tonight in the chapel on my knees." He surveyed the meal hungrily, his eyes huge in his thin face. I saw his struggle plainly written in his features, before he turned away.

"Vittore, you are troubled." I removed the temptation of the bread, finished my own meal discreetly. I secretly hoped he would not tarry long; I wished to do some reading before I retired to my couch. I had borrowed Sebastien's *Treatise on the Myriad Aspects of the Demon* from Gioletti, and I was eager to delve into it. I felt it might shed some important light upon the current crisis in our city.

"My lord, I find myself returning to the scene this morning in the *piazza*...." He shifted on the bench, his slender body trembling. I was overcome with pity; I knew he was in pain.

"When we encountered the unnaturals." I had seen only the faintest glimpse of them, two men. Vittore had been at the forefront of our gathering. "I understand, Vittore." I laid a hand upon his shoulder. "You had not seen such evil until this morning. Yes. The gleam of Satan in their eyes. Doubtless they had just returned from some debauched tavern where they took their pleasures."

"It wasn't merely that, my lord." He swallowed, his throat contracting painfully. His hesitation was annoying me; I could think only of the volume I had loaned from Gioletti, and how much I wanted to read it before the bell tolled me to vespers.

"Yes, what was it then?" I slipped my spectacles on, the better to see him. Mother of God, he looked *terrible*—

"They drank his blood, my lord, and the taller one, I saw him delve into the boy and—" He leapt and bolted out the door. I heard the sound of retching, violent and strained.

"Vittore, it's all right, all right...." I rubbed his back while the spasms passed, gave him a linen towel to wipe his mouth. "Come inside and take a little wine."

"But Fra, I am fasting—"

"A little wine for thy stomach's sake, you should listen to the exhortations of St. Paul." I poured him a cup of the hot wine I'd dined upon, waited in silence while he drank it gratefully, and then gave him some more. I had no idea what he was talking of; I had seen nothing but two wayward scoundrels creeping home before the daylight.

"Abominations, my lord!" He leaned forward and broke into a fit of noisy weeping. "I saw it with my own eyes, their lips wet with blood...."

I dried his tears and sent him off to Brother Frederico, who was adept at handling upsets of the mind. And then I closed the door gratefully, barred it from the inside. I wished no interruptions, and truly, Vittore's outburst had upset me more than I could admit, even to myself.

I took Gioletti's volume from the drawer and lit a candle, settled myself at the table. Outside, the wind wailed and screeched, scratching at the shutters, but I ignored it. Sebastien's treatise was my immediate concern.

"There are a myriad of demons that exist within the natural world, and these should not be confused with gentler spirits, they which issue from Jesus Christ our Lord. It is most useful to query the spirits, to discover the origin of their issue, and to apprehend them based solely on this. But there are monsters, wholly unnatural, of which only the greatest caution can avail.

Foremost of these is the devourers of the living, which are those heretics who have died unshriven. At death, these emissaries of the Evil One are transformed by his power into blood-drinkers, whose fate is to roam the Earth and prey upon the living, and most especially the holy, however there is a most efficacious—"

I laid the book down softly, got up from the table. I needed most of all to feel the flagstones underneath my feet, to assure myself that I lived and thought, and was wholly in command of my senses.

My mind flashed immediately on Vittore's fantastic story, those two young bravos we had seen this morning in the piazza....

They drank his blood, my lord.

I found Vittore in the chapel, praying with his arms outstretched, his face turned toward the heavens. I knelt beside him and prayed the *Ave Maria*, then leaned and bestowed him the holy kiss. "You are blessed of the Lord, Vittore."

The bell was tolling vespers when I crossed the Ponte Vecchio, hastening toward Gioletti's palace.

THE cardinal was resting, I was told, and not to be disturbed, but this was too important, and I would not be put off by some pewling, beardless novice. I pushed past Gioletti's coterie of handsome boys and burst into his rooms.

The sight that I encountered apprehended me completely, drove breath from my body. I sagged against the doorsill, while hot and cold flushed rapidly upon my face.

Cardinal Gioletti was lying spread upon the bed and fully naked, while Niccolo manipulated his erection by mouth. Another boy, a near-perfect copy of the pale sylph at Gioletti's groin, thrust himself vigorously in and out of the Cardinal's mouth, while a third boy, some years younger than the others but also blond, sucked on Gioletti's toes.

"My lord, I had no idea…." I bowed, although he couldn't see me, and backed away. The boy at Gioletti's head thrust strongly once more, grunted, and spilled his seed into the Cardinal's mouth.

"Ludovico, I pray you, don't run away." Gioletti wiped his face upon a linen towel, shooed the boy away. He passed me grinning, slipped into the antechamber, and was gone. "Come and join our little celebration." He patted Niccolo on the back of the head. "Go on now, Nicco. You can finish later." Niccolo took the other boy and also left, vanishing into the outer suite of rooms.

I was embarrassed beyond measure, but also powerfully intrigued. This was obviously some fault of my nature; I would be certain to perform absolution as soon as I made my next confession. I realized that, while I was by necessity immersed in the most heinous evil, I must be careful to bear no taint of it myself.

"As you can see, my young novices were benefitting from my spiritual instruction." Gioletti rolled his bulk off the bed, wrapped himself in a gaudy brocade robe. "Come and take a sup with me, Serenola." He waddled to the table and poured us both a cup of wine, drank it gratefully. "Ah! That gets the taste out." He fixed his gaze on me. "Now. What was it you wished me to understand?"

I blurted out what Vittore and my group of flagellants had witnessed that morning in the piazza, and related how Sebastien's treatise mentioned monsters such as these. "This is the abomination that has called the wrath of God upon us, my lord. Such sin and apostasy as this! We are lucky He refrains from raining fire on us." I deliberately avoided mention of the acts that Gioletti himself had just now committed, in this room. My mind still clamored with the images, and I wondered how he could explain the sin away.

"Ludovico." He passed a tray of sweetmeats, but I declined. It was my habit to take nothing in the evenings. "I impress upon you most strongly: please desist." He swallowed a handful of figs, farted lustily. "It is not my belief that the current pestilence is the punishment of your most vengeful God."

"But Sebastien—"

"Is an ascetic flagellant and a fool. He sees ghosts and spirits where there exists nothing but air." Gioletti's fingers lingered over the tray, plucked a candied apricot and sucked it thoughtfully.

"Then why did you give me his manuscript to read?"

"Purely for enjoyment, perhaps some slight erudition. Sebastien is not to be taken seriously, Ludovico, and *you*—" he tapped my cheek with two fingers, "—need to find some lithe young piece and spend an evening fucking." He sucked a great draught of wine, belched with obvious enjoyment.

Hot color mounted into my face; my cheeks burned. I realized at once that I was furious with him. "You filthy sodomite!" The center of my chest throbbed painfully; I was a hair's-breadth from sobbing. "How can you continue like this, when every holy syllable ever written—"

"Ludovico!" A whip-crack warning in that single word. The air around us pulsed with some discrete malevolence. I did not doubt that he would kill me if he could. "You will say nothing of what occurs here in my home, and when you arrive within my gates, you will *desist*—"

"Cardinal Gioletti—"

"You will *desist* to rant at me of apostasy and sin!" He slammed one meaty fist into the table and rose, towering above me like an angry bull. "You despicable, small cretin!" He was nearly apoplectic, stammering with rage, his spittle splattering my cheek, the collar of my cassock. "You know nothing of the dictates of the Holy See! I am a Cardinal of the Holy Church, and this luxury about me is my reward for my service here on earth...."

He was still ranting as I left. I turned at the staircase and saw Niccolo and the others slip in silence back into the room. The door closed softly behind them.

Chapter 9

DANTE

IT WAS evening. I awoke hungry, the blood-thirst sighing and moaning along the shadow of my bones. I could discern a slender thread of daylight, as bright as blood, and I watched as it slid along the casement's edge, disappeared into the advent of the night.

The body beside me in the bed was warm, burning with the peculiar heat that is so characteristic of our kind. I tilted his sleeping face and gazed into it: yes, he was a beauty! And changed now, by the blood, his features refined and sharpened, even more lovely than before. A beautiful young man, forever young now, and immortal unto eternity.

Rouen was sleeping opposite, curled up on a makeshift pallet in the corner, the blankets clutched against his chest. His long, dark hair was spread upon the pillows, silky and disheveled. His eyelids fluttered as if he were dreaming. The house had taken on its evening aspect, and pools of darkness gathered in the corners. Shapes that were familiar by candlelight were obscured, surreal. It was my favorite time of the night, that cusp of darkness when the day is dying.

"Valentin." I spoke to the heated bundle in my arms, "Time to wake and hunt." I shifted, pulled him closer to me, pressed his skin against mine. *Oh yes, I can see why Rouen loves you.*

He murmured, burrowed into the blankets, his palms against my chest. His fingers were long and slender, graceful. "Save me...."

"Valentin." I pressed my lips against his cheek, against the rosy spot where it had lain pressed against the pillow. "Wake up, *tesoro*."

Across the room, Rouen lifted his head from the pallet and gazed at me, eyes sleep-hazy, his expression indistinct. "Did he survive?"

I nodded. "Yes. And he is perfect."

"Why does he not awaken?" Rouen propped himself upon his pallet, clutched the covers against his naked chest.

"Valentin." I tilted his face up to mine and pressed my opened mouth against his. Immediately, his body curled around me, he returned the caress with eagerness. His pale eyes flickered open and focused into mine; a slow smile slid across his features.

"Have I recovered?" His fingers went to touch his own face, probing his flesh for signs of disease.

"Yes. You are whole again, and well."

Rouen slid off the pallet and moved across to us, his bare feet soundless on the tiled floor. He knelt beside the bed and hugged us both, his green eyes bright with bloody tears.

I lifted Valentin, helped him to sit upright. "How do you feel?"

"As if I were born again."

I lifted his upper lip with my fingers and probed the gums; his fangs were just beginning to descend, tiny points of whiteness, razor-sharp. "He is ready," I told Rouen.

Rouen smiled, reached out to help the pardoner to his feet. "Come, Valentin. Dante and I will show you how to hunt."

THE streets were unusually crowded as we made our way back from the outskirts of the city. Rouen and I chose our victims from diverse areas, so as to avoid the risk of detection. At this juncture, it would not do for us to come under any kind of suspicion.

We hadn't heard anything of Lilith now for weeks; the previous furor seemed to have died down a little with the coming of the winter, although the mad priest Serenola still followed the carts and preached about the Judgment.

"Valentin, keep up." I reached behind me and pulled the pardoner in step with us. "If you can't keep up, you'll have to hunt by yourself."

"Dante." Rouen shot me a warning glance. "Please."

"Where are you taking me now?" Valentin had fed well, but was now sated to the point of sluggishness. It is so often the way with the young ones, the new-made vampires who glut themselves on blood until they fall into a stupor.

"Home!" I snapped. I was short-tempered and ill at ease, and I didn't understand why. I had a terrible presentiment of danger, although I couldn't identify any specific peril. I wished to return to our lodgings as soon as possible. We could pass what little remained of the night in a game of bones or dice.

"It's still dark!" Valentin caught Rouen's arm, pressed against his side. The sight irritated me. "Please, Rouen, can we stay out a little longer? I have never seen the night this way—"

"Rouen...." There was something happening up ahead, just around the corner. I was suddenly possessed of a strong desire to turn and run the other way....

"Valentin, it will be soon be dawn. The darkness is deceptive. See there," Rouen pointed to the sky above the housetops, already lightening with the first streaks of false dawn "The night is weakening. We must hurry home."

My heart began to hammer in my chest, a resounding clatter in the bony cage of my ribs; my throat was thick and it was suddenly difficult to breathe. I was as afraid as I have ever been.

"Dante..." Rouen turned to me, a question in his eyes. "Do you smell something burning?"

I did. It smelled like flesh.

Valentin looked as if he might be sick. "What is it?"

"They're burning someone," I whispered. "Rouen, has it already gone this far?" My stomach contracted painfully, clutched in a fist of ice; cold thrills scampered down my spine.

We could hear the sounds of shouting, and the drums, as we moved closer. And Serenola, the mad, red priest, preaching the Judgment of God. "I want to go home," Valentin hissed, his fingers clamped around my arm. I could feel the tension in him, his body drawn taut like a bowstring.

"Shut up!" I shook him off me and slid around the corner, my back against a wall. I could feel Rouen's breath against my neck.

The crowd had assembled in the square, crouched around a cart upon which bodies had been piled, some already badly decomposed. A swarm of mosquitoes rose and fell above the bodies and the crowd; the cart exuded a foul stench, like filthy breath.

"The fools!" Rouen whispered, "They should incinerate the bodies, they'll all be infected!"

We understood what the mortals gathered there did not: that even casual or accidental contact with the plague meant certain death; prolonged exposure, such as this religious demonstration, was a headlong rush into the arms of the reaper. It was no threat to us, of course.

And there was Serenola. "There is a plague of evil rampant upon the land!" His voice was sonorous and loud, and carried well across the square. The inhabitants of the houses opposite made no objection to his bellowing on their doorsteps at dawn; I wondered if he had already gained so much in power that people feared to oppose him, as they feared to go against the will of God. "Evil has risen and walks among us!" He stopped, looked about him for a moment. I could see his expression, the question in his eyes. Something occurred to me, with certainty.

"He knows we're here," I told Rouen. "He recognizes me." I could see the crackle of the flames behind the platform; the smoke rose, an oily stench. I pressed my hand against my mouth and gagged.

"*Mio Dio*, how?" He stared at me, his mind working furiously behind his eyes. "Unless...." He swallowed several times, his throat flexing painfully. The smell was making us all sick.

"No, he's not a vampire," I replied. I'd sense him otherwise; our kind can recognize each other, even across great distances. "But he senses us, he knows us. Rouen, we have to get out of here." I cast a gaze across the crowd, the dun-clothed mass of Serenola's mad disciples. Wait—

"Rouen, is that a cardinal?" I pointed to a stout man crouched behind the platform, a tubby prelate with the small, dark eyes of a mad pig.

He followed my pointing finger, eyes narrowed. "Yes." He glanced at me. "So Serenola has the blessing of the Church?"

I shivered. "I don't know. I hope not." I chewed my lower lip. "He's a priest, isn't he? Some mendicant order. Perhaps that gives him credence."

"Who's that priest?" Valentin had pushed between us to see what was going on. I noticed that the front of his doublet was splattered with blood from his kill. *Damn!* "Perhaps he knows Cardinal Gioletti, I should speak with him—" He blinked, eyes watering against the greasy smoke. "What's burning?"

And before I could stop him, he had pushed his way into the crowd.

"Rouen! *Jesu Cristo!* Get him back here!" I watched Valentin's silver head slipping through the crowd, his bright, strange hair illuminated by the first rays of the rising sun....

The sun!

Rouen was pale with fear. "Valentin...." He turned and grabbed my arms. "Dante, he'll be incinerated...." We looked as the crowd parted to let Valentin through, saw the scaffold outlined against the sky, the bodies lashed to stakes, already—mercifully—dead. "*Madre de*

Dio!" Rouen turned away, retching.

The crowd had fallen silent, awaiting its cue. As if in some ghoulish tragedy, they stood ranged about the scaffold, arms folded resignedly against their chests. Each one bore upon his or her forehead a bright red cross. "What the hell is that?"

Up on the platform above our heads, Serenola gazed at Valentin with undisguised irritation; his fingers were white-knuckled where they gripped the edges of the pulpit. He wore spectacles, small glass ovals that caught the glare of the rising sun. "How dare you approach me?"

Several of the gathered mortals turned to stare at Valentin; they could not fail to notice the dark pattern of blood upon his clothes.

"I am a pardoner, Ser... perhaps you know me?" Valentin's voice carried well across the square; he hadn't learned how to modulate it, it was many times louder than a normal human voice. I stared at him, standing there, realized that he was as good as finished, that there was no way in earth or heaven that these mortals would look upon him and know him as anything human. The blood had burned away every vestige of Valentin's mortality; his appearance now was unmistakably vampiric, unnatural.

The crowd began to murmur... *Blood, there's blood on him... Killer, I've seen him in the taverns... Plague, he's one of them... Evil....*

"Rouen, we have to get him out of there." I peered over my shoulder; the sun was peeking over the housetops, the stream of daylight lengthening. In a moment, all three of us would be burned to cinders.

It takes about half an hour to die from burning, a little more if the wood and coals underneath your feet are slow. And every moment is an agony.

It takes but a moment for a careless strike of sunlight to kill a vampire. And then you are in agony for all eternity.

I watched the crawl of daylight as it advanced above the housetops. Serenola murmured about the edges of my senses; the crowd was closing around Valentin. Rouen seemed to float beside my vision as he moved slowly through the throng; his long hair drifted on his shoulders like a halo.

"Verily, I say unto you, you shall not suffer a witch to live! And what is this, standing here before us, an apparition pale as death and splattered with the blood of innocents?" Serenola had focused upon Valentin; the realization was unmistakable. Valentin was in grave danger, and so were Rouen and I! "What is this pale demon, but her hand outstretched to reap the Judgment? She is upon us, the Red Madonna… behold!"

There was a sudden, vicious crack as a burning timber exploded at the stake. Rouen leapt upon the platform, his hands about Serenola's throat, eyes flashing like bloody gems in the impending dawn. The crowd shrieked and murmured, stumbled over one another and bumped into the carts; a body slithered off the pile and slid onto the cobbles, damply dead, disgusting. Everything was a chaos of confusion: Valentin stared, mouth agape and fangs clearly showing, as Rouen grappled with the priest, Serenola's terrified followers buffeted the platform, threatening to dislodge them both. And Valentin was assaulted on all sides, slammed back and forth between unyielding mortal bodies. He had no knowledge of his own considerable power, the power I'd poured into his dying mortal body with my blood. They were attacking him, slapping and kicking, pronged fingers reaching for his eyes. *This is insane!* He could have killed them all with merely a thought….

"Valentin!" I roared with all my might. He was pushed around the other way by the stampeding mob; he craned his neck to see me, and as he did so, stepped backward, unthinking, and stumbled unwittingly into the first deadly pool of sunlight.

The psychic shock wave seared the surface of my brains, and I was pinioned in agony, helpless against the platform's edge. *Burning, I'm burning, burning….*

The morning sunlight cut a bloody streak across his face, sliced into his flesh, seared his eyelids and cheeks, the bridge of his nose.

I gasped, a burning breath that filled my lungs with the scaffold's oily smoke. Valentin was there, I could feel him; the agony of one of us feeds directly into the soul of each.

I put out my hand and pulled him into the precious darkness, cast about me wildly. "Rouen!"

He had disappeared; there was nothing now about me but the screaming, surging crowd. The mad red priest crouched on hands and knees, retching on the platform, while the bodies burned behind him. The wind changed suddenly, an icy blast that drove the smoke the other way, toward the crowd. I wrapped my arms around the pardoner and rose into the air.

She was there before me: the Unholy Madonna, rising from the smoke and ashes. I blinked, eyes streaming in the cold light of the dawn. *Mystery, Babylon the Great, Mother of Harlots....*

"Dante...." She opened her mouth, and annihilation yawned there, implacable, ancient. "You cannot escape me, Dante. I am your destiny."

"Leave me!" I roared, slashed the air with my free arm, my fingers passing through her apparition as through smoke.

"This is but the advent of a myriad of horrors."

She disappeared.

I closed my eyes against the rising sun. Below us, Florence writhed in the grip of another evil dawn. The smoke rose, obscuring my view. I turned my face toward our quarter of the city and flew, the unconscious pardoner lying in my arms.

THIS indeed was the beginning, as Lilith said, of a plethora of horrors: persecution, torture, death. As the winter waned and slid slowly into a cold, early spring, the abominations committed by Serenola's followers were manifold. By the middle of March, Florence—indeed, the entire country—was in the midst of a religious revolution.

A squad of soldiers chased an entire village into the forest at

Calabria and systematically hacked them to pieces, upon the orders of a Cardinal, who—it was rumored—was a follower of Serenola. In Florence, hundreds were lashed to the rack and pulled with ropes until their bellies burst, spilling their bowels on the ground to be eaten by dogs. Others were stripped naked and whipped to death with iron rods, until skin peeled off the bone like paper. Some were buried alive. Others were covered in pitch and set afire, a variation on the burning scaffold that Rouen and I had seen that morning in the square.

They were looking for a scapegoat, and I knew that there were not "unnaturals" enough to satisfy their hunger. There was another, much more dangerous element to the madness: Serenola and his followers now professed the Sacrament of the Red Madonna, the she-vampire that I had known as Lilith. Blessed be her name.

I HAD lain all day in a sleep as deep as death, Valentin curled in my embrace, insensible to the horrors going on around us.

There was still no sign of Rouen. I had been tormented by dreams of him, lashed helpless to the scaffold, burning, dying in the full glare of the morning sun. But I had been sunk so deeply into unconsciousness that there was no relief of waking to shake the nightmare; I must needs endure it, until the sun had safely set and I would rise again. Thus is our sleep so very like mortal death: each morning we die with the new-born sun; each night, we rise.

"Dante." Valentin's fingers on my face, the scent of Valentin, the warmth of him. "Wake up, *mi amore*."

I swam up through the clinging layers of unconsciousness, feeling frightened and suffocated. It was late evening; the sun had been gone for hours. I had overslept. "Where is Rouen?" My voice was a husky whisper, my throat seared by the oily smoke of the burnings... I could still taste it, in my mouth. "Rouen."

I caught Valentin's face between my hands; his flesh was healed, undamaged. He was whole again. "Your face... are you quite all right?" I remembered how the stray beam of light had struck him as he stumbled backward: sunlight slashing across his face, the delicate bridge of his nose. He should have been killed.

"Yes." He came into my arms, a compact package of bones and muscle, blazing with the eternal heat that so marks us as immortal. He was liquid fire in my arms, a burning wraith that leaned close to kiss me, mouth wide and hungry. I could feel his desire pressed against my leg, the blood throbbing inside his naked limbs, his belly, his sex. *Oh, where is Rouen?*

He slid wordless down my body, left a trail of fire drawn from the tip of his tongue. His lips pressed against my belly, each hip, the tender inside of my thighs; his mouth closed around me and swallowed me whole.

I gave myself to him and closed my mind against the horror that danced there; I slid my fingers into his eerie, silver hair and let him pleasure me. His wise mouth tugged at me, tongue swirling, his palms hot against my thighs. *I can see why Rouen loves you....*

I drove myself into his eager mouth, again and again, until a bright shard of pleasure drilled a spindle through my brain. I arched up into his mouth and erupted in release, shouting; spilled myself into his throat. I retreated for a time into a place of silence, and trembled. I was shivering with cold. I still could see the scaffold, in my mind; I could taste the greasy smoke.

"Cover yourself...." The blankets slid over us both and he curled into my arms, his bright, silver head close to mine, our faces touching. "Dante."

"Where is Rouen?" I kissed him savagely, my lips hard against his. "Where is Rouen?"

"Dante, don't...." His palms against my chest, pressing, resisting me, he was resisting me, the little bastard, *me, he was resisting me*!

"Where is he? You know where he is." I slammed him flat against the bed, caught his wrist tightly in my hand. His flesh smelled wonderful, delicious. He was a juicy thing, a precious new-made vampire. My fledgling. *Mine.*

"Dante, stop!" His body cracked like a whip, rose against me, muscles strained to throw me off of him.

"Where is Rouen, Valentin?" I was like a man possessed; I knew that he knew nothing more of Rouen than I did, but yet I couldn't stop. I wanted to torment him; he so begged it, with his large, pale eyes and his darling innocent face—

"Please." A whimper. Eyes filling up with bloody tears, pleading with me not to hurt him, even as his erection pressed against me, underneath.

I felt my fangs descend, sliding down out of my gums slowly, with a pleasure that is just the other side of pain. *Love me, yes you do....*

I bit into his wrist savagely, eyes wide open; watched as his body bucked underneath me, his eyelids jerking, shocked. I clamped my mouth over the bloody gash and drank from him, pulling his blood into my body, taking back from him what I'd given. His blood felt like nectar, it tasted like light; oh yes, he was innocence, but through and through, he could no more kill with malice than kill his own mother....

Valentin. The true believer. An iconoclast; an honest Pardoner.

I lifted my lips from his wrist, gazed down at him, my mouth wet with his blood. *Love me, yes you do.* "Do you want me to stop? Have you had enough?"

His eyes, half-lidded, were rolled back in his head; his breath came shallowly, rasping in his throat. I was alarmed; perhaps I'd killed him?

"Let me. Please." He was reaching for my wrist, but I guided him to my chest instead, slit the corrupted nipple for him and gave him suck. He curled against me as he had the night that I'd first made him; slowly laid me flat against the bed and rubbed himself on me.

I disengaged him, drew his mouth away from me and kissed him, tasting my own blood. His tongue slid into my mouth, teasing the tips of the fangs, testing their sharpness. "You must love me...." His mouth left bloody kisses on my throat, my chest and shoulders.

I took his clubbed foot between my hands and caressed it gently; ran my fingers over the deformity that so defined him, slipped into the spaces between the crushed and damaged toes. He was beautiful, *yes you are*, I could see why Rouen loved him. *Oh where is Rouen?*

I pleasured him slowly, with my mouth, as he had done for me, brought him panting time and again, trembling on the edge of climax, only to draw away from him, return to open the wound in his wrist and suck the blood, a little at a time. His naked body writhed beneath me, sheened with bloody sweat, dampening the bedclothes; his hair was sticking to his forehead, dark-silver. *Please....* His swollen member throbbed in cadence with his heartbeat, engorged with his lovely blood, the blood I loved.

He trembled when I at last took him into my mouth, lips wet with his blood, and brought him swiftly to his pleasure. He spent himself, writhing deliriously beneath me. He lay panting, eyes pressed shut, for a long time.

I covered him, bent to bring the candle, and as I did so, passed it glimmering beside his eyes. His eyelids flickered, eyeballs rolling, as his back arched into that familiar rictus. His jaw snapped shut, fangs slicing into his lower lip as his neck extended back at an impossible angle. "Valentin!" I caught his head between my hands and tried to force the corner of the sheet between his teeth, but he was already too far into the swoon, and I would have had to break his jaw to force his teeth apart.

His fingertips clutched, clawing, at the mattress, blood streaming from his lips. I backed away, still holding the candle, remembering what Rouen had said about not touching him when the seizure was upon him. "Valentin...." It was infinitely painful to see him this way, straining and trembling in the grip of it, his slender body bent like a reed in the wind. And what of my powerful blood, that so far had perfected him, had it no power to save him from the swoon?

And as quickly as that, it was over.

"Valentin." I went to him, caught him into my arms. "It's all right, *mi cuore*, you're safe." I rocked him, like a child.

"I saw her." He turned his gaze to me, his pale eyes fever-bright. "The Red Madonna."

Lilith.

"Riding on a dragon. I saw her." I wiped his bloody mouth on a corner of the bedclothes. "In the spring, it will come again, and there will be more burning, and Serenola—" He gasped, his eyes wide, stared at something past my shoulder, something I could not see.

"*Tesoro*, what is it?" I peered behind me; there was nothing there but the familiar shapes of our apartments, bathed in darkness.

"Her."

"No, Valentin, you're dreaming." I wrapped the blankets around him, held him tightly to stop his trembling.

"You don't believe me," he whispered. His eyes closed slowly, the seizures exhausted him. "I can see it, Dante. She is the hand of vengeance."

There was silence. The tiny hairs nearest my scalp prickled; I had a very real sensation that we were being watched.

I laid him carefully on the bed and turned slowly toward the doorway, took the candle in my hand. "Who's there?" My voice boomed out at freakish volume; inhuman, unnatural. My skin crawled with possibilities. I spun slowly in a circle, peering into every darkened corner, every crevice.

"Dante." A figure in the doorway. *Rouen.*

Chapter 10

ROUEN

THE embrace of those familiar walls was welcome after the sight of Serenola's scaffold, the tumult of the crowd. I had walked until I had seen the candle in the window, and I knew that Dante at least was here, and perhaps Valentin. The smell of incense led me to our lodgings, our nearest neighbors burned it, it was the latest "cure" for plague.

"Where have you been all day?" His hands upon my shoulders, he was naked underneath the blanket he held clutched against him. I surmised he had been sleeping.

"I found a place to sleep, I went to ground." I embraced him gladly, held him to me for a moment, savoring the throb of his heart against my chest. "I love you."

He drew back a little, his dark eyes quizzical. "Hmmm."

"Dante, please." I was weary beyond all dreams of stupor; all I wanted was to fall down on the bed and stay there, forever. I lowered myself gently to the floor, laid my head in my hands. The room, the universe about me, all was spinning.

"You haven't fed." He replaced the candle in the sconce and sat beside me. "I've warned you about that, Rouen."

I sighed. I had no answer to give him, my mind was whirling with the memory of all I'd heard and seen. There was nothing to say, no way to sufficiently exorcise myself of it. Serenola following the carts, bellowing the cry of Judgment, the demented masses that followed him, governed only by their bloodlust and the promise of redemption. I wondered, in a vague sort of way, if indeed this heralded the end of the world.

"Don't be a fool," Dante hissed. He had correctly discerned my thoughts, as usual. "Serenola and his followers are fanatics, as you well know, with not a grain of truth in any of his teachings." He arranged his blanket about his shoulders. "A little dogma is a dangerous thing." He said this with an odd sort of intensity, as if he were trying to convince himself of it.

"You're afraid of him—Serenola." I laid my hand on his shoulder, against his burning skin. "Why?"

He shrugged elegantly, the blanket falling off his shoulder. "There's something about him, Rouen. Yes, I am afraid of him." It seemed to be a difficult admission for him.

Valentin was sleeping, resting on his belly with his cheek pressed against the pillow. I moved over and laid my hand against his neck, slid my fingers into the silky softness of his hair. "How is he?"

"Sleeping." Dante moved to kneel beside me, his blankets trailing like ceremonial robes. He leaned his elbows on the bed and watched me in silence for a moment.

"Serenola is crying now for recompense." I drew my palm slowly down Valentin's pale skin. "He claims that this plague is a punishment from God."

Dante snorted. "Certainly. And the darkness is the stronghold of the Devil, and you and I and Valentin are his emissaries." He crossed his arms upon his chest. "*Fanatico.*"

I nodded. "Of course. Indeed, he is mad. But it doesn't matter." I thought about the crowds gathered around the platform, eagerly hanging on his every word. "Serenola has captured their acclaim. And the Church is giving serious credence to his theories."

Dante's eyebrow crept toward his forehead. "Indeed?"

"I'm serious." I felt old, in a manner that I had not since Dante made me what I am. The city had become a hotbed of fear and mounting political pressure, the wellspring of Serenola's madness. "He is sanctioned by the Church. That was a Cardinal we saw."

The candle sputtered, the only sound. Dante took a deep breath, let it out slowly. "We are in trouble, Rouen."

"How so?" As ominous as Serenola's noisome preaching was, I didn't see that it impacted on us directly. Apart from the fracas in the square this morning, we had had no contact with him whatsoever.

"Serenola sees Lilith."

"He does not." This, I did not want to contemplate; this would mean that—

"She said that she was come to bring about the end of the world, Rouen. She will do as she says." Dante shivered inside his blanket. "Serenola is the perfect instrument; he has the ear of Church, he has the attention of the people. Rest assured that she will use him as she sees most fit."

I drew the covers over Valentin, pondered again something that had been sliding across the surface of my mind for ages now. "Dante…."

"Hm?" He was occupied in picking something from the sole of his foot.

"That day that I first met you." Mere days before the Christmas feast, the holiest of days; Dante freezing in the market. Selling himself.

"Hmm." He continued picking, refused to look at me.

"I don't understand." The words fell from my lips and into silence, rolled away into the darkest corners.

"What do you not understand, Rouen?" His head snapped up, eyes flashing fire. "That I was allowing myself to be buggered for money?"

"No, that I understood—"

"I assure you, you do not." Cold as ice, and as sharp.

"Yes, but…," I sighed. "You were a vampire then."

"Indeed." His gaze was once again suspicious, hard; the gaze of the market whore shivering against the cold stone of the arcade.

"So why did you allow Leonardo to rape you? When you could have killed us both."

His head came up slowly, his eyes looking everywhere but mine. His mouth was trembling, as it does when he is trying not to weep. "I was making recompense."

My skin prickled violently, a sudden flush of shame like heat. "My God, *why*?"

"Because all of it was my fault, if I hadn't lured her to Salvatore's house—" He was up and pacing, quickly back and forth, his hands gesturing madly. "—She came looking for me, and everybody *died*!"

I was stunned. I hadn't realized that underneath his contained exterior there was a soul capable of that kind of needless guilt. Truly, Dante was a paradox. "You cannot possibly believe that."

"I *do*!" Voice trembling, dark eyes filling up with bloody tears. "I do, Rouen."

"You believe that your master and his household died of plague because of you." Incredible.

"Yes." Turning, his back to me, hugging himself, his shoulders trembling violently.

"It isn't your fault." My throat felt as if I'd swallowed sand. "You cannot carry this guilt with you throughout eternity!"

"Rouen." Absolutely calm, he was contained again. His voice was clear and precise. "Lilith came to Salvatore's household because it was me she sought. If I had not been there, if I—" He was seized with a violent fit of weeping, body trembling, tears running in bloody streaks down his face. "If I did not *exist*—"

"Then you would not have made me. And I, too, would be dead of plague, and so would Valentin." I went to him, gathered him into my arms and kissed him. "I'm sorry I stood by and let him hurt you—"

"I deserved it."

"No! You did not!" I hated myself, at that moment, that I had allowed him to be so violently mishandled. "You have suffered enough."

He drew back a little and gazed at me. "If Serenola is correct, then there are manifold sufferings yet to come."

"Serenola is a madman." I kissed him gently, drew him over to the bed where Valentin lay sleeping. "Tell me of Valentin. Did you fly away with him?" The pardoner's face had healed perfectly, but such is the power of her ancient blood, the blood that flows in each of us. We could withstand tragedy such as would kill an ordinary mortal.

"Rouen, we should arrange to leave the city as soon as possible." Dante had moved away from me and was busy pulling on his clothes. "I have a bad feeling about this. We should leave." He slipped into his shirt, fastened his hose quickly, buckled on his purse. "Valentin is having fits again; I passed the candle by him this evening and he swooned." He adjusted his doublet, shoved his feet into his boots. "And Rouen—" He clasped my shoulder to gain balance as he fastened his laces. "His visions are stronger than they ever were." He grunted softly. "He sees Lilith. He says there will be another upsurge of the plague this spring, and more burnings. Already it is March, the days and nights grow warmer. How much longer till it strikes again?"

I thought, suddenly, of something Dante had said a while ago, at the advent of Serenola's madness. *Have they been to question your father yet? Lying in that fusty bed and fucking his own sister....*

"How much is there left of the night?" It was suddenly vital that I go.

Dante peered at me strangely. "It is but the stroke of eleven. Why?"

"I am going home." I shoved my hands into my gloves. "I have to warn them."

"Rouen—" Dante's hand on my arm. "You cannot propose to journey to Prato this hour of the night.... I'm coming with you." He shrugged into his cloak, tucked a small dagger into his belt.

"You won't need that." I felt uneasy at the sight of it, it assumed a certain threat. "Villa di Francisci is well fortified."

"Rouen." Dante patted the dagger against his hip. "Stop nattering and come along."

"What of Valentin?" I glanced to where the pardoner, exhausted, lay sleeping.

"Stoke up the fire and cover him. He'll be fine until we return." Dante's grin came and went like lightning, "He knows enough now to stay out of the sunlight."

I WOULD have preferred to walk, but Dante insisted that we travel his way, and so with great trepidation, I allowed him to take me with him into the air.

He was more practiced than he had been the last time, more able to negotiate the capricious winds and retain his essential course. We flew high above the housetops, streaking past the sleeping city at great speed, until I pointed out the villa that my father owned. "There, it's right down there." The house, with its sprawling gardens and stables, its adjoining groves, was massive; I had never fully appreciated it until I'd seen it from the air.

Dante's flight took us in a meandering course over the countryside; it was near midnight when we landed, and the house and grounds were deadly silent. I supposed the servants to have gone to bed: the stables were all dark, there was no footfall in the courtyard. It was eerie.

I passed through the antechamber into the foyer, moving through the great swinging wooden doors, imposing with their heavily inlaid panels, their impressive brass fitments. But then, my father married right back into his own family's money. I could not imagine how my grandfather had permitted such a thing to come to pass; it was inconceivable to me.

"He was dead, very probably, and could give neither his blessing nor his veto."

Dante's voice startled me momentarily; I had quite forgotten that he was there, behind me. "Refrain from reading my mind without my consent, *cretino*." I reached for his hand and pulled him close to me. "You must show me that technique." I forced a tone of levity into my voice, when, if the truth be known, I was filled with a horrible foreboding. I knew that somewhere, around the next corner, I would see it—the disaster that I anticipated. *Have they been yet to question your father? Lying in that fusty bed and fucking his own sister....*

I shuddered.

"Rouen, what is it?" Dante stopped, tilted my face toward him. "You're trembling!" He pressed his gloved hand against my cheek. "*Tesoro*, what's the matter?"

"Let's go in." I pulled away from him. Whatever it was, I might as well see it and get it over with.

THE smell assaulted me immediately when I entered: blood, soaked into the rushes, blood soaked into my mother's carpets, blood splattered on the walls. "There has been a struggle here," I said. My own voice sounded strange to me, strangled.

Dante made no reply. His eyes looked peculiar: impossibly wide, huge.

The first one that I found was my brother, Paolo—he is an idiot, an eternal child. When he was born, the ancient *nonnas* said he was God's punishment upon my mother for her sins. But my mother always said God smiled on him, and that God loved him most of all, because He had given Paolo the gift of eternal innocence. He went everywhere with my mother, his wrist attached to hers by a long silken cord; he guided her, because she was blind.

They had cut his throat. I could see the edges of it, gaping like a pair of lips, like a grin. They had stabbed him in the stomach, sliced his abdomen across so that his bowels bled onto the floor. They had cut the cord that bound him to my mother.

He was lying in his own excrement, foul and bloody, stinking like shit. I was seized with a sudden vicious anger—why didn't he resist them, why didn't he save my mother, why....

Behind me, Dante retched quietly, leaning against the wall. There was something pressing at the underside of my tongue, a pressure at my throat, like choking. I felt like I would smother.

I found my parents in their bed. Their throats had also been cut, but they had sliced off my mother's breasts... and her hair. My mother always had such beautiful hair, and now it was shaved nearly to the skull and scattered about the room like leaves. She had been raped, I saw, her thighs streaked with blood, smeared with filth. They had severed my father's penis and shoved it in her mouth.

And written it in blood, all around the room: *Mystery, Babylon the Great, Mother of Harlots.*

I turned to look at Dante. A great roaring had started in my head, like the noise of many rivers, and something throbbed within my guts, a violence.

His eyes were immense and held all the sorrow of the world. I hoped he would keep silent, for if he did, then I myself could turn and depart in silence, and not speak of it. I knew this. I knew that if only he kept his mouth closed, I could seal this horror forever and it would never find me. I would run from it. I would hide.

But he spoke. One word, my name. *"Rouen...."*

And a roar exploded out of me, torn screaming from my throat, a wail of horror, violence and bloodshed. I slapped my palms against his chest and roared, a rending, animal wailing.

I fell and fell and fell, the darkness opening before me, and Dante with his arms about me like a band of iron, rocking me and kneeling in my mother's blood.

"I could have made them one of us," I told him. I recall that I was dipping my fingers in the blood and licking it, doing this over and over, between the words as they trickled out of me. I slapped my hands in it, sucked it from my fingers, until Dante screamed that I must stop, and I kept on doing it, scooping up their stolen blood and licking it off my hands, until finally he sank his teeth hilt-deep into my hand.

"*Stop it!*" He was shaking, his face as white as bone. "Come away from here." He took me by the hand and led me stumbling into the courtyard, wrapped his arm about my waist and rose into the air.

"Drop me," I begged him, "loose hold and let me fall." And I struggled with him, but he was and is the stronger of us, and he did not let me fall. The wind drove his tears against my skin as he wept for me, but I was silent. There is some sorrow that is far too deep for tears.

"Valentin!" Dante roared up over the stairs, half-carrying me, half-dragging me. His hose and doublet were speckled with the blood of my dead family; his face was wet with bloody tears. "Valentin!"

He stumbled into the main room, kicked the door open, stood trembling on the threshold.

Valentin was there, dressed in clean and rich attire, talking to the cardinal that we had seen that morning in the square.

The disciple of Serenola.

A murderer, like him.

I launched myself at him, and the world dissolved in a roar of blood and vengeance.

Chapter 11

VALENTIN

I AWAKENED, and he was there, sitting in the room, indistinct against the darkness. And I was tired, heart-heavy, as I so often am when the visions come.

The dim shape of him alarmed me; I thought for an instant that I still was dreaming, that the phantoms from my visions had somehow taken weight outside their world of forms.

I sat up, clutched the covers to me, shamefully aware that I was naked. I felt like I did when he first stumbled upon me in the whorehouse. "Valentin."

I blinked. "Messer Gioletti—"

"Don't get up." He said. He glided toward me, the rustling of his robes the only sound. "Gentle, pardoner." The bed compressed beneath his weight. "Don't be afraid, Valentin…."

I shivered as his fingers slid into my hair, pressed against the smooth skin of my face. "So soft…." He leaned toward me, the scent of cloves heavy on his breath. "You never have grown a beard, your downy cheeks as smooth as a maiden's. Why?" A hint of menace. My new senses caught the quickening cadence of his heart, the barely perceptible quiver in his voice.

"You dishonor me, Ser." I jerked away from him, slid further back until I rested against the wall, my feet stretched in front of me. "Pray, what business do you here? And how did you know the address of my lodgings?"

Cardinal Gioletti had bothered me of late. I still met with him regularly, as dictated by the conditions of my holy service, but each one of our meetings was fraught with insinuation and veiled threat; I suspected he had hired spies to scrutinize me, to satisfy his own misgiving. He claimed I did no service to the Church and wondered where I had disappeared. The habitual offering that I had agreed to make was long since tardy, he reminded me, and of what account the pardons that I sold? Where was the money that I made by showing holy relics, and since when was I free to wander as I chose? I had duty; I must attend. I recall that he even mentioned something about excommunication.

I last had seen him the night before our unlucky meeting with the followers of Serenola, in the square.

"I have nothing to give you." I had met him in the foyer of the Duomo, standing far back against the shadows so that he would not discern my unnatural pallor. The thing that Dante had done had changed me: I had in life been pale, but now I looked a thing unearthly, and each infusion that I took of mortal blood rendered me paler still, till I resembled but a walking corpse. My eyes, always gray and ghostly, were now nearly colorless, an eerie silver in which swirled myriad reflected hues. My hair crackled when I touched it, as if it were a living thing, and my fingernails were opaque, as hard as glass.

"You have nothing to give me?" He advanced, his voice heavy with intimidation. "How so?"

"Exactly as I said." I felt the throbbing in the back of my skull, forced myself into an essential calm. "I have not sold indulgence now for many weeks." Indeed, I had not offered pardon since I arrived in Italy, over a month since.

"And where is the portion that you promised to me?" he demanded, his voice escalating shrilly. He clamped his fingers around my upper arm. "Did you think our agreement void, simply because you discerned some alternate vocation?"

"Loose hold of me," I whispered. A terrible violence pulsed along my limbs; I knew that I could kill him if I wanted, and yet it seemed a finer thing to hold him here a little while, to torment him if I could.

"So innocent, your darling angel's face." He pressed two fingers against my lips. "Gentle pardoner...."

I slapped his hand away with a force sufficient to shatter the bones of his wrist. While he was cowering on the floor, I knelt and grabbed him by the surplice, towed him close to me. "I am no longer in thrall to you, Messer Gioletti. Listen and be warned."

"*Sodomite!*" Anger twisted his stout features into an ugly mask; he cradled his shattered wrist with his other hand. "I elevated you to the esteemed position you now hold, and rest assured, I can crumble your foundation—ah!"

I had seized his broken wrist lightly between my fingers, allowed it to dangle in my grip like the stem of a flower. "I will no longer sell pardon."

"Please, I beg you—" He trembled violently, this sturdy man, and his face was blanched and damp with sweat. "—I inquire only after the state of your soul!"

I rose slowly, peered down at him, kneeling there in agony. I laid the sole of my clubbed foot against his chest and pushed. "I have seen you following me. I have heard you asking for me. I have seen you in the taverns and the inns." It was true: there were many times that I went out at night to feed that I discerned him, just out of range of my vision. I suspected there were others, also, that followed me and reported according to his orders.

"I question only because I am worried about my Valentin!" Obsequious, fawning now. He knew I had discovered the truth of his investigations, and wished to spare himself from damage.

"You question far too much, and what sorts of questions do you ask, Ser?" I dropped to my knees in front of him, my gaze level with his. I could smell fear emanating from him like a foul odor. "I would know."

"You would know!" He sneered, *"You!"* And when I made no reply, "I worry about the standing of your acquaintances, their reputation. I worry that you sully yourself by associating with the underclasses...." He was speaking quickly, out of breath, clearly afraid for his life.

"Rouen di Francisci is a nobleman, and Dante is of the house of Salvatore di Tuscano." I blurted this before I realized that he was baiting me, and now I had given him priceless information, the names of my comrades. *Damn!*

"Rouen?" He peered at me as he struggled to his feet, painfully. I did not aid him, merely watched with some faint interest, the difficulties of this pithy mortal. Dante was correct; they hardly warranted our consideration. "Of the house of Francisci of Prato?"

I moved to go; he followed me toward the door. "I have ways of knowing, Valentin. Perhaps it would be best if you allowed me to restore you as pardoner." There was a rustling as he moved closer, the scent of cloves swirled around me, spicy. "I think we ought to each protect the interests of the other, don't you?"

In that instant, I divined his thoughts, and they were most unsavory. For he intended to collect his share of my illegal pardoning and to then betray me to the courts: Rouen, Dante, and myself he would see racked and then burned, just as I had seen the enemies of Serenola mortified. "You are in league with him," I whispered. I was not at all surprised.

"I serve only our Lord and Savior, Jesus Christ," he replied, in a tone as mild as milk. "I would resist the urge to do me damage, Valentin." He gestured around the foyer. "The Spirit of God bears witness here, and I know you value your immortal soul above all else."

I felt as if a trap door had opened underneath my feet.

I felt that way now, with him in the room.

"Valentin."

I snapped out of my reverie, peered at him across the darkness. "I repeat only what I told you in the Duomo: I will no longer sell pardon.

As for the business of my soul, I have been newly shriven by an authority much higher, and am content with that." I got out of bed, dropped the blanket, and, standing naked there before him, dressed at my leisure. I watched him from out the corners of my eyes, saw his greedy glance linger on my buttocks, my flat belly, the long muscles of my thighs. "There is a charge for looking," I informed him, my tone succinct.

But he deflected my sarcasm, turned instead to other things. "Your esteemed companions… where are they this night?" His voice pressed against me, threatening. I saw that his wrist was wrapped in linen, the wrist that I had broken. "They have departed and left you all alone! For shame!"

I flushed hot and cold; I wondered if I should kill him then and drink. "Get *out*!" I roared, my voice redoubling in the containment of the apartment. "You will lay no suppositions at my threshold!" I yanked my hose up around my waist, tied the laces savagely.

"Such fine grasp of language you have now…." His small eyes narrowed. "When first I met you, you could barely speak, and stuttered out the Offertory so that I was obliged to tutor you… how came you by this schooling, Valentin?" He slid off the bed, stepped close to me. "You still cannot answer me the question: where are your good companions?"

Something dark and ugly slithered through our midst, some evil premonition, and I knew with abject certainty that he had worked some sinister plot. "What have you done?" My voice cracked as it forced its way out of my throat, paralyzed. Time hung suspended, waiting.

There was the clatter of boot heels on the stairs, and I heard the doors swing open. "*Valentin!*"

Dante.

He was dragging Rouen, who had collapsed against him like a mishandled doll. His eyes were terrified and empty. "Who is this murderer?" I heard his voice, and it was terrible, awesome in its grief. Rouen roused himself and looked about him, eyes focusing slowly on

Gioletti. He gazed at the priest for an eternal moment, gained strength from it, pushed himself away from Dante, and stood quivering beside the doorsill.

"Murderer." His wooden boot heels rang against the tiles as he drew closer. The scent of cloves was strong upon the air.

"And here you see, Valentin, your good companions have returned to y—" His speech was cut off in mid-phrase, as Rouen put out a hand and stopped his breath, fingers clamped around Gioletti's throat. The Cardinal kicked and struggled, his mouth working silently. A slender thread of spittle slid from the corner of his lips, dropped quivering into the air, a strand of spider silk.

This evil, the abomination of which I had a premonition, sifted down into our midst: it slid in through the casements and crawled gibbering upstairs; it oozed between the spaces in the bricks, and incarnated as a chilly breath that hung between us all, a scent as sickening as cloves.

I glanced at Dante, standing speechless against the farthest wall, lips white with shock and some recently remembered horror. He seemed to be whispering something, over and over, just underneath his breath, something that I could not make out....

Mystery, Babylon the Great, Mother of Harlots....

Rouen held Cardinal Gioletti dangling by the throat, eyes bulging, soundless as a statue. "I am lately come from my father's house in Prato," he said. His words rang hollow, emerged from out of a damning emptiness. He gazed at me, eyes flashing, slid the memory into my mind along that link that only our kind possess....

Jesu Cristo....

I began to tremble, fighting against the pictures in my mind, resisting it, but Rouen would not allow escape; he forced the images into my brain until everything around me swam with it, and I was sickened.

He drew his hands up underneath the Cardinal's jaw and, staring deep into Gioletti's eyes, snapped his neck with one brutal gesture.

Rouen shivered, mouth wide open as his fangs descended, turned and struck at Gioletti's dangling body.

His action freed us all to movement; I darted for the doorway but Dante curtailed my flight, slammed an arm against the jamb and caught me underneath the chin. He dragged me with him, dropped me in front of Gioletti's body.

"The heart." His lower lip trembled, his voice quivering with sorrow, the horror he had seen at Rouen's father's villa.

I stared at him. "What?"

"The heart." He slapped a fist against the back of my head, driving me down against the body. "Take it."

A fire ignited in my belly; I made a fist and slammed it into Gioletti's chest, clutched my fingers around his still-beating heart. I jerked it from its moorings, the greasy network of arteries and veins, ligaments and sinew, took the spasmodic spurting of the blood against my face and neck. The smell of it tormented me, rich and meaty, and I was very hungry, but I did not drink.

I reached out, the bloody heart upon my palm, and handed it to Rouen. "Signore." It was indeed an offering, a most poignant sacrifice.

He took it, sank his fangs into it and drained it of blood, sucking greedily, then turned without ceremony and tossed it out the opened window. His lips and face were smeared with blood, an obscene carnival mask.

The dead cardinal lay spread-eagled, as if impaled on spikes, his sightless eyes bulging from his head. His inanimate face was set in an expression of profound wonder, the mouth slightly open. The chest was caved in around the hole my fist had made: it appeared as if some monster had burst out of him, breaking through the ribcage and out into the open air.

Dante spoke, dropped words into the awful silence. "May God have mercy on his soul." He wept, tears making bloody streaks against the paler landscape of his face. He turned to Rouen, inquired, "What shall we do with him?"

I assumed he meant the cardinal.

Dante caught and held me as Rouen stripped me, forced me down upon the floor.

"*No!*" I struggled, lashing out with arms and legs against them, my fangs bared. Panic washed over me in suffocating waves. I saw them come and go above me: first Rouen and then Dante, flashing through my field of vision, dark as ravens.

They took blood from every place on me that they could find; it seemed I felt fangs slide in and out of me a thousand times and then again, the sucking pull as they drank, draining me to the point of weakness.

"Valentin."

I fought unconsciousness to look at him, raised my eyes, the flickering beginning as it always did inside my skull. "Rouen." I sobbed dryly, reached my fingers to touch his face. "I swear to you...."

He tarried over me, swaying, then leaned and pressed his bloody lips against my forehead. It felt like a benediction; it seemed like absolution. *Valentin, Te absolvo....*

But he was cold as death.

I watched through half-lidded eyes as they dragged the corpse upright between them, carried it down the stairs and into the street. I knew where they were going; they would display him in the square so that Serenola and his disciples, arriving with the carts at first light, would see Gioletti hanging there. Serenola had taken much from Rouen, and Gioletti was the instrument.

"BUT they cannot escape the fate that attends us, Valentin."

Her voice floated to me across a sea of blood and agony; I turned and saw her, drifting between the opened casement and the wall. Her form was translucent, a shadow-creature, but her eyes were bright with possibilities. The Madonna of Impruneta, the Holy Virgin crowned with a ring of stars. "*Far tacere*, you do not swoon this night. I am come to bring about the final act of this destruction."

I turned my face toward the opened window, to the faint paling of the darkness as dawn slid across the sky. I was aware that I was weeping, soundless. I knew, as I have often known since, that there was no way for us to stop her. She was and is the Consort of God, and manifold is her power.

"Look towards the west, Valentin, and as the sun so rises on the empire now defeated by the Moors, so will I effect again my destruction. Already the believers there are massing to prejudice my purpose!" She drifted close to me, took my face into her hands. "Already the seasons turn towards the spring and it will come again. Already He instructs His purpose."

I heard the murmur of their voices, Dante and Rouen returning from the square where they had mounted Gioletti's body.

She drifted to the casement and hovered for a moment, insubstantial as a ghost. "*Ricodare*."

Remember.

If I died this night, I would remember little else.

"IT HAS become far more dangerous than I expected." Dante and Rouen, returning from the square, their clothing and their hands greasy with Gioletti's blood. I heard them summon Emilia to bring water, listened to the splashing and their quiet murmurs as they washed their hands and faces, stripped off their bloody clothes and exchanged the soiled garments for others. "Rouen, I think the time has come for us to take flight."

I started up, eyes snapping open. Did they include me in this escape, or was I too much suspect, and therefore not involved in the consideration?

"Where will you go?" My voice felt hesitant and thready; I

experienced the profound loss of blood in much the same way as a mortal does.

"I think it best if we leave before the light." Dante ignored me, drying his hands on a towel. I saw him reach a gentle hand toward Rouen, standing naked and shivering near the basin. "Best for you, Rouen."

"Indeed." Rouen pulled on a clean set of drawers, layered dark hose over this, the color of blood. He slipped a clean white shirt over his head, and over this a heavy knee-length robe, buckled on his purse. He pulled his boots back on, and wrapped a velvet cloak about himself.

"Where are you going?" I asked again. I flinched, shielded my eyes against the sudden flare as a candle sizzled into flame. "I insist you tell me."

I saw them exchange a look, some agreement that passed between them; I knew that it had some sinister thing to do with me. Dante brought the candle closer, knelt beside me on the floor. "I would request a little favor, Valentin."

I gazed up into the depths of his dark eyes, and saw nothing there, except my own tiny reflection. It frightened me. "I pray you, do not bleed me again... I can't stand it!" I slid backward, away from them, my palms flat against the floor. Dante's smile was falsely beneficent. He leaned toward me, and passed the candle flickering beside my eyes.

"Please, don't—" My speech choked off as surely as if there had been a hand about my throat. I felt the claws come down and slice into my skull, heard the hollow thud as my head slammed into the floor, spine arched at an impossible angle. I fought against the tremors, but it was useless. Perhaps they had drained me so that I could no longer resist them; perhaps they had planned it that way all along.

The swoon split along lines of rupture, and I saw her: majestic, wonderful, riding down from Heaven on a flame of fire.

A voice slid along the edges of my madness. "Valentin." But it was glorious here; there were sensations that I rather liked to feel, and there were colors and there was comfort. I could tarry here; the timbre of this place pleased me.

"Valentin." A different voice, pleading. Then, "Dante, stop it, leave him alone!"

"What do you see, Valentin?" The high sides of the bed pressed into my back; I was sitting on the floor, but I was blind! Some strange alteration of the swoon… I didn't like this at all.

"She is approaching." I put my hand out, felt the wavy softness of fine velvet. Rouen's shoulder. "The Queen of Heaven. Coming this way." I heard them slip away from me, drift whispering into the corners of the room. I put my hands out, fell forward into space, slapped my palms and my cheek against the floor. The blow cracked my skull, sent me reeling into dizziness. Lilith was coming back.

"Valentin!" A scuffle, then a pause, warm breath against my cheek. "Rouen, what's the matter with him?"

"Valentin." A different presence; I could identify them now by the preternatural nimbus of energy that encloses those of our kind: it is a thing sensed, rather than seen, and it differentiates each of us from our fellows. "Dante, he's *blind*!"

There was a tiny creaking noise. I cocked my head toward it, sought vainly to identify it. All other noises stopped.

I felt the room spin about me, and then there came a sound like a violent rushing wind. My vision flashed back into being, a sudden streak across the brain. I knew that she was there.

The casements exploded inward, their wooden shutters blown in splinters into the opposite wall. The basin shuddered, slid off of the table, spun along its rim until it smashed itself trying to hasten down the stairwell. The single candle flickered and went out.

"She's here." I groped my way along the floor, found Dante lying near the door, stunned and bleeding from a gash in his forehead, but otherwise unhurt. Rouen was pinned against the wall, terrified, his lips as pale as the whites of his eyes.

A thread of flame appeared, burning hot and blue, and revolved slowly in the center of the room, midway between the ceiling and the floor. As we watched, it coalesced into the shadowy outline of a woman's form: tall and slender, with long hair streaming in the wind. She became solid before our very eyes, flesh building onto the phantom outline, eyes forming first in a face that resembled nothing human.

"Valentin." Her hand, outstretched toward me, drew me to her, slid me unresisting along the floor to where she floated, an inch or so above the tiles. "*Mi amante….*" My body drifted up, suspended in the air above her, as if I were dangling from strings. My head tilted toward her, eyes closing, mouth open and connecting with hers….

I do not will this!

The connection snapped, and I tumbled to the floor. The residue of her power crackled through me, sizzling along my limbs and dispersing into the air around me. My crippled foot began to ache.

Her head turned slowly, a leisurely survey of the room, and the halo of energy around her began to change. It throbbed, malevolent, descended through the spectrum to dark purple as she saw Rouen.

She flashed across the room, slashed his face with her fingernails, fastened one hand around his throat, and lifted him kicking into the air. "I will destroy him for you." Her whisper sounded like a thousand sighing devils. "Infidel."

"*No!* Not him, let him go!" I clawed my way across the floor, fingers scrabbling for purchase against the tiles. "I beg of you, please… *let him go!*" Fear throbbed in my temples; it felt as if my brains would burst.

She turned to look at me, and I saw that she had fangs extending past her lower lip, and fully razor-sharp. "You do not wish this?"

I was sobbing, bloody tears dripping off my cheeks, falling in spatters on the floor. "No!"

She let him down, gently; erased the damage with a wave of her hand. "Don't weep so, gentle Pardoner." She lifted my face, kissed each cheek in turn, as if I were a child. "Blessed are the pure in heart."

She drifted out the casement and was gone.

"Rouen." I went to him, lifted him up, scrutinized his features for any sign of injury, but She had healed him completely.

"How is it that she obeys commands from you?"

I turned. Dante was there, the wound in his forehead rapidly healing, closing before my eyes, the cut edges of the skin sealing together.

I stared at him. "What exactly do you mean?"

"You saw! You tell her that you do not wish a thing, and she obeys." Dante yanked me to my feet. "How is this so, Pardoner?"

"Dante, leave him alone."

"Seriously, Pardoner." He crossed his arms on his chest, stared at me. His expression was cold, unforgiving as old stone.

"I have no... *pact* with her, if that's what you are asking!"

"I think you are a traitor."

"*Dante!*" Rouen's outrage was manifestly obvious. "Have you taken leave of your wits?"

"It's the truth, Rouen." He shoved me, so that I stumbled backward, my clubbed foot unable to find purchase on the slippery tiles. "You are a traitor, aren't you, Pardoner?"

"*Bastardo!*" This was so glaringly unfair, "How dare you accuse me?" I had just saved them both from the full force of her wrath.

"Dante, I think perhaps...."

Rouen's intended warning died away to nothing as Dante's rigid right arm bunched and struck me in the mouth. My head snapped back, teeth clattering, my fangs lancing into my tongue, a nasty little jolt of pain.

I recoiled, caught him under the chin with the heel of my hand, slammed him back against the wall. Rage flashed inside my skull, multicolored and precise, as cold as stone. "—kill you—"

"*Stop!*" Rouen, furious, wedged himself between both of us, pressed me back against the wall, pushed Dante away from me. "This is madness!" He stared at us both, panting at each other like a pair of trapped bears. "Fighting each other this way! Has everyone gone mad?" His voice trembled, dissolving into tears. He retreated to the bed and sat down, his head in his hands. I felt as if I were the central figure in an elaborate farce.

"I am in no league with Lilith," I hissed. I glanced toward Rouen. "Whatever you may think."

Dante stared at me with eyes full of hatred. "You stupid little bugger," he said. "You think everything has something profound to do with you." He laughed bitterly, went to Rouen and crouched beside him. I heard them whispering, saw Rouen nodding once or twice. I was terribly afraid, for I knew that if they disappeared and left me, I might not survive for very long.

Dante and Rouen knew the demands of our preternatural existence; they could anticipate the difficulties, turn troubles aside as soon as they arose. They knew where to hunt and which victims they might take; Dante could even call them to him, draw them unresisting into his embrace. He and Rouen had been transformed by the blood, they had become new.

I was still Valentin, the Pardoner. I was still naive and really rather stupid, a stone's throw from illiterate. I didn't know how to find a willing mortal, and took my victims in violence. I forgot to hide the bodies. I killed clumsily, and made a mess of myself. I drank too long and deeply, and fell into a stupor. And in the final figuring, what was I to them? *Some dithering boy whore that you buggered at Tralini's for a florin, now and then.*

I had heard Dante say that. I remembered the contempt in his voice, his hands, as he washed me and put me to bed.

And what else was there for me, now that I was changed and could no longer expose my unnatural flesh to daylight?

I thought about Messer Lorenzo, wondered if I could make some bargain with him. I thought about the Church, wondered if perhaps I went back to England, could I still sell pardon and thus serve the God I once professed?

I realized, then, that there was nowhere for me to go.

Weighted by this unhappy thought, I went to the casement, leaned my forearms on the broken sill and peered out. I could see the scaffold in the piazza, its evil skeleton erected as a reminder to anyone foolish enough to appear impious, in these dark days. I watched the false dawn draw light around it, the rich darkness of the sky behind it gradually fading into gray. I loved the dawn, even though I knew that it could kill me.

There was a sudden clatter on the stairs; Dante started up, glanced around in panic. Some portent of disaster.... His face changed, his haughty expression melting slowly into disbelief. *"Jesu Cristo... Serenola!"*

The stairwell....

They flooded up the stairs, a multitude of Serenola's mad disciples, a sea of enraged faces, pitch-coated torches held high above their heads.

They will destroy us.

Dante gaped at them, open-mouthed, while Rouen tugged at him. "The trapdoor... the trapdoor!"

I helped him push the bed toward the advancing minions as we both hefted the heavy door, slapped it open. A great cloud of foul dust arose, pungent with the stench of filth. "We have no choice," Rouen shouted, "we must go down!"

I started down the ladder, careful in my haste to place my clubbed foot in the center of each stair. Above me, I could hear the panting scuffle of the crowd, as they poured into our rooms, shouting and screaming. I glanced above the hatch once more, took one last look around the room. *Jesu Maria....*

"Dante!" I roared at him with all my might, just as Serenola leapt on him and plunged a torch into his hair; his chestnut locks took light, burning....

"My God!" Rouen grabbed Dante and shoved him down the hole; he tumbled into me and knocked me off the stairs. We landed squarely, flat against the earthen floor. I wrapped his cloak around his head, smothering the flames, but he was screaming and I knew that he was badly burned.

"The sun, the sun, oh God, Rouen, the sun...." The door slammed shut, muffling the sounds from up above.

"Shh—" Rouen cast a glance at me, his mouth a thin white line. "—not the sun, Dante."

"The sun, burning me, burning, burning me...." He was delirious, clawing at the cloak that covered him, screaming in agony.

It was horrible.

"Shhh." Rouen wrapped the cloak around him, turned to me. "Now we have to dig, Valentin. Else they will be down and find us! The sun is rising and soon we'll sleep." He was forcing himself to be calm, and this calmed me. I would listen and agree with him, whatever it was that he would have me do.

I stared at him. "I don't understand...." I felt riven, emptied.

"Dig!" He shoveled at the soft earth, using his hands for scoops, moving at an incredible rate. I watched as he excavated a hole large enough for both Dante and himself, sank into it, and disappeared from view. The earth assembled itself over him as if it had never been disturbed.

I was horrified. I could not allow myself to sink into the earth, be subsumed underneath a mountain of stinking soil, in which crawled all manner of filth and insects. The thought of it repulsed me.

But Serenola and his acolytes still thundered, up above.

I found a great iron tub with a lid that fit like the lid of a pot, and it was within this that I secreted myself, pulled the lid against the teeming crowd. I heard the trapdoor open, once, smelled the unmistakable scent of mortal blood. But they did not descend the ladder. God had seen fit to spare us, after all.

I waited, fighting sleep, until I could hear them no more above me. I crouched in silence in that fusty tub, fingering my sheaf of pardons and remembering when life was simpler and I was Valentin the Pardoner, riding the darkness between London and Canterbury. Life had been a simple process then, a daily round of eating, sleeping, working, a cup of water in the morning to fill my aching belly until I could earn my bread.

I realized what I must do.

I lifted the lid and came out of the tub, rummaged in the dark underground until I found a bundle of old rags with which to cover myself. These I wound carefully around my face and head, and around my hands. The rest of me was covered by my clothes.

I would go back to the one place where I knew I always belonged, the fate that I knew was mine from the beginning. Surely, I was fit for little else. And it was something that I well knew how to do, and to which I would give myself until I died, if ever I would be granted the release of death.

The rising sun led the way and I followed it, through the winding streets of Florence, until the lodgings and my immortal companions were but a distant memory.

Chapter 12

LUDOVICO SERENOLA

I HAD ceased to rely on Gioletti. His sin had become too great for me to bear, and I had my own acolytes now. Just this very morning, we had led an attack upon the stronghold of the unnaturals. I knew it was scant time before we were rewarded for our timely and sacred endeavor.

I had made Vittore my respected companion and my confidante, but I realized that none other of our new-made order recognized the sacred mission as I did. Sadly, we had lost Italo to the plague, as heralded merely weeks before by the notorious appearance of the rash upon his arm. I accepted it as God's will. He takes whom He must, and it is not for us to say Him otherwise.

But nonetheless, our numbers had swelled with the devotion of the faithful, and I made it my business to seek out unnaturals and vanquish them, wherever they might be. I made it my business, also, to stand in the Piazza del Duomo at just the hour of vespers, and instead of praying (as was previously my custom) I would preach to all who happened by. At these times, I felt the anointing of the Holy Ghost, the Spirit of the Lord descend on me. I knew that I, above all others of our order, had been chosen by the Savior to spread His message. And as always, I was alert and wary for the presence of unnaturals.

This particular nest had existed for some time in a crumbling neighborhood close to the Duomo. Cardinal Gioletti had informed me (before our untimely rift) that a former protégé of his (an illiterate

English pardoner) was now living there, in sin and open sodomy with two others. Gioletti informed me also that the primary companion of this pardoner was none other than Rouen di Francisci—lately of the house of Francisci of Prato.

This last aroused my interest, for Francisci was a nobleman, and such types are prone more than the simple folk to sin. I decided to make a day's journey to Prato to investigate the doings of this Rouen, find out who his people were. Perhaps there was sufficient evidence to mount a purge in Prato.

Prato is but a short distance from Florence, a pleasant day's ride at half-gallop, and so I packed my saddlebags with bread and wine, and set off, with Vittore as my company. The morning dawned clear and bright, with a fresh breeze, and the quiet splendor of the countryside was a welcome respite after the squalor of the city. I rode for some time in silence, reciting matins to myself as the sun climbed and the sky turned that unclouded blue that heralds good weather. It was a glorious morning, and I was doing God's work. Truly, I had attained my proper place within the universe.

"Do you think he is one of these unnaturals, my lord?" Vittore's voice shook in time with the cadence of the horse; he rode badly, as befit a barefoot monk.

I turned, jolted from my contemplations. "He is, Vittore." I folded back the hood of my cassock, breathed the clean air deep into my lungs. "He lives in open sodomy with two other men, in rough lodgings behind the Duomo." I had no doubt as to the types of sin they perpetrated there; my mind was filled with a plethora of debauched images, courtesy of Cardinal Gioletti.

"But my lord, you and I live in company with other men." Vittore pointed this out with his usual maddening simplicity. "And we do not engage in sodomy. Cardinal Gioletti lives also with other men—"

"Vittore!" I had already begun to regret bringing him. "I pray you, desist of this." Gioletti was the least of my concerns. He could rot in his rich *palazzo* with his herd of lissome boys. "It is my sacred duty—*our* sacred duty—to discover and apprehend these unnaturals, wherever they may be, Vittore. Such miscreants as these are the whole nature and cause of pestilence, and like the Jews, spread filth and noisome squalor, poison wells, and corrupt the children of our citizens!" I forced myself calm, but I was annoyed that he would dare to question me. "If we do not purge the nation of their filth, then we deliver our faithful into the hands of Satan!"

"I would think the greater sin is to accuse the innocent where there is no taint, my lord." Vittore's level gaze seemed a blatant denunciation. It left me with no reply to make, and so I turned my horse's head toward Prato and rode in silence. But throughout the journey, I noticed Vittore watching me with a dawning apprehension, eyes narrowed. I decided I could no longer trust him. I would wait till nightfall, and dispose of him on the journey back to Florence. I knew that I could not allow anything to interfere with my sacred duty.

WE ARRIVED in Prato just after the noon bell tolled, and made our way to the markets, where the most useful of information is often found. Vittore and I tethered our horses at an inn and continued to the marketplace on foot, passing through the dwellings of the town, the small mean shops. The arrangement of the entire town annoyed me, so obsequiously pastoral.

"Do you think there is evidence of plague here, my lord?" Vittore was much occupied in gazing about him. "For all this village seems such a peaceful hamlet." His words, I was certain, concealed his nascent cynicism, an irritating suspicion that flicked me on the raw.

"The presence of evil is so often masked in good, Vittore!" I snapped. "If you were to attend more closely to the writings of the Church fathers, I am certain you might discern it for yourself." I turned a corner past a shop, stumbled over a young peasant woman with three filthy children. Vittore, of course, paused to give them blessing, for which they were obscenely grateful, bobbing and bowing. They were little more than grubby animals, crawling with lice and covered in sores.

"Remember my instructions to you." I unwrapped the provisions and handed him a chunk of bread. "I am to ask the questions only. If we seem too eager, we will never uncover the devil's nest in this place." I would have gagged him with a cloth if I thought it would successfully stop Vittore's mouth.

I discovered a smithy near the market, stepped inside to ask uninterestedly about the Villa di Francisci. I hoped that, by appearing profoundly casual about the subject of my inquiry, I might learn more. The smithy was a horrible, clanging place, full of smoke and fire and hellish noise. "What, old Jacopo's place?" The smith stretched his back, rested a moment from his labors. He scratched his chest thoughtfully, chewed on some anonymous object in his mouth. "What d'you want to know?" He was a fat, garrulous, old man with an enormous chest and a bull neck. His face was red and leathery, deeply seamed as a result of exposure to all weathers. "Nobody asks much about *them*."

I offered a hasty explanation of ecclesiastical census, prayed underneath my breath. "We are numbering the faithful, in the face of this new pestilence, that none be denied a Christian burial." Vittore watched me keenly, his mouth set in a straight white line. Yes, I would have to dispose of him on the return journey, or else I risked his exposing me to those wayward unbelievers of the Church in Florence— namely, Gioletti's minions who saw no cogent threat in this new plague.

"Jacopo di Francisci?" A younger man had joined us, possibly the smith's son, and leaned against the doorsill chewing on a blade of grass. His face was the same ruddy hue as that of the older man, and his forearms were like oak saplings. I was certain he could bend a bar of iron in his teeth. "Married his own sister." He passed the older man a look and the two guffawed, much hidden meaning incipient in their laughter.

"What do you mean?" I glanced from one to the other while Vittore shifted uneasily behind me. "Such a union could not possibly be countenanced by the Church!" A keen thrill of shock ran up my spine, shivered in the roots of my hair. Had I indeed discovered the very nest of vipers in this place? Perhaps it was from Prato that the plague initially erupted!

"T'wasn't." The mason reached into the fire with his tongs, laid a chunk of red-hot iron on the anvil and began hammering lustily. "Jacopo and his sister went away to some relative of theirs in Siena. When they came back, they were wed and she was with child." He plunged the metal into a bucket of water, shouted above the hissing steam, "Of course it's no secret about these parts, but not much is." He nodded toward the younger man. "Enrico, my son, used to play with Rouen when he was a child. And their other son, the idiot. Paolo." He tossed the finished horseshoe upon the pile.

"There is an idiot son?" Certain evidence of sin! "Where is he now?" I had to see the monster for myself.

"He still lives there." The smith jerked his head in the general direction of the hill. "Not good for much, though." He peered at me with that curious candor of the common folk. "You here to baptize him or something?"

I was quivering so violently that I could scarcely speak. "The child has not received the rites?"

"Huh." The mason scratched his head. "Don't rightly know." And the expression on his humble visage declared he wouldn't tell me anything more. But he had told me enough already, and I smiled, blessed him silently. This honest smith with his broad leathery face, and his humble peasant's manner, had given me everything I needed. Such is the utility of the common folk.

VILLA DI FRANCISCI was a tall, imposing fortress, set at the top of a hill, walled about with stone. A set of ornate inlaid gates provided entry, and it was to these gates that Vittore and I appealed.

"Ho, the house!" My horse whickered in the silence, shying from the gates. "We are emissaries of the Church!"

Nothing. I darted a glance at Vittore. "I am certain there is life within these walls." The cypress trees waved gently in the breeze, but there was no other sign of movement. I approached the gates, called again. After a little time a man appeared at the casement, and then the gates swung open. I will admit to some small sense of triumph as I rode through that day. I knew that my endeavor was surely blessed by God, since He made certain that I garnered access where needed. I was confident that before long, we would have eliminated those unnaturals that so contributed to the spread of deadly pestilence. And this holy land would once again belong to God.

"MY LORD, we bid you welcome." A woman's voice, elegant and cultured, an accent that owed much to the graceful Siennese.

I turned from my contemplation of the luxuriant tapestries that adorned the spacious salon to see a slender woman, hair as black as a raven's wing, green eyes set like emeralds within the pale perfection of her face. My heart fluttered within my breast, for one glorious moment, I thought I was in the presence of the Virgin.

But there, tied to her wrist, a monster. A lumbering giant, overlong of limb and wholly insensible, a ghastly miscreation. "*Madonna.*" I bowed deeply, blessed her fortitude in the presence of such ugliness. "I am Fra Ludovico Serenola, and this is Vittore."

The monster shivered, grunted. His gaze ghosted around me, slid off into nothing.

"Forgive me, Fra Ludovico, but—" She smiled brightly, and the monster at her wrist wavered, his pale eyes fixed upon us both, "—I am blind."

I was stabbed to the heart, and for a moment my resolve wavered, doubt flickering deep within my brain. I ought not to have come here; I ought to have left well enough alone—

"But Paolo guides me very well. Indeed, I am blessed to have him." She waved toward the monster at her wrist, and he nodded at us, a great, simpering behemoth whose mouth hung open, drooling. "You will forgive Paolo, he cannot speak."

I cast a look at Vittore, who had turned a pasty shade of pale. "Of course, Madonna. I pray you, where is your husband?"

"Jacopo is away on business, visiting with family in Siena. But will you take refreshment with us?" She sketched a graceful curtsey, her brilliant eyes sweeping the blankness before her. "Paolo will summon the boy." And she loosed him from about her wrist, allowed him to pull a bell-cord. A servant appeared with a tray of wine and sweetmeats, vanished into the vast recesses of the house. I sat with her and ate, but each bite stuck in my throat. I could not swallow any of the wine. Throughout this interlude, the monster knelt beside his mother's chair and gaped at us, his watery eyes rolling uncontrolled inside their sockets. The sight of him was making me ill. I wished she would send him away.

"Madonna, we must needs soon depart." I could stand it no longer, the lovely blind woman, the lumbering idiot tied to her wrist. My head throbbed abominably; I felt as if I were trapped in some egregious nightmare. My eyes were stinging. I could not find my spectacles. I signaled to Vittore that he should finish his cake and come along.

"Will you bless us before you go, Fra Ludovico?" She fumbled for the purse at her waist. "I will make you a donation." She opened her hand, and a gold florin glistened on her palm.

"Madonna, I cannot accept it." My throat ached, words forced past its constriction. I closed her fingers about the coin, gazed deep into her sightless eyes. "We are a simple order, and I have taken vows of poverty. Your hospitality is enough." I turned to make my hasty exit. I had erred badly. I would leave now and never return. I would refuse all thought of this place. I would erase her name, her lovely face, from my mind forever.

"How goes the pestilence in Florence?" Her voice rang, clear and bell-like. "My son is living there and my thoughts turn often to him."

She was weeping, her lovely pale face working. She was weeping without making a sound, and she was beautiful, like the Blessed Virgin. Something stirred within me, some vestige of carnal feeling I thought I had long since banished. I remembered when I was a young man and lay with maidens, and I had a vivid, sudden desire to lie with her, to slip between her thighs. The image slapped against the inside of my mind, *yes*....

All that long, raven-dark hair, that flower-petal mouth. Her breasts would be like silk to touch, as white as milk. I wondered if she had given this great monster suck.

"Come along," I told Vittore harshly. I could not linger here, looking at her lovely face and her pretty blinded eyes, allowing carnal lust to surface in my soul. I turned away.

"A blessing, Fra Ludovico?" Her voice caught me as I tried to leave. The idiot started up, lunging at his tether. I wondered if what the surgeons of the college said was true, that idiots sensed danger in a manner quite like beasts. I wondered if he could smell my lust, throbbing underneath my skin like pain. I wondered, in an agony of perversity, what he might do if I were to take his mother here in front of him.

"I bless you in the name of God," I choked, muttering. I waved my hand before her face, turned on my heel and left them. The smell of their family sickened me; I wished to put Villa di Francisci behind me and never have to look at it again.

"YOU did not truly bless her." Vittore pulled his horse's head level with mine. "She asked you for a blessing and you did not give it."

"Desist of this!" I hissed at him. It had begun to rain, great drops of cold and driving moisture. My cassock was soaked through to my skin, and my feet had turned to lumps of ice inside my sandals. "You will not question me." I thought about Madonna Francisci, her lovely face, her emerald eyes. My lust quivered in my belly, and my brain was filled with unthinkable notions. For the first time in years, I considered whether I might seek release. Perhaps Gioletti was correct. Perhaps what I needed most was to "spend an evening fucking".

I realized that I was horribly confused.

"I *will* question you! I will question you because I think you did wrong in Prato this day, Ludovico!" Vittore was as angry as I had ever seen him, his pale amber eyes flickering.

I was silent, sunk in my own thoughts, unable to move or frame an answer. I realized that Vittore had become a very real danger, now that he was no longer allied to our mission, our sacred point of view. I wondered what I was to do about him. It seemed that the answers I had once summoned readily now evaded me. I could think of nothing but Madonna di Francisci, the idiot giant tethered to her wrist with a braided cord.

"And you will not answer me, will you Ludovico?" Vittore bent to gaze into my face, waiting for my reply, but I ignored him.

IT WAS dark before the solution sprung fully formed into my brain, and only because I stopped my horse upon the brink of a chasm. She had been trotting at half-gallop for some time, carrying me where she would, trusting that I would give her head to find her own way. And now her hooves slipped and slid in mud, and I started up in time to pull the reins. She had stopped a mere hand's-breadth from the edge of a gaping ravine. I could see nothing below me but jagged rocks, could hear nothing but a great sucking pull, like rushing water.

"Fra Ludovico, what is it?" Vittore's voice behind me, pierced through the freezing rain. I slid off my horse's back and walked quickly toward the lip of the chasm, bent double at the waist as if I were in distress. I had decided what to do about Vittore.

God give me strength to do this vile thing! I recognized that, in some other context, it could be seen as the most heinous sin imaginable....

But Vittore was a problem. And he threatened my most sacred

mission, the missive given me by God.

I waited till I felt his hand upon my shoulder, and then I caught his arm and hurled him with all my strength into the chasm. I loosed his mount and drove her back toward Prato.

And then I mounted my horse and rode toward Florence, and I did not look back.

Chapter 13

DANTE

I WAS on fire, burning from the inside, smothering in thick smoke that filled my eyes and ears, and nose that clotted in my throat like blood. "Rouen!"

I felt myself rising up through layers of earth, pulled by some outside force, until I lay gasping on the musty floor. I remembered that we were underneath the house, that we had been forced to flee Serenola's hordes. "I'm burning, Rouen."

"Shh, *tesoro*, you're safe." His arms came around me, held me tightly to him. I felt the reassuring thud of his heart, knew that I was indeed safe. At the very least, we had escaped Serenola, and that was something. "We've been in the earth all day."

"Serenola...." I touched my fingers to my face, felt the raised edges of my wounds, the melted tissue that had scabbed into scars. "What happened to my face?"

"You were burned, Dante. Do you remember Serenola with the torch?"

I didn't—that is, I didn't remember the torch specifically. I merely remembered the sudden searing pain as my hair caught fire, as flames burned my face and neck. "I can't see out of my other eye."

Rouen touched my lid gently, pulled it back so he could see the eyeball. "It's been burned as well." He sat back on his heels. "Do you think this will heal itself?"

I didn't know. There was so little I knew about the properties of our special blood, this legacy of Lilith's. When she had made me, she had told me nothing, and so everything since then that pertained in any way to our preternatural existence, I'd had to discover for myself. "Only time will tell, I suppose. I can't say for certain." The blinded eye throbbed painfully, a throbbing matched by the pain in my face. "How bad is it?" I asked Rouen.

He grimaced, turned to hide it from me. "I expect it feels rather worse than it looks."

I knew at once that he was lying. "Rouen…," I sighed. "I am not a child. Tell me."

"Dante, you're bald."

"Oh." Well, that was most unsavory. "Completely?"

"No." He shook his head. "Merely on one side—the side where the torch was thrust in. And your face is badly charred on that same side." His fingers traced the damage, gently. "Even if it does heal, I don't see how there cannot be a scar."

"Let's go up." I pulled myself to my feet. I knew there was a mirror in our rooms. "I want to see it for myself."

"I'm not sure that's wise." Rouen frowned. "Besides, are you certain you're strong enough to climb the ladder?"

I grabbed the rungs and hauled myself up. "Well, we'll soon find out, won't we?" I grunted, pushed open the trapdoor with one hand. "At any rate, if I fall off this ladder, I still have you to fall upon, now that Valentin…."

Rouen's face froze, as static as an image in a fresco. He turned, called softly, "Valentin?"

The basement chamber gave back nothing but an echo.

"Perhaps he rose first, and has gone out to hunt," I said. I saw an expression cross Rouen's face, flash quickly into nothingness. "What is it?"

He shook his head. "Nothing. You must go up."

I levered myself through the trapdoor's square hole and into our rooms, resting for a moment on the floor. My head swam dizzily, and I had difficulty catching my breath. I knew I needed blood, and badly.

"Dante?" Rouen's face peered at me through the hole. "Are you all right?" He pulled himself up into the room, took a slow look around him. "*Jesu Cristo!*"

Our apartments had been sacked, and someone had tried to burn the furniture. Our bed had been ripped apart, the sheets torn, the pillows scattered. The feather mattress had been disemboweled, and great white mounds of goose down lay about the floor like snow. The brocade coverlet—belonging to Rouen's mother—had been shredded into strips.

I pulled myself to my feet and looked about me, disbelieving. There were burn marks on the walls, along the floor, even on the ceiling. The chests containing our clothing had been smashed, our garments tossed away, probably out the window.

I gazed at Rouen, standing silent in the middle of the room. "Valentin?" I asked.

He shook his head sharply, once. *No.* "I suppose—" It caught in his throat. He swallowed rapidly, tried again. "This is a warning from the followers of Serenola." The rims of his green eyes filled up with bloody tears, and I knew that he was remembering the atrocities against his parents.

"Rouen…." I put my arms around him, gathered him to me. "*Mi amore.*" I was rigid with hatred.

"Ah, Dante." He laughed softly, freed himself from my embrace. "Always the strong one." He dashed his tears away with his fingertips, took a deep breath, as if drawing strength. "Well then."

"Rouen, where is Valentin?" I sensed no trace of him anywhere around here; if he was in the immediate vicinity, I would know; I would feel his presence, the proximity of his mind to ours.

"I don't know." He moved across the room, turned, knelt in front of the fireplace. "Dante."

"What is it?" I peered at him, trying to make out the object he was holding in his hand; it was damnably difficult, considering I only had the one good eye, but it looked like some kind of jar, a thin porcelain cylinder with a silver top.

"His relics." Rouen unscrewed the top, tipped the contents into his hand. "Bones." He smiled. "Animal, judging by the look of them." He dropped them back into the jar, bent to peer into the ashes. "Oh, *no*." An abrupt ejaculation that slid off into silence.

"Rouen?" I went to him, knelt beside him, resisted the urge to scratch the burned skin of my face. It itched abominably!

"There are his indulgences." He handed them to me: charred scraps of paper, curled about the edges, some with only the Church's seal intact, the rest indistinguishable from the other rubbish burnt up in the grate.

"I don't understand." I took the crumpled scraps, rubbed them between my fingers. Immediately, they fell into ashes and were gone. "Why did he do this?"

Rouen shook his head. "I don't know."

I rose stiffly to my feet, passed before the mirror hanging on the wall, stopped abruptly, and steeled myself to take a look.

Rouen had not been lying when he said that I was bald, for I was indeed as bald as an egg on the same side that I had been burned: my naked scalp was visible, blistered and burned black in places, some of the skin already sloughing off. The remaining of my hair rose like a cock's comb from the middle of my skull, fell away in feathers against my face, the way I had always styled it. But it was singed about the edges, white and curling, and when I touched it with my fingers, it too fell into ashes—like Valentin's burnt pardons—leaving me with hair as shaggy and uneven as if it had been gnawed by a goat.

My face was still another matter altogether, for Serenola's torch had done its damage there as well: the flesh above and below my distorted eyeball was badly puckered, drawn tight like the strings of a purse. My eyebrows were gone. The blinded eye was seared white, the iris showing milky underneath the damaged lid, and my eyelashes had burnt, as well. The flesh of my cheek and nose had bubbled, collapsed into waxy ridges that rose from the smooth surface of my face like mountains. A wide red band of burnt skin extended from the corner of my mouth and down against my neck.

Taken for all in all, I supposed it wasn't that bad.

"Rouen, look at this!" I gestured at him. "I'm a monster!"

"Dante, come away from there—" He pulled me back from the mirror. "—there's no need to scrutinize yourself like this."

I pulled away from him, stalked to the casement, and stood there for a long time, breathing heavily, willing the tears away. I would not give in to this, I would not let Serenola and his minions destroy me, when *I* was the only thing that I could count on—

"*Mi cuore....*" He embraced me gently from behind, pressed his lips against my neck. "I love you."

My chest caved in. I turned and buried my face in his chest and sobbed like a child, overwhelmed with hopelessness, terrified of what I didn't understand. "Rouen, I'm ugly—"

"You will never be ugly to me." His lips soothed the hurt, pressing gently against my burned and tormented flesh; his arms held me and would not let me go. "Please don't cry... you will only make yourself upset." He lifted my chin and gazed at me with quiet understanding.

"Help me." I felt suddenly cold all over, sickened. "Rouen, I need blood...."

He nodded. "I think perhaps that would be the best thing for you, yes."

I watched as he tore his wrist with his teeth and offered it to me, pressed his skin against my lips and let me drink. "My wounds," I whispered, "rub it on the wounds."

He smeared his blood against my cheek, the burned skin of my neck, the bald portion of my head. "Your beautiful hair," he said, "pray God it will grow back."

I drank until I sensed that he could give no more. "Enough." I pushed his wrist away, afraid to take so much that I would weaken him. "Thank you, Rouen." I kissed his palm, pressed my lips against each of his graceful fingers. I knew I still needed more, but I could not—would not—take it from him.

I removed the burned sheets and lay down on the vandalized bed, feeling the blood course through me, the light and heat of him. The burns on my face and neck tingled ferociously; my scalp pulsed as his blood nourished it. "Rouen…." I called to him.

"It's not enough, is it?" He leaned over me, a graceful shadow. I saw that he had lit a candle, its light throwing the image of his form against the walls and ceiling.

"No." I wept, tears leaking from my eyes and soaking into the savaged mattress. "I'm sorry." It was because of Serenola, all of it, and I knew that we were no longer safe here. "We have to leave, Rouen— he will be back to see if his minions have destroyed us!"

"I'll go and get the blood for you." He rose, laid the candle on the bedside table.

"No! It's too dangerous…." I was terrified that he would leave and never return to me, and I could not bear to lose him.

"I will be exquisitely careful," he promised. He bent to kiss me, his long hair brushing my cheek. "I will be as quick as I can," he whispered.

I watched him disappear down the stairwell, his cloak about his shoulders.

HE WAS as good as his word, for he returned with a companion, a slender boy with curly auburn hair and large brown eyes. *Very nice…* "Rouen?"

"Dante…." He hastened to me, helped me to sit up. The infusion of his blood had healed me somewhat, but the flesh of my cheek and my blinded eye had not responded to his treatment. "This is Giovanni. I met him in the arcade."

Ah. The very same arcade, no doubt, where he had met me on Christmas past. How appropriately circular, I thought. "Messer Giovanni," I inclined my head. "Welcome to our home."

He cast a wild look about him, eyes wide and strained. I saw his gaze linger on the shredded bedclothes, the burn marks, the smashed chests, and ruined paintings. "What place is this?"

"You forget your manners, Ser." Rouen nudged him from behind. "Pray, greet Messer Dante properly."

He laughed shortly, a guttural braying, not unlike an ass. I disliked him, then and there. He perused my damaged face with an air of one inspecting a particularly odiferous tub of shit. "He is a *monster!*"

A chill ran through me, and I was ashamed. "How much do you charge, boy?" I fumbled for my purse, sifted through it, clinking coins between my fingers. "I would prefer that we negotiate price as a matter of priority."

He stared at me, horrified, turned angrily to Rouen. "You told me you would entertain me! You said nothing about being expected to service a monster!"

My eyes narrowed. *Filthy little baggage.* "I assure you, Ser, my cock is the same as yours. No scales, feathers, or fins."

Rouen smothered a grin. "Shall we begin?"

I rose from the bed, a single smooth movement. Already my old grace was coming back; the infusion of Rouen's blood had helped enormously. "A florin?" I asked. "Is that sufficient to your purpose?" I caressed his cheek with my fingers. "You are a handsome, young bravo, now aren't you?" My hand crept around the back of his neck as I pressed the coin into his palm.

I took a deep breath, and everything slowed. Anticipation crept along my skin: already I could taste him, the seductive bouquet of a mouthful of fresh blood.

My hand tightened on his neck with a grip like iron. There was no hope of escape for him now. "Allow me this pleasure...." A slow heaviness throbbed, deep in my belly, as my fangs descended. *Oh yes, now the dance begins....*

I cradled his head between my palms and brought him to my mouth, kicking helplessly, all his senses engaged in his hopeless struggle. My mouth watered at the smell of him—the tangy aroma of sweat that clung to his shirt and cloak, the dusty fragrance of his skin, the delicious stink of him.

Love me, yes you do....

The vein burst underneath my teeth, popping like the skin of an overripe grape. His blood spurted, washing against the back of my throat, sliding down to warm the inside of my belly, and I groaned. Pleasure pounded in my temples, streaked across my closed eyelids: *Oh so good, so good....*

Far more than nourishment, the kill is a seductive dance, like sex; a delicate negotiation that must be conducted properly, with all due attention to the unwritten formalities that so govern our existence. Above all else, it is an act of beauty, the perfection of predation. *This is my body, this is my blood.*

I felt the death come down, and I disengaged, dropping him abruptly on the floor. I felt suddenly uneasy, as if every nerve were being stretched. I backed away from his inanimate remains, flicked a gesture at it. "Rouen, get rid of it...." A great excitement went scampering along my limbs. I could hardly bear to stand still.

The blood soaked into my broken body as rain into a parched landscape. It seeped into my skin, it pooled behind my eyes, was drawn into the marrow of my bones.

I was racked with excruciating sensation, pain and pleasure bursting in my brain. I clamped my hands to the sides of my head and spun in circles, trying to dilute the sensitivity as my body screamed for release.

The rhythm of my heart increased, a pounding furor in my chest, hammering against my ribs as if it would burst out of my body. My vision expanded and contracted, sight returning to my damaged eye with an unexpected *pop!* as the skin of my face sealed over, healing itself. A great flush of heat shivered up, tingled in my scalp, and a mane of chestnut hair fell about my shoulders. "Rouen! *Dio*, what's happening?"

I stepped backward, slammed into the wall, palms flat against the surface. My garments were suddenly too tight, constricting me, I felt as if I were choking. "Get it *off*, Rouen...." I tore at the closure of my shirt, raked my nails over the skin of my arms. A profusion of sensation shimmered across my flesh as a bubble of pleasure burst deep within my brain.

"Rouen...." I reached out for him with both hands; more than anything, I wanted him to touch me. "Make it stop."

"Dante, what is it?" He hovered close to me, concerned. "Are you in pain?" His fingers pressed against my face.

"*No*...." I grabbed his hand, took his fingers into my mouth and sucked on them. His skin was tangy, delicious. I nibbled on the pulsing tip of his index finger, felt the minute throb of blood flowing through the digit, tickling the underside of my tongue. "Rouen, *touch me!*"

He pressed himself against me, slid full-length down my body to his knees, laid his cheek against my belly, his breath seeping through my hose. He was hot, he was pulsing, I wanted to crawl inside of him. I felt his fingers fumbling with my laces, sliding my hose down around my knees.

"Please." My fingers trembled in his hair. In a moment I would shake myself to pieces.

Carefully, deliberately, he opened his mouth and closed its warmth around me. I was immersed in him, I could read his thoughts with greater clarity than I ever could before, I knew Rouen more intimately than I ever had. And I was *with* him, inside his skull, I was experiencing our lovemaking from each separate perspective, I knew precisely what he was thinking in the instant that his mouth began to pleasure me. *Dante, I love you....*

I trembled against him, the wall cold against my naked back, as his lips moved on me, his arms around my waist. My senses had stopped their screaming with his touch; my body's rhythms settling into their normal cadence. I moved with him in silence, felt *with him* the pleasure that he was giving me, until at last my climax trembled in my belly, and I surrendered to it.

His hands on my face, his mouth pressed against mine. "Rouen...." Precious thing, my immortal beloved. Stay with me, never leave, stay with me forever....

And cradled in his arms and held next to his desperately beating heart, safe within the nimbus of his power, and loved.

And loved.

"WE HAVE to search for Valentin."

I turned sleepily, my head against Rouen's shoulder, our bodies pressed together in the bed. "Of course." I raised myself on one elbow. "Rouen, tell me truly, am I restored completely?"

He smiled. "Yes. Completely."

"Truly? There are no scars?" I wasn't entirely convinced that my face had healed, that my hair had grown back, as thick and lustrous as before.

"Dante, you are beautiful." His hand caressed my cheek. "And I love you."

I smiled.

"Dante." A shadow crossed his face; his beautiful green eyes were thoughtful.

"What is it?" I turned his face to mine and kissed him. "Rouen?"

He gazed at me, and I guessed that there was some interior debate going on. "Why is it that you never profess to me, as I do to you?"

I was jolted, to be sure. And not quite certain how to answer him. "You misunderstand, Rouen," I replied, forcing a note of levity into my voice. I tossed aside the covers. "I think perhaps we should seek

Valentin before the dawn."

"Dante!" He caught my wrist. "I require an answer."

"Rouen, there is no need for such a scene, if you would just—"

"Do you love me?" Eyes filled suddenly with fear so intense it shamed me. I bit down hard against my lip, pressed my fingers to my mouth. It was no use. The first sob escaped me, a choked hiccup, as I curled around myself, my shoulders shaking. God *damn* my traitorous emotions! And now I would make a fool of myself in front of Rouen....

"*Mi amante*, what is it?"

I told him again about Salvatore, but this time I revealed how his love for me became, finally, his religion. I told Rouen how Salvatore smothered me until I railed against his benevolence. I told him how I had killed my master, if only to ease his final suffering. I told all this to Rouen, sobbing bitterly, until finally I had cried myself empty.

He was silent for a long time, his fingers stroking my back in the same pattern, over and over. Finally, he stirred himself and looked at me. "I am... deeply ashamed," he said. I made to speak, but he pressed a finger against my lips. "No. Dante, I tried to wring a profession out of you because I felt that it would come as easily to you as it does to me. I decided that you could pronounce your love as I do mine, yet you cannot. And in my blindness and my ego, I force you, again and again, to do the thing of which you are most incapable." He smiled crookedly. "I apologize."

I was speechless. But he turned from me, hopped out of bed and began pulling on his clothes with rather unseemly haste. "Come. We must seek Valentin."

ROUEN led the way through the narrow streets and dubious back-alleys of Florence, while I merely followed in silence. I had no idea where Valentin might have gone, but Rouen clearly did, so I surrendered our investigation to him.

We eventually arrived at an unprepossessing tavern, set far back at the end of a narrow street, poorly lit and filthy. "What is this place?"

Rouen smiled. "Welcome to Tralini's whorehouse."

The scene inside the doors was one of complete cacophony: directly to our left, there were a clutch of musicians, all strumming and banging away on their various instruments, seemingly liberated from any notion of harmony or tune. They were all very young, all recently emerged from puberty, smooth faced and nubile. The hair of each was carefully combed and curled, their faces heavily painted, as if for a carnival. The effect was unusual, to say the least.

To the right was a huge round table, set about with benches, at which sat about a dozen or so young men, playing dice or cards. Several of the younger boys appeared to be in the advanced stages of drunkenness; I recognized the sweetish smell of *hasheesh*, it reminded me of Salvatore. The whole interior was crudely furnished and rather haphazardly decorated. The only visible ornament was the series of lewd paintings that adorned the far wall, each one a depiction of some unusual sexual act, many of which I knew to be anatomically impossible.

"Rouen!" A shriek from one of the furthest corners; I squinted my eyes and peered through the sickly smoke. "We thought you were never coming back to us!"

A figure came toward us, mincing with tiny steps; a tall slender woman with a strange voice posed and addressed us in the most familiar terms possible. Or at least, she addressed Rouen.

"Tell her not to put her tongue in *my* mouth," I instructed him *sotto voce*, as he unobtrusively wiped his mouth on his handkerchief.

"Dante, this is Fernando. Fernando has been with Messer Tralini for many years now."

This was a *man*? I peered at the heavy skirts, the long wavy hair, the jewels that winked on his fingers, at his ears. His face-paint was a masterpiece. I stared, for only a moment, and then I was dazzled and amazed. I took his hand, bowed deeply. "Messer." I smiled. "Your...

illusion is a masterpiece. I am greatly indebted to you for the privilege." I did not intend this as an insult, I absolutely meant it: the transformation that this man had effected was incredible.

His large, soft eyes opened wide in pleasure, and then he smiled. "Thank you." He swept a careless hand across the front of his gown. "Really, it is quite an easy feat. I am certain you could do it."

I felt Rouen nudging at my mind. *I never realized you preferred the female guise....*

I parried it with a retort of my own, *You chose me when you could have had them? For shame, Rouen!*

His laughter slid into my mind, warming me.

"Fernando, I wish to speak with Messer Lorenzo. Is he about this evening?"

"There—see, playing a game of cards." Fernando pointed to a table set against the far wall. "Rouen, you should visit more often!" He winked at me, behind Rouen's head. "There was a time when it was supposed you boarded here!" He swept a curtsey, was gone into the crowd.

Tralini was a largish man of vigorous middle years, with the high forehead of nobility and the ruddy cheeks of a peasant. He rose and shook our hands, bowed stiffly from the waist. "Rouen! Such a pleasure to see you again, and this young friend of yours." He indicated the benches to the side. "Sit, sit—Alison!"

A young woman appeared, in gown and apron, bearing a tray of wine and a selection of sweetmeats. "Anything you pleasure, Ser?" She leaned over me to pour the wine, and I saw that her plump young breasts were free inside her gown.

"*Dante.*" Rouen shook his head, once, turned to Tralini. "I'm looking for a friend, Lorenzo. He used to be one of your boys— Valentin—remember him?"

Tralini's smooth white brow furrowed. "Is he in trouble, Rouen? Has he offended you?"

"No… he's become rather a good friend to us, and we're worried. He left our lodgings this morning and we haven't seen him since. Dante and I wondered if he had come here."

But Valentin hadn't been there, Tralini assured us; no, he hadn't seen Valentin since that day he sold him into the care of Cardinal Gioletti.

"Thank you." Rouen rose to go, clearly disappointed. We had hoped that we'd find Valentin here, and I knew that Rouen's worry was now redoubled. He bowed gracefully, collected his hat. "I am certain we will find him elsewhere."

"Rouen." Something in Tralini's voice stopped us cold. "I was very sorry to hear about the tragedy that befell your family. May God support you in your sorrow." His face bore an expression of the utmost sympathy as he blessed himself slowly, deliberately.

Rouen stared at him, mouth open. The tiny hairs on the back of my neck prickled. "How did you learn of it?" he asked. His tone was dangerous, suspicion riding underneath the surface. "I did not allow it to be noised abroad." His spine straightened underneath his cloak, his fingers balling into fists. As if sensing danger, the boys at the table nearest ours scattered, scampering up the stairs like frightened rats. The musical cacophony near the door ceased, a lute string twanging as it broke.

"Well—" Tralini's yellow teeth clamped into his lower lip; his hands fumbled at his doublet. Beads of sweat stood out upon his forehead, glistened on his nose. "—if I see Valentin I will certainly give him your message." He spun about and disappeared.

"Rouen." I grabbed his arm and steered him toward the door. "What was that all about?"

We stepped into the murky darkness, breathed until our lungs had had their fill of fog. "There is no way that Tralini could have known about the murder of my parents," he said, "unless he was somehow privy to that information."

I stared at him, the street seeming to cave beneath my feet.

"Rouen, do you mean—"

"Dante, I mean that there is nowhere safe for us, not now. I have known Lorenzo Tralini ever since I was aware of my own unnatural desires. He has never lied to me." He stalked away from me, his shoulders stiff underneath his cloak. I had to run to catch up with him. "But Dante—" He clutched my arm, peered into my face, "—he has lied to me tonight."

"And if he knows this—"

"Then he knows *all*." Rouen's mouth was white about the lips. "Dante, I do not know who betrayed me to Serenola, but I know it was not Valentin."

How?

"Valentin I would trust as I trust my own soul, but I fear he has been played about like dice. This Cardinal of his, this Gioletti that we killed, this *vermin* who was in league with Serenola, first found Valentin whoring for Tralini. You can rest assured that he saw opportunity there—"

"And when Valentin ceased to do him service—"

"Yes!" Rouen began walking, slowly, feet slipping on the slimy cobbles. "Gioletti did some small nosing of his own. Or perhaps sent Ludovico Serenola."

I recalled Tralini's agitation, the beads of sweat that sat upon his brow, and I recognized the connection that Rouen had made, realized with sickening swiftness that he was right. "Rouen, you don't think that Valentin told Serenola of your parents, betrayed their illegal marriage?" It was inconceivable, since Valentin would have had no motive except malice, and of that, I knew he was incapable.

"No. Valentin did nothing wrong. But Gioletti...." His face hardened. "Dante, I am glad we killed him."

"But Rouen...." Gioletti might indeed be dead and now rotting spectacularly on a pike in the piazza, but Tralini was very much alive. "Tralini is the common link in all of this, Rouen. Gioletti found

Valentin and knew he'd make a splendid pardoner. Tralini let Valentin go, but he and Gioletti struck some sort of bargain. And when Serenola rose to power, Gioletti knew that here was his opportunity to advance his own position in the Church."

Rouen nodded. "Yes. Since the Church so completely supports Serenola's politics. Yes." He gnawed his lower lip thoughtfully. "So Gioletti surmised—and rightly so—that Tralini, being a man of his position, and thus privy to all sorts of damning information, would make the perfect conduit."

"Tralini takes his patrons' money, hires out his whores—"

"And collects a handsome stipend from Gioletti, for his prowess in listening at doors."

I felt sick. I leaned against a nearby facade and pressed my eyes shut, fought for breath. This was horrifying. Now that we had pieced it all together, the danger to us—to Rouen especially—was paramount.

"I have known Messer Tralini for many years, Dante." Rouen's eyes were huge, great haunted pools of fear. "I am certain it is he who told Gioletti about my parents."

"And Serenola's inquisition," I said, "Rouen, you know that he is hunting those of our kind." I did not mean the vampires, the creatures that people the night. I meant those like Rouen and I, who preferred the love of a strong young man to that of a pretty maid. I meant all those who lived somehow outside the usual circle of existence, who were governed not by the dictates of the Church, but rather by their own unique morality.

"Indeed." He turned away from me abruptly, fist pressed against his mouth. "Dante, we are in danger here."

"Yes." Serenola knew the address of our lodgings, and he had seen our faces. I recalled the vandalism that his minions had done to our apartments, and realized for the first time, their sickening symbolic gesture. "Rouen, they tore apart our bed...." Doubtless Serenola distinguished us, and those like us, as the cause and spread of plague; considered it his holy mandate to eliminate our kind. *I am come to bring about the end of the world....*

"Tralini has no protection now that Gioletti is dead." He puffed a breath, mind flickering so rapidly that I could not follow it. "And neither do we." We turned a corner, crossed the Ponte Vecchio in silence, our boot heels ringing out the long traverse against the bridge's wooden span.

"Rouen, Valentin was but a pawn in all of this."

And yet I had accused Valentin of betrayal.

"We must find him, Dante." His eyes filled up with crimson tears. "Upon my soul, we owe him recompense for what we have wrought! Valentin is innocent."

Gentle Pardoner. And how I betrayed you with a kiss....

"ROUEN." We had walked for some time in silence. I suppose we could have flown, but I preferred the mortal mode of travel when I needed time to think. "Do you suppose Valentin went back to England?"

We were passing in front of the Duomo, on our way to our lodgings but a little distance hence. "It is possible, but—Dante, is that someone... *singing?*"

I stopped, listening intently. Yes, it was indeed singing: high, pure and sweet, an angel's voice. *O Quam Mirabilis...* The devotions of St. Hildegarde. It was coming from the Piazza del Duomo. *What in God's name...?*

We came upon the scene: a remnant from a carnival farce, for there, in the middle of the piazza was Valentin, surrounded by a crowd of people, some of whom were throwing stones at him. The younger children had jostled to the front, yelling and spitting, while the adults crouched around him, whistling and shouting obscenities. It was well past dark, and there was still the hysterical fear of plague, but this spectacle had drawn them out into the darkness. They flocked to see him here in just the same way as they flocked to hear the mad rant of Serenola. Such rabble is inevitably drawn to a public profession of shame.

"Oh my God." Rouen stared, his face crumpled into lines of agony. "Dante, it's him...."

We fought our way through the crowd, were cursed and elbowed for our trouble. "Valentin!" I caught his arm, turned him around to face me. "We've been worried sick about you. *Mi cuore*, where have you been?" His psychic mantle, the cloak of energy that surrounds a vampire, was ragged and insubstantial. I wondered when he had last fed. "Valentin?"

His gaze roamed my face: vacant, senseless. His eyes held a holy glow, the madness of the mystic. "You must purchase pardon." He thrust a piece of paper at me, a page torn from a book, upon which a crude cross had been daubed. "Inscribed by Pope Clement. Genuine pardons." There was nothing else written on it, of course; Valentin was illiterate. He spat on the paper, swirled it about, and I saw that the cross had been marked in blood. His own, no doubt. "I have relics... come see." He thrust his hand into his purse, brought it out clutching a fistful of small stones. "These are the bones of St. John the Baptist."

I swayed, caught Rouen by both arms. "Rouen, he's *mad*!" Behind us, Valentin was addressing the crowd, exhorting them to purchase an indulgence. Two children ran forward, grabbed his hose, and tugged them down about his knees. The crowd howled with delight. "I can't stand this!" It was physically painful for me, having to watch him being humiliated this way. "I'm taking him home with us...."

"Valentin, come along." I pulled his hose up around his hips and tied his laces, straightened his purse about his belt. "It's time to come home now."

"I'm not going with you... heretic!" He recoiled, spat in my face.

He didn't recognize me. Or Rouen either, probably.

"Dante, come away." Rouen tugged at my sleeve. "*Please.*"

"No!" I shook him off. "Valentin, come along!" I wiped the spittle off my face. "Please come home." Behind me, the crowd roared, and there was something animal in it, some undifferentiated savagery. It horrified me to think what might happen to Valentin if we simply walked away and left him.

Dante, we have no claim upon his loyalties. Rouen was gazing at me intently, his expression remote and sad.

"Leave hold of me, Ser!" Valentin slammed his palms against my chest, slapped me backward. "I am in service to Monsignor Serenola, and I do God's work."

Rouen's lips were white, his face working furiously. He was struggling, I could feel it in him. "Dante...."

I caught Valentin's chin between my fingers, nearly lifting him off the ground. His pale blue eyes gazed emptily into mine, his eyelids flickering. "You sold out to him, *didn't you?*" I shook him like a doll. The crowd howled, obviously enjoying the performance. "*Didn't you?*" I considered whether I should kill him quickly, slip my thumbs underneath his jaw and snap his neck, as I had seen Rouen do. I wondered if I were strong enough.

"I serve Jesus Christ our Lord." Something flickered in his eyes, some thread of memory... *Valentin, come back to me!* "Loose hold of me, Ser." Struggling in my grip like a landed fish.

"What business do you here?" A roar from behind me; I turned and was face-to-face with the largest mortal I had ever seen, a hulking behemoth with hair and beard so black that it was blue.

I considered whether I dared kill him, here, with the crowd looking on.

"Dante, come away." Rouen pulled me backward, hissing in my ear, "*Il Scorpino—the Summoner!*"

Il Scorpino, known variously as the Summoner, or merely as the Sting. It was said that, if you were served summon by him, it were far better that you kill yourself than allow him to escort you. A vicious emissary of the powerful ecclesiastical courts, it was rumored that he now worked chiefly for Serenola.

As did Valentin.

It was over. Our preternatural kinship had thus ended.

I stumbled away into the crowd, blinded by tears, sensible only of Rouen's hand upon my arm. I sobbed, fumbling on the cobbles, tripped over the threshold and crawled up the stairs in darkness.

"Dante, stop this, you'll make yourself sick."

But I couldn't stop: I was compelled to go on sobbing, haunted by the image of him, standing defenseless in the piazza with his hose down around his knees. People laughing at him, throwing stones. That horrible, hulking Summoner, lingering over Valentin to see that he enacted his farcical duties.

"Serenola knew that Valentin was our good companion." Rouen came and sat beside me on the floor, his arms clasped about his knees. He had lit no candle, and I was grateful; darkness was better for this.

"What's the matter with him, Rouen?" I turned to him, my vitals clutched by an awesome fear. "Did we do this to him? Did we drive him into madness?" I thought about the times that I had induced his seizures, in order that he might inform us, by his visions, of what Lilith intended.

Rouen pulled me into his embrace, cradled my head against his chest. "No, Dante. I think that the burden of existence weighed heavier on Valentin than it did on others."

I had wanted to love him, I had tried. And not merely out of pity, although I pitied him as well. Valentin had been sorely tried by life, as Rouen had said. I wondered if I did right by him when I decided to give him the ancient blood. Perhaps if I had not interfered with him, he would have long since died and entered into rest. There would be no such rest for Rouen and I, nor for others of our kind. Damnation flies in both directions.

I remembered when he first came to us, scant months ago, freezing in midwinter and dying of the plague. I remember bundling him inside my cloak and hurrying him through the darkness, certain that if this feeble mortal would but cling to life for another instant, I could save him. And then caring for him, peeling off his filthy clothes and washing him, tucking him into bed and praying that he would survive the night, that he would survive the winter. That he would stay with us.

And now it was spring, and everything had changed, turning on that imperceptible spindle about which all things spin. Valentin was mad, and forever lost, and Florence was no longer safe for us.

"Rouen, let us take our leave of this place." I shifted, pressed my lips against his cheek. He was weeping. "I am weary of it. Spain is lovely in the summer and it is nearly that. Let us go there, and leave this place and Serenola...." I choked, leaned forward, my forehead in his lap. I waited for his hand to slip into my hair, his fingers to slide around my neck and comfort me, but he was silent, and when I tried to read his mind I found it cold and empty.

Chapter 14

ROUEN

THE darkness snapped me out of my sleep, a fitful sleep that had taken me through the day mired in memories of Valentin's humiliation. I turned aside the bedcovers and laid my feet against the cold tiles. Dante was still sleeping, curled in a lump under the covers, and I left him there. Tonight, I wished to hunt alone.

I dressed quickly and in silence, my fingers cold with lack of blood, fumbling. I pulled my boots on, splashed a little water on my face, and went out.

I was incredibly angry with Dante, a vast unreasoning resentment that forced me out into the night, away from him. For despite what I had said to him earlier, I did very much blame him for Valentin. And while I stood by and allowed him to create Valentin as one of us, to bring him into the ancient blood, I realized now that it had been a vast mistake.

I hurried through the streets, crossed the Ponte Vecchio, moving in a southerly direction from the Duomo. I was very hungry, and some dark emotion throbbed deep within my belly. I became as part of the darkness, slipping through the night on silent feet, a fatal shadow.

I found a street-front house, the entryway obstructed by a heavy door, barred with an oak timber. I broke this easily, cast the fragments away, and hastened up the stairs. There were mortals sleeping here, I could smell them: a mother and her child.

I found the woman resting on a makeshift pallet beside the dying fire, the child at her side. A little boy, not more than an infant, perhaps eight months of age.

I sat beside her, drew my fingers through her hair, auburn, lustrous, streaming unbound around her shoulders. Her skin gleamed ivory in the darkness. "*Mi beneamata....*" Beloved. I waited until she rose smiling out of sleep, and then I caught her by the throat. "Struggle but a little." I crushed her plump cheeks between my hand, leaned down to kiss her lips. Her palms pushed against my shoulders, uselessly. Her eyes flamed fear at me, an animal terror. "Just a little kiss for Death...." I forced her mouth open, kissed her brutally, sliced her tongue with my fangs. Her eyes grew wide as she felt her own blood filling up her mouth. I pressed her back against the pillows, my hand across her throat, watched with interest as she choked on it, struggling, the color draining slowly out of her face.

The child woke, pressed mewling against her, rooting for the breast. I caught him to me, joggling him in my arms, tossing him into the air. "What a precious little son you have, *signorina.*"

She coughed, blood burbling in her throat, and reached for him, fingers outstretched. She clawed wildly at me, her fingernails raking uselessly. I held him high above me, raised him between my hands. "The perfect sacrifice... would you give your son to God?" And then I tore his throat, sucked back the blood and tossed his body onto the hearth, tore off the child's swaddling cloths and fed them to the dying flames. His foot was clubbed, turned back into the ankle, distorted. Like Valentin's had been. Valentin's clubbed foot, that so fascinated and aroused me.

A great violence was building in me, pulsing through my bones, my muscles, with a cadence like a drumbeat. *Would you give your son to God?*

Would you turn him out into the streets because he could no longer serve you? Would you sell him into whoredom, would you sacrifice his immortal soul or would you send him gently into the arms of the mother Church?

The child's body stiffened slowly, his little eyes staring up at nothing."He was imperfect." I shrugged. "Pity."

She moved, a sudden sideways motion, leapt off the bed and went scrabbling across the floor, on hands and knees. "Cannot leave just yet, *signorina!*" I caught her wrist and yanked her back toward me. "What did you intend to do with him, this child?" It was vital that I know.

Her mouth opened, spilling blood upon her night robe, the ivory perfection of her skin. "He was to go into a monastery, Ser. When he was old enough." Her eyes trembled, spilling tears. "Ah!" I tore her robe, ripped it down the front. Her breasts, unbound, tumbled out into the air, rosy-tipped and heavy with milk. Something stirred in my belly. "Where is the child's father?" I demanded. I pulled her toward me, pressed the heat of her against me, this warm delicious mortal. "Has he abandoned you?" I realized that I could take her, have knowledge of her, and she would not resist me.

"No, Ser." Her palms slid up the front of my cloak, fingers reaching to cup my face. The smell of her rose into my nostrils, enticing. "He is in service to the Church, and cannot attend us as he wishes." She pressed her bloody mouth against my neck. "Pray let me go, Messer, and I will pleasure you."

So she would bargain. "What is his name?" I tilted her face up, gazed deep into his eyes. "And what is his profession? Is he a priest, and have you committed sin with him?" I smiled. "There is much less tolerance for sin these days."

"My husband does not sin," she whispered. She began to rub herself on me, spreading the animal scent of her all over my clothes. The smell of her blood was nearly overwhelming, and my head swam dizzily. I would kill her quickly and get it over with. "My husband is a pardoner. His name is Valentin." Her hand slid down, fumbling with my codpiece.

I killed her quickly, broke her neck and drank her blood, dropped her body on the hearth. I ran down the stairs and out into the street and I did not stop running until I reached the river Arno.

I prowled the back streets for the rest of that night, and killed two beggars who slept beside a tavern. I came upon an old man with a bundle on his shoulder, and I drained blood slowly from his wrist, drank a little, and left him there to bleed. I found a whore walking near the markets and I tore her throat out, simply to see if I were sufficiently divorced of essential human feeling. I was aware of a new quality within me, as if every life that I took from now on would be in recompense to Valentin, as payment for the colossal wrong that we had done him, by bringing him into the ancient blood when he had not been strong enough to stand it.

My husband is a pardoner... his name is Valentin....

He must have traveled often, returning here from England, no doubt to meet with Gioletti, to pay the illegal tithes that he'd collected. And he would have met her, perhaps seen her in the market, and she, seeing his luminous pale eyes, his angel's face....

Betrayed. Oh, how Valentin had been betrayed by us, and I was wrong to think that it was all to do with Dante and naught to do with me! If there were any such thing as sin, then I had sinned this night, when I supposed myself to be pure and blameless in this matter.

Hypocrite. A shimmering vibration, a floating thought.

I spun around, seeking the source of it. "Who's there?"

Laughter: hollow, mocking. The calling card of some mischievous young god.

Hypocrite.

"Have you been following me?"

"Only since I awakened." He fell into step with me, jauntily.

"You might stop smirking," I said stiffly.

"Ah, poor, Rouen, so very disillusioned." He skipped a little ahead of me, executed a dance step on the slippery cobbles, and leapt high into the air. "I presume that up until this night you supposed yourself a creature of certain purity. Unsullied by existence, untouched.

Residing in some protective tower, the Campanile, perhaps. Hmmm?"

"Dante…." I turned up a narrow side street, hoping to get away from him.

"Come, Rouen! Don't be so down in the mouth." He twirled, balanced on the balls of his feet and flipped backward, landing with perfect precision. "So you have discovered that you are not so very different from me, that Valentin was as much your doing as he was mine." He caught my arm in his, pulled me into the dance. "*Bravo!*"

"*Stop* this!" I jerked away from him, my face burning. "How dare you make sport of me in this manner?" I was trembling with humiliation, remembering Valentin in the piazza with his hose down around his knees, passing out blood-smeared bits of paper.

"Did you know he had a wife, a young son?" The little boy's clubbed foot, turned back into the ankle, his tiny body lying on the hearth.

"Yes." He had stopped a few feet ahead, leaning against the facade of an inn, and floated some small distance above the ground. "I did."

"How?"

"I read his thoughts. You should, too, Rouen. It's a skill that you should practice."

"Why did you not tell me?" I lashed at him, but he floated away, bobbed out of my reach, infuriating. "*Dante!*"

"Welcome, Rouen, to the ramparts of the damned!" he called, drifting. He bumped against the eaves of a house, disrupted a flock of nesting pigeons, set them to fluttering and cooing.

"Come down!"

He settled beside me, feet firmly on the ground. "There's no need to shout. What outrageous manners!"

I stared at him, cold and trembling and close to tears. "Why do you do this to me? Why do you torment me so?" I was flying apart.

"Oh, belt up, Rouen!" He sneered, his smooth white face folding into ugly lines. He has the most moveable face I've ever seen, so entirely incapable of disguising its expressions. Dante is a most imperfect liar, for that very reason. "Do you think I devote my entire existence to torturing you?"

"Tell me what it means," I whispered. I stopped beside a flight of stairs, sat down on the bottom step.

"What it *means*?" He laughed, incredulous, came to sit beside me. "Why, it means nothing." He laughed again, slapped his knees.

"Stop laughing," I said miserably, "I find nothing funny in it." For I had been betrayed, as much as Valentin, had gone willingly into the arms of my damnation. Perhaps I thought to escape my own dark past, my father's incestuous secret marriage, the burden of my family's evil secret. Perhaps I believed the promise in Dante's soft dark eyes when he touched me that night and whispered, "*You need me*".

"Do you think, as the Church elders do, that we exist here on this earth for some divine purpose?" Dante got up, walked a little ways back and forth. "*Assurdita!*" He knelt before me, his face beautifully earnest. "Rouen, this place is just some stop-gap way station, until He discovers what to do with all these souls—if indeed He has any plan at all!"

"Dante, that is blasphemy." The timbre of this conversation was making me distinctly uneasy.

"Blasphemy?" He snorted. "As if He cares anything for us, now."

"Then you believe Lilith's lies—that He will wipe us off the face of the earth?"

He regarded me, his head on one side, looking very much like a painting: contemplative, still. "Yes." He started off again, walking in the opposite direction to which we had come.

I hurried to catch up with him, not wishing to be left behind in the dank and empty streets.

THE inn at Tralini's was crowded to capacity tonight. I supposed that the onset of the warmer weather had drawn people out of the safety of their homes, into the streets. Dante and I slipped inside the door, took a seat at a table by the wall.

"Rouen, do you think this is such a good idea?" Dante glanced about him, warily.

"Don't worry, this won't take but a few moments," I replied. Besides, Lorenzo Tralini was nowhere in sight.

"Rouen." A tall, slender young man slid into the chair next to mine, impeccably clad in a velvet doublet, crisp white shirt, and fine, dark-blue hose. "It is not safe for you to be here, we must needs leave at once." He produced a bag, obviously very heavy, laid it on the table. "Come along. I will accompany you to your lodgings."

"Rouen, who is this?" Dante asked. "We do not know you, Ser. I pray you, be gone. We have no business with you." He flicked his wrist impatiently, turned away.

"Dante...." I smiled, grinned at our companion. "You do not recognize our good friend? Take a closer look."

The young man moved his chair further into the light, propped his chin upon his hand. His clear hazel eyes were smiling, beautiful jewels set into the pale perfection of his face, about which fluttered wavy, dark auburn hair. His brow was high and fair, his chin indented with a dimple.

"I do not know him."

"Perhaps because you have not seen me in this guise." He shifted a little in his chair, cleared his throat. "I ought to have appeared to you as I did before." When he spoke this time, it was with a woman's voice.

"My *God*!" Dante leaned across the table, caught a strand of dark auburn hair between his fingers. "And this is yours?" He yanked on it.

"Ouch! Yes, it is." Fernando grinned. "You see, I am not a

woman all the time."

"My God...." Dante said, again.

"Your mouth is hanging open," I told him. "Pray shut it unless you wish to capture flies."

"But...." He shook his head, confused by the information of his senses. "I had no idea you were so very... masculine, Ser."

Fernando laughed, revealing pearly white teeth. "Ah. Well, we all hide behind our various guises, now and then." He rose, picked up the sack. "Now let us hasten. I have no time to waste this night."

FERNANDO followed us through the dark streets to our lodgings, his sack over his shoulder. We did not speak as we went, but concentrated on making our way as quickly as we could. There were scant hours left before the daylight, and Dante and I had to be out of the country by then.

I lit a candle and closed the door behind us, bracing the broken frame shut with a brick. I led Fernando up the stairs, ushered him into our rooms. "Here. Bring your things in here." I pulled the dining table—certainly unused by us—over to the wall, laid the candle in the sconce.

"Rouen." Dante's face was taut with worry. "They will see the light. We cannot fight them all."

"It's all right." I kissed his cheek, drew him over to the table. "Fernando has aid for us."

"Dante, would you prefer to be first? Or perhaps Messer Rouen." Fernando was busy pulling gowns out of his bag, ladies' kirtles, high-heeled shoes. He tossed a pair of fine, white stockings carelessly over his shoulder, picked out earrings and necklaces, gorgeous wigs of lustrous, shining hair.

"Rouen...." Dante slid close to me, laid his arm across my

shoulder. "Why did you not tell me he was beautiful?"

I glanced at him, uneasily. "Don't."

We stripped down to our drawers, handed our clothing to Fernando, who secreted it inside his bag. He took our cloaks, our boots, even Dante's tiny silver dagger. "We can allow no trace of anything that would identify you," Fernando said. "If Serenola's people are expecting you in Spain, they are already well-versed in your appearance." He grunted softly as he tugged a silken kirtle over Dante's head, fastened the laces.

"Too tight!" Dante tugged at the neck of it, grimaced. "This is damned uncomfortable."

"Really?" Fernando glanced at him, eyebrows raised. "I've always liked the feel of silk against the skin."

Dante shot me a look, one which was mercifully smothered by a gown as it went over his head.

"STOP talking, please." Fernando smoothed color on my lips with a tiny brush, his tongue between his teeth. "You have beautiful lips, Rouen. You should wear paint." He tilted my head into the light, brushed soft green color onto my eyelids, stained my lashes black. "Your wig, Ser—" He dropped it over my head, pressed it into place, adjusting it against my skull. "—drape the curls about the neck, like so... *perfetto!*"

He clapped his hands and grinned, "Here, look at yourself," passed a mirror before me. "Beautiful."

I did not readily recognize the person in the glass, but I did agree with him, she was very beautiful. The green that he had brushed on my lids shimmered like a peacock's wing; my lips, outlined in red and painted, were pouting, sensuous. "How do I look?"

"Like a practiced courtesan."

I frowned. "A whore."

"Well...." Fernando shrugged, his broad shoulders lifting underneath his elegant clothes. "No lady of distinction would be seen in that much paint, but it does suit you. And you are less likely to attract attention if you are disguised as a common whore."

"Rouen cannot abide the common, it rubs him so."

I turned to address the speaker, and saw a gorgeous young maid, sitting decorously on a chair directly opposite. Her hair fell in glistening apricot ringlets about bared shoulders that were as white as milk. Diamonds glistened in the hollow of her throat, matched the shimmering of the gown. Rings sparkled on her fingers. "Dante!"

"Yes, Rouen." He rose and came toward us, drifting gracefully across the tiles, one hand pinching a handful of his drapery. He bent low over me, exposing the tops of plump white breasts, a steep and dangerous cleavage.

"How did you manage that?" I asked Fernando, incredulous.

He smiled. "A little padding here and there, a nip and tuck."

I went to him and embraced him warmly. "I can never repay you for your kindness." I moved to kiss him.

"Ah!" He pushed me away, laughing. "Desist, or you will ruin all that lovely paint." He gathered his bag, stuffed our belongings into it. "I promise that I'll retain this in safekeeping until I hear from you, Rouen."

"Fernando, thank you." Dante embraced him, ruffled his hair. "I like you much better this way, Ser."

"Hmmm." He laughed. "And I like you better in that gown."

He took his leave of us, bundled the sack underneath his arm, and disappeared. Dante and I were left alone with our single candle, our sacked apartments, and each other. "So we are leaving," he said. He walked slowly about the room, went to gaze out of the casement. His expression was pensive.

"Dante, we must hurry. Already it comes dawn."

"Fernando is lovely, Rouen." He left the casement, closed the shattered shutters. "Do you not see the marvelous spirit in him?"

Something in his tone pricked me. "What are you getting at, exactly?"

"Rouen...." He caught my hands in his, eyes gleaming. "Think what an immortal he'd make!"

I stared at him, flushed hot and cold. "Don't you *dare* loose another mistake like Valentin upon the earth!" The image of his dead son rose to haunt me, the little body with its twisted foot, lying on the hearth. "You stupid bastard, you ignorant, selfish *peasant*!"

He drew back his hand and delivered me a stinging slap across the mouth. Not with the closed fist, as one man would strike another, but a slap, such as a woman makes. I recognized the insult.

Immediately his eyes grew large, his face paling underneath its paint. "Rouen, I'm sorry." He pressed his fingers to my mouth, the paint bleeding off into his skin. "God forgive me!"

I realized that he wanted me to apologize to him. But I would not. Dante had never before struck me, had never laid a hand on me in anything but love. Even on the night that I first met him, when Leonardo raped him and Dante could easily have killed us both, he didn't touch me. I had always thought it was because of his professed desire to "make recompense" but now I recognized the essence of his ostensible restraint, and it was his large and dangerous ego. I surmised that the continued adoration of Salvatore di Tuscano had somehow warped him, had convinced Dante that he was a wondrous thing, a superior creation—the very Son of God. Dante expected certain things from his existence, and was therefore willing to endure certain other horrors. It was his trump card.

He had allowed Leonardo to rape him, and me to watch it, because he knew that I would pity him, and that that pity would tie me to him forever.

Once again, he had gained the upper hand.

"Come along, Rouen." He buckled on his purse, the only item of his possessions that Fernando had allowed him to retain. "It grows late, we must be going."

I snuffed the candle, followed him in silence down the stairs. The sky above the Duomo was just lightening, night dying into daylight, the streets shivering to life again after an evening of repose.

Dante put his arm about my waist, and we rose high into the air.

Chapter 15

1348

Seville, Spain

DANTE

THE Torre del Oro was the first thing I saw, floating in the darkness above Seville, Rouen clutched tightly in my arms. I drifted closer, over an expanse of dark water, the River Guadalquivir, until the great round tower with its gilded tiles was gleaming in my sights. "Rouen, we are in Spain."

He stirred himself, lifted his chin from my shoulder. "Indeed." He glanced down, at the dark water rushing past beneath our feet, swallowed. "Perhaps I shall not look down until we land."

WE FOUND lodgings in the Juderia, the obscure ghetto where the Spanish Jews had formed their community, and where we would be the most secure from interference. Rouen and I discarded the female guise for the time it took to bargain out the rent, took care to disclose the location of our rooms to no one. Our lodgings were small, but not unpleasant, and very clean, with cool tiled floors into which had been laid an elaborate Moorish mosaic. We had a rooftop garden, with nasturtiums and jasmine, and several kinds of herbs, a winding stone staircase that led through a wrought iron gate into the yard. Our comings and goings were supervised by an old grandmother who seemed mainly occupied with sweeping, and always at the foot of our stairs. Thankfully, she never saw us in our female costumes, else we might have found ourselves summoned by the courts. For a stretch of time, we lived in peace amongst our Jewish neighbors, and came and went without hindrance. For their part, they took care to learn our names, to greet us in the street or in the square, till we found ourselves absorbed into their community, into their peaceful sphere. Unfortunately, the remainder of Seville was not engaged in the pursuit of peace.

It had become evident to us, shortly after our arrival, that Serenola's fanatic influence had spread; the main instrument of dissent was an archdeacon named Martinez. Like Serenola, Martinez believed the plague to be a punishment from God. Also like Serenola, Martinez was occupied with finding a probable cause. For the several weeks that spring that we were in Seville, Rouen and I were careful to avoid him.

"BUT Dante," Rouen remarked, one evening as we were dressing in our rooms, assembling our female disguises, "there is no evidence that this Martinez is in league with Serenola." He grunted, pulled a pair of stockings up around his knees. "He may well be operating on his own, spreading his own message of dissent." We had been in Seville some several weeks now, and as time wore on through the month of April, we realized that the same kind of religious hysteria was in evidence here as in Florence. We recognized also, that the deacon Martinez, after the model of Serenola, was looking for a scapegoat on which to blame the horrors of the plague. It was murmured that the Jews were his favored target. Here, as in Florence, they were readily identifiable by the circular yellow badge sewn into all their clothing.

"Rouen." I fitted my wig over my own hair, combed my curls about my shoulders. "Nothing happens in this world that is without coincidence. If Martinez is at the head of this new inquisition, then either he is connected in some fashion with Serenola, or he has caught wind of his ideas." I stretched my lips, applied paint with the tiny brush that Fernando had given me. "Lilith's influence is felt here as well." I rubbed powder into my neck and shoulders, pressed a flower into the bodice of my dress. I felt ridiculous, dressed this way. I hated it.

"Very nice." Rouen had come to stand behind me, watched me in the mirror, a tall, beautiful young woman. We had retained our female costumes on the premise that Serenola's spies were not expecting two young Italian courtesans, and therefore we could pass unheeded through the crowds. And we had taken employ, both of us as serving-wenches in the same small tavern, a poky, low-class wine-house in a disreputable section of the city.

"Thank you," I replied sourly. I rose and wrapped a shawl about my shoulders. "Rouen, be sure to keep your ears open tonight. I want to glean everything I can about the actions of this Martinez."

He frowned at me. "Truly, do you think he is some sort of weather-cock for Lilith's movements? I hardly see it warranted."

"He is," I insisted, "now hurry, please. Already it grows late, and Rouen, you are annoying me." I caught his arm. "I insist only that you listen well this night... there are secrets to be had, when men are in their cups."

We went out, closed our door behind us.

THE tavern in which Rouen and I had found employment was a creaky, street front house, little more than a large open room set about with tables and rickety benches, unsanitary, and smelling strongly of urine and offal. It had at one time been a gorgeous monument to Moorish architecture, but that had been a long time ago. Now, it was but a crumbling ruin, its clean lines and graceful arches falling into dust.

Many of the buildings about Seville were in the Moslem fashion, but the Giralda tower so reminded me of the Campanile that every time

I saw it, I was pierced with a desire to flee back to Florence. I felt I had been away a hundred years.

"Rouen, take a tray of ale to that table over there." A company of Gypsies, loud and boisterous, played their strange music near the door. "And pray tell them to cease that ungodly racket!" My Tuscan ears were unaccustomed to the Spanish strains; to me, it was merely so much noise.

We had contracted to serve wine and ale between the hours of sundown and midnight; after the tavern closed, it was customary for Rouen and I to part company and hunt. We did, after all, still need mortal blood for our survival. But the tavern, despite its certain drawbacks, was the perfect place for us to hear the news. But like any sort of gainful employment, it was fraught with certain complications....

"*Carina*...." A meaty hand, sliding up my haunches. "You look delicious tonight."

"Pedro, please." I slapped the hand away, swore fluently in Spanish; I had gathered enough of the language to put together a serviceable vocabulary. "Did you order another cask of the port? You have distinguished guests who prefer it to all else." Rubbish, of course, since the only patrons that Pedro's tavern serviced were the street-front vendors and the noisome Gypsies by the door.

"Why not let me take a little taste of you, hmmm?" His hot breath scorched my naked shoulders, seared the back of my neck. *Go away or I'll kill you!* A mental directive, as strong as I could make it. Thank God for preternatural ability....

"*Ay!*" He backed away as if he'd been burnt. "Little testy tonight? Not your moon-time, is it?" His nose twitched, above his long black moustache. "I can smell the blood...." He shuffled off into the back room, muttering.

Rouen appeared, mercifully, with a tray full of empty glasses. The Gypsies had switched to something a little more subdued, and were alternately singing and crying. I sighed. "Rouen...."

"Shhhh!" He caught my elbow, pinched it painfully.

"Of course—uh, Emilia—" I had difficulty remembering to use our female names. I was tiring of the whole adventure, the weariness of wearing dresses.

"Look the other way, pretend you are cleaning underneath the bar." Rouen laid the tray down, took exquisite care in removing each dirty glass, one by one. "Those Gypsies by the door, do you know them?"

"Not personally, no. And I thank the saints for it." I swiped at the dark wood with my cloth, flicking crumbs and bits of dried food.

"But you recognize the group I mean?"

"How could I not?" I retorted, hissing, "They have been creating that cacophony ever since they came in. I feel as if I'm in Tralini's whorehouse again!"

"They are talking about Martinez."

Immediately, my ears were pricked. I leaned close to Rouen, gazed at him. *Are you saying they are allies, or enemies?*

Enemies, absolutely. They are discussing whether it is safe for them to attempt escape. The fiddler is very worried, I can feel it. He thinks Martinez and his oppressive dogma will soon be a force to reckon with.

"Emilia!" Pedro's booming voice. "Go tap the cask and fill some jugs with port. We are expecting distinguished guests." He lingered behind me, his hands about my waist, his body a mere hair's-breadth from my own. "I do not like your friend; she is not a comely *señorita*."

Something warm and wet flicked out, slid against my skin—it was his tongue, painting a trail of spit up and down my neck. *Jesu Maria....* I spun about, smacked him squarely in the face with my opened palm. "Loose hold of me!" I felt hot color mount into my cheeks, a knot of anger tighten in my belly.

"A little fiery one...." He pulled me to him, rubbed himself against me. "How can you resist? And I would make it worth your trouble, *cara*." He smelled of sweat, an excess of cheap wine. The whites of his eyes were yellow, jaundiced. I suspected some disease of the liver.

"Let go." I pushed him away, turned to move out from behind the bar, was suddenly apprehended and slammed facedown against the polished wooden surface. His fingers splayed against the back of my neck as he forced my head down, pushed himself against me.

"Such a darling little one...." His tongue drew a wet streak down the back of my neck, dipped into the collar of my gown. Where was Rouen? "Come and let me purchase of your pleasure...." His hands slid around the front of my body, squeezed the padding that he supposed was breasts. I knew that if his hand dipped further, I would be in trouble. For I knew he wouldn't find a woman's rounded love-mound, but the organs of one who was very like himself. *Rouen! Jesu Maria, where are you?* I needed to distract him, until I could disable him sufficiently to get away. "Come into the back, where we can dally." I reached around, caught his hand in mine. "This place is far too public, *Señor.*"

THE back room of the tavern was Pedro's private rooms, as bare and ugly as the rest of it, and absolutely filthy. A brazier burned continuously in the corner, sending out clouds of vile smoke; the windows were tightly shuttered and no candle burned to provide illumination. A makeshift pallet was located against the wall, on which was heaped a bundle of dirty rags that masqueraded as his bedclothes. A pair of boots, heavily crusted with mud and filth, crouched underneath the single chair, poised to walk away.

"Come here, pretty one." He grabbed my arm and yanked me toward him, violently. "Can't escape me now!" He fell down upon the pallet, pulled me into his lap, fingers delving underneath my skirts.

"You are far too fast for me, Señor...." I pushed his hand away, with effort. A warning sounded in my brain: for a mortal, he was very strong. I wondered if he might possibly detain me against my will?

He rolled onto his back and pinned me against his chest, his lips rising to meet mine. *Oh God, I'm going to be sick... Rouen!* I turned my head away, fought to escape him. "No, Señor, you'll ruin my paint!"

He rolled again, and this time I ended up beneath him, choking on the foul odor of his body, the collective stink of his sweat. I wondered if this was how a woman felt, taken by force. I brought my knees up, pushed against his chest, and was successful in knocking him off me. I leapt up, made for the door, was caught and slammed head down into the stinking blankets of his pallet. My face slid greasily, slick with paint; I was gagging in the fusty blankets....

Hands fumbled at my skirts, hands rippling in my petticoats, lifting my kirtle, pulling my stockings down. I flushed hot and cold with rage, fighting him; I deliberately withheld the full force of my attack in order to maintain the illusion that I was but a mortal female. It was an effort.

His fingers slid along my skin, cupped my buttocks, spreading me apart, and I knew what was to happen next. Time slowed to an inky crawl and the room darkened about me: I had a choice. I could allow this, therefore protecting the illusion that Rouen and I were women, or I could resist him, with the full power of my preternatural nature, and expose us both irrevocably.

I felt suddenly sickened, cold. I remembered the anonymous inn where Rouen and Leonardo had taken me. I remembered Leonardo, mocking me, *Dance, boy! I, Leonardo di Sforza, command you!* And being violated by him, allowing it because of my own misplaced guilt.

I will endure it. It will be over in a moment. I will let him take his pleasure and pretend that he has conquered me, and then I will go about my business and it will all be over. I can endure this, if it means that I gain precious information....

I had nearly convinced myself that I could tolerate any assault he chose to make, when I felt the throbbing tip of his erect member, probing my entrance, pushing into me.

'Leonardo, stop it, you're humiliating him'!

I waited, tensed beneath him, as he grunted and pushed, forcing himself past the tight ring of muscle at my entrance. He panted above me, sweating like a bull, his fingers flexing and opening around my waist. He withdrew, paused, his member bobbing against my buttocks, the back of my thighs....

...and then my hand was at his throat, and I was crushing him inside my fist, squeezing off his air as he kicked, gasping. I felt my fangs descend, sliding down out of my gums as the blood-thirst flooded upward, invading my brain. "You are *mine*...."

I struck at him savagely, burst the artery, and sucked the blood back into my throat. It slid burning into my stomach, drove heat into the chill marrow of my bones, burst inside my skull like carnival rockets. I tore his throat, spilling blood greedily down the front of my gown, staining myself through to the silken kirtle that I wore against my skin. *Mine.*

I rolled him underneath the table, covered his body with the heap of filthy blankets from the bed. Then I stripped off the sodden gown, tore away the kirtle, removed the wig and the necklace, the earrings and the high-heeled shoes, tied it all into a bundle, and tossed it out the back window.

I stood naked in the middle of the room, my body throbbing with a covert excitement as the blood coursed through me, filling my head with light. I felt like laughing and I did, throwing my head back, slapping my own knees.

"Dante!" Rouen.

"Close the door." I pulled him into the room, slammed the door behind him and bolted it.

"But there's nobody—"

"Shut up." I knotted my fist in the front of his gown and pulled, tearing a wide swath down the front. "—sick of seeing you in that woman's dress, you're a *man*, dammit—"

"What did you do with your costume? Why are you naked? Dante!"

I scraped his face clean of paint and my own as well, tore the wig away and let his soft dark hair flutter about his shoulders. "Beautiful, you're beautiful." I walked him backward until he rested flat against the wall, arms high above his head and pinned within my grasp. And I kissed him, hard and desperately, and I felt free again, as I hadn't felt in ages.

"Dante...." His fingers pressed against my face, his eyes hazy with desire. "I love you."

I cupped his face between my hands and kissed his cheeks, pressed my lips to the perfect center of his eyebrows, the soft underside of his sculpted jaw. "I love you, Rouen. Yes, I'm saying it. Now come along."

"Where?" He allowed me to tug him, naked.

"Home. Back to our lodgings. And we will dress as gentlemen, which is what we are, and we will hunt together." I was tired of running from Serenola and his minions; coming here had been a vast mistake, and I was completely weary of this pretence. I had lived for six weeks now as a woman, and I wanted my old life back. I wanted to be myself again. And I was a vampire, after all, with not a little share of talent. I was certain I could stand up to Serenola if it came to that.

"Dante." He stopped me at the door, his mouth curved in a mischievous grin. "Has it occurred to you that we are both completely naked?"

I stepped out onto the veranda, a shaky platform jutting off from Pedro's rooms. "Come along." I held out my hand to him, and he took it.

If any of the good citizens of Seville noticed two naked men flying overhead that night, nobody mentioned it.

THE plague had taken a disastrous toll in Spain, just as it had in Italy. As April lingered on the cusp of May and spring moved into summer, the number of deaths increased dramatically. With this new onslaught came renewed hysteria: it seemed that Martinez was indeed a disciple of Serenola, in that he preached the Judgment of God, followed the carts, and murdered those he suspected of apostasy. His minions rioted on Ash Wednesday, sacked and burned the Jewish section where Rouen and I had taken rooms. They were repulsed and flogged as an example, but all of us knew that it was but a matter of time before the hysteria again reached a fever pitch.

"HO, DANTE!"

I glanced up from my book, smiled in response to the cheerful greeting of Isak, our neighbor in the Juderia, and our good friend. Rouen and I had taken to sitting outside of an evening, just after sunset, accompanied by a lamp or two, for light. "Isak, good morrow to you. Come, sit beside me and tell the news." I moved aside, cleared a space for him on the steps where I was seated. I had amassed a collection of books and papers on the topic of various diseases and spent my spare time in the evenings perusing them for some clue as to the cause of the plague. So far, I had found nothing, and I was inclining more and more toward my previous, morbid sympathies: perhaps Lilith really was the author and the cause of it.

Isak lowered himself gingerly to the steps, breathing heavily, his white brows lowered over dark eyes of an astonishing depth and intelligence. It pained me to watch him struggle as he moved his body, but I knew better than to help him. I had offered him my arm one night, shortly after Rouen and I arrived, and had been soundly rebuffed, and rather roundly cursed. "What do you have there?" He inclined his head toward the volume in my hand, squinted. I moved the lamp a little closer, so he could see the title. The last of the sunset had died away to a thin pink streak in the western sky.

"It is a treatise on the plague, a piece by Messer Boccaccio. I am curious as to why the illness strikes." I placed my finger between the pages, closed the book upon my lap.

"Ah." He nodded. "Some things are the province of the Lord God, Dante, and subject to His jurisdiction. Don't you think that this pestilence is but another test upon the holiness of His faithful, as was the pestilence in Israel?" He paused, breathing in the scent of jasmine that filtered through the soft summer darkness.

"Ah, but why would a loving God need to test His faithful?"

And we were off on another of our spirited theological debates.

"Enough!" Rouen's clear voice rang out; he descended the steps and seated himself near us, a little above, placed another lamp beside me. "Good evening, *Rebbe*. I trust Dante has talked your ears off?" He picked up one of my books, flipped it open and quickly shut again.

"He seeks answers to the ways of the Almighty, when the ways of Adonai are known only to Him."

"Leeches," I said suddenly, if only to tease him a little. "I am certain we could achieve success with leeches."

Rouen raised an eyebrow. "Indeed. Isak, don't listen to him. The next thing, he'll convince you he can let blood, cut hair, and shave." He shifted himself, slid down a step until he was level with us. The air was warm, and beautifully calm; it was a perfect summer's evening. "It has been thankfully quiet around here lately. What has it been now? Six weeks, seven? I wonder if Martinez has finally learned the error of his ways...."

"Today is June sixth," I said, "so nearly seven weeks. Perhaps the peace this time is a lasting one." Even as I said it, something niggled at the back of my mind, warning me. I shook it off, returned to our discussion, but I had been distracted by it, and had lost the thread of what I had been saying.

"Isak, Rouen tells me your nasturtiums are fully as large as trenchers. Is this so? I wish I had your secret; Rouen claims that a little

THE EYE OF HEAVEN

wine placed at the roots is nourishing, but so far, all he's done is kill them all." I nudged Rouen with my hand. *There is some danger afoot here. I can feel it.*

"Some say a little wine is useful." The old man shifted, easing his bones. "But I have always found the ground bones of animals most efficient." The lamplight reflected off his dignified old face, settled in the heavy creases between his brows and around his mouth. He was immensely old, especially for a mortal, and I wondered how much misfortune he had seen in his long lifetime, and what small sum of joy.

Dante, what is that sound?

"Animal bones? Is that so? I have never heard of it before."

Rouen, it's coming closer… do you think we should sit here in full view? We were identifiable in the lamplight; should anyone who knew us hasten close enough, we would be discovered. And our neighbors had never seen us in our female costumes; Rouen and I had crept out to the tavern under cover of the darkness, slipped away into the night. Besides, I'd destroyed the dresses weeks ago, in a fit of pique, and I had no intention of finding any more.

"Dante…." Rouen spoke aloud this time, raised himself up to take a look. "That noise…."

Isak turned toward it, squinted into the darkness.

"Señor, I think you had best return home." I stood back while Isak rose, handed him a lamp. "Please take this to light your way."

"What is it?" he asked. "Is it coming this way?"

"Please, Señor." I stepped back from him. "I think for your own safety it would be best if you—"

A multitude spilled into the street, a vast wave of humanity, borne along the darkness. I watched, open-mouthed, as they poured into the square, a flood of mortals borne along the rising tide of their collective insanity, waving torches and screaming.

"*Rouen!*" I grabbed his sleeve. "Get into the house, *now!*"

"Dante, they are merely mortals—"

"And we are but two, and we cannot fight them all!" I remembered that night in Florence, the siege of Serenola's forces, a burning torch thrust into my face, *I'm burning, oh God, the sun, the sun!*

They crashed toward us, burning and slashing anything that crossed their path, bursting through the doors of houses and harrying the occupants within. The house directly opposite to us glowed a dull and eerie orange, throbbing for an eternal moment in dead silence, and then exploding in a ball of flame. A streak of fire raced up the outside wall, ran along the roof, shot sparks against the sky.

In moments, the entire block of houses was aflame. The street had become a tumult of cacophony, people screaming and running every which way, an outbreak of hellish chaos.

"Rouen, where's Isak?" I cast about me wildly, he had been here but a moment ago, I had given him a lamp and sent him home, where was he?

"Dante—" Rouen had bundled our belongings into a sack underneath his arm; his traveling cloak was slung over his shoulder, a dagger stuck into his belt. "—come along. This is no place for those of our kind."

He was right, of course. For fire destroys us as nothing else can, and a vampire destroyed by fire cannot be resurrected. I had been lucky once—Serenola had merely damaged me—but I could not depend so blindly on good fortune, not this time.

"I can't just leave him!" The wind shifted, blowing smoke in my direction; I coughed, heaving. My eyes watered, bloody tears seeping out into my lashes. "He's around here somewhere."

"Dante." Rouen slung my cloak around my shoulders. "Come along. This place isn't safe for us." The crowd surged closer, manic faces highlighted by the eerie orange glow of numerous fires; someone climbed upon a nearby house and set the rooftop gardens alight. The block of houses crouched around us, menacing, their hulking dark shapes backlit by the flames.

"Isak!" I cupped my hands around my mouth and called him, desperation beating in my breast. It was vital that I find him, I could save him, whisk him away somewhere, snatch him from the menace of the mob.

"Dante, come along!" Rouen was furious; he grabbed me by my arms and pulled me toward him, hissed into my face. "These mortals will make wrack of us if you do not *come along*!"

I stared at him, his pale face streaked with bloody tears, his green eyes glistening in the light from hundreds of fires. His fangs had descended, as they so often do when we are feeling threatened or afraid; they gleamed pale ivory behind his parted lips. "I have to save him, Rouen."

"You *cannot* save him." His fingers dug into my arm just above the elbow. "Now fly."

"One quick look…." I pulled my arm from his grasp. "I swear to you, Rouen, it will be but a moment, please!" I gazed at him in silence, sorrow gathering underneath my breastbone. "*Please*."

He followed me into the street, cursing.

I felt as if I had stepped into hell: the houses along both sides of the square were burning freely, casting blood-red sparks into the air. Behind us, a great tower of smoke rose, billowing into the night, the collective dispensation of a community's mortal possessions. Animals shrieked and bleated, ran freely or were trampled underfoot, were killed randomly, or set on fire. I caught a small dog that had been burned; it still lived, but was in agony, its great dark eyes rolling in its sockets, pink tongue hanging from its mouth like a sodden rag. I broke its neck swiftly, ending the misery, laid it gently down upon the cobbles. I felt like sobbing.

"I cannot find him," I shouted to Rouen amidst the furor. "Perhaps he escaped when the riot started."

"Dante…." Rouen's hand upon my shoulder, a damning kindness

in the midst of hell. "He was a very old man—"

"Stop it!" I slapped his hand away, furious. "He lives, I swear to you...."

He regarded me with an infinite patience, his eyes wide and full of sorrow, the eyes of an ancient illuminated Christ. "You could not save him." Smoke billowed out behind him, an inky cloud against the darker backdrop of the night. A child staggered down a flight of steps and subsided in the gutter, choking on the oily smoke. Rouen offered me his hand. "Come away."

I walked into his embrace, wrapped him in my arms and rose into the air, wheeling slowly northward, rising out of the chaotic scene to freedom, while beneath us the Juderia burned.

I am come to bring about the end of the world.

I wondered if Lilith waited for us, somewhere beyond the end of our journey.

WE WENT to ground in a forest some miles outside of Calais, spent the day in that state of unconscious exhaustion that is so much a feature of our unnatural lives, and rose at sunset, refreshed and invigorated. The stink of burning still clung to me, and I wished for water that I might wash it all away.

"Rouen. Come see this." I found a little stream, stripped myself, and bathed in the icy water, joyful and rather a bit hysterical that we had escaped.

"I am not coming into that, it's freezing." He pointed, rather tactlessly, at my male parts. "Look how shriveled up you are."

"I am obliged to you for pointing it out," I replied, bowing deeply from the waist. "Pray, come and bathe your stinking hide, Ser." I reached and pulled him into the water with me, stripped his wet clothes away and embraced him underneath the chilly spray of the waterfall. The water was indeed cold, but he was warm, burning with the ever-present fever of the vampire. It delighted me to pleasure him, out there in the open forest, to love him underneath the stars.

"Where will we go?" he asked this, when we were lying on the grass, our bodies drying slowly in the evening breeze. "Northwards there is England, which may be safe haven, at least for a little time." His expression grew thoughtful, as he sank into himself, gazing with the inner eye. "If indeed there is safe haven."

We were immune to plague, we knew that much by now, since we had traveled out from Florence, spent time in Spain, and had not been affected in the least. Mortals similarly exposed dropped like flies around us.

We were not immune, however, to the madness and hysteria of the people. We had faced Serenola in Florence, and the demented minions of Martinez in Seville. What was there in England for us?

"Valentin."

I glanced about me, alarmed. "Where?" Had he appeared to Rouen, as Lilith had to me?

"Valentin is in England."

"You do not know for certain." And Valentin was mad, demented with the strain of his apocalyptic visions, a raving lunatic. "We last saw him in the piazza." Passing out pardons.

"Dante, I know for certain that once you have the bit between your teeth, I could move both Earth and Heaven without the slightest hope of influencing your mind." Rouen regarded me wryly, his head propped upon his hand. "You will not let it rest until you find him." He twirled a stalk of grass between his thumb and finger, slid it between his teeth.

"You are talking nonsense." I sat up, clasped my knees against my chest. "I think we ought to go to England to see how far things have progressed, and if the madness that influenced Serenola has found similar repository there. That is all." I turned my face away from him. "Mayhap Lilith is appearing there, as she appeared in Florence. I wish to know her actions, to ascertain how we must proceed."

"Do you still think we can stop this thing, reverse the judgment of a vengeful God?" He leaned close to me, his hair brushing my bare shoulder. "Some things are beyond your power, Dante."

"A vengeful God?" I laughed bitterly. "Guard your tongue, Rouen. You begin more and more to sound like Serenola."

"What do you think it is?" He pressed his lips against the skin of my neck. "Or have you ascertained that yet?"

He was distracting me with his caress. "I know that it is not some kind of holy judgment." I caught his face between my fingers and kissed him. "Theology aside, there cannot be so many of us upon the earth that God must needs destroy us."

"Why then a flood for Noah?"

"Rouen!" I tired of all this theological dispute; his lips were traveling along my skin and I was too distracted to follow the argument. "I wish only that I could discern Lilith's movement. I could then decide how I wish to proceed." I moved away from him, curled around myself.

"Perhaps if you induced a swoon in me, I might see visions."

My head snapped around. "I beg your pardon?"

"Like you did in Valentin. He served your purpose, Dante, for as long as he withstood. Pity that he wasn't strong enough."

I rolled onto my knees, faced him, my chest constricted painfully, hot color mounting into my cheeks. "What say you now, Rouen? More accusations?"

He smirked, and something ugly flickered in his face. "Merely truth."

I hissed, recoiled from him. "I have examined your truth, Rouen. It strikes me rather curious. Have you ascended again into the protection of the Campanile, or do you truly recognize your part in all of this?"

He blanched, mouth opening on nothing. I got to my feet, moved away. I was so very angry that I feared I might do him harm. I remembered how in Florence I had struck him when he had insulted me, and I realized that that same anger simmered, close to the surface.

"I was not the instigator. I merely stood by—"

"*Precisely!*" I spun and shoved him. "You stood by, Rouen, as you always do, waiting until you deem it appropriate or safe enough for your participation. But know this—" I caught him by the shoulder, shook him. "—you have committed sins plenty of your own. I remember, Rouen, and I will not forget as mortals do, the times that you stood by and allowed catastrophe to continue all around you." I spat on the ground, walked away.

Silence grew up and thickened all around us. I heard Rouen collect his clothes, move away into the forest. And I was alone.

I felt it before I heard it, and I am not certain even now if what I heard was anything at all. There was a sound emanating from the forest, like someone singing, and for one horrified moment I thought it might be Valentin, singing the devotions of St. Hildegarde, as he had in the Piazza del Duomo.

But this was different: high, pure, and sweet, a sound like a thousand voices, like imagined angels. A sense of bliss descended over me, set something pulsing deep inside my belly.

Do this in remembrance of me....

She was here.

I turned, mouth open to call Rouen, and she was on me, her mouth closing over mine, her hands sliding on my skin. My body rose to meet her, floating above the ground, perhaps a hand's-breadth, perhaps a little less. She knelt, and I descended slowly, till I was lying on my back against the grass, arms and legs extended. "Dante...." She leaned over me, her breath hot against my body. She smelled of spices, exotic things.

She summoned me to hardness with her mouth and hands, and

lowered herself down upon me, till I was buried in her. I could feel her throbbing, the blood-heat of her deep insides, enfolding me.

Love me, yes you do....

Behind her eyes, I saw terrors such as I have never imagined, and the sight of it forced me into silence, my mind collapsing down into a truncated horror. Words passed behind my eyelids, the names of abomination, the designated tortures of those who defied the prevailing social ethos. *Strappado*.... Heretics strapped onto wooden frames and stretched by means of weights attached to arms and legs... *Aselli*.... Unbelievers, throats filled with water, suspended in a semiconscious state for hours, sometimes days, cords tightened about their limbs until veins burst.... *Auto da fe*... The stench of burning....

Her body shivered and slid on mine, hips pumping, her head thrown back, long hair streaming in the wind. Her fangs descended, curved wickedly about her lower lip, gleaming ivory daggers. Her skin burned me like acid.

I watched from a great distance as she ground herself against me, as I arched up into her and spent myself, mouth open in a soundless scream. My mind split along its hidden inner fault-lines as her climax exploded in my brain. Darkness opened under me, and I fell into it.

"DANTE... for the love of God, answer me!" Rouen, a shadow above me, hands against my face. "Dante, please."

I blinked, peered up at him. "Rouen, it was her. She was here!" I shivered, cold and naked on the ground.

"It's all right, *tesoro*." He wrapped my cloak around me, kissed my forehead as if I were a child. "What did she do to you?"

I stared at him, suddenly ashamed. "Rouen, she—"

"What? What did she do to you?" His gaze met mine, quizzical.

"She...." I dropped my voice in shame, although there was no one else to hear. "…seduced me."

He drew back, eyes wide. His mouth opened and then closed, opened again. "What do you mean?"

"Rouen!"

"Oh!" He frowned. "*Oh.*"

"Where are my clothes?" I took them from him, dressed shivering in the darkness. "I'm starving, we should hunt." I fumbled with my drawers, drew my hose on with shaking fingers, slipped quickly into my shirt. "There is a village, we might find something there." I didn't want to think about Lilith and what she had done; I didn't want to speak of it.

We walked for some time in silence, until finally Rouen said, "What was it like?" He refused to meet my gaze.

I thought about this for a moment. Was there anything in my experience that I could compare it with? "I'm not sure what you mean," I replied. I could not tell him what I had seen, held in her thrall. I could not reveal the horrors that I knew would come to pass. I worried that if I disclosed what I had seen, if I discussed it further, it would rise to haunt me, and fear of the future would render me ineffective. No, it was better if I kept it to myself, told Rouen only what he needed to know, and nothing more.

"Well." He stopped, peered pointedly at me. "You have loved her, and you have loved me." His fingers fumbled with his doublet, fiddled with the closure of his cape. "What was it like?"

It struck me, then. "Rouen." I started laughing. I couldn't help myself. I laughed and laughed, there in the middle of that tiny road, in the middle of that dusty little village, somewhere near Calais. I howled with delight, slapped my knees, and spun in circles till tears started to my eyes.

"I don't see what is so funny," he said stiffly. "I merely asked a simple question."

"Well, Rouen." I paused, flicked tears from the corners of my eyes. "You are merely a new-made revenant, and Lilith is the consort of God."

"What are you saying, exactly, Ser?" His tone was very much aggressive, but there were tears standing in the rims of his eyes. I was ashamed, then, that I had teased him so unmercifully.

"Rouen...." I caught him to me and kissed him. "I do love you."

WE SLIPPED into a house at the edge of the village, found an old farmer and his wife and dispatched them both into the arms of a darker Morpheus. I had rarely seen Rouen kill, since we usually each hunted alone. I was astonished at the viciousness that he displayed. Truly, I had done well with him.

But the night was wearing on, and I knew that there were scant hours left until the dawn. If we were to go anywhere, we had better hurry. "Come, Rouen." As we had done so many times before, we clasped ourselves together and rose into the air.

"Where are we going?" His voice dissolved into a whisper in the wind, his long hair streaming back against my face. He no longer feared flying with me, in fact, he seemed to relish it.

"Rouen...." Something occurred to me. "Have you ever attempted it yourself?"

"Don't!" His fingers dug into my shoulders, painfully. "I pray you, don't drop me." His lips were white with fear.

"You probably have the same abilities as I do." I shifted him in my arms. "It takes but a thought to rise into the air."

"I... can't do it." He hid his face against my shoulder.

"Rouen...." I lifted his chin. "Have you ever tried?"

"No. I wouldn't be able to do it like you do."

I spun him out, a little distance away from me. The wind rose around him, lifted his hair into a dark halo, fluttered the edges of his cloak.

"Dante, please—"

"Hold tight to my hand," I told him. "I promise, I won't let you fall." I felt a little bit like Christ, balancing the Apostle Peter so that he might walk on water.

"You are *not* Christ, despite what you might think." Rouen's face was twisted with fear and clearly horrified. "Dante, pull me in!"

"Go out a little farther, to the extent of my fingers. Go on." I stretched my arm out, our fingers laced together, opened my hand and reeled him out into the night. He floated there in front of me, a vision. "You belong among the stars." I eased my wrist, slid my fingers out of his, whispered to him along the summer winds, "*Fly, Rouen!*"

He disappeared from view.

"Jesu Cristo!" I spun full about, turned a complete circle. He was nowhere in sight. I flipped so that I was head downward in relation to the ground, peered down through the layers of darkness—he was falling, I knew it, and it was all my fault, my *arrogance* that pushed him when he wasn't ready. "Oh *God....*" I pressed my hands against my eyelids, praying madly, although I don't know why—I didn't believe, in those days, that He ever heard the pleas I made. I wasn't mortal, after all.

A pair of hands went around my waist, drew me backward till I came to rest against another body. "Rouen! Oh, thank God...." I turned in his embrace, lay against him gently. "Very nicely done, Ser." I was shivering with relief.

"Dante, this is a miracle!" His eyes gleamed with delight, smiling into mine; his expression was jubilant. "I wish I had tried it before now." He cupped my face between his palms and kissed me. "What things we could do aloft, *mi amante....*"

He had a point. I returned his embrace, and for a few blissful moments there was silence, the caress of hands and lips, the weight of my immortal darling in my arms. "Rouen, look down there—" I pointed to the large dark island, directly beneath us. "That expanse of water is the Channel, and that is England." I flipped onto my head and dove, streaking through the air, then reversed and bobbed back up beside Rouen. "It is your choice. We can stay aloft or we can go down."

"How long can we stay like this? In the air?" He stepped sideways into nothing, as if dancing, put out a hand and felt among the stars.

"I don't know. But I wouldn't recommend it when the sun rises." I moved to where he was, took his hand in mine. "Shall we descend, Messer?"

He gazed at me, eyes large and beautifully reflective, his face the cool perfection of a statue. How I loved him! "Is there a technique to landing, also?"

"Just hold my hand," I told him, as we dropped through layers of air, "and I promise it will be all right."

"*Dante!*" A stream of frustrated swearing, several inventive curses. "I am standing in a *bog*!"

I scrambled down off the hillock where I'd landed, skidding on my hands and knees. He was indeed standing in a bog, and it smelled foul. "I think perhaps—"

"Pull me out! Now!"

"Right away, Messer. On my word, Messer." I grunted, yanked him out. "Will there be anything else, Messer?"

"Oh, shut up!" he exclaimed crossly. "How is it that you can land perfectly well and I fall into that... that... stinking cesspool!"

I wrinkled my nose. "Rouen, my darling, you smell of shit."

WE SLIPPED anonymous into the teeming mass of London, safely ensconced in a land where Serenola's influence—at least so far—was unknown. Periodically, news filtered out from Florence, reached our ears by way of traveling minstrels, the captains of ill-fated plague ships who had dumped their cargo on some Italian shore and fled. The plague was becoming worse, the death toll mounting easily into the thousands. Rouen and I heard how there was no help to be had in Florence now: if anyone was afflicted, they died alone, without succor. I thought of Salvatore, was grimly glad that he had died in the early days of this tribulation.

Despite the spread of plague, now rampant at the height of summer, London was a very cluttered town, busily engaged in its affairs without heed of outside catastrophe. Indeed, pilgrims still traveled from London to Canterbury, much as they had before the onset of the plague. I supposed that there is that place in the human soul that desires spiritual sustenance, and thus requires a regular demonstration of faith.

"Do you think Valentin is among them?" Rouen asked this one evening, as we were sitting in a tavern in Cheapside. There was a group of pilgrims across from us, gossiping and telling stories, a motley collection of personages from various social stations.

I shook my head. "No."

"Why not, Dante?" He gestured at the group. "They are a motley bunch… Valentin could well be among them, in another guise."

"Rouen, you are clutching at false hope." I could see a knight among their number, a miller, a couple of nuns, an obese friar with a face like the rising moon. There was no pardoner. "If Valentin were there, I am certain we would see him." I turned back to my ale, pretended to drink. I wished that Rouen would stop mentioning Valentin every chance he got, as if the erstwhile pardoner would suddenly materialize before our astonished gaze.

"Hail and well met!" A hearty, booming voice captured my attention. I glanced up to see a sturdy young man with ruddy cheeks, well dressed, smiling at us. "Are you to make pilgrimage yourselves?"

I shot a gaze at Rouen. "No—that is, we are but visiting."

He cocked his head. "Ah… I recognize that accent. Italian?"

Rouen, make him go away! "Quite correct, Ser."

He pulled out a bench and sat down. "I hear the incidence of plague is very high in Florence. How do the people fare?" I noticed the strand of beads, twined around his fist. He was slender to the point of gauntness, but with beautifully sculpted bones; his nose was thin, a trifle pointed on the end, but this was offset by his large, clear eyes that wavered between blue and green, and the elegant arch of his brows.

"We have been away from Florence since well before the plague, Ser," I replied. Rouen nudged me, a painful jab with his elbow. "But I hear the death toll is mounting daily."

"That is most unfortunate." Sadness flickered briefly across his narrow, pleasant face. "I have traveled often to Florence, it is a lovely city." He grinned, suddenly remembering his manners. "Oh... forgive me, Messer. I forget myself. I am Geoffrey."

We nodded, bowed across the table to each other, ridiculously. "I am Dante, and this is Rouen. I see you are making pilgrimage... to Canterbury?"

He smiled. "Yes, to the shrine of St. Thomas à Becket. Would you choose to join us, Messer? We are a lively company, and there is plenty room in our little group for others."

"Thank you, that is very kind, but we have other business at this time." I sighed inwardly—the very last thing I was wont to do right now was to go gallivanting off to seek God in some fusty English shrine. How would his band of gentle pilgrims react when Rouen and I started feasting on them? I chuckled at the thought.

"You seem a merry sort... come and join our company. We are telling tales to pass the time before we depart for Canterbury." He stood, waited for Rouen and I to join him, until it would have been an outright affront to refuse.

"WE HAVE new friends to join our company, if only for the telling of the tales." Geoffrey waved us into seats, throwing his arms about effusively. "This is Dante, and Rouen, visiting from Florence."

Immediately the crowd drew back. I saw the knight reach instinctively toward the handle of his sword; the nun nearest us went white with fear.

"Please, do not trouble yourselves. Dante and I have been away from Florence now for some several years. We have not come to bring the plague to you." Rouen smoothed things over with a facile lie. "Now pray, continue with your tales. Dante and I will listen."

The miller launched into a bawdy tale that, as far as I could see, expounded on the art of cuckoldry, an impending flood, and a young bravo by the name of Nicholas who farted at inappropriate times. "Rouen, I cannot see—"

But Rouen was laughing uproariously at this, clearly enjoying it all tremendously. "Dante, it's *hilarious*! Can you not picture it with the mind's eye? Young Nicholas, being branded on the arse for his trouble!"

"Rouen, I've heard enough; pray come along—"

And then I saw him. A flash of short, cropped silver hair, at the edges of the crowd, a flicker as he went past, too fast for the mortal eye to discern. I felt as if the floor had fallen out from under me.

"Dante, what is it?" Rouen spoke to me aside, whispering. "Are you unwell?"

"Rouen, I saw him!" My scalp prickled; there, I glimpsed him again, moving in and out of the crowd.

"Who?" He touched my arm, concerned. "Who did you see, *mi cuore*?"

"Valentin!"

He glanced around him, frowning. "Dante, I doubt it. He is not here."

A flicker, Valentin slipping past us. Rouen went rigid, his eyes as large as trenchers. "Dante, did you feel that?"

"Yes," I whispered. "Rouen, he is here, and he is summoning our attention." I rose from my seat. "Gentle pilgrims, Rouen and I must needs depart." I bowed gracefully. "But we thank you for your most entertaining company." I laid a handful of coins down on the table. "Pray, have meat and drink with our kind compliments."

"Must you depart so soon?" Geoffrey's hand upon my arm. "We have so many other tales to tell, and the evening is new."

"I'm sorry, but we must." I squeezed his shoulder. "I wish you a pleasant journey to Canterbury."

"May God bless you, Sir." He grinned, bowed, and returned to his company of pilgrims. I was unutterably thankful that we had not aroused his curiosity.

"Rouen, where is he?" I looked for him amongst the crowd.

"Dante, he is standing by the door—no, there!"

I bolted from the table, Rouen at my heels, stopped short of actually crushing Valentin in my arms. "Valentin?"

He was badly dressed, his cloak tattered and dirty, his hose ripped in several places. His boots were badly scuffed, the leather gaping around the soles. He looked wretched. "Dante...." He peered at me curiously. "What is this place?"

"Valentin, you are in England." Rouen moved toward him, hands outstretched. "You have been ill, and we have been looking for you."

Valentin flinched away from him, eyes huge in his pale face. "I have not been ill!" he retorted, scornfully.

"How are you?" I asked gently. I wondered if he had been feeding, and on whom. "We have missed you, Valentin."

But already his gaze was sliding away from us. "I must go."

"Valentin!"

His presence flickered into nothing and was gone. I stepped outside, took several deep breaths, willed the tears away. My throat felt tight, as if stuffed; it was difficult to breathe.

"Shhh, it's all right, *tesoro*." Rouen pulled me into the alleyway, took me into his arms, held me while I clung to him and sobbed.

"Why is he doing this?" I demanded. "Rouen, we have to find him!"

"Dante, we cannot force him to come with us." He lifted my face, wiped my cheeks with his handkerchief. "He is a liberated being. We have no claim upon his loyalty."

"Exactly what you said in Florence," I told him bitterly. "And here he is, running mad in London." I backed away, tripped over something lying on the ground.

"*Jesu Cristo!*" Rouen gagged, pressed his hand against his lips.

It was a body. I bent to peer at it, saw that the throat had been torn out, the eyes gouged, the chest ripped open and the heart extracted. I remembered Cardinal Gioletti, Valentin plunging a hand into his chest to pull out the still-beating heart. I knew that this body would have been completely drained of blood. *Valentin....*

"It's his victim, isn't it?" Rouen had flattened himself against the wall. "Valentin did this, didn't he?"

"Yes." I smiled grimly. "He did a fine job of it... the only problem is that he took no thought to hide the body."

"Then he's forgotten what you taught him."

"Perhaps." It was not something I wanted to contemplate. I knew that Valentin would be driven to take life in order to survive, as we all were, but I worried about this evidence of carelessness. "If it continues, he may well be discovered."

"In a city this size?" Rouen's disbelief was evident. "I hardly think it likely, Dante."

"If he is killing randomly and being careless about the bodies, then he will be discovered, Rouen, by someone who knows him, who sees him going in and out." I straightened, nudged the body with my foot. "It is but a matter of time until he betrays himself."

"We have to find him."

"We will not find him if he wishes otherwise." I wondered where, in all the teeming mass of London, Valentin kept lodgings. I knew that there must be some place for him to sleep during the day, unless he merely went to ground.

"Dante, we have some responsibility to him."

I stared at him. "In what manner? Valentin is hardly our responsibility." I resented Rouen's attempted moral lesson.

"You made him, Dante. You owe some regard to his wellbeing."

"Rouen—" I took his arm. "For God's sake, come out of this stinking alley." We stepped into the street.

"Dante!" His tone stopped me cold. "Either seek him and return him to health, or destroy him completely!" He was shaking, his slender body taut and rigid as a bowstring. "You have a duty to him!"

"A *duty*? To destroy him, Rouen?" I could not believe what I was hearing. "So in the future, should you take with some immortal brain fever, I should destroy you out of kindness?" What a monstrous notion!

"If I were incapacitated, then yes... I would prefer that you destroy me." His mouth quivered at the corners. "It is not a fate I like to contemplate, but it is a possibility."

I was stunned into silence.

"I am certain that if you were similarly disabled...."

I turned on him. "I pray you, stay your reason, Rouen! You and I are not so similar as you fancy!" It horrified me, the thought that he would dispose of me once I was no longer perfect.

"You are talking nonsense."

"I am talking truth! Come down from the Campanile, Rouen—"

"Gentlemen!" A different voice, beckoning us from just beyond the corner. "Come here."

Rouen glanced at me, brows knit. "Make known your intentions, Ser."

The robed figure glided to us, slid between Rouen and I and slipped an arm around our waists. "Why are you no longer in your female guise?"

I recognized the voice, finally. "Fernando!" I pulled him to me, embraced him joyously. "What brings you here?"

"I had no word from you and it worried me. I wondered if perhaps something had gone wrong." Fernando related how he had gone as far as Spain, and finding our apartments in the Juderia destroyed, had tracked us here. I dared not ask how, or inquire as to what methods he had used. Fernando, I'd discovered, was a man of unparalleled innovation. God only knew the ways in which he'd bargained his way across the continent.

"Why are you dressed this way?" I examined his drab, dark robes, not unlike the clothing of a priest. "Have you taken vows?"

"I am in disguise, buffoon." He posed for us, one foot pointed as if he were standing for a portrait. "I am a Cathar."

Rouen snorted. "Fernando, there are no Cathars in England. Indeed, I wonder if there are any left in Italy." He referred to the alternative group of religious who, designated as a threat to the established Church, were mercilessly hounded into extinction.

"What is the news from home, Fernando?"

"Florence is riddled with plague, and Serenola's followers have evolved into hysterical madmen. There are tortures and burnings regularly." His face clouded. "Messer Tralini died last week—"

"May God have mercy on him," Rouen interjected, bitterly.

"—and the inn is closed. Therefore, you see why I am free to wander."

"Fernando...." I took his hand. "Have you any means?" I would not see him go without, not when Rouen and I could sustain him.

"Oh, indeed." He patted his purse. "I am a man of many means."

"You need not be coy with us, Ser." Rouen clasped his other

hand. "If you have need, then you must tell us."

We had reached our lodgings, and I ushered Fernando upstairs to the tiny suite of rooms we kept. "Rouen, light the fire." Despite the height of summer, London was drab and foggy this night. Too long used to the heat of Tuscany, it chilled my bones. "Now Fernando, tell me. Have you need of anything?"

"Dante, please!" He laughed, slapped at me playfully. "My family name stands me in good stead, and we are rich. Indeed, the rate at which the plague is decimating us puts florins in my pocket."

Ugh. That was rather grim. "Are all of you so mercenary?" I asked. I offered him a cup of wine.

"Indeed. Mercenary is our business." He supped it gratefully, held it out for more. "I am a Medici."

"Fernando...."

He held up a hand. "Please, Dante." He cast his drab robes aside, revealed a rich velvet doublet, fine embroidered hose. "Do you think my family would rush to claim me publicly if they knew how I made my living?"

I could not comprehend his choices. "Fernando, pray tell me why—"

"Enough, Dante." Rouen shot me a glance. "There are those of us who, being sons of prominent families, must hide the truth of our lives. Pray, do not belabor this." His eyes begged me, *please*.

So Rouen knew of Fernando's background. Perhaps this was why they had bonded to each other as such good friends. "I see." I could just imagine the reprisals of the Medici if they knew that one of their well-born sons preferred to spend his time dressed up as a lady. Granted, Fernando made just as beautiful a lady as he did a handsome man. "Well, then." I was at a loss for words, and I felt awkward.

"Come, Fernando." Rouen adroitly stepped into the gap. "Tell us news of home."

AFTER Fernando had departed, Rouen and I lingered, sated on good conversation and congenial company, before the dying fire. I was thinking about Valentin; indeed, I had not ceased to think of him since last we'd seen him in the tavern.

"What is it?" Rouen rolled onto his stomach, gazed at me, his chin propped in his hand. "You have been pensive all evening."

"I am thinking of Valentin. Rouen, what do you suppose will become of him?"

"I don't know." I felt his mind withdraw from mine. "He is a wretched thing, indeed."

"Rouen, what if Lilith finds him?"

"Lilith has no use for Valentin. In his present state, he could be of no service to her." He patted my arm, smiled. "The dawn comes, and I am tired. Come along to bed."

Chapter 16

July 1348
Florence

LUDOVICO SERENOLA

"WHY have you come here?" I rose from the table to confront him, standing in the doorway of my cell, resplendent as always in his clerical robes. The sight of him sickened me; I was too pure, now, to sully myself by associating with such as his kind.

"Fra Ludovico, I pray you, do not be so hasty." He slid sinuously into the room, looking so very like Gioletti that I forced myself to remember.

Gioletti was dead. Of course. He had been found murdered, with his heart ripped out. His flyblown corpse rotted in the Piazza still....

I wondered which of his scurrilous minions had done it.

"Cardinal Prosti, I beg of you. The hour is late." I had been drowsing at the table with my copy of St. Thomas. I wondered what possessed him to disturb me now. Tomorrow was Sunday, and the faithful of God would expect me to deliver the most recent of His missives. I could do no less.

"Ah, but Ludovico...." He seated himself opposite me, reached and took the book out of my hands. "This morning I received inquiry from the family of Fra Vittore."

I stiffened. My chest began to throb, a painful beating like a wound. "Truly?" I slipped my spectacles off, laid them on the table. It was easier to feign indifference if I were nearly blind. "Regarding what?"

"Regarding his disappearance." He leaned back, considered me through slitted eyes. Yes, the resemblance to Gioletti was indeed there, so much so that it was eerie. "And Fra Ludovico, I would give gentle reminder also from the Holy See."

"Indeed."

"His Holiness is most… *concerned* with the tenor of your most recent preaching. His Holiness wonders if perhaps your zeal outstrips your wisdom. His Holiness—"

I rose and walked rapidly away from him, stood at the casement to compose myself.

"—wonders if perhaps you might desist."

Rage drew me taut as a bowstring. I turned to face him slowly. "I am the instrument of God. I deliver such message as He gives me, and who are you to say me otherwise?"

"I would warn you—"

"You would *warn* me?" I rounded on him savagely. "You come waddling in here, dressed in your luxurious excess, and suppose to warn me about the tenor of my preaching?" I couldn't believe this; surely the Holy See had taken leave of reason. Didn't Prosti know that all of Florence flocked each Sunday to the Duomo to hear me? "Such gaudy excess as you flaunt is the greatest sin of all!"

"Fra Ludovico. I pray you, stay your reason." Prosti rose and moved toward me, a great lumbering shadow in the candlelight. "The Holy See is not without compassion." His gaze flickered over my face. "Fra Vittore was a novice under you instruction, yes? But so often novices do stray."

I wondered where this was leading. "Of course. We are all

capable of sin, each of us." I remembered my lust for Madonna di Francisci. I treasured the lock of raven hair that my acolytes had brought me, and I was glad that their holy purpose had dispatched her into Heaven.

"And Fra Vittore, I am told, was of your company when you traveled to Prato?"

A great shroud of fear dropped about my shoulders, weighed upon my neck. "Yes."

"Ah." He spread his hands expansively. "And never did return from Prato. His mount was found wandering in the hills."

I swallowed with great difficulty.

"Fra Ludovico, I see that we are at an impasse." His arm slid about my neck. "But there is a way out of it, as I am certain you yourself can understand."

"What do you want?" I thought about the crowds that would throng the Duomo tomorrow morning, overflowing into the Piazza. I thought about the mounting death toll from the pestilence, the corresponding corruption and apostasy that surely drew fire down from Heaven. And I knew what Prosti would ask of me.

"The Holy See values her holdings both here and abroad. Indeed, such material wealth as she now owns has come to her through the dedicated efforts of such faithful as yourself." Prosti's arm tightened perceptibly about my throat. "Fra Ludovico, pray limit your zealous urgings to the sins of common folk. His Holiness desires that your criticism of the Church would stop."

I stepped away from him. "I bring such message as the Lord Jesus Christ Himself would bring. You have no place to threaten me in this manner!" I took myself firmly in hand; I would not be cowed by such as him.

"And it is not meet that you should rain damnation down upon the heads of those who serve the Holy See!" he thundered, lunging at me. My head began to throb, my eyeballs seared. "Fra Ludovico, I tell it to you plain: there are those of us who know the conditions of your soul.

And I assure you: Fra Vittore speaks aloud, even from the grave!"

"Get out." I drew a quivering breath. "Leave me!"

The door swung open and he was gone. I trod a wavering path into the garden, leaned over a hedge of roses, and vomited till I was empty.

THE Duomo was full when I ascended to the altar, laid my trembling hands on either side of the pulpit. I glanced out over the sea of faces, wondering if the treacherous Prosti was among them. I was still shaken by my confrontation with him last night. He reminded me too much of Gioletti, and Gioletti was something I would sooner forget.

But I was here now. And I paused to invoke Him, request the honor of His holy anointing. He is so often visited upon me of late, His grace descending like a dove.

"My brothers." My voice cracked; I swallowed and began again. "The time has come for us to cast off the material vagaries of our unholy nature, to refuse the excess of luxury such as we have grown accustomed to."

There was a flicker of red at the edges of my vision. Prosti, slipping through the multitude.

"It is time to purify ourselves by burning." I felt the excitement mounting, His holy anointing at work within my spirit. And I didn't care about Prosti, or the sins of Gioletti, and I knew that Fra Vittore was in Heaven and I was God's ambassador. And I flung wide my arms to encompass the whole of them, and I loved them, as Jesus loved them. "My friends and my companions—"

Prosti was standing before the pulpit, his face a mask of stone.

"—it is time to ignite the bonfire of the vanities."

They poured into the Piazza and heaped their possessions high: rich velvet garments, gold and jewels, fine plates of brass and cups of silver. Women tore their earrings off, took the rings from their fingers, unclasped their necklaces of pearl and flung them onto the pile. A novice of our order uncorked a pot of pitch and poured it on the wealth.

And then I struck the tinder. The fire roared like all the fiends of hell, consumed the idle wealth. We clasped hands about the flames and danced and sang, our tears streaming down our faces.

Truly, I had been born for this.

Chapter 17

July 1348
London

ROUEN

"ROUEN, I cannot stand it anymore."

I turned from the window, shaken from my contemplations by this abrupt pronouncement. "Dante?" It was high summer, a glorious evening, and I was amusing myself in observation of the mortals passing on the street below. We had been in London for some weeks now, and the parade of strange and motley individuals that nightly passed below our casements never ceased to interest me. Watching them had become a favorite habit of late.

"Lilith. I cannot know what her next injunction might be, and yet I am supposed to wait until she sees fit to render judgment!" He tugged at the neck of his shirt, pulled the laces. It was abominably hot, even for us. "I want to *do* something, Rouen!" This had become Dante's constant complaint.

"Dante, I'm sure I don't know what you mean." I pulled my shirt over my head, loosened the laces of my hose. I had opened all the windows, but in vain; there was no breeze. I considered whether it was proper to loll about in only my drawers.

"We have to do something." He spoke in that decisive tone that I knew so well, and which I dreaded, because it so often heralded some unreasoned action. "If Lilith will not come to us, then we will go to her." He brushed his hair off his forehead, peevishly.

"Are you mad?" I laughed, astonished. "Or are you so desirous of disaster that you run to meet it headlong?" I reached to press my fingers against his face. "No fever… it must be madness."

"Stop patronizing me!" He slapped my hand away. "Rouen, I am stewing here in this infernal English cesspool! We come and go, and seek our pleasure in the tavern, and talk to Geoffrey and his company,"—The pilgrims had returned but days ago—"and listen to the carts rolling underneath our windows."

"I can do nothing about the carts," I told him vaguely. This aimless conversation was annoying me. "Look, Dante, if you are bored why not seek company more congenial than mine? I am certain Geoffrey is at this hour in the tavern."

I glanced about as there came a tap upon the door. "Ho, within!" I tossed a blanket over me and went to answer it.

"Rouen—" It was Fernando. "Mother of God, it's hot!" He stepped into our rooms, "What amuses you this evening, Dante?"

"Fernando, I was just about to go down to the tavern."

This was news to me. "But a moment ago you were noising loudly about your boredom. Why the sudden sea-change?" I hoped that his comrades in the tavern would amuse him sufficiently to drive the idea of Lilith from his mind.

"I thought perhaps I might seek company more congenial than yours." He stuck out his tongue as he passed behind me, disappeared down the stairs, leaving Fernando and I alone.

We had seen much of Fernando since he first appeared to us, a familiar face in a sea of strangers. Thankfully, he had abandoned his Cathar disguise for his normal dress, and anyway, I suspected that he first affected it as much for novelty as for any other reason. Fernando possessed that sense of drama, and truth be told, I suspected he rather enjoyed dressing up in costumes.

"So how goes it, Rouen?" He slid gracefully into a chair, tossed his cloak upon the bed. "Have you adapted well to the English climate?"

"Dante is rather disaffected with our present status," I told him. That was an understatement, to be sure. Dante at the best of times was fractious, unrestrained. I did not relish another lengthy stretch of time in these small rooms with him.

"Ah." Fernando gave me a knowing glance. "So the bloom is off the rose?"

"I beg your pardon?" I went to the cupboard, poured him a cup of wine. "I don't know what you mean."

"You and Dante… no longer the feckless young lovers, drowning in each other's eyes?" He swigged the wine, trapped me in his speculative glance. "Because if not, there are others, Rouen, who would cherish the privilege…."

Laughter caught me unawares. "*You?*"

"Yes, of course." His tone was hurt. "Why not me?" He passed me his empty cup, waited while it was refilled. "Dante is obviously enamored with his poet friend…."

"Geoffrey Chaucer?" I stared at him. "Oh come along, Fernando! Dante's admiration of Geoffrey is purely intellectual, a mutual admiration. Besides which, Geoffrey is not of our sort." I felt slightly queasy; I didn't like where this discussion was going. "Enough," I told him. "What is the news from home?"

"Rouen, the news from home is very bad." He leapt into it, without preamble, and I was thankful that he accepted my refusal of his overtures. "The pestilence is worse, and I fear that Serenola's madness is heading this way soon. Already there is talk in the taverns of God's holy vengeance.'" Fernando made a face, blessed himself dramatically, eyes rolling. "I fear these doughty Englishmen will soon begin to hunt those whom they suspect have taint." He snorted, quaffed another mouthful of the wine. "You know, these Christians do quite tickle me,

Rouen… all this talk of hellfire and damnation. You'd think we were all damned for eternity if we refused the final Unction."

"You speak as if you are not Christian." I wondered what, if anything, Fernando believed. He had never spoken openly of faith, but then, neither did any others of my acquaintance. I did remember attending Mass when I was a child, my mother nodding over her Book of Hours on a Sunday. I suspected Fernando had no deep religious feeling, nor had ever had any.

"I speak as if I knew the convictions of my soul." His hazel eyes caught and held my gaze. "You know truth as well as I, Rouen. If there is a loving God somewhere, why does He allow this damnation of pestilence?" He made an irritated noise, set his cup down on the table with a clang. "So much nonsense." He moved to where I was. "You realize that the madness you fled in Florence is now creeping into England."

I understood him utterly. "So we are neither more safe here than we are anywhere." Was there any place on earth for our kind?

He blinked. "Well, you could travel southward to the new lands, there are ships leaving daily. I am certain you might book passage, even tomorrow morning."

"Fernando…." I bit my lip. "There are limits to the times when we may travel. Dante and I move mostly in the night. I am not certain we could endure a sustained sea voyage." I shuddered to think where we might hide ourselves on a crowded vessel, where on earth we would find shelter from the sunlight, never mind the necessity of blood.

"But surely you could arrange your itinerary, to travel till you had reached safe port." He frowned. "Rouen, is there something that you aren't telling me?"

I was silent.

"Rouen." He touched my arm. "No secrets. We are friends, very nearly brothers. Tell me what it is."

"I cannot."

"But surely—" He moved around to face me as I moved away. "But surely it cannot be so horrible! Rouen, you must trust me!" His gaze wandered over my face. "You don't trust me," he said flatly.

"It's not that—"

"No, please." He took a deep breath, biting his lips. "Make no apologies to me." Damn him! He pretended hurt so skillfully that I was forced to capitulate, offer him some kind of explanation.

"Dante and I are afflicted with...." How to phrase it? "A... condition of the skin that precludes our exposure to sunlight." I swallowed hard. "Pray, question me no further."

"Well, then." He peered at me. "Is it contagious?"

"No. Dante infected me with it, but can communicate it to no one else." My God! I made it sound like some kind of exotic venereal disease....

"Do you mean...?" And Fernando was thinking exactly that. "Does it affect the male parts, then?"

"Fernando!" I tried to keep from laughing, gave up and roared. "What a filthy mind you have!"

He pulled me to him, suddenly, his hazel eyes alight. "Rouen, we are alone."

"But Dante—"

"Is in the tavern with his poet friend, that Chaucer fellow. And you and I are here." As he spoke, he walked me back toward the bed, pushed so that it caught behind my knees and felled me like a tree. He caught my face between his hands and kissed me with a consummate skill; desire rose and broke in me like waves. "Pray, Rouen, do you like to play rough?"

I had no idea what he meant, until he drew back and slapped me in the face. I gasped, recoiled and slapped him hard, drove him against the wall. *Jesu Cristo!* I had forgotten my preternatural strength. "My God, Fernando, I'm sorry!"

"Rouen, you ought to check that slap, *tesoro*. You nearly killed me." He felt his jaw ruefully, slipped a finger inside his mouth. "I think

I'm bleeding."

"Let me see."

This was my fatal mistake. For as I drew near to him, the scent of his mortal blood rose into my nostrils, enticing, a smell that surpassed all fleshly desire. I caught his face to mine and kissed the corner of his mouth, flicked his bleeding lips with my tongue. My fangs slid down out of my gums; I was blinded with the hunger, I could smell the blood in him....

"Rouen...." He resisted, his palms pressing uselessly against my shoulders, naked fear standing in his eyes. "Please, don't...."

I rolled, pinned him beneath me, this delicious morsel of humanity....

"Rouen, for God's sake, *stop*!" A shoulder slammed into me, rolled me off Fernando, pushed me against the wall. "Stop!"

My eyes focused slowly. Dante. "I thought you were in the tavern," I said thickly. Fernando crouched against the opposite wall, terrified and shaking.

"Rouen, do you realize...?" He cursed me bitterly, turned to attend Fernando. "Come and sit over by the window, Ser, you need fresh air."

"Don't touch me...." The young Medici gripped Dante's shoulder, stared at me with eyes glazed. "Don't let him touch me, Dante, he's a monster."

"Well then, darling Fernando, so am I." Dante pulled a chair for him and pushed him into it. "And now you know our little secret." *Rouen, you are an idiot and a very great fool!*

"What are you talking about? I don't know what you're talking about." Fernando's lower lip quivered uncontrollably, and without warning, he burst into noisy sobs.

"Bravo, Rouen." Dante straightened to glare at me. "Another tactful handling of a delicate situation. Truly, for one well-born, you have an appalling lack of skill."

"This is why you fled, isn't it?" Fernando moved to where we were, crying noisily. "It has nothing to do with plague, with Serenola. You're a *monster*!"

"It has *everything* to do with Serenola!" I snapped. "He killed my family."

"Then why did you not destroy him with your strength, disperse his minions?" Fernando sniffed, rubbed a hand across his nose. His lower lip still bled freely.

"Because Rouen and I are only two and we cannot fight all of them ourselves. And there are larger matters at hand." Dante mentioned nothing of Valentin, and I was grateful. Fernando did not need to know there was another of our kind; it was enough that he had discovered us.

"What kind of a... *creature* are you?" He glanced at Dante and at me. "Are you devils?"

"Yes," Dante replied ruthlessly. "We enjoy a certain distinguished damnation, you might say."

"Have you been cast out of the Church? Is that what this means?" His mind riffled through the alternate possibilities, found nothing it could fasten upon.

"Fernando." Dante sat down upon the floor. "Rouen and I are nothing mortal." And he proceeded to tell Fernando the entire tale, sparing nothing. I listened with a growing uneasiness; I felt rather less than certain that this was the correct thing to do. By imparting to Fernando at least the partial truth, we opened ourselves up to deeper scrutiny. I wondered vaguely if perhaps it might not be best to kill him.

"So you must take blood to survive? Is this correct?" Fernando glanced from Dante to me, back again.

"Precisely." Dante caught my eye, shook his head abruptly, as if to warn me from saying otherwise. He seemed to have once again discerned my stream of consciousness. "It is really more like a disease of sorts. A physical condition."

I shot him a poisonous glance: *Liar.*

"Oh." Fernando hugged his arms against his chest, an unconscious gesture. "Well, then." He seemed to accept our explanation easily. Something about that unquestioning acceptance bothered me, but there was nothing upon which I could readily fasten my suspicion.

"But don't worry, we won't harm you." Dante smiled crookedly, his mouth twisted in a travesty of humor.

"I'm glad to hear it." Fernando grimaced slightly, pressed a hand against his cheek. "But truthfully, Rouen, I would not wish to come against you, that slap nearly killed me!"

Damn! I flushed hot, suddenly embarrassed. "Fernando." And now Dante would discover everything, and there would surely be a scene....

"What does he mean, Rouen? Did you slap him?" Dante gazed at me, lips pursed. "Why?"

I thought furiously, plumbed the depths of my imagination for some suitable rejoinder. "Dante, Fernando and I—"

"You were going to fuck him, weren't you?" The accusation splintered like broken glass into the midst of us. "While I was in the tavern, talking to Geoffrey Chaucer. You were going to have him, weren't you, Rouen?"

He had caught me out. "That's rather an indelicate way of putting it, but—"

Dante laughed.

Fernando shifted uneasily. "Perhaps I should be going," he said quietly. The tension in the room tightened, the walls contracting in on us.

"No, Fernando, I pray you, stay. Rouen is quite a spectacle when he is angry—all that righteous indignation. Isn't that so, Rouen?"

"Dante." I was miserable, deeply ashamed. "Please."

He stalked across the room, caught my face between finger and thumb. "Look at him, Fernando. Is he not a beauty?" He squeezed my cheeks cruelly. "For all that he is a demon."

"Stop it!" I slapped his hand away. "The heat has disturbed your brains."

"Rouen, I will speak with you later." Fernando edged toward the door.

"No!" Dante caught his arm, wheeled him savagely back into the room. "I insist you stay."

"Dante, leave him alone!" I shoved him backward, angrily. "You have no quarrel with him, your dispute is with me."

"And who is to say me otherwise, Rouen? You?" He slapped me, an irritating little cuff, with the back of his fist. "You, the highborn son of the house of Francisci who buggers boy whores at Tralini's?"

"I warn you, Dante!"

"Do you indeed, Rouen? Do you warn me?" He laughed uproariously, spun in a circle. "Do you hear, Fernando? He *warns* me!"

"Dante. I pray you, go no further." My belly throbbed painfully, like hunger.

"How much further?" He slapped me again, another annoying smack, a dry cuff against my cheek. "How far do you want to take it, Rouen?" He turned to address Fernando. "What about you, Fernando di Medici? How far would you like to see us take it, hmm? Would you like to see Rouen beat me? Would that suit your fancy? Perhaps it excites you, to see us fighting. Or, wait! Perhaps it would be better if we both were stripped." He yanked his shirt over his head, tossed it away. His powerful torso was sweat-soaked, the muscles rippling underneath the skin. "Come strip, Rouen, and we will battle in the Greek fashion."

"You stop this, and you stop it *now*!" I was furious, my vision clouded with blood. "How dare you insult me, Ser?" Rage roared deep within my brain and I slammed him back against the wall, my fingers clamped around his throat. Oh yes, he was beautiful, he was so very beautiful like this, dangling helpless at the end of my extended arm.

"Beg mercy, Dante." Heat flooded up from deep within my belly, spilled into my loins, tingled along my limbs.

"Loose hold—" He choked, sputtering, his torso streaked with bloody sweat. "—Rouen!" His fingers wrapped around my wrist, prying my fingers loose.

"Beg for it, you filthy ill-born bastard."

"Rouen—"

"No mercy, Dante. Not this time." From the corners of my eyes I saw Fernando, sprawled upon the bed and watching us with keen astonishment. He was clearly deriving pleasure from the spectacle, fingers spread inside his codpiece. "Beg, *bastardo*."

"Please...." The rims of his eyes filled up with dark blood tears, his chest heaving. "Rouen." His mind slipped a tendril into mine, *I love you, why are you hurting me like this?*

My lip drew back, exposing my descended fangs. *Because I can! Because I enjoy it.*

His body whiplashed in my grip, legs kicking, and he freed himself, his sweat-slicked skin sliding from my grasp. He bolted but I caught him, slammed him back against me, tore his hose away, yanked his drawers down, exposing his naked buttocks. "You suppose I like to bugger strong young men, Dante...." I pressed my hand against his neck, forced his head down. "Pray you witness this—" I freed myself, slammed into him, buried myself hilt-deep within his body.

He jerked, pushed back against me, his hands sliding on my thighs, my waist, scrabbling for purchase. He was desperate, and he was ashamed, I could feel a myriad of dark emotions throbbing underneath his skin. His mind flickered evil, as his fingertips dug into me, fighting to force me off him.

I plunged into him, the delicious friction creating a frisson of sensation all along my limbs, withdrew, plunged into him again. I controlled him, and I enjoyed it; he was mine, I owned him as surely as if I had paid for his service. I considered, cruelly, that perhaps this was what he was best suited for, Dante.

It's Christmas, take it.... A handful of florins tinkled to the floor beside him, Dante shivering in an anonymous inn. *It's Christmas... take it....* Covering him with my cloak, easing the hurt I'd caused him, by standing by and watching it be so. *Why are you hurting me like this?*

Because I can... Release shivered in my belly, erupted in a powerful climax as I spent myself, pounded into him, shouting hoarsely. A great wave of dizziness washed over me, and I rested against his sweaty, naked back, panting. I felt sick to my stomach.

"Rouen...." Fernando rose and came to me, caught me in an incongruous embrace and kissed me, his turgid sex a bulge inside his hose. "Let me...."

"No." I pushed him away, wiped my face in my sleeve. "Go, now." I was desperately ashamed; I wished he hadn't seen it.

"But, Rouen—"

"I said, go!" I turned on him, fangs flashing, the blood-thirst rising in me as it so often did after consummation of fleshly desire. "If you value your mortal life, I bid you go now."

"I want you...." His opened mouth pressed against mine, tongue flickering, a point of heat. "Let me pleasure you."

"Go *away*, Fernando." I shoved him, stepped away. "Please."

He stood back, stared at me, his face expressionless. Small beads of sweat stood out on his forehead; his doublet was wet underneath the arms.

"Go."

He disappeared down the staircase, regret lingering behind him like an odor.

"Dante." He was trying to dress himself, pulling his drawers up over his hips, clutching the edges of his tattered hose with shaking fingers.

"Don't you touch me!" His head came up, eyes flashing fire, fangs curved wickedly above his lower lip. "Don't ever touch me again, Rouen." He was as I had seen him in the marketplace: angry, feral, his eyes a wild gleam in his pale face.

I noticed that his desire rose stiffly beneath the thick linen of his drawers. "You are still unsatisfied," I said.

"Don't touch me." He moved toward the casement, stood with his back to me, his shredded hose around his knees, an absurd flag. I had badly wronged him, made him ridiculous in both our eyes.

"Take this off. I'll get you new ones." I tugged at his hose, pulled them down and off. His skin was burning hot. Regret churned within my guts, a guilt so paramount I marveled that I could withstand it.

"Are you sorry, Rouen?" He watched me, leaning against the casement, a dark young god. I wondered if, again, he had allowed this assault upon himself, if he had deliberately provoked it by his accusations. I wondered why he thought he needed such ammunition of emotion. I wondered if I had done anything to make him feel this way.

"I am not sorry," I said. I regarded him, my head on one side. "You deserved it. You provoked it." I would not be drawn into the dangerous dance of pity with him, not this time. We had outgrown those roles.

"Yes, I suppose I did." Cautiously, eyes narrowed, gauging my reaction. "*Bravo.*" He moved into my embrace, a heated bundle in my arms. "How the dance has changed, Rouen." So he had divined my thoughts.

"Humiliating me in front of Fernando like that." I lifted his dark hair away and kissed his neck, nipped his earlobe between my teeth. He turned his face and took my lips, kissed me brutally, his hands against my waist. "I love you, Dante…." And I did, the sweat-slick heat of him, the delicious flesh. The evening was new; I could sink myself in him and forget everything else for a time….

"Rouen?"

A rustle near the door, an unaccustomed voice. I turned and there he was, standing at the top of the stairs, silvery and insubstantial as a shadow. His eyes were large and haunted, great translucent pools.

Dante started up, rushed toward him. "*Valentin!*"

"I have come to give you penance." Valentin regarded us calmly, yet with no hint of recognition. "You have sinned against God." His presence now was so diminutive as to be almost nothing at all, a slender immortal skeleton, flesh cleaving to his bones. He made no explanation as to why he had suddenly appeared here.

Dante glanced at me. "Valentin, won't you stay for awhile? Tell us what you have been doing." His voice was strained with horror; he could barely speak.

Valentin's pale hands dipped into his wallet, withdrew holding a small silver knife, and I watched in fascinated horror as he slit the white skin of his wrist.

"Rouen, don't let him do that!"

"Leave him." I couldn't tear my eyes from Valentin, this bizarre thing that he was enacting.

"I absolve you in the name of Jesus Christ our Lord." Valentin dipped a finger into the dark well of his wrist, drew a crude cross on Dante's forehead. Dante's eyes were huge, astonished; a muscle at the corner of his mouth twitched sporadically. "You can go to heaven now."

He advanced on me, his bloody finger outstretched. "Come receive pardon."

"Valentin, stop it! Please stop!" I caught his wrist, held him away from me. His body felt frail, creaking like old bones.

"Rouen, don't let him leave… he can lead us to Lilith, tell us of Serenola…." Dante moved to bar the door.

Valentin paused in the middle of the room and gazed about him, as if pondering his purpose here. I wondered if he perceived the danger to himself, merely being in our presence.

"Rouen, bring the candle."

I could not believe what I was hearing. "Dante, this is insanity, look what this has already wrought!" Valentin reduced to madness, selling pardons for Serenola.

"The *candle*!" He snatched it from the table, moved around behind Valentin, the flickering flame shielded behind his hand. "He will tell us all he knows. He will have no choice."

"I will not be privy to this." I moved away, caught my cloak from off the bed.

"Rouen, come back! You come back here, Rouen... don't you run away from me!" Shouting, furious, literally spitting with rage. "You participate in it, Rouen! The eradication of the species. *Rouen!*" He paused, stared at me, his features twisted with fury. "Then run, *coward*!"

I hastened down the stairs, unbarred the door, and passed from that cursed place. Behind me, I heard Valentin's agonized breathing as his body bent itself into that obedient rictus.

THE tavern's lights enticed me from the street, and so, casting off my heaviness, I went inside. At the very least, I thought, I could buy a pint of ale and sit among the people. The room was very full this evening; those that could go about had done so, and there was much cheer. I envied them, those feckless mortals who could so easily cast off trouble. I would give nearly anything to regain my own mortal nature.

"Rouen." A kindly voice, a hand upon my shoulder.

I looked up, saw Geoffrey standing there. "Oh!" I blinked, struggling to free myself from the morass of my own dark thoughts. "Geoffrey, I pray you, sit and have a cup of ale with me."

He was very finely dressed, in a gorgeous velvet doublet, embroidered hose and leather boots. He sported a new cap with a curving ostrich feather, evidence of some familial largesse. "How does this evening find you?"

I opened my mouth, closed it again without uttering a sound.

"Rouen, are you in distress?" He leaned toward me, touched my arm. His clear eyes were kindness itself, but I could not confide in him.

"Geoffrey, I want to say how precious it has been to me, knowing you." I clasped his hand, suddenly terrified by some dark premonition. "I will never forget you."

He drew back, smiling. "Why, Rouen… whatever is the matter? Are you determined to cast off the mortal coil?"

I braced my head against my hands. "No, nothing like that." I felt tears start behind my eyelids. "He's going to do it, he's going to plunge us into the midst of hell." I was mumbling, hardly aware of anything that I was saying, but I needed to make some sort of noise, or else I would take leave of myself.

"Who are you speaking of?"

"Dante." I started up, suddenly. "Geoffrey, do you know about this plague?"

"Rouen, drink your ale, and take good cheer, my friend. You are talking as if you have taken with a fever."

"Dante is trying to destroy me."

"Oh, come now! I somehow doubt that. He is your friend and good companion." Geoffrey impaled me with his penetrating gaze. "Rouen, is there something about Dante that troubles you? You have my bond of confidence, I assure you." He smiled, clasped my hand. "It distresses me to see you so distraught."

I caught his hand in mine, squeezed his fingers gently, pressed the smooth skin of his palm. I pondered whether I should disclose the truth to him, or if I ought better to keep silent. I trusted him, and I genuinely liked him, he was a fine young man of good conscience and unsullied morals.

And yet, he was but a mortal. How to explain to him the devastation that had yet to be unleashed upon the earth? I became immediately frightened; perhaps the plague might kill him. Perhaps I might pass this way in five years time, or ten, and inquiring after Geoffrey Chaucer, be shown a handsome stone laid in the churchyard.

I wanted to say something to him, something profound and memorable. I wished there were some small gift to give him, in gratitude for his unquestioning friendship.

"Geoffrey…." A thought occurred to me, a germ of an idea. I felt as I had that night that Dante encouraged me to fly. "What is your heart's desire?"

He laughed, rather uncertainly. "Why, Rouen. What encouraged this largesse?"

"No, my friend, I pray you, be serious. I am a man of means."

"My heart's desire?" He thought for a moment, his face contracted in concentration. When he again met my gaze, he appeared a little shamed. "It is a fool's wish. I cannot tell it to you, you would laugh at me."

A fist of ice squeezed itself around my heart, a chilly pain. "I would never laugh at you, my friend. Pray, tell me what it is."

His gaze slid away along the tabletop, his fingers tracing the pattern of the grain, nervously. "I…."

"Please." I was conscious of time running down, as sand sifting in the glass. "What is it?"

"I wish to write," he said quickly. "Poems and such, fine tales." He would not meet my gaze. "I fancy that I might like to be a man of letters."

I was charmed, and not surprised. I had suspected there was more beneath his solid, middle class exterior. "That is a fine wish," I whispered. In a moment, I would weep. "Perhaps tales of your pilgrimage to Canterbury."

I drew him near and laid my palm against his face. I wondered if it were within my power, or did it matter? Perhaps the gesture was enough to make it so. *I give you words….*

"Rouen, what is the matter with your eyes?" He drew back from me, alarmed.

"It is nothing, Geoffrey, not plague. It is another illness that I have had since childhood. It cannot harm you." I leaned quickly and kissed his hand. "I must go." I slipped away from him, hastened to the door. I was shaking badly; in a moment I knew I would collapse into weeping.

"Rouen." His hand upon my arm, turning me slowly toward him. "What did you do, just now?" He pressed his fingers to his face, his eyes shining with unshed tears.

There was no way that I could explain it to him, not in any terms that he would understand. "My gift of gratitude," I whispered. I clasped his hand, overcome with emotion, ducked my head and moved out into the night.

OUR rented rooms were the scene of devastation: the table overturned, legs broken, the glass windows smashed, the shutters wrenched from their hinges. It looked as if some beast had used it for a rampage. I wondered vaguely if Serenola had paid a visit.

"Dante, what is the meaning of this?" He was sitting on the bed, his back against the wall. A series of livid scratches, like finger marks, faded slowly on his cheek. His fangs were down. "What has been going on here?"

"I have come to a decision, Rouen." He got off the bed, unfolded his body slowly, drifted to the casement. "I induced the visions in him." He drew his hand along the broken glass, watched with interest as blood welled up and dripped down his fingers, the wounds sealing over quickly.

"I told you—"

"Valentin is allied with Serenola, and Lilith is preparing for the final blow." His voice was flat, curiously without inflection. "And I find, Rouen, that I can no longer sit and wait for the advent of the apocalypse." He picked the broken glass with his fingers, tossed it down into the street. "You may do as you wish—"

"—what do you mean? Are you deserting me?"

"—but I am going back to Florence." He came and caught me by the shoulders, his expression peculiarly intense. The pupils of his eyes were dilated, black, like chunks of onyx. "Come with me, Rouen! Fight with me! I know that if we can—"

"If we can what, Dante?" I spun away from him, jerked my arms from his grasp. "If we can stem the tide of this continental pestilence? How do you propose we do that?"

"I will take the battle to the source."

"You will seek Lilith, provoke her. Draw her out into the open." So he was insane.

"Lilith is but the instrument." He was suddenly behind me, his lips against the side of my neck. "I intend to address the fount and wellspring of this holy vengeance, Rouen."

Did he intend to confront Ludovico Serenola? "You cannot mean it. He has infected you with madness, Dante!" I turned and caught his face between my hands, peered deep into his eyes. "You have somehow received Valentin's affliction!"

"No, Rouen." Gently, he took my hands away, held them in his own. "It merely stands to reason. If evil exists, there must needs be a foil."

"So you do believe in God."

"Yes, Rouen." He kissed my lips gently, the gesture a benediction. "And I intend to take the battle to His very doorstep."

Chapter 18

August 1348
Florence

LUDOVICO SERENOLA

FLORENCE was mine after that. The Bonfire of the Vanities was noised abroad, was spoken from the pulpits of many churches. Soon towns and villages like Prato, Pistoia, Empoli, and Fuccechio imitated this great act, called all their citizens together, and bade them burn their finery. There was not a bauble left in all of Tuscany.

Prosti came to see me the day after I had incited the Bonfire, slipped into my cell with all the uncharacteristic silence of a fat man. "Fra Ludovico."

"Yes." I was resting on my knees, contemplating the Cosmic Egg of St. Hildegarde. I wondered if I might initiate a fresh round of flagellation in my acolytes. We had gained in prominence, my young novices and I, following the carts and preaching judgment. We had garnered a mighty reputation for ourselves, and those commoners who watched our efforts from afar had dubbed us "The Weepers." It was wholly undeserved, I assure you, since not one among had any need to weep. No, we rather proclaimed the will of Jesus Christ our Lord, and gloried in Him, as is His desire for us.

"The Holy See is less than pleased with your bonfire. An entire fleet of carters has been scrubbing the flagstones all day to try and get the burn marks off." He seated himself, grunting on my bench. The heat very much affected Prosti.

"Better burn marks on the flagstones than the flames of Hell upon the soul," I said, and rose from my knees. "Is there else you came to say, or did you merely arrive to apprise me of the sanitary conditions that exist in Florence?" I genuflected to my small shrine. "And further to that, I would certainly recommend the reintroduction of swine to the streets of this good city. Given the amount of refuse, of course." Despite council ordinances to the contrary, Florentines still insisted upon emptying garbage out the windows. "Since the plague has so decimated the carter's guild, the cobbles are as slick as monkey shit."

Prosti grimaced, no doubt annoyed by my plain speaking. "I came to apprise you once again of the instructions of the Holy See. You are to desist, Fra Ludovico. That is all. Simply desist and we will forget this unholy bonfire—"

"That bonfire was the ordinance of God Himself!"

"That unsacred conflagration was the product of your arrogance. You will desist this; you will cease your noisome ranting...." Prosti blubbered, red-faced and sweating.

"My noisome *ranting*?"

"Fra Ludovico, you are mendicant of a simple order. I pray you, it is far more fitting that you apply yourself to the kind of good and humble service that is doubtless suited to your station." Prosti rose to go. "Besides which—" He leaned close to me, scrutinized me with his keen, small eyes, "—I cannot understand the need you have, Ludovico, to perform these acts of public outrage! You defy the soul and purpose of your holy vows, posturing and preening before your adoring masses...."

Yes. Indeed, they did adore me now.

"... and Fra Ludovico, I will tell you also: such power as you now possess cannot possibly last!" He shuffled toward the door, breathing heavily. "Take my good advice. Desist of this. You are still within the jurisdiction of the ecclesiastical court. Pray, let me not have to send a summoner for you."

A great flush of heat suffused my face. "You would dare to threaten me here, inside my own cell? How dare you?"

"This is no threat, this is a *warning*, from one who has sufficient position to either redeem you, or to damn you." He paused, as if to say something else, but turned abruptly and left me, his unspoken words trapped in his throat.

I wandered to the open doorway, leaned for a moment against the sill. It was a beautiful day, clear, bright, the light as hard as marble. Would it be vanity to wander a little in the rose garden? I could do with a little sun upon my face.... Yes, I would do that. I would take my psalter with me, and have my contemplations outside today.

"Fra Ludovico." A whispered voice with a cadence like the thunder.

She had returned.

My fingers froze upon my psalter. I dared not turn about, lest I see her. It was enough that I now heard her voice every moment of every waking hour. She was driving me slowly mad, this insane apparition; I knew that Madonna di Francisci was dead.

"Fra Ludovico. How goes the plague in Florence?" A lovely woman's voice, a pure alto, ringing clearly like a bell. "My son lives in Florence, and I do wonder how he fares."

I knew that if I turned, I would see her as I always had of late: drifting near the casement, her garments floating behind her like ocean waves, her blinded eyes beseeching me, her raven hair shaved close against the skull.

"I cast you out in the name of Jesus Christ our Lord!" I made the Cross behind me, clutched my psalter to my chest. I could not bear the images she conjured in my mind. She was dangerous, as I had known from the beginning: she summoned memories, which I had fled into holy orders to escape. She was forever the woman that I couldn't have, the woman who would not have me, because I was sad and poor and really rather ugly, and she was beautiful and young.

"Go away." I pressed my eyelids closed.

The demon was gone.

I would linger in the garden, contemplate the Holy Mysteries, take pleasure in my gorgeous, illuminated psalter. Yes. And all would be well when at last the tolling bells called me back to vespers.

Chapter 19

August 1348

DANTE

"THIS is madness, Dante!" Rouen stalked and raged, his shadow thrown large against the far wall, his long hair wild about his shoulders. "Think of what you are saying!"

"Why is it so insane, Rouen?" I was throwing clothing into a bag with studied haste, my thoughts centered on one thing only: my return to Florence. Oh, how I would embrace the joyful sights, the Campanile and the great hulking shape of the Duomo! How I would linger in the Piazza and dance with glee across the Ponte Vecchio. "I will bring the battle to its very source!"

"You cannot hope to battle God Himself!" Rouen crouched beside me. "Dante, please. I beg you... reconsider! This is madness, running back to Florence like this. What if Serenola's minions find you? He has the blessing of the Church, the masses."

I smiled at him, reached out a hand to touch his cheek. "This is a most necessary evil, Rouen." I dropped my hand, turned away. "I pray you, collect your things and come along. The dawn comes, we must be away." I hoped Rouen wouldn't raise a fuss about this, there simply wasn't time. About the last thing I needed at this point was Rouen's over-intellectualizing. Damn him, he could ruminate along the way if need be.

"Have you at all exposed this to rationale?" Rouen climbed upon the bed. He was wearing a favorite pair of bright red hose, a flaming orange doublet.

"I have all the rationale I need, thank you." I fastened my bag, slung it over my shoulder. "I have you, Rouen, the perfect rational mind." I took a quick look around our rooms, but there was nothing else that I desired to take. I seriously couldn't imagine myself flying over Europe carrying a dining table....

I went to the sconces and blew out the candles, plunged the room into darkness. "Come, Rouen."

I felt him approach me on silent feet. He took me into his embrace and kissed me, lingered but a moment, his mouth on mine, before he drew away. "Goodbye, Dante."

I didn't understand.

"I have decided to remain here, in London." His voice was resolute, as firm as I have ever heard it.

I was astonished. "Rouen, you cannot be serious! Really, if this is a joke, I find it in rather poor taste... I pray you, come along!" I was becoming distinctly uneasy, and really rather frightened. It was inconceivable that he would allow me to leave here without him.

"No, Dante," he said, and to my mind he whispered, *Not this time.*

"Well." I affected bluster, but truth be told, I was deeply shaken. "This is a fine thing." My mind was a desperate flutter of activity, my errant thoughts glancing off of this and that in some attempt to frame a persuasive argument. He *had* to come with me! There was no other alternative....

"It matters not whether this thing is fine or no." Rouen's shadowy form flickered past my eyes; I saw him silhouetted in the broken casement. "I will not go with you."

"Rouen!" I yielded to the raw anguish, felt tears sting the backs of my eyes. "How can you do this to me?"

"Dante, this is utter lunacy." His voice was tight as a drum head, but I could feel the tension in him. "I cannot countenance it... I will not!"

"Rouen, we are comrades in this fight!" I went to him, lingered near the casement, willed him to look at me, but he did not turn, only continued staring steadfastly out into the dying darkness. To touch him I would have to reach across a gulf as vast as time.

"There is no fight, Dante. There is merely your own dark delusion. You think you can command God himself, but I tell you, it is arrogance!" He looked at me then, bright crimson tears standing in his eyes. "*Arrogance*, Dante. Your arrogance. As always."

I felt a cold descend over me, like a mantle. "You do not love me." The idea of it hurt me more than I could ever have imagined. If Rouen did not love me, then there was nothing else on earth for me. I might as well go silent into Hell.

"Yes, I *do*!" He took my hands in his, squeezed my fingers. He was cold. "Dante, please reconsider."

"No, Rouen." I pulled my fingers from his grasp. "I have made my choice." I stepped away from him, moved to gather my cloak. "Are you certain you will not reconsider?" I waited in the gathering silence, knowing even as I waited what his response would be.

"You amaze me, Dante." Contained, utterly calm. "You think it is so easy."

"It is easy, Rouen. Merely mount into the skies and project your body toward Florence. I've shown you how to do it, and I must say, you've become quite accomplished." The words had scarcely left my lips when I realized that he meant something quite different.

"You *think* I can go back there, be easy in the company of my countrymen, when my parents lie in unconsecrated ground, murdered by a madman who claims to do the will of God!"

Ah, blindness. "I cannot force you to go with me," I told him, "I can merely request it."

"And my response is, now and always, no."

I slung my cloak over my shoulder, tucked my gloves into my purse. He caught me to him, kissed me brutally, his hands cupping my face. "Dante, take good care!" His fingers burned their imprint into my skin. "Always take good care."

But there was no suitable rejoinder. I stared at him, hoping that some small part of him felt some necessary pull toward me, and then I left him, heartsick.

FLORENCE rose out of the darkness for me like a lover, beckoning me onward through the last of the night. I wheeled over it, wishing to see it unsullied like this, from a distance.

I first saw the slender tower of the Campanile, rising into the early morning sky like a finger from the hand of God. There, just opposite, was the great bulk of the Duomo, Brunelleschi's masterpiece, halted in construction by the plague. And there was the Piazza del Duomo, and directly across, our old lodgings, so lately destroyed by Serenola. The scaffold also remained, its dreadful skeleton outlined against the rapidly brightening sky. I wondered how many Serenola had so far burned.

I set down just inside the Piazza, glanced toward the eastern sky. In a moment, the sun would be across the horizon. I must needs seek shelter.

I found a crypt beneath the Duomo, in which I secreted myself against the sunrise. It was little more than a fusty marble box, filled with dusty old bones, the bodies of postulants long-dead—such lovely, saintly relics as Valentin would doubtless treasure. And here I was, enacting desecration by settling my bed among them. The thought amused me, and I was glad, because I had need of some small amusement in these dark times.

I pondered, before I slipped into sleep, whether Rouen had followed me, or if he had remained in England, true to his resolve. I allowed myself to feel the tiny pang of hurt that I had carried all the way across the sea from London, like a needle in my breast. And then the pain grew larger, became a great dark pool that swallowed me, as I fell to weeping. I thought to rise and immediately go to seek him, but the dawn was approaching, and it stole the last of my power.

Sunrise lowered a lid of darkness over me, and I knew nothing.

I AROSE early the next night, climbed out of the crypt just after sunrise, and, wiping my garments clean of the saintly dust, slipped into the city to seek this evening's victim.

I was still thinking of Rouen.

I found a serving wench lolling outside an inn, drunk on small ale and stinking of vomit and piss, a pretty little *signorina* whose entire family now probably resided on a cart. She was so drunk as to be nearly unconscious.

But I wasn't as choosy in those days as I am now, and I knew little of how the drink she had taken might affect me. I drained her swiftly, left her body in the alley, and staggered out into the streets. It was my first mistake of the evening.

The drink hit me like a hurled stone, turned my brains to water. I could no longer see where I was going; the streets had taken on the surreal quality of some barely lucid dream. I was drunk, as drunk as I had ever been when mortal. Had I been sensible enough to appreciate it, I'm certain I would have found it wildly amusing.

I stumbled into an inn, collapsed before the fire, suddenly cold, as if taken with a chill, despite the heat of the evening. "Cold, I'm cold, more fire." I took hold of a log and tossed it into the flames, watched the fire leap around it. It was mesmerizing. I could stay here all night.

"You there! On the floor!" A heavy foot caught me in the side. "Get out!"

A behemoth crouched above me, a great fat woman with eyes like a demented swine and a mouth full of rotten teeth. An odor emanated from her, a great rancid stink.

"I was merely warming myself...." I wished she'd move so that I would no longer have to smell her.

"Out! Lolling around in here as if you owned the place!" I felt a pair of hands grip into my collar; another pair clasp the seat of my hose. I wondered, vaguely, what would happen. I wondered if I would be surprised.

I wondered how I landed on the cobbles, facedown.

"God!" I rolled over, hands sliding on the slippery street. My doublet and hose were stained with all manner of foulness; my clothing stank of offal. I had forgotten the myriad charms of my native city, this cosmopolitan town whose hearty villains still emptied pisspots out of windows.

I realized I could not drink from drunken mortals, else the drink poison me as well. I had thought myself immune to things like this. It now appeared otherwise.

I had to cleanse myself, somehow; there was no way I could endure this stench and filth. My senses, always very keen, had been heightened by the blood to an unbearable sensitivity. I wondered sometimes how I managed to endure the world at all, but then, I did sometimes fancy my own courage overmuch.

I had taken no lodgings; there was nowhere I could go to bathe. I thought briefly of the public baths, immediately dismissed the notion. God only knew what strange and various vermin were swimming in those waters. Besides which, I couldn't imagine splashing there naked in the middle of the night. It would certainly attract unwanted attention.

I wandered aimlessly for a little time, as the effects of the drink dispersed, until at last I found myself in front of the very inn where I had first encountered Rouen. It was a shock of nostalgia, to be sure. I wondered what had become of Leonardo di Sforza, if indeed he had succumbed to plague, as I'd told Rouen.

I chuckled a little to myself. Yes, I had told Rouen that Leonardo was infected with the plague in order to seduce Rouen, to draw him to me. And Rouen, so evidently trusting, had believed me.

Of course it was dishonest. Well, did you expect I would be otherwise than the monster that I am?

I missed Rouen so very poignantly that I began to weep there on the cobbles, sniffling and bawling and making a mess of myself. I seriously considered flying back to England, finding Rouen and *forcing* him to come with me.

But in the end, I didn't do it.

I found a serving girl sewing by herself before the fire, and for a few coins I secured a room. With a little stealth I secured a suit of clothes from a wealthy banker sleeping in the room next door: fine silken hose, a crisp new shirt, a fine velvet doublet, cap, and leather boots. Even clean linen drawers.

I stripped and threw my soiled clothing out the window, sank into a tub filled with hot water to my chin. It was glorious, such an absolute creature comfort that I all but keened aloud.

And I remembered Rouen, filling the tub for me in his father's rooms, sitting there and watching me in the mirror while he totaled up his father's earnings in a ledger. *You need me....*

Suddenly, I was weeping. I laid my forehead on my knees and sobbed like a child. My bloody tears stained the water a delicate roseate crimson, like wine. *This is my body, this is my blood.*

I got dressed and went back to the Duomo. It was past three, and the streets were nearly deserted. I wanted to see no one; I preferred my solitude, because privacy was best where grief was concerned, and this certainly was sorrow.

I thought about what I had proposed to do. I wondered if Rouen was correct, if I was indeed insane. For it was an insane idea, by any measure, looking for God. I remembered trapping Valentin in our rooms, inducing his swoon to discover Lilith's movements. I remembered how he'd fought me, clawing in his delirium. I wondered where he'd gone, Valentin, now that he no longer resided in his large gray eyes. I prayed that I had not caused him to be so. Perhaps I might petition God for Valentin's release, once I found Him.

I realized that I was seriously considering this.

I wondered where I might find Him, if indeed He could be found at all. I considered, gazing at the frescoes and the icons, the great altar crucifix, if this were indeed where God existed, in the twisted, dying body of His son.

There was a rustle, no louder than a breath, and I turned.

Serenola.

I would have recognized him anywhere, and yet I was stunned into a momentary silence. What capricious turn of events could have brought him here tonight, of all nights? And what quirk in my own auspicious fortunes had contrived to place me here before him!

"Forgive me, Ser, I did not mean to interrupt your contemplations." The priest deferred to me, genuflected quickly before slipping into a pew beside the altar. At this small distance, he was not nearly so imposing as I had conjured him: he was but a slight man of middle years whose thinning hair was combed straight back over his high forehead, his contemplative face. He was wearing spectacles.

I wondered what he was doing here, at this hour, when other mortals were asleep. He seemed distracted. And something else, also, some other prevailing impression....He didn't recognize me.

Interesting.

I moved a little closer, pretended to be contemplating another fresco. I watched him praying with his eyes closed, lips moving rapidly, his fingers flickering on his string of beads.

I realized that he fascinated me. I couldn't stop looking at him.

After a moment, he sat up in the pew, gazed into the middle distance. He was passing something through his fingers, and it looked very like a long, dark ribbon, or a strip of cloth.

Until, jarred, I realized that it was a lock of raven hair.

"Do you hear her singing?" He tilted his head, as if listening to phantom music. "She sings all the time, now."

"Are you unwell, Signore?" He kept passing the hair through his fingers: now over them, now under them, now between each separate digit in turn. It was a ritualistic thing, a repetitive act to ward off evil, like counting crows....

"One for sorrow, two for joy...." He nodded in time with the ghostly music. "My bonfire of the vanities." He spoke as if to himself. "I thought to appease God."

I remembered Rouen's parents, the horrors that had been committed in this man's name. I thought about the atrocities, the veritable witch hunt that this priest had incited, all in the name of his misplaced devotion. "We so often think to appease the darkest cravings of our hearts."

His lips twitched. His face was utterly immobile, a mask of stone. "I told Prosti about the pigs. And I told him about Gioletti." He turned to me, appellant. "Do you think I left anything out?"

"No, Ser." A thousand questions pressed, underneath my tongue, and I could not ask a single one. I was fascinated with the blankness of his face, his unprepossessing demeanor, so elegantly nonplussed. I wondered what sorts of thoughts passed behind his mild, kindly eyes.

"Would you hear my confession?" He asked it without turning his head. "Since there is no priest present but myself, and we are two believers in these dark times."

The irony was as a tang of bitterness within my mouth.

"My soul is heavy." Plaintive, his voice sodden with pity for his own self-inflicted sins. Pleading with me, like Lucifer begging God not to toss him out of Heaven. If only he knew to whom it was he spoke! If only he knew the terrible flight that Rouen and I had made, the horrors that we endured, all because of him.

"Perhaps destruction is the will of God, Ser." I had no real idea what His aberrant will might be. He had no discourse with those of our kind, least of all with one as godless as myself.

"Then His will is paramount." He slipped out of the pew, then, a shadow taking to the air. I watched him genuflect again, saw him disappear, vanish into the long, narrow darkness of the nave.

I WANDERED for a long time about the streets that night, lingering in the places I had loved and missed the most. I passed the Campanile, drifted northward into the belly of the city, walking slowly as a mortal might, savoring the journey for its own sake. I lingered in the streets until the first streaks of dawn began to paint the eastern sky, and then I returned to the crypt beneath the Duomo, curiously light-hearted and joyous.

I would find God. I believed that He existed. I would request an audience with Him, and I would make Him understand that He must stop the devastation.

'New-made revenant, I bless you....'

I fell into an uneasy sleep, through which passed images of Lilith.

Chapter 20

August 1348
London

ROUEN

LONDON was an empty place after Dante left. This was a truth that I recited to myself, each night when I rose alone to hunt. The thought of him pained me; I wondered how he fared in Florence, and yet, I didn't dare send word. I knew that Serenola's spies were everywhere, and I had no wish (however much I might disagree with him) to see him land in any danger.

I thought about him constantly, however. The pain of his absence was so great that I deliberately avoided his old acquaintances, and steered clear of the tavern, lest I run into Geoffrey. I wished to make no explanations, but to continue along my chosen course until existence had revolved into its natural end. What that might be, I had no idea, and I didn't particularly care to find out. I had descended into a dangerous state of spiritual emptiness—what moderns call "nihilism." And I deliberately kept myself friendless, because I preferred to keep my sorrow hidden; I didn't wish to have it openly dissected like some vulgar display. The only person that I did see was Fernando de Medici.

"Rouen, come in!" The heavy oak door swung back on its hinges, and I was ushered into a sumptuous room, about which was stationed a collection of young men—Fernando's friends, I assumed. "Let me take your cloak… sit down, sit down!" It was a very warm evening, but for all that, a fire burned in the grate. Oddly, all the windows had been thrown open to the night air. I thought this rather a strange arrangement, until I saw the water pipes and smelled the sickly-sweetish odor of *hasheesh*. Trust Fernando to have found a supply of it in doughty London.

For all that my welcome was so gracious, I was immediately uncomfortable; I had expected that Fernando would receive me alone, and that we would spend a quiet evening. "Fernando… well met." I embraced him warmly, clung to him for but a moment. That I missed Dante was evident to us both.

He introduced me to his friends, all of them young gentlemen of good families, all of them splendidly clothed, all of them either quite drunk or intoxicated with *hasheesh* smoke. And one of them—the shortest and slightest—a young woman, elegantly dressed in men's clothing. "This is Melina."

I bowed low over her hand. "*Madonna….*"

They had been dining, it seemed, on fruit and sweetmeats, heavily augmented with copious amounts of wine. The smell of mortal food sickened me; I wished he would take it away. The stench of wine was a miasma in the room, a drifting cloud about my head.

"I have made good acquaintance here in London." Fernando poured himself another cup of wine, emptying the flagon. I suspected that he had imbibed as heavily as all the rest, yet showed no ill effects. "All of these people that you see before you, Rouen, are the first-fruits of an English Renaissance, the elect of my companions, those who have been redeemed. I would not go back to Florence now if someone paid me!" That the wine had loosened his tongue was evident, but not surprising… Fernando often waxed eloquent. In a man of lesser presence, it would have appeared vainglorious. "I am come to lead them to glory like Christ among the heathen!"

There was collective laughter from the room in general, a resultant polite patter. I saw the young woman, Melina, watching me carefully. I returned the gaze.

"Fernando says you are a free soul." She was at once crouched beside my chair. Her legs were long and slender, her feet small and neat in fine leather boots. I could discern no breasts underneath the man's shirt she wore. "May I read your future?" And she took my hand, turned it palm up.

I studied her carefully as she traced the lines in my palm with the tip of a finger. Her hair was dark auburn, and had been trimmed about her shoulders, cut to feather about the face, in a young man's style. She wore no paint. Her face was heart-shaped, exceedingly serious; with dark, straight brows framing brown eyes that reminded me of Dante. There was a tiny scar in the form of a half-moon, underneath her right eye. "You have a curious future," she said, "and a strange past." She turned her gaze on me for a long moment, probing me. "Are you named after the city, Rouen?" She moved her head and I saw the cords in her neck, straining against the skin. She was very slender.

I shrugged. "I don't know, but I think not. More likely it was a collection of sounds that pleased my mother's ear." I had never wondered about it, until she mentioned it. I realized that now I would wonder about it forever.

"Fernando says he would like to bed you." She pointed with her chin. Fernando stood against the far wall, his fingers buried in the thick blond hair of a seated man. "Would you allow him?"

The thick *hasheesh* smoke drifted, blinding me; the smell was curiously intoxicating. "Melina, I hardly think this is appropriate conversation in mixed company." I had never heard a lady speak to a man in this manner; it was disconcerting.

"Mixed company?" She laughed, a shockingly masculine guffaw, and slapped her knees. "Rouen, we are all gentlemen here." She climbed into my lap, her legs across my knees. She weighed scarcely anything at all. "You are very beautiful. I think I would like to bed you, also. Will you give your consent?"

I stood up, spilled her to the floor. This was insupportable....

"Rouen, where are you going, friend?" Fernando caught me by the door. "Come, now! Stay a little longer." A clatter behind me, a perceptible pause in the conversation. I saw Melina watching me from behind a post, her eyes glassy, doll-like.

"I have no wish to sit about and discuss indecent acts with your young friend!" I felt hot color mount into my face; I was absolutely mortified that I should even address such things with Melina, angry that she should be so bald-faced as to introduce it. "I can believe you discuss such things in my absence—"

"Which things?" He gazed at me blankly, and then his brows twitched. "Melina." He sighed. "Rouen, you must forgive Melina. Oftentimes, she is so very eager to emulate the ways of men that she forgets the social delicacies. I pray you—" He closed the door, ushered me back into the room, "—return. We will have some amusements, perhaps a game." He bent near to me, his hand at my elbow. "And Rouen, I beg you, forget your prudery! There was no place for it at Tralini's inn, and there is no place for it here!"

Fernando produced blindfolds for us all, and we engaged in a spirited game of hiding and finding each other. I heard the others scramble away to various places about the house; I felt my way into a vacant bedroom and hid inside a wardrobe.

"Get *off*!" A pair of hands slammed into my chest and shoved me; the wardrobe rocked violently, threatening to overturn. I scrambled for a handhold, fingers slipping on the smooth sides of the chest, bashed into the door, which flew open, spilling me into a heap beside the bed.

"Melina." I untied my blindfold, rolled it into a ball. "It seems I cannot avoid you."

"Have you wish to avoid me, Sir?" She clambered out of the wardrobe, sat upon the edge of it, legs splayed unconsciously. Her resemblance to a lovely, smooth-skinned boy was unnerving. "Have I given offence?"

"Pray sit like a woman, close your legs."

Twin spots of color appeared, high up on her cheekbones. "For all intents and purpose, Sir, when I am in this guise, I am a gentleman!"

I sighed. Trust Fernando to have found her. It seemed I could never be certain which of his acquaintances honored their true gender... "And those others out there... I suppose they are ladies, also?"

"Huh!" She tossed her head, set her short hair to flying. "They are Fernando's pretty boys. They merely masquerade as ladies." Her contempt was manifest; I wondered why she engaged in their society.

"Are you masquerading as a lady?"

A strand of hair was caught in the corner of her mouth; I reached out and removed it. We gazed at each other without tenderness, without the taint of gentler concern. It was rather a perusal, the kind of blatant assessment such as animals make toward each other.

And then I caught her in my arms, crushed her slender boy's body to mine, inhaled the sweet scent of her skin. She was hard, throbbing, a single compact muscle. Her little arms were like cords of leather.

She buried her face against my neck, groveled into me. Her hands tore at me, opening my shirt, her fingers tangled in my hair. "Bar the door," she whispered, and I did.

I pulled her shirt above her head, pressed my face into the hot space between her tiny breasts, my fingers splayed around her ribs. I fought with the complicated fastenings of her hose and tore them off, discarded the jeweled codpiece that she wore.

She moved into my lap, her legs wrapped around my waist, and whimpered softly as I entered her, resting on my knees. Her hands clenched the back of my neck, pulling on my hair; her knees pressed against my sides, hard and brittle like the bones of birds. She rocked against me, our bellies pressed together. She cupped my face between her palms and kissed me, then arched her back and climaxed, her mouth stretching itself wide, eyes rolling in her skull. Her body was almost unbearably hot, burning like blood.

We rested for a time at the throbbing center of it, insensible. The stone floor was cold against my back as I lay with my arms flung wide,

Melina perched atop me like a bird.

"Why do you pretend to be a boy?"

"I am a boy." She slid, skin rasping on mine, a frisson of excruciating pleasure.

"You are not. And if you are, you must be some new sort of boy, because I've never met a boy like you."

"Have you had many boys, Rouen?"

I ignored the question. "Where did you get this scar?" I traced it with my fingertips, the tiny demilune underneath her eye.

"Fernando cut me."

"Liar."

"Truth. I said he was a sodomite." She tilted her head, an eerily birdlike motion. "Are you a sodomite, Rouen?"

I pretended not to have heard her.

I SAW her often after that, whether in Fernando's company or not; she seemed to be a fixture about London, and she appeared in odd places, at times when I least expected her. I would be walking late at night and I would turn a corner and she would be there, standing calmly in the darkness gazing at me. When I looked again, she would have disappeared. Or, I would mount the stairs to my lodgings only to find her waiting at the top, her little heart-shaped face remote and inscrutable, her figure heartbreakingly beautiful in her boy's clothes.

She was inordinately clever. She was often in my rooms when I was out, prowling about, for my nearest neighbors reported her movements, all unwitting of her true persuasion: "your cousin called for you last evening, the young sir."

I would find tokens placed upon my pillow: a lock of hair, a scarlet ribbon, a handful of fragrant posies. And cryptic notes, scribed hastily upon torn bits of parchment, illegible.

"I want you to devour me," she said, coming upon me in an alley just before dawn. "Slit my wrists and drink me, Rouen; I want you to crawl inside me and listen to the drumming of my heart."

Such protestations bothered me; I wondered if Fernando had revealed my secret to her. I wondered if she suspected it herself. I wondered if she had followed me, if she had seen me kill. I took care to feed on the outskirts of the city, far from Fernando's lodgings, and to hide the bodies well. I became rather paranoid, obsessed with the threat of discovery, and to that end, developed little rituals centering around my hunt, certain acts I would be obliged to perform before I killed. If I omitted any of it, I would be wracked with guilt, tormented by insane imaginings. I began to believe that God was watching me, and He knew everything I did.

But there was Melina, and the privacy of my lodgings, and our fierce and frantic coupling in the last desperate moments before the dawn. "Why does this take you, this daylight sleep?" she asked me. I often fell into unconsciousness while she was there, locked myself in day-sleep, careless of the risks. I never knew if or when she would discover my aberration and expose me to the sunlight. I simply never knew. She came and went according to her own desires, wandered freely about the streets. I marveled that she had no fear of plague.

"It does not frighten you, Melina?" We lay wrapped together in my bed. "This plague?"

"We protect ourselves, Rouen."

I had no idea what she meant.

"Fernando, Geraint, Alan, and I." She caught my fingers in hers, spread my arms above my head. "We have a special ritual that we enact, and we have been spared." Her legs moved, slid to enclose mine. "Let me be the man this time, Rouen." Her moist, hot mouth moved on mine as she rose and impaled herself on me. I thought to ask what this ritual might be, but my mind wandered in the tumult, and moments later, in the full glare of desire, I had forgotten it completely.

"Sometime soon, I'll show you," she whispered.

THERE was an utter absence of light. Darkness pressed in on me, smothering; darkness enveloped me, an airless space.

The snapping retort of a tinderbox, and a candle flared into life. A circle of light throbbed outward from the tiny wick, glowing deep orange, violent yellow. The hand holding it placed it on the floor, slipped back into the circle.

"What is this place?"

"Silence, Rouen." The figure beside me nodded, dwarfish in the long black robe. A second candle flared to life, went clockwise around the circle.

"We beg His presence here." I recognized the voice; it was Fernando, his theatrical flourish.

The room around me was swathed entirely in black, the windows draped with heavy buntings, the furniture covered in the same black stuff. The heavy dining table with its marble top stood just beyond our circle. Atop it was a silver basin, and a silver, half-moon knife. I wondered uneasily what the implements were used for.

"And He comes, Jehannum, He who is the voice of reason: Belial, Beelzebub, Satan the Destroyer." Fernando's voice grew in volume, till it rolled about the room like thunder.

"*All Hail!*" The circle chanted as one.

My scalp prickled; I had no idea what was to come, and I wished suddenly with all my heart that I could leave. The ceremony was at once threatening, and patently absurd.

"Easy, Rouen." Melina's hand upon my arm. "So tense, and you will snap your laces." Her fingers curled around my thigh, a secret caress. "You are among friends."

I wished fervently for Dante. "What is going on?"

"Hush. You will see in but a moment."

It was some sort of ritual—nothing I had seen before, and certainly nothing I had ever heard about. I refused to think it merely harmless; it occurred to me that the basin and the knife were for some sinister purpose.

"Come look."

I slipped into the line behind Melina, was immediately immersed in a sea of rustling robes. I had thought myself among some small several of Fernando's friends, but there were perhaps dozens here. I watched as the first one approached the table, took the knife, and nicked his wrist. A bright bead of blood welled up, slid slowly down, pooling in the bottom of the bowl.

My pulse seemed concentrated in my throat.

My God, they're blood-drinkers!

"What is this?" I caught Melina's arms, shook her. "What does it mean?" A plethora of possibilities hammered in my brain; I wondered if they were others of our kind, immortals.

"We protect ourselves," she said, smiling. And she took the bowl, tilted it to her lips, and drank a great draught.

The smell of it was overwhelming, sweet and rich. I felt my fangs descend, the great throbbing of the blood-hunger beginning, deep within my belly. It pulsed in my fingertips, the soles of my feet, pulsated in my temples, the tip of my tongue.

"You see, Rouen, we are not so very different from you." Fernando stood before me at the table, spoke softly through his bloody lips. "The blood is the life."

I stumbled backward, horrified, bumped into Melina. "Why didn't you tell me?" I whispered.

"We are like you, Rouen." Fernando reached for me, but I hissed at him, fangs fully descended. The hunger had reached its apex and throbbed inside my skull like murder.

"You are *not* like me!" I was walking as I spoke, moving away from them, propelled toward the door. Everything about the edges of my vision was stained with blood. "And you could burn for this!"

"Rouen, we have welcomed you inside our circle!" Melina caught my arm. "We are a coven of believers, as you are!" Her bright, dark eyes shone, vivid in her pale face.

"No." I pulled away from her. "You don't understand."

"Then show me," she said. The smell of blood was in my nostrils, maddening me.

Show me....

I turned and caught the blond one, Geraint, crushed his throat between my fingers, held him dangling like a broken doll. And there, before their terrified and disbelieving gazes, I slammed my fangs into his throat, drained his blood and let him drop. The body tumbled to the floor, landed with a wet, fleshy slap. The open eyes regarded the ceiling with an expression of wonder and surprise.

I gazed about the circle, at the silent ring of faces. "Come... who's next?" The bitter irony of it, these mortals and their sacrifice. "Or shall I take you one by one?"

I had thought they would resist me, but I was wrong. They behaved like no mortals I had ever known.

One by one, they presented themselves to me, collecting in a line before the table. They unfastened their dark robes and bared their throats, and stood silent and unblinking, waiting. I could have taken each of them in turn, and there was none to say me otherwise.

"What are they doing?" My voice rang out into the silence. "What do they want?" I roared. "*Melina!*"

She drifted toward me, coalescing out of the darkness. "My lord." She bowed gracefully, a sweet aberrant boy. "We are at your service. We have always known that you would come!"

My heart froze within my chest. *My God....*

They thought I was the Devil!

I rushed toward the door, bolted down the stairs and out into the street. I ran as fast as I could, feet pounding on the cobbles, until at last

I collapsed against a wall.

They thought I was the Devil!

I braced my head in my hands, mind spinning. "Oh God, oh God, what do I do, what do I do?"There was nowhere left for me to go, there was nowhere safe for me to hide; no matter where I went, they would find me—

"Rouen!"

A slender, graceful boy emerged out of the shadows, cloak slung over his arm. He approached on silent feet, took my face between his hands and kissed me, his lips wet with blood. It was Melina, of course. "Let us honor you."

I was plunged into a morass from which there was no escape, unless I killed them all. And if I did, there would arise others to take their place. I swayed dizzily; put out a hand for support. The walls about me seemed to shift and move; the street tilted dangerously.

"How long has this been going on?" I deliberately closed my senses to her, lest her dangerous allure pull me in again.

"We have practiced our art as long as I can remember. Fernando has traveled here from time to time to partake of our sacraments." The voice was calm, without inflection; neither male nor female, nothing human. It might have been a spirit talking.

"Are you some sort of witches?"

"No. The Wiccans serve the Goddess, do good to all, and never take life if they can at all avoid it. We are different."

"This is monstrous," I whispered. I felt cold and sick.

"Why is it so monstrous? We only seek to guarantee our continued existence, as you do. You require blood as we do."

"No! It is not the same thing!" I pressed my hand to my mouth, distress clawing at me. Dante would know how to deal with this, if he were here. I did not.

"Rouen." Her fingers caught me underneath the chin, tilted my face. "Since we have practiced these devotions, not one of us has fallen to the plague."

"Coincidence," I replied bitterly, "you deceive yourselves that you have discovered the fount of life."

"And why do you drink blood?"

"Because I must. I cannot survive without it."

"So we are more alike than unlike." She smiled thinly, bowed from the waist. "Bravo."

"Go away," I said miserably, "and leave me!"

There were no retreating footfalls, but when I looked again, she had vanished.

I DIDN'T know where to go or what to do; I knew only that I must get out of London. I could no longer count Fernando or his coven among my friends, in truth, I had no friends. I was as alone as the day I was born.

I walked, immersed in trance, until I saw the first streaks of dawn slide across a steel-gray sky. The air was ominous, heavy with anticipation, too close to breathe. Sweat stood upon my skin in beads.

The first rumble of the thunder caught me unawares, a monumental boom that rocked the heavens. And then the rain came, a torrential flood, water streaming from the eaves of buildings as if poured from a flagon. I clutched my cloak about my head and ran underneath an awning.

The clouds were thick, but I knew the sun was coming, I could feel its advent pulsing all along my skin, like pain. My bones began to ache, like the bones of old mortals. I must seek shelter.

I ran as far along as I could, underneath the awnings of shops, and I ducked into the dark and narrow alleys, where the overhanging top story blocked the sunlight. But it was coming, I knew it. I could feel its deadly warmth, its warning.

It caught me in front of my door, daylight searing my eyeballs, screaming. It poured into my mouth and nose, struck daggers into my flesh. I clawed at the handle, ripped the door open and stumbled up the stairs. I was burning—

Rouen, I'm burning, burning, the sun!

I burrowed into the bedclothes headfirst, clawing at the mattress, tearing the blankets into strips. I tore the mattress ticking and crawled inside it, buried myself deep inside the feathers, still feeling it burn me.

Rouen, I'm burning....

I turned once, before the darkness took me, and I knew no more.

I AWOKE to an unfamiliar ceiling, smooth wooden walls. There was a slow, steady sound, like water dripping into a basin, or rain into a barrel. "Where am I?"

My voice echoed in the emptiness. I lifted my head off the pillow and was assaulted with weakness, a sharp feeling in my stomach as if I would vomit. The room swam before me. "What is this place?"

A hand fastened onto my arm, someone bending over me. I saw the head and shoulders of a man I didn't know. Outside, it was dark.

"Who are you?" He wore the robes of a doctor, or perhaps a barber-surgeon, I couldn't be entirely sure. I heard the door close softly behind him.

I felt along the sides of the bed, my fingers coming into contact with the smooth metal rim of what I discovered was a basin. Before I even lifted it, I knew what I would see, and indeed, it was filled with blood. My blood.

My torso heaved and I retched painfully, a dry coughing that brought up nothing. I found the tube and tore it out of my arm, pressed my thumb to stanch the wound until it sealed itself.

Someone had been bleeding me. There was no question as to who had done this.

"Ho, Rouen!"

It was Fernando, and Melina was behind him, dressed as usual in men's clothing. A fearsome rage rose clawing at the insides of my throat. "Tell what the meaning of this is, and you tell me *now*!" I leapt off the bed, wavered, and collapsed. The floor rushed up to meet me with sickening speed. I was astonished that I was so weak.

"Rouen, you must rest." Melina knelt above me, struggled to lift me into an upright position.

"I don't remember...." I began to weep, feeling that this was the end, the demise that my nihilistic expectations had wrought. "Where am I?"

"You are in Melina's house. Get up." A boot in my ribs, a pair of hands pulling me upright.

"You've been bleeding me—" I gasped, swung at him, but he stepped neatly out of my way. "—admit it!"

"Yes, Rouen, we have been bleeding you. And we are nearly done." He lifted the basin, peered into the dark liquid that moved and shifted glossily, like oil. "You must tell me all about this wondrous substance of yours." His eyes narrowed to slits; this was a side of him that I had never seen before. "So that we can reproduce the effects in ourselves. Melina says you kill people to achieve this most miraculous condition."

My face twisted painfully, a grotesque spasm. The loss of blood was affecting me, draining my strength and my control. *"To hell with you!"* I spat at him, clawing. My hand floated out before my eyes, comically slow, subsided back against my side uselessly.

"Oh, stop that, all that nonsensical hellfire and brimstone." He slapped at me with his gloves. "Come now, Rouen...what happened to your good cheer?" He spoke lightly, as if we were once more trading banter around a gaming table.

"My 'good cheer' is resting in your basin, Ser." My shoulder twisted, muscles spasming, my head pulling to the side. The cramps were agonizing. I wondered how long I could endure it.

"Melina says you cannot stand the sunlight." His gaze was speculative, dissecting. "So your Dante was not lying when he related that fantastical tale to me."

I was silent.

"Oh, Rouen, please! Stoicism doesn't suit you. Pray, open that lovely mouth of yours and tell me what you think about our plans." He laid the basin down upon a table, within arm's reach of me. "I'll hear your confession before you die."

"Fernando, you are boring me." I braced myself against the bed. "And you are a liar."

Behind him, Melina scribbled busily upon a paper. "What is she writing?" I asked.

"A message to your Dante."

"Telling him I'm dead." This was monstrous. I had to get out of here, I'd had as much as I could stand.

I needed to create an intrigue....

I sighed, allowed my eyes to roll back into my skull, and collapsed across the bed, my feet hanging off the side, my hands outstretched toward the table. It was a lovely swoon. The basin was within reach, just beyond my fingertips. Perfect.

"Rouen!" His palm rested in the center of my back, as he bent over me, his breath against my skin. I knew that I must act now.

I slammed my body backward, my head and shoulders connected with his face. There was a pronounced crack as his nose shattered. I leapt for the basin, grabbed it and drained it in one draught, the blood spilling down my throat like nectar.

I caught Fernando and crushed his ribcage with my hands, snapped his neck and drank from it, sucking back his blood as fast as I could take it. Somewhere behind me, I heard Melina screaming, and I turned in time to see her vanish down the stairs.

"Rouen—" It was Fernando. To my astonishment, he attempted speech, formed words with his crushed and bleeding mouth. "—I beg you, mercy!"

"You wish mercy of me?" I drew back and slammed my foot into his broken ribs, a savage kick. "You, who kidnapped me and drained my blood!" I knelt beside him, caught his face between my fingers, forced him to look at me. "Melina thinks I'm Satan." I tilted my head, regarded him. The blood was making me stronger by the minute. "Tell me, what do you believe?"

His head rolled in my grasp, blood and froth bubbling on his lips. "Mercy...."

"Go to hell."

I went to the wardrobe and selected clothing for myself: fine embroidered hose, a crisp linen shirt and drawers, a velvet doublet with dagged sleeves, a cap. I dressed myself in this, took a scarlet cloak and a pair of slim dark boots, buckled a leather purse about my waist.

I took one last look about me, prior to departing. Fernando lay where I had tossed him, his body smashed, unrecognizable. I poked him with my foot, made certain he was dead. I had no desire to see him ever again.

Yet, something made me pause on the stairs and look back.

A slender man with short-cropped silver hair was bending over Fernando, taking the battered body into his arms. The scene was at once so tender and so entirely strange that it enthralled me; I watched it as I might regard a pantomime.

The man looked so much like Valentin that I feared I had taken with a devil. I ran some several steps, peered into the room, called his name, "Valentin!"

The empty chamber echoed back my voice.

Chapter 21

September 1348

Florence

LUDOVICO SERENOLA

I, FRA LUDOVICO SERENOLA, write these words with my own hand, so that, in the dark days after the coming of the Apocalypse, let anyone who reads this be comforted by the faithfulness of Jesus Christ our Lord, even unto death.

I did my best to deliver the word of the Lord. Even when late this madness wracked me, and those who would oppose my holy cause rose up on every side to discount me, still I stood steadfast. This is what history must have to say of me.

I WAS not surprised.

I was resting in my cell, having tossed all the night before, bereft of sleep. The sun was sinking just below the great shadow of the Duomo when I heard them, a great coterie of Prosti's, a dozen trampling feet. I rose and let them in.

"Pray, be careful of the roses." A last few fragile blooms, those sturdy bushes planted by Fra Vittore's hand. The sound of my fellows, chanting vespers, drifted to me through the opened door.

"Fra Ludovico." Prosti approaching me, hands outstretched. His red cap gleaming in the dying light, the fine satin of it. "I have orders from the Holy See." And he unrolled a papal bull, indeed sealed by His Holiness, as I could clearly see, even though my spectacles had been lost these weeks since. "Ludovico...." And pausing, wanting to say something to me, "...please come along."

"My spectacles." I felt along the tabletop, certain I had left them there, or perhaps along the shelf; no, they were beside my bed, I had removed them this afternoon to rest—

"Ludovico!" Their hands upon me, roughly, caught me dangling between them. I must not lose my dignity; I must at all costs retain my composure. I thought desperately of every pleasant and sacred thing. I thought unashamedly of Madonna di Francisci.

"You are hereby charged and convicted of heresy, of spreading pernicious doctrine, of subverting the populace of Florence, of disobeying the prohibition of your preaching...."

His voice uttered off into nothing. The opened casement caught the last rays of the setting sun, set my tiny cell gloriously alight, a vision of sacred fire. I felt the press of lips against my cheek and there was Fra Vittore. "I must ask that you give me all your books and papers."

I went quietly to the cabinet and gave him what I had. There was no thought within my mind at this time. I was incapable of framing any such cognizance. I was astonished at my tranquility, and regarded myself as if I were not party to these dark proceedings.

"Is it necessary to bind you?" Prosti, silhouetted near the doorway, his face inscrutable.

"No." I said this, and held my hands out to him, as if waiting for the rope to pass between my wrists. "Let come what may, I have no fear."

If I must suffer, I wish to suffer for the truth. What I have said, and these things that I have done, I have received from God.

All thanks and praise to you, Lord Jesus Christ. I will go with them, and I will gladly suffer whatever it is that I am made to suffer for His sake.

Fra Ludovico Serenola

September, 1348

Chapter 22

September 1348
Florence

DANTE

I THOUGHT often of Rouen, in those dark days, when I wandered all alone in the still temple of the Duomo, or when I was lying in the crypt beneath her floor, awaiting the advent of the dawn. I missed him terribly, longed for him with the longing that is a physical pain. Florence was not home without him.

And Florence suffered still, devoured by the plague, by religious hysteria, by ignorance. The Church whose truth he had professed had tortured and murdered Serenola but a fortnight ago, had hacked his body to pieces and dragged it round the Piazza del Duomo before finally hanging him from his own scaffold. He resided there in great pomp and splendor as birds picked out his eyes.

The carts rolled at dusk and dawn, hauling bodies to the makeshift mass graves that had been dug behind the church. There, the *beccamorti* would shovel the bodies into the hole and cover them with but a sprinkling of dirt. They knew, as did the rest of Florence, that tomorrow there would be more bodies, and the day after that, still more, till there was not ground enough to hold them. The sheer number of daily deaths was astonishing; I was amazed that a people could endure such unending tribulation, yet there seemed no end to their strength. And I admired them, these frail and finite mortals, whose influence over their universe was tenuous at best. Their numbers decimated by the plague, they were preyed upon by a vast variety of socially sanctioned thieves, commercial cutpurses. The Medici realized that as the plague progressed and civility declined, so too did legitimate commerce disappear; they finally threw up their hands and left the legislation of trade to the councils, the Church, and the *beccamorti*.

This profligate number of funerals necessitated an increase in the production of mourning cloth, which both the merchants and the *beccamorti* sold for exorbitant prices. A mourning outfit, (cloak, mantle and veil) which in previous times cost two to three gold florins, climbed in price to over thirty florins, and then higher still. The illegal commerce of those unscrupulous enough to practice such desperate usury remained unregulated; in time, the price of cloth, of bread, of wine, became incredibly inflated as merchants, cognizant of the death that danced around them, strove to gather wealth. In time, Florentines could not afford the garments necessary to honor their dead, the bread to feed the mourners, the wine to still their sorrow. Yet, it was considered a disgrace to keen the dead unless properly attired. So the modest middle classes switched to linen, and sewed weeds of their own; the very poor wrapped themselves in rags.

The entire city had gone insane, all notions of civility and order sacrificed to the mounting horror. The plague became the great taboo, the judgment of a vengeful God, that which it was indiscriminate to mention. The sight of a swelling bubo was cause for hysteria. No one dared enter a house where someone had died, and there was no aid rendered to the sick.

Because of the overwhelming fear of plague, as well as the exorbitant cost of death, the council passed edicts forbidding the sale of bells, burial benches, winding-cloths. The dead were wrapped in bed sheets, their deaths heralded by keening mourners. They traveled to their final resting place atop a plank of wood. And the inhabitants of Florence carried on, despite the plethora of edicts passed on their behalf. They lived, and died, were carried to their God and laid in His sacred ground, secure in the knowledge that this was His will, somehow.

I was not convinced that this was sacred edict, but then, I had never been possessed of a particularly sturdy faith. I wondered where God was, in all of this. I wondered why He had not seen fit to show His face to those who professed Him, even unto death. Serenola had screamed and broken under torture, racked and roped until every bone in his body shattered, and there still existed a hysteria in Florence—a very real feeling that the plague was the result of some forgotten transgression. It was but a matter of time before the Florentines selected another scapegoat, or a savior. I shuddered to think from which disparate section of their ranks they would cull another Serenola.

I kept my own council in those days, rising at dusk to hunt and feed, always returning to my beloved Duomo to contemplate within its perfect silence. It was, ironically, the only place where I felt safe, there in God's house. I hoped He did not object to my presence.

I was sitting by myself one evening, drifting in a meditative state among the hundreds of votive candles that flickered near the altar. Each one was some mortal's plea for the intervention of the divine, the casting of stale bread upon the waters. All day, as I lay in an unconscious half-sleep, I heard mortals as they moved above me, drifting into the Duomo to place a candle, mutter a prayer. Their oft-repeated petitions, their whispered buzz of retribution, hummed about my head, a miasma of misery. I discerned their sorrow from the clicking of their beads.

The streets outside were eerily quiet this night, empty save for the ragged whores who peddled their disease, beggars seeking alms. Florence languished, crushed by pestilence.

I was experiencing what I had come to think of as a crisis of faith: a curious emptiness of spirit, a haunting lack of purpose. My faith in my own immortal nature had been progressively eroded, worn away by disaster and despair, and the dull horror of my nightly existence. It was not surprising, given the sheer numbers of mortals who sickened and died about me; yet, I had thought myself unaffected by it all. Untouchable. But I knew it was not the plight of mortals that was bothering me; I knew it was something much more intimately personal. I had had much latitude of late to ponder on my soul, and when I looked into the shadows of my own heart, what I saw frightened me. I feared that I had lost my mortal nature, become fully the thing that Lilith made me. A blood-drinker. *A monster.*

I moved into the long darkness of the nave, pacing, my mind working frantically. I disliked feeling this way; it presented emotions that were of no use to me, ethical problems that weighed heavy on my overburdened brain. I had become obsessed with wondering about myself, the status of my spirit, whether I did indeed possess a soul and if so, if it were sanctified. These questions so obsessed me that if there had been a priest present, I might have offered my confession. How very amusing a notion! *Forgive me Father, for I have sinned. I have drunk the blood of countless mortals....*

I was tormented, too, with thoughts of Rouen, worried for his safety. Although our minds were linked and we could communicate, he had been silent for some weeks—a silence that produced its own prescient dread.

"Ser?"

I turned, shaken from my reverie by the unfamiliar voice. "Yes? What do you want?" It was a boy, a ragged street Arab, with a crumpled piece of parchment in his hand. He was filthy, riddled with disease, his mouth encrusted with weeping sores. A wretched, finite mortal.

"I have a letter for you, Ser. From London." He slipped it into my hand.

The seal was unfamiliar to me; it wasn't Rouen's family seal, it was nothing that I recognized. "Just a moment, I'll give you something." I knew he would expect it, his large and hungry eyes gazing at my purse. I reached for a coin, but he turned suddenly, as if summoned, and was gone. His abrupt disappearance left me curiously shaken.

I took the letter with me into the sanctuary, sat down on a pew, and pulled the seal apart.

My hands were trembling. I unfolded the paper and peered at what was written there:

Rouen di Francisci is dead.

My mind stuttered into silence, refusing thought.

I stood up, walked rapidly toward the altar. My heart began throbbing, low and deep, a vast booming drum inside my chest, a damning cadence that echoed in my brain.

Rouen di Francisci is dead.

I strode on shuddering knees toward the giant crucifix, the twisted body of the dying Christ. I stopped just short of crying out, of begging Him for succor....

Rouen di Francisci is dead.

I decided that I didn't believe it. Not for a moment. He hadn't broken our link, he had merely been silent. I was certain there was an appropriate explanation. Rouen had perhaps been very busy. Yes, that was it. Doubtless he was gossiping with Geoffrey in the tavern, adding to the sum of tales the pilgrims told. Or, he had met some new friend and spent his nights in learned discourse. Yes, that was the explanation.

My mind was overtaken with a jeering, violent laughter. *He can't possibly be busy if he's dead!*

"He's not dead!" The exclamation, echoing, startled me. I realized that I had spoken it aloud. "Rouen is strong." Rouen was a vampire, he couldn't be destroyed—And yet along the link I heard a distant cry, a vampire in pain, *I'm burning, burning, the sun!*

I fell across the altar, hands outstretched at the foot of the cross. I reached through the altar rails, slid my hands on the chilly stone, pressed my fingers into the indentations in His feet, the nails that protruded brutally from His marble flesh.

Forgive me father, for I have sinned.

Rouen is dead. It burned behind my eyelids like a remembered curse. I repeated the word, over and over, *dead dead dead dead....*

Rouen di Francisci is dead.

I did not believe it. It was an idea too enormous for my mind to hold.

I WALKED the streets all night, driven by the darkness that coiled and festered in my soul. I summoned Rouen frantically, screaming down the link to him, was answered only with a damning silence.

Rouen di Francisci is dead.

I found my way into a tavern where a group of laughing youngsters was making merry, oblivious to the death surrounding them. A brace of minstrels played while couples danced, and a jolly fool ran in and out, bells jingling.

"What is your pleasure, Ser?" He hopped upon my table, a nimble dwarf. His hands were tiny and perfect; his teeth like little pearls. He smiled, and the skin of his face split and shifted like old leather.

"Go away." I swept a hand at him, thinking to knock him off, but he leapt and tumbled gracefully into a somersault.

"You seem so very sad, Ser." He snapped his fingers and a blue flame danced above his hand. "Will you join our party?"

My head throbbed abominably, my temples pulsing as if my skull would burst. I called Rouen, again. Again, there was no answer.

I was terrified beyond belief. This was worse than the stories I'd been told in church, tales of hellfire and damnation, the Day of Judgment, the Rapture of the Blessed. This was worse than Serenola, preaching with unholy conviction, steadfast in his heresies. This was worse than anything. I realized, with sudden cold clarity, that this was my punishment from God. Because I was such a fiend, He had taken Rouen to punish me. It made perfect sense.

The dwarf was dancing on the floor beside my table.

"A friend of mine has died," I snapped. "I pray you, leave me!" The horrific implications held me galvanized; I wondered how He would address the remainder of my myriad transgressions. If there was indeed a Hell, then I was in it.

Behind us, the celebration continued unabated. A young man rose and joined the minstrels, began singing lustily in a bright, clear tenor. A musical version of the epic, *La Roman de la Rose.*

Rouen di Francisci is dead.

I fumbled in my wallet for the letter, drew it out and held it to the light. The writing was small, childish and crabbed, drawn hastily upon the paper with a badly sharpened pen. I had no idea where it had come from, or indeed, how the messenger had found me. I wondered briefly if it had come from one of Serenola's spies... but the followers of the dead priest had scattered like leaves before a driving wind. There was no one left to forswear our existence, none remaining to persecute our kind. Now that Serenola was dead, it was safe for Rouen to come home.

The merriment was making me physically sick, filling my glands with black bile, dangerous humors. I catapulted out of the chair, tossed the table over, dashed toward the door. Nausea clutched a hand about my throat, strangling me, and I vomited spectacularly in the middle of the floor, retching great gouts of congealed blood. I fell to my knees, gagging, began to weep, wished desperately that there was someone to help me. "Oh God, Rouen...." I clenched my teeth against it, wiped my mouth with a trembling hand, leaned against the wall. The music stopped, and several of the party turned to stare at me. Someone whispered, *Plague!* I clutched the letter to my chest and ran.

I screamed. And screaming, ran through the streets of Florence like some horrific voice of the damned. And screaming, roared across the Ponte Vecchio, crossed the Piazza, bolted into the dark nave of the Duomo, carried forward upon a wave of agony.

The great figure of the Christ regarded me from His monument of torment, His empty eyes blinded, His head twisted painfully on His corded neck. I staggered forward, smashed through the altar rail and fell down at His feet.

I promised Him that I would never kill again. I promised that I would bring them all back to life. I promised that I would visit the graves of Rouen's parents, force the Church to recognize them, consecrate the ground. I promised I would destroy myself. I pledged money, effort, I promised Him my blood. I allowed that all of this was my fault. I acknowledged that I deserved to be destroyed. But He remained up there, cold and silent on his great marble cross. And there was no succor for me.

The doors of the Duomo swung slowly open and shut again. I dared not turn around. I knew the Devil had come for me, or the ghost of Serenola, and I was afraid.

"You seek God, Ser." A tiny hand upon my shoulder. It was the dwarf from the tavern, the merry fool.

"Who are you?" I was weeping, eyes streaming blood, crouched against the altar like some grotesque martyr. Where was Valentin, now that I wished to purchase pardon?

"You seek God, Ser, and indeed, you see Him." He advanced on me, his stunted arms outstretched. "For God is higher than we are, Ser." He knelt beside me. "I pray you, seek him upon the mountains, seek Him in the heights!"

It sounded like so much nonsense. "Go away."

He genuflected, bowed to me, and smiling, danced away.

I DREAMED of Rouen all the next day, twisting in my sleep underneath the Duomo. I dreamed that we were mortal again, and walking together in a grove of cypress in the daylight. "I have good news, Dante." Rouen turned to me, his green eyes glistening like gems. "I am getting married!" A slender woman hovered behind him, her large dark eyes very like mine. I drew close to Rouen, to embrace him, but the woman stabbed at me with the claws that protruded from the ends of her fingers, and I was forced to fall back.

I awoke with a start, eyes snapping open in the darkness of the crypt. It was just dusk outside.

I rose and went out, found my first victim of the evening, dispatched him quickly. I did so without remorse.

I spent hours walking about the city, imprinting each aspect of it upon my memory. I wanted to remember it this way, frozen in the moment, perfect. I wasn't sure if I would ever see it again.

I slipped silently into the sumptuous houses of the rich, lingered in the salons while elevated conversation swirled about me. I was careful to notice the details of rooms, of clothing, the attitude of bodies, the expression on a face.

I wandered among the whorehouses, lingering near the shops on the Ponte Vecchio, observed in silence as the harlots plied their wares. They were beautiful to me, these sad and tragic mortals. It was important that I remember them all.

Finally, I went back to our old lodgings near the Duomo, climbed the rickety stairs to our rooms. There had been little change since we'd left here, fleeing Serenola: the table had been overturned, and someone had used the corner of the room as a latrine. The ravaged bed was still in place, bleeding great gouts of goose down, the mattress ticking slashed. I sat down upon it, remembering how I would fall into the day-sleep, Rouen wrapped in my arms. We had been happy here, for some small stretch of time.

When I had seen everything, I rose into the air and headed south, to Sicily, where Etna smoked and rumbled. I halted at its foot and waited, listening to the great grumbling of its primordial guts. I laid my hand against the rippled ground of its lower slopes, felt the ancient warmth penetrate my skin. Here was a monument most suited to my purpose.

I began to climb.

I could have easily mounted to the air and negotiated it thus, landing on its smoking top with minimal effort. But it was important that I *feel* it underneath my hands, experience the pulse of it, deep in the soles of my feet.

The heat increased exponentially as I climbed, until sweat streaked my face, soaked my shirt and doublet. I stopped, stripped off the doublet and cast it away, wiped my forehead in the sleeve of my shirt. It was important that I continue, for the day was growing. I must be at the summit by dawn.

I clawed with fingertips, desperate among the scattered scree, scaled the side, panting. Bright spots streaked across my vision; my breath came hard in my side. There were active fires all around me, flames fountaining out from the mountain, blossoming into the naked air. It was hellish, surreal, an ascent into the Seventh Circle. Demon shapes danced and shifted, indistinct, in the smoke about my head.

At the mountain's base I could see the hardened lava layers, centuries of rage laid down, a frivolity of multicolored lava tracing the edge of the sea. To the east, the Ville del Bove carved a great cavernous gash deep into the bowels of the mountain, a vast scar in its side.

The air was thin up here, scant distance from the summit, and stank heavily of sulfur, acrid smoke that stung the eyes and burned the skin. I coughed, choking, sought foothold on the crumbling edges of the crater. Below me, a lake of fire, a sea of molten rock as red as murder. I would crumble instantly to ashes if I so much as ventured near it.

Fire is the thing we fear the most; only the flames of Hell destroy us. But fire also beckons, seduces, with its promise of the light, till like the hapless moth we embrace the candle that will kill us.

I pulled my shirt off, stripped my hose away, tossed my boots into the crater. My clothes evaporated in a curl of smoke. I opened my purse and scattered the coins, made an offering, a recompense, to this God that would not have me. I danced, screaming, on the lip of Etna's crater.

The heat drove me back, scorched my naked skin and seared my eyebrows. Sweat rose in beads and broke, slid in rivers down my body, trickled onto the heated stones and evaporated, hissing. Fire throbbed in the tips of my fingers, behind my eyeballs; fire pulsed in my belly, my sex, my skull. I bowed to it, made ritual my awe. I was a pagan priest, presiding over sacrifice.

I raised my arms high above my head, a supplicating gesture. And I called to him, above the tumult of the flames, above the primordial roar of Etna's rage....

I will remain here until You come to bargain or until the sun destroys me!

I waited, panting, sweat rolling off my body in dark rivulets of blood.

To the east, the sun was rising over the Mediterranean.

Chapter 23

September 1348

ROUEN

"MY DEAR Rouen...." His hand upon my shoulder, this dearest friend that I had so shamelessly shunned of late, his clear dark eyes smiling at me. "...where have you been? I thought you long since flown!"

I glanced about me; the marketplace was crowded with all manner of man and beast: women with withy baskets jostled for room among a gaggle of geese, a flock of filthy sheep. The air fairly hummed with the stench of life, the bustle and the detail. "It's awkward, I'd rather not—" I stepped back a pace, neatly avoiding the ratty children that ran between us, one clutching a mangy puppy underneath his arm. I wondered if the animal was a pet or somebody's dinner....

"I understand." Something closing down behind his eyes, his face becoming shuttered. Murmuring, prepared to move away.

"Geoffrey." I caught his hand in mine, drew him back to my side. "I'm sorry. Have you dined yet? May I treat you to a meal?" It was just past seven in the evening, the cusp of twilight. The streets were crowded with Londoners hurrying home, the markets closing for the night.

"I'd like that, Rouen." His gaze fixed itself on me, a question forming in his expression. "If you're certain that it's not an imposition." He spoke cautiously, as if wondering about my intentions. I couldn't blame him; I hadn't been in his presence since our last meeting, when I seemingly took leave of him. But that was before Dante's flight to Florence. So much had changed since then.

"It would be my pleasure," I told him. "I pray you, come along."

He took a meal in the tavern of the inn that we most often frequented, and after he had satisfied his hunger (and Geoffrey ate most lustily and well) we fell to talking. Or rather, Geoffrey probed me gently, and I responded as obliquely as was possible.

"I would know the truth, Rouen." He leaned forward and scrutinized me keenly. "Since we last spoke, I have had scant word of you. Is there something wrong?"

"Not at all," I responded easily, "but Dante has left England."

"Ah." He nodded. "Is this why you took your leave of me? Because you had planned to accompany him on his journey?"

"I had assumed I would be… welcome on his voyage." I made no mention of why Dante had left so abruptly, nor his purpose in Florence, both of which were sufficiently crackbrained as to warrant serious investigation.

"Rouen." Geoffrey paused, and I could see his sharp mind working in the interim, his white teeth nibbling at his under lip. "You friend Dante… this is a different sort of friendship, is it not?" He patted my arm, as if taken aback by his own boldness. "I mean no disrespect, of course."

"And there is none taken." I smiled at him. "Geoffrey, I love Dante, but I am certain you have discerned that for yourself."

"I had." His face fought to maintain its solemnity, but lost to his rising humor; he grinned broadly, then burst into gentle laughter. "Did you think me too entirely restrained to comprehend the quality of your understanding with young Dante?"

"Well, yes. I saw no need to offend your sensibilities, and

Geoffrey—" I leaned across to whisper to him, "—there are severe penalties for such as Dante and I have committed. It was not a thing I wished noised abroad." I did not add, of course, that Dante and I were immortal and could doubtless fend for ourselves, as we had against Serenola. There were some things, I felt certain, that my enlightened friend would *not* understand.

"Of course. You have my word of honor—"

I patted his arm. "No need, my friend. I trust you as I would trust myself." Inexplicably, a knot of pain uncoiled inside me. I sat across from him, gazing into his broad, honest face, talking comfortably with him, in friendship, and yet I realized at once that he was mortal and I was not; that he would one day pass into dust while I might well exist forever. I hoped that he would write his poems, as he had promised. His spirit ought not to pass into nothingness; there should remain something of Geoffrey Chaucer to delight the ages. All this passed through my mind in the space of time it takes to blink an eye.

"Rouen... why so suddenly pensive?"

"What do you mean?" I asked.

"Your face, it simply... *changed* just now."

"I was merely musing," I said airily, "it is nothing. I was wondering how Dante fares in Florence."

"The dispatches indicate that the plague is rampant there as well... nothing unexpected, I assume...."

I nodded, motioned for him to continue.

"...and the Council passed an edict concerning the sale of mourning clothes. Oh, and that Serenola ingrate, I hear they've hanged him from his own scaffold." Geoffrey shivered, drew his robe about him. "I know he terrorized the city; indeed, a little dogma is a dangerous thing."

Dante had said that, once. *A little dogma is a dangerous thing.* I was struck with a sudden, sickening loneliness, a longing for him. I had whispered to him along our link for days now, but there was no answer.

I supposed he was angry that I had not followed him into the teeth of Hell, as he expected.

Geoffrey was saying something to me. I focused my attention with an effort. "Did you say Serenola is dead?"

"Yes." He clutched my fingers. "Rouen, are you certain you have not taken with an illness?" He pressed his hand against my forehead. "You are considerably pale."

"I'm all right." In point of fact, I was significantly shaken.

Serenola was dead. Which probably meant—and this was mere assumption—that his ideas had died with him. That his minions had been scattered and there was no one to lead them in their madness.

"Rouen." Strong hands upon my shoulders. "What did Serenola do to you?"

I shuddered, swallowed past the lump forming in my throat. "He killed my mother and father, and my brother Paolo." *And he terrorized my lover, and he destroyed my home, and wrought havoc in my city....*

Geoffrey blessed himself, tears standing in his eyes. "I'm so sorry. Rouen, you cannot know—" He turned away, a hand pressed to his mouth.

"It's all right, my friend." I got stiffly to my feet. "I... have to leave." My face and hands felt numbed, the words humming in my brain. *Serenola is dead.* "I need to make... an offering...." I laid some coins upon the table. "Geoffrey, I thank you for this." I squeezed his shoulder, turned and walked away. I knew I would never see him again.

I ARRIVED in Florence the next night, set down in the Piazza del Duomo. It was just past midnight, and raining; the streets glistened with moisture, reflected the glow of late lamps that still burned in windows. I felt Dante's psychic signature all about me, lingering in the air like smoke. I knew that he had been here recently. I wondered if he were still here now.

I wandered into the Duomo, genuflected in the darkness. The great statue of the Christ regarded me with empty marble eyes, from His perch above the altar. The aura of sorrow was very distinctive here, it weighed about the altar rails, a subconscious pulsing, like a beacon. An immortal had suffered badly here.

There was someone sitting in the front pew, directly to the right of the altar, someone so heavily gowned and cloaked as to be unrecognizable, but who projected an immortal aura. I approached cautiously, not daring to hope, yet with my heart hammering deep within my throat....

Oh my darling—

"Well met, Rouen."

Recognition shattered itself against my brain, a psychic sound like breaking glass. "Lilith."

"Come greet your immortal mother." She slid toward me, clasped my face between her hands and kissed me, her lips as cold as marble.

"You are *not* my mother!" I stumbled backward, tripped, and was floating in air, rising toward her, light as thistledown.

"Stop this!" My limbs flailed uselessly, I was as helpless as an infant. "I beg of you, stop!"

"Your unholy consort, do you know where he is?" Her hand floated atop my body, and she gestured, like a conjurer. A frisson of fear twisted in my guts, an icy shard.

"Please put me down."

"Do you know what he has done?" Her eyes were blue, glowing incandescent in the darkness, an evil flame. Everything within me recoiled from it, yet I could no more escape her than a mortal escapes Time. "Are you privy to his sick imaginings?"

"I have not seen Dante for weeks," I gasped. She made some small gesture, a flicker of her fingers, and I was suddenly on fire, my nerves screaming with the pain. I writhed like an insect impaled upon a pin, mindful always of the elated glitter of her strange eyes, her expression of delight. "You're hurting me!"

I slammed into the floor, was smashed against the tiles, held there by some incredible force. My lungs labored under it, and I couldn't breathe, I saw dark spots form before my eyes. I spun clockwise, legs grappling for purchase, but it was like trying to crawl uphill in a hurricane.

She fell to her knees before me, claws digging into my temples, her mouth a rictus of rage. "Your unholy consort desires discourse with me, and I will give it to him!" Hissing tendrils slid into my mind, curled themselves around my brain, manufactured images: Dante standing on the lip of a great, flaming cavern, naked and screaming into the wind. "He thinks to call down God! What say you about this impudence?" Her fangs descended, great ivory slivers, curved wickedly about her lower lip. "Perhaps I will destroy you...."

There was a sudden small sound, a whispering within a whirlwind. I turned toward it, fastened onto it as some small hope.

Lilith heard it, also.

Her voice ceased, as utterly as if her throat were cut, and her eyes snapped wide, bizarre and doll-like. A whistling rattle passed her lips, a desperate near-whisper, before she was sucked back into the whirlwind, enveloped by it. She vanished abruptly, snatched out of existence.

I climbed gingerly to my feet, breathing heavily, clutching my sides with both hands. I felt bruised, as if I had been beaten by a gang of brigands, and my head swam with bizarre after-images. I didn't dare quantify what had just happened; I suspected it was somewhat beyond my ken.

I found the letter near the altar. It was indeed what Melina had been writing. It said what I had suspected: *Rouen di Francisci is dead.*

It was crumpled, creased in a dozen places, mottled with the stains of bloody tears. I pressed it to my face, knowing that his hands had held it, he had possessed it, if only for a time. I rubbed it between my fingers, crushed the bloodstains deep into the parchment. *This is my blood, which was shed for you.*

I wandered out into the street, traced my way back to our old lodgings, mounted the rickety burnt stairs, sat down upon our ravaged bed. His signature was here, also, that discreet lingering energy that signals the past presence of an immortal. I knew he had returned here before he embraced what he perceived as destiny, had tarried in these rooms, remembering how we had been before, when we were happy, and Valentin was whole, when Lilith was but a distant presence, wreaking havoc in our absence....

She had shown me an image of a fiery mountain.

I sat upright, as if pulled on strings. *A fiery mountain....*

My boot heels clattered on the stairs as I bolted into the street. I caught the sleeve of a passing peddler, swung the astonished man around to face me. "What do they say about the man on Mount Etna?"

His eyebrows knit savagely as he wrenched his arm out of my grasp. "Ser?"

"Mount *Etna!*" I insisted. "Is there anyone on Mount Etna?" I waited for his protestations, his affirmation of my madness.

"I know little about him, Ser, but in my opinion, he's insane. Of course, that's my opinion only, but you can test it if you like. I haven't seen him, but they say he's been there days now, raving and mother naked."

I nearly fell down weeping at his feet. "Thank you, thank you...." I pressed a gold florin into his palm, turned and ran into the city.

The news had traveled from Sicily in hours, the story growing and evolving as it passed from mouth to ear. The man on Mt. Etna was the Christ, some said, come to save the world from the scourge of plague. Others maintained that he was Serenola, resurrected from his untimely death and ready to ignite another Bonfire of the Vanities.

I knew who it was. And I hugged the blessed knowledge to my bosom like a holy relic.

HOVERING above it in the darkness, I conceded that it truly was a metaphorical Hell. Myriad fires blossomed from its rippled sides, belching sparks and smoke; rivers of ancient lava pooled and puddled around the trunks of ruined trees, the roots of blasted scrub. It was a massive stony fist, thrust up out of the bowels of the earth; gestural, obscene, crowned at its summit with a wreath of shredded clouds. The vast fiery pit at the crater's mouth glowed brilliantly red, a primordial lake of molten rock. I knew that nothing could venture near it and survive. Even at this height, the smell of burning sickened me, an ever-present stench of sulfur that seared my nostrils, the lining of my throat.

But he was here, I could feel him, his presence weak and fading, flickering inside Etna's greater fire like an uncertain candle flame. I concentrated all my energies and howled to him, summoned his attention. And then I waited, drifting in the night sky over Etna, listening with all my being for a whisper, some small recognition.

There was nothing but the mountain's gusty rumble, the hiss and crackle of a dozen spurting fires. I briefly entertained the notion that he might be dead, wondered if my quest was hopeless. Perhaps I should fly back to Florence, mourn him properly, and go to ground until the ravages of this age had passed.

Rouen....

My head snapped up so fast that I lost my equilibrium and tumbled end-over-end, a ridiculous juggernaut. What was that? That infinitesimal whisper, weak and fading....

Rouen....

It was him! It was Dante, definitely....

But drifting dangerously into insensibility.

I descended as fast as I could manage, plummeted through layers of smoke and soot, acrid sulfur. My eyes burned, ran with bloody tears, the inside of my nose and throat were seared, as if by acid. I could barely breathe; I was choking on it, my chest heaving, ribs straining to expel the foul air. "Dante!" I cast wildly about me, peering through the smoke. "Dante… where are you?"

I turned a full circle, eyes strained to glimpse him. There was no sign. I wondered if perhaps he had fallen into the crater. I didn't see how he could survive in there.

"Dante!" My throat closed together as if clamped, I stumbled, retching, eyes streaming. My foot caught on some invisible obstacle, and I fell heavily, my chin striking a patch of hardened lava, my fingers dangling scant inches from the crater's lip. A great blackness rose up to overtake me.

I wavered dizzily, slid tantalizingly close to the edge of unconsciousness, yanked myself back by sheer force of will. My nerves shrieked the pain in a repeating sequence, a knife-edged sliver in the brain. It felt as though I'd sheared all the edges off my teeth. "Dante!" I doubled over, seized with a violent fit of coughing.

And then I saw him: the naked figure of a man, lying in a heap some small distance from the crater's edge. I started up, scrambled toward him, stumbling on the sooty rocks, the razor-edges of the scree. I fell down beside him, shaking frenetically. "Dante… oh my God!" I caught his shoulder and gently turned him onto his back, cradling his head in my palms. "Oh God…."

He was badly burned, as if by the sun: his face a mass of bloody blisters, blackened skin. His smooth forehead had cracked and split, ravaged by the sunlight; the skin of his cheeks had separated into strips like rotten cloth. His lips were swollen, black and crusted with hideous sores.

He was entirely naked, burned from the top of his head to the soles of his feet, his skin cracked and bleeding, or crusted with dark pus.

I didn't see how he could possibly survive.

I gathered him into my arms and held him as gently as I could manage, rocked his ravaged body like a child. He keened with the pain and clung to me, the burned skin of his fingers peeling at the tips. "Dante…." I slid my fingers through his singed hair and told him how much I loved him. Sitting there, in the midst of Hell, and holding the ravaged body of my lover, willing him to live and love me, I wept tears of bitter remorse that I had sent him off to Florence, heedless of the danger lurking here.

"Rouen." Dark eyes flickered open, focused on my face. His voice sounded like stone grating on stone, his ravaged lips parting slowly, painfully. "Rouen."

"Don't speak." I had to get him off this mountain, before the sun rose and finished him. "I'm going to take you home." Sorrow trembled in my chest, leaked out of my eyes. I could hardly see.

"Rouen." His fingers clasped my wrist. "I saw the Christ." His eyes rolled back into his skull, his spine arching with the pain, and he shuddered gratefully into unconsciousness. I gathered him into my arms and stood. I had to get him away from here, get him off this hellish mountain….

"Rouen!" Another voice. "How impolitic of you to leave me there for dead."

"Fernando." The ancient blood enriched him, he fairly glittered with it. I wondered who it was had brought him over.

"Indeed." He sketched a bow, gestured to Melina, who of course accompanied him. "And there is your Dante." He tilted his head on one side. "Looking rather worse for wear, is he not? I'd say your darling ought to stay out of the sun!" And he laughed uproariously.

"Tell me how this is possible," I demanded. Dante shifted in my arms and moaned, shivering. I unfastened my cloak and covered him with it. "Who brought you over into death?"

Melina simpered at him, smirked, regarded me with a certain cool contempt. The blood had aged her curiously, had invested her with authority while retaining the childlike simplicity of her face and form. It was eerie, altogether unsettling. "Rouen, you are a clever fellow." And her eyes told me the tale.

I clutched Dante to my chest as a great frisson of horror slid along my bones. "Valentin the Pardoner."

Fernando nodded. "Yes."

I took to the air.

He followed, rising off of Etna's fiery peak, Melina clutched against him. So she couldn't fly… I wondered if perhaps Fernando had brought her across himself, thus weakening the tincture of the blood.

"Rouen! Don't flee, my darling!" He tumbled, hands outstretched like an acrobat, flipped over and drifted in the air before me, Melina clinging to his back like a monkey.

"Go away, Fernando. I have no quarrel with you." I canted sideways, caught an up draft and rode it higher.

"Ah, but Rouen—" He tumbled again, crested higher. "I have issue with *you*!"

"I said *leave me*!" I waited for him to tumble, stuck out my foot and caught him square in the chest. The impact sent him hurtling away, Melina clinging desperately by her fingertips.

"Rouen, help me…." Dante pressed his face into my neck, his arms tight about me. Above all else, I had to protect him; I doubted he could fly in his present condition.

"It's all right, *tesoro*, don't worry." Fernando was approaching, driving headfirst through the air toward me, Melina on his back. I pushed off with my heel, danced away from him.

"Rouen!" He roared with rage, face contorted. Melina's dark eyes glittered as he swung past me. "You owe a debt to me!" He redoubled, turned back upon his flight path, caught my shirt in his fist.

I shook him off, shoved him away from me, rocking dangerously through a passing thermal. I scissor-kicked like a swimmer, maneuvered away from him. "Go away."

"You left me for dead!" He swung an arm, palm open, and slapped me, a ringing smack in the face. My body swung wildly, a dangerous backward arc, and I fought to hold Dante.

Below us, Etna's hellish glow carved a sliver of the darkness. I could stare directly down into the crater's flaming mouth. I had to get him away from me, the sun would soon be rising and *I must find shelter, aid for Dante.* I thought furiously.

Melina could not fly.

"Rouen!" Fernando concentrated all his energy and drove toward me, head-down, his arms tight against his sides. I waited until we were nearly face-to-face, and then I reached out and caught Melina's arm, wrenched her off his back and flipped her out into the empty air.

She fell like a stone, arms and legs outspread, her mouth wide in a soundless scream, straight toward Etna's flaming cavern. Fernando turned about, flipped and dove after her, raging straight into the ancient mouth of Hell.

I turned my face to Florence and flew against the dawn.

Chapter 24

DANTE

I HAD thought to summon God, and I was prepared to tarry there as long as necessary. It turned out that I had not long to wait. For after I had stripped myself and turned my face toward the heavens, the sun rose over the sea.

There was nowhere for me to hide, and it caught me, the first full glare of morning. The sunlight struck me, a deadly shaft that lifted me off the ground, held me suspended, burning, twisting in its grip, and finally let me drop.

I groveled into the ground, desperate for shelter, clawing at the hardened earth, the solid lava of Etna's unyielding face, reckless in my search for respite. I could not break through that impermeable skin, although I shredded my fingers to the bone.

The sun rose higher, unstoppable, ascended into the faultless blue of the morning sky... that sky! that huge expanse of blue above me, a great wide swath from horizon to horizon. It seemed eons since I had seen the morning, and even as the sun blackened me, burned my skin to blisters, I marveled at it, gave myself to it. I turned onto my back and lay full-face upon the mountain, bared my body to the sun.

It was a rapid devastation, and after the first unearthly shrieking pain, it faded to a kind of muted throb. My pale skin turned red, bubbled into blisters, stretched and broke, cracked into great open wheals, subsided into black, the color of charred meat. My hair curled and shriveled, crumbled into ash as it had under Serenola's torch. The skin of my fingers contracted, split around the nails, tore like ancient paper. My palms split asunder along the lifeline. I pulled myself upright, tried to walk around the side of the mountain's northern slope, and left the soles of my feet like bloody prints upon the ground. I began to shiver, as the damage spread throughout my system, my bones shuddering as if my body would collapse into a heap of dust.

I was very afraid, and I began to cry. I was going to die, it was but a matter of moments. I pressed my hands against my eyes, those fleshy stumps of ruined meat, and waited for the end.

The scene atop the mountain clouded before my eyes, and I faded into nothing.

"DANTE." He was calling me.

I rose up on my elbow and looked about me: behind me, Etna smoked and rumbled, belching fire to the heavens, but I could not feel the heat, or hear the noise. There was no sensation of ground beneath me. "Who are you?" A great tumult of fear began beating in my breast; perhaps I was already in Hell!

I glanced about and saw a perfectly ordinary man seated on the ground opposite, his legs crossed, turning a glittering piece of lava over in his hands. He smiled, but there was something quirky in it, some hidden humor lurking at the corners of his mouth. "Well met. Are you rested?" He was wearing a robe, dark hose and leather boots, all of it curiously nondescript. He wore no jewelry, carried no seal of any noble house. His hair was cut in the style like mine, his lips fringed with a tidy beard. He might have been anybody.

"Tell me your name." I felt that I should know him, as if I had seen him in a dream, passed him in the street. "Do I know you?"

"Let us merely say that I'm a friend." He reached a hand to me, clasped my fingers. "You wished a voice in discourse. Here I am."

My scalp prickled. "What happened to the mountain?"

"The mountain is still there. You are still on the mountain." His face softened as he drew me near to him. "Dante, please don't be afraid of me." He wavered, insubstantial in the smoke, a trick of the light. His reassurance only made me fear him more, and I sobbed like a child, not understanding any of it. I wanted to go back to Rouen, I wanted life to be the way it was when we were happy together in Florence. "It isn't my time, yet—" I clutched the front of his robe, frantically, "—please, let me go back!" My fingers slid without purchase, passed through him. The fires of Etna flickered about the edges of his being.

"Dante." He wiped my tears away, gently, with his fingers, his flesh pressing mine, even as it vanished against me. For the first time, I noticed the hideous scars in the center of each hand, a great circular wheal, as if a metal rod had been forced through the flesh of each palm.

Or a nail.

"You're not real, I don't believe in you!" I backed away, gibbering with fright. "I don't believe in you!" I watched him from a secure distance, terrified to be near him. "What scars are those?" I had never seen anything like them; they were the result of no tortures such as I knew.

"A reward for my agenda. A necessary sacrifice." He shrugged. "It doesn't matter now. Dante, you want to speak to me, I know you do. I pray you, continue."

I told him about Lilith, about Serenola, about Rouen's family, about the bubonic plague. I told him how we had fled from Florence into Spain, and from there to London, hoping to escape the rising hysteria that stalked the continent. I told him about the thousands upon thousands of innocents who'd died, and how others had become scapegoats of the plague. I told him all this in great sorrow, and in scarce the time it takes to draw breath. Time passed differently in his presence.

He took me by the hand and led me through this place, strolling slowly past melted gouts of steaming lava, stepped with me through still ponds of molten rock, iridescent pools of fire. "I'm in Hell, aren't I? You're punishing me." I wondered why I wasn't suffering, why I didn't feel the pain of burning.

"No." He slanted a gaze at me, a gentle humor in his face. "Rather an in between place where contemplation is possible." He nodded to the flaming crater, still belching fire behind us. "The mountain exists as ever it did, but you do not exist."

My brain set up a great clangor of alarm. "Do you mean I've *died*?" I pressed my hands against my chest, felt the slow beating of my heart.

"Dante...." He considered how to phrase it, a smile playing about his lips. "Let us merely say that I've slid you out of Time."

I gazed at him, suspicious of this explanation. Who was he, that he could affect such convincing magic?

"Now about Lilith." He settled himself without preamble and began his story:

"This woman that you know as Lilith is in fact the consort of the Father God, He whom you know as Jehovah, although He has other names as well. And He has other aspects, appearing in the faith of many cultures under many different guises. Lilith was created as the wife of first man Adam, but was unsuited by her temperament to that task. And so she petitioned the Father God for her release, and this was granted. Lilith was allotted space beside the Red Sea, where she might contemplate and consider where she best fit within the scheme of things.

"Lilith behaved unwisely, in that she did consort with demons, and gave birth daily to scores of immortal offspring—beings such as you are, Dante. We thought that these immortals might well serve a useful purpose on the earth, to cull from the ranks of man those who engendered evil in their souls, who sought to harm their fellows, who did injury to innocents. But the children of Lilith were too many, and instead of fulfilling this most excellent purpose, they began to turn against each other, feeding on the blood of their fellows, so that some small several of them became too powerful and mighty. These ones then turned to preying upon innocents.

"Lilith was summoned into our presence, and the Father God requested how we might mitigate this scourge that she had brought into our midst. And Lilith decided that she would create a pestilence, to affect these evil ones who attacked innocents and drank the blood of their fellows."

My vision misted over. "Plague."

"Yes." He touched my shoulder. "Dante, we are sorry. We entrusted Lilith with this task, and she erred. We have tried to influence her, to convince her to recall the pestilence, but she insists that she cannot." He spread his hands, a gesture of helplessness. "We have made a pact amongst ourselves that stands ever since the creation of the universe. We cannot interfere with what Lilith has wrought, but we must let it run its course unhindered."

I could not believe what I was hearing. "So you can do nothing about the plague. You propose to allow the death of tens of thousands, and you will do *nothing*?" I stared at him, aghast. "Then we are truly damned!"

"You are not damned." His voice was firm. "We would never damn an innocent creation, certainly not your kind." He caught my elbow. "Dante, walk with me." It was not entirely a request.

"I cannot see how you can allow this!" I laughed bitterly. "Were you listening to me praying in the Duomo? Is that why you brought me here?"

"I brought you here because you petitioned me for audience." His elegant brows twitched. "Perhaps you should be cautioned in what you wish for."

"I don't believe in you," I snapped. I felt as if I would fly apart at the seams. "Send me back to Etna."

"Dante, I cannot stop what Lilith has brought into existence, but I can mitigate your pain!" He stopped, peered through the drifting smoke toward the ocean. "You and your kind have a purpose, but you must promise me—"

"What?" I turned on him, suddenly enraged by his futile attempt to mollify me. "What must I promise you? How many souls must I save? What sacrifices do you want? How many candles should I light in the Duomo?"

"None of that has anything to do with me."

"None of *anything* has anything to do with you... not anymore! What are you to me, to those mortals who profess your name and kill each other? A statue in a chapel, a dead man nailed to a cross, a haloed saint in a religious fresco, the long-dead Son of God!" I was quivering with rage, standing outside myself and watching this immortal called Dante conduct a heated argument with Jesus Christ. "You can't save me, you can't save any of us!"

"I never intended to save anybody." A mask of sorrow slipped down over his features, sadness welling in the darkness of his eyes. He looked nothing like an icon or a cold and chilly statue; he looked like a sad and lonely man. "It had nothing to do with that."

Inexplicably, I started sobbing. "Then it all means nothing." I wrapped my arms about myself and wept.

"You have a task. You, and Rouen, and all the others of your kind that remain. You are a predator, and your purpose is to serve us, as all others serve us, and thereby, serve yourselves. Dante—" He gathered me into his arms, "—it is your task to seek out the darkly sick and desperate, who torment and kill their fellows, who do evil in the darkness, who commit murder, who prey upon the innocent. And Dante, when you find them, you are to take their lives from them and do it swiftly, draw that evil into yourself." His embrace was a well of sanity and safety into which I would sink and remain forever. Was this the thing toward which Serenola strove? "This is a sacred trust, not an easy task. I am asking that you become the repository of all evil on the earth."

"And thereby contain it." I understood. But it frightened me, this purpose.

"Yes." He drew me to him, pressed his lips against my forehead. "Go, now. One who loves you waits below." He released me and I was falling backward, drifting down and down and down....

"Dante!" The voice sliced through the hell of smoke and sulfur, as keen as quicksilver. "Where are you?"

I lay facedown upon a pile of ashes, near the summit of Mount Etna, badly burned and drifting in and out of consciousness. It took a massive effort of will to project to him, *Rouen....*

And there he was, at my side, lifting me into his arms. "Oh my God, Dante...." Blood-tears dropping onto my burnt and ravaged skin, his precious arms about me.

"Rouen." My arm reaching, fingers splayed, toward his face. "I saw the Christ."

A great wave of agony engulfed me, and I passed into the blackness.

Chapter 25

January 1349

VALENTIN

I HAVE seen the face of holy vengeance, blessed be her name! And though I wander through the wide world dreaming, dispensing pardons to each and all, my bag of woes is heavy. For I am separated forever now from those whom I have so lately loved, my masters both mortal and immortal. I do service solely to my Queen.

My name is Valentin, and I am a pardoner of Rome, and were my will my own I might make pilgrimage, indulging those who sin against Jesus Christ our Lord. But I have not will to take myself away. She holds me here beside her throne, and I am hers.

Blessed be her name.

JoAnne Soper-Cook was born on the island of Newfoundland and grew up in the tiny village of Hant's Harbour, where she was raised by a carpenter and his wife and spent her days gazing out to sea and roaming the forest. At age eight, she published her first story, The Magic Elf, and, thus bitten by the writing bug, went on to fail miserably for the next twenty years.

In between times she managed to earn a B.A. and an M.A. in English Literature and a B.Ed in post-secondary education. She now makes her home in St. John's, North America's oldest city, with her husband Paul and their two spoiled rotten dog-children Lola and Sheppy. She likes travel, food and wine, river rafting, hiking, and failing to learn complicated foreign languages; Egypt and Romania are next on her list of countries to visit although Newfoundland is her favorite place, followed closely by the Deep Southern states of Louisiana and Mississippi. She is a Newfoundland nationalist with a deep and abiding love of her island home. She believes in reincarnation and is currently involved in working off the karma incurred from certain 19th century wars.

Visit JoAnne at Facebook: http://www.facebook.com/profile.php?id=100000376814472&ref=name and LiveJournal: http://joannesopercook.livejournal.com.

Paranormal Romance from DREAMSPINNER PRESS

Historical Romance from DREAMSPINNER PRESS

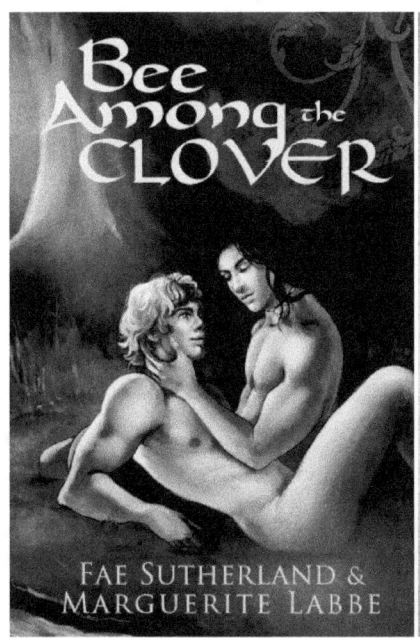

http://www.dreamspinnerpress.com